THINGS
WE HIDE
FROM
THE
LIGHT

Center Point
Large Print

Also by Lucy Score and available from
Center Point Large Print:

Things We Never Got Over

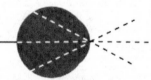

**This Large Print Book carries the
Seal of Approval of N.A.V.H.**

THINGS WE HIDE FROM THE LIGHT

LUCY SCORE

CENTER POINT LARGE PRINT
THORNDIKE, MAINE

The text of this Large Print edition is unabridged.
In other aspects, this book may vary
from the original edition.
Printed in the United States of America
on permanent paper sourced using
environmentally responsible foresting methods.
Set in 16-point Times New Roman type.

ISBN: 978-1-63808-780-9

The Library of Congress has cataloged this record
under Library of Congress Control Number: 2023934112

In memory of Chris Waller, the reader husband who reached out and asked me to include the word "gusset" in a book just so he could win a bet with his wife. Kate, I hope it makes you smile when you find it again inside.

1

Tiny Little Embers

Nash

The federal agents in my office were lucky for two reasons.

First, my left hook wasn't what it had been before getting shot.

And second, I hadn't been able to work my way up into feeling anything, let alone mad enough to make me consider doing something stupid.

"The Bureau understands you have a personal interest in finding Duncan Hugo," Special Agent Sonal Idler said from across my desk where she sat with a ramrod-straight spine. She flicked her gaze to the coffee stain on my shirt.

She was a steely woman in a pantsuit who looked as though she ate procedures for breakfast. The man next to her, Deputy U.S. Marshal Nolan Graham, had a mustache and the look of a man forced into something he really didn't want to do. He also looked like he blamed me for it.

I wanted to work my way up to pissed off. Wanted to feel something other than the great, sucking void that rolled over me, inevitable as the tide. But there was nothing. Just me and the void.

"But we can't have you and your boys and girls running around mucking up my investigation," Idler continued.

On the other side of the glass, Sergeant Grave Hopper was dumping a pint of sugar into his coffee and glaring daggers at the two feds. Behind him, the rest of the bullpen buzzed with the usual energy of a small-town police department.

Phones rang. Keyboards clicked. Officers served. And the coffee sucked.

Everyone was alive and breathing. Everyone but me.

I was just pretending.

I crossed my arms and ignored the sharp twinge in my shoulder.

"I appreciate the professional courtesy. But what's with the special interest? I'm not the only cop to take a bullet in the line of duty."

"You also weren't the only name on that list," Graham said, speaking up for the first time.

My jaw tightened. The list was where this nightmare had begun.

"But you were the first one targeted," Idler said. "Your name was on that list of LEOs and informants. But this thing is bigger than one shooting. This is the first time we've got something that could stick to Anthony Hugo."

It was the first time I'd heard any kind of

emotion in her voice. Special Agent Idler had her own personal agenda, and nailing crime boss Anthony Hugo to the wall was it.

"I need this case to be airtight," she continued. "Which is why we can't have any locals trying to take matters into their own hands. Even if they've got badges. The greater good always comes with a price tag."

I rubbed a hand over my jaw and was surprised to find more than a five-o'clock shadow there. Shaving hadn't exactly been high on my priority list lately.

She assumed I'd been investigating. Reasonable given the circumstances. But she didn't know my dirty little secret. No one did. I might be healing on the outside. I might put on my uniform and show up at the station every day. But on the inside, there was nothing left. Not even a desire to find the man responsible for this.

"What do you expect my department to do if Duncan Hugo comes back here looking to shoot holes in a few more of its citizens? Look the other way?" I drawled.

The feds shared a look. "I expect you to keep us apprised of any local happenings that might tie in to our case," Idler said firmly. "We've got a few more resources at our disposal than your department. And no personal agendas."

I felt a flicker of something in the nothingness. *Shame*.

I should have a personal agenda. Should be out there hunting down the man myself. If not for me, then for Naomi and Waylay. He'd victimized my brother's fiancée and her niece in another way, by abducting them and terrorizing them over the list that had earned me two bullet holes.

But part of me had died in that ditch that night, and what was left didn't seem like it was worth fighting for.

"Marshal Graham here will be staying close for a while. Keeping an eye on things," Idler continued.

Mustache didn't look any happier about that than I was.

"Any particular kind of things?" I asked.

"All remaining targets on the list are receiving federal protection until we ascertain that the threat is no longer imminent," Idler explained.

Christ. The whole damn town was going to be in an uproar if they found out federal agents were hanging around waiting for someone to break the law. And I didn't have the energy for an uproar.

"I don't need protection," I said. "If Duncan Hugo had two brain cells to rub together, he wouldn't be hanging around here. He's long gone." At least, that was what I told myself late at night when the sleep wouldn't come.

"All due respect, Chief, you're the one who got himself shot. You're lucky you're still here," Graham said with a smug twitch of his mustache.

"What about my brother's fiancée and niece? Hugo kidnapped them. Are they getting protection?"

"We have no reason to believe that Naomi and Waylay Witt are in any danger at this time," Idler said.

The twinge in my shoulder graduated to a dull throb to match the one in my head. I was low on sleep and patience, and if I didn't get these two pains in the ass out of my office, I wasn't confident I could keep things civil.

Mustering as much southern charm as I could, I rose from behind my desk. "Understood. Now, if y'all will excuse me, I have a town to serve."

The agents got to their feet and we exchanged perfunctory handshakes.

"I'd appreciate it if you'd keep me in the loop. Seein' as how I've got a 'personal interest' and all," I said as they hit the door.

"We'll be sure to share what we can," Idler said. "We'll also be expecting a call from you as soon as you remember anything from the shooting."

"Will do," I said through gritted teeth. Between the trifecta of physical wounds, memory loss, and the empty numbness, I was a shadow of the man I'd been.

"Be seein' you," Graham said. It sounded like a threat.

I waited until they'd strutted their asses out of my station before snagging my jacket off the coat rack. The hole in my shoulder protested when I shoved my arm into the sleeve. The one in my torso didn't feel much better.

"You all right, Chief?" Grave asked when I stepped out into the bullpen.

Under normal circumstances, my sergeant would have insisted on a play-by-play of the meeting followed by an hour-long bitch session about jurisdictional bullshit. But since I'd gotten myself shot and almost killed, everyone was doing their damnedest to treat me with kid gloves.

Maybe I wasn't hiding things as well as I thought.

"Fine," I said, harsher than I'd intended.

"Heading out?" he prodded.

"Yeah."

The eager new patrol officer popped up out of her chair like it was spring-loaded. "If you want lunch, I can pick something up for you from Dino's, Chief," she offered.

Born and raised in Knockemout, Tashi Banner-jee was police academy fresh. Now, her shoes gleamed and her dark hair was scraped back in a regulations-exceeding bun. But four years ago, she'd been ticketed in high school with riding a horse through a fast-food drive-thru. Most of the department had skirted the line of the law at some point in our youth, which made it mean more that we chose to uphold it rather than circumvent it.

"I can get my own damn lunch," I snapped.

Her face fell for just a second before she recovered, making me feel like I'd just landed a kick to a puppy. *Fuck.* I was turning into my brother.

"Thanks for the offer though," I added in a slightly less antagonized tone.

Great. Now I had to do something nice. Again. Make yet another I'm-sorry-for-being-an-asshole gesture that I didn't have the energy for. So far this week, I'd brought in coffee, doughnuts, and—after a particularly embarrassing loss of temper over the thermostat in the bullpen—gas station candy bars.

"I'm heading out to PT. Be back in an hour or so."

With that, I stepped out into the hall and strode toward the exit like I had business to attend to just in case anyone else had a mind to try to strike up a conversation.

I blanked my mind and tried to focus on what was happening right in front of me.

The full force of northern Virginia fall hit me when I shoved my way through the glass doors of the Knox Morgan Municipal Center. The sun was shining in a sky so blue it hurt the eyes. The trees lining the street were putting on a show as their leaves gave up the green for russets, yellows, and oranges. Pumpkins and hay bales dominated the downtown window displays.

I glanced up at the roar of a bike and watched Harvey Lithgow cruise by. He had devil horns on his helmet and a plastic skeleton lashed upright to the seat behind him.

He raised a hand in greeting before rumbling off down the road doing at least fifteen over the posted speed limit. Always pushing the bounds of the law.

Fall had always been my favorite season. New beginnings. Pretty girls in soft sweaters. Football season. Homecoming. Cold nights made warmer with bourbon and bonfires.

But everything was different now. *I* was different now.

Since I'd lied about physical therapy, I couldn't very well be seen grabbing lunch downtown, so I headed for home.

I'd make a sandwich I didn't want to eat, sit in solitude, and try to find a way to make it through the rest of the day without being too much of a dick.

I needed to get my shit together. It wasn't that fucking hard to push papers and make a few appearances like the useless figurehead I now was.

"Mornin', Chief," Tallulah St. John, our resident mechanic and co-owner of Café Rev, greeted me as she jaywalked right in front of me. Her long, black braids were gathered over the shoulder of her coveralls. She had a grocery tote in one hand

14

and a coffee, most likely made by her husband, in the other.

"Mornin', Tashi."

Knockemout's favorite pastime was ignoring the law. Where I stuck to the black and white, sometimes it felt like the rest of the people around me lived entirely in the gray. Founded by lawless rebels, my town had little use for rules and regulations. The previous police chief had been happy to leave citizens to fend for themselves while he shined up his badge as a status symbol and used his position for personal gain for more than twenty years.

I'd been chief now for nearly five years. This town was my home, the citizens, my family. Clearly I'd failed to teach them to respect the law. And now it was only a matter of time before they all realized I was no longer capable of protecting them.

My phone pinged in my pocket, and I reached for it with my left hand before remembering I no longer carried it on that side. On a muttered oath, I pulled it free with my right.

> **Knox:** Tell the feds they can kiss your ass, my ass, and the whole damn town's ass while they're at it.

Of course my brother knew about the feds. An alert probably went out the second their sedan rolled onto Main Street. But I wasn't up for a discussion about it. I wasn't up for anything really.

The phone rang in my hand.

Naomi.

It wasn't that long ago that I would have been eager as hell to answer that call. I'd had a thing for the new-in-town waitress riding a streak of bad luck. But she'd fallen, inexplicably, for my grumpy-ass brother instead. I'd given up the crush—easier than I'd thought—but had enjoyed Knox's annoyance every time his soon-to-be wife checked in on me.

Now, though, it felt like one more responsibility that I just couldn't handle.

I sent the call to voicemail as I rounded the corner onto my street.

"Mornin', Chief," Neecey called as she hauled the pizza shop's easel sign out the front door. Dino's opened at 11:00 a.m. on the dot seven days a week. Which meant I'd only made it four hours into my workday before I'd had to bail. A new record.

"Morning, Neece," I said without enthusiasm.

I wanted to go home and close the door. To shut out the world and sink into that darkness. I didn't want to stop every six feet to have a conversation.

"Heard that fed with the mustache is stickin' around. Think he'll enjoy his stay at the motel?" she said with a wicked gleam in her eyes.

The woman was a glasses-wearing, gum-chewing gossip who chatted up half the town every shift. But she had a point. Knockemout's motel was a health inspector's wet dream. Violations on every page of the handbook. Someone needed to buy the damn thing and tear it down.

"Sorry, Neece. Gotta take this," I lied, bringing the phone to my ear, pretending like I had a call.

The second she ducked back inside, I stowed the phone and hurried the rest of the way to my apartment entrance.

My relief was short-lived. The door to the stairwell, all carved wood and thick glass, was propped open with a banker box marked *Files* in sharp scrawl.

Still eying the box, I stepped inside.

"Son of a damn bitch!" A woman's voice that did not belong to my elderly neighbor echoed from above.

I looked up just as a fancy black backpack rolled down the stairs toward me like a designer tumbleweed. Halfway up the flight, a pair of long, lean legs caught my attention.

They were covered in sleek leggings the color of moss, and the view just kept getting better. The fuzzy gray sweater was cropped and offered a peek at smooth, tan skin over taut muscle while highlighting subtle curves. But it was the face that demanded the most attention. Marble-worthy cheekbones. Big, dark eyes. Full lips pursed in annoyance.

Her hair—so dark it was almost black—was cut in a short, choppy cap and looked like someone had just shoved their fingers through it. My fingers flexed at my sides.

Angelina Solavita, better known as Lina or my brother's ex-girlfriend from a lifetime ago, was a looker. And she was in my stairwell.

This wasn't good.

I bent and picked up the bag at my feet.

"Sorry for hurling my luggage at you," she called as she wrestled a large, wheeled suitcase up the final few steps.

I had no complaints about the view, but I had serious concerns about surviving small talk.

The second floor was home to three apartments: mine, Mrs. Tweedy's, and a vacant space next to mine.

I had my hands full living across the hall from an elderly widow who didn't have much respect for privacy and personal space. I wasn't interested in adding to my distractions at home. Not even when they looked like Lina.

"Moving in?" I called back when she reappeared at the top of the stairs. The words sounded forced, my voice strained.

She flashed me one of those sexy little smiles. "Yeah. What's for dinner?"

I watched her hit the stairs at a jog, descending with speed and grace.

"I think you can do better than what I have to

offer." I hadn't been to a grocery store in . . . Okay, I couldn't remember the last time I'd ventured into Grover's Groceries to buy food. I'd been living off takeout when I remembered to eat.

Lina stopped on the last step, putting us eye-to-eye, and gave me a slow once-over. The smile became a full-fledged grin. "Don't sell yourself short, hotshot."

She'd called me that for the first time a handful of weeks ago when she'd cleaned up the mess I'd made of my stitches saving my brother's ass. At the time, I should have been thinking about the avalanche of paperwork I was going to have to deal with thanks to an abduction and the ensuing shoot-out. Instead, I'd sat propped against the wall, distracted by Lina's calm, competent hands, her clean, fresh scent.

"You flirting with me?" I hadn't meant to blurt it out, but I was hanging on by sheer will.

At least I hadn't told her I liked the smell of her laundry detergent.

She arched an eyebrow. "You're my handsome new neighbor, the chief of police, and my college boyfriend's brother."

She leaned in an inch closer, and a single spark of something warm stirred in my belly. I wanted to cling to it, to cup it in my hands until it thawed my icy blood.

"I *really* love bad ideas. Don't you?" Her smile was dangerous now.

Old Me would have turned on the charm. Would have enjoyed a good flirt. Would have appreciated the mutual attraction. But I wasn't that man anymore.

I held up her bag by the strap. Her fingers got tangled around mine when she reached for it. Our gazes met and held. That spark multiplied into a dozen tiny little embers, almost enough for me to remember what it was like to feel something.

Almost.

She was watching me intently. Those whiskey-brown eyes peered into me like I was an open book.

I extricated my fingers from hers. "What did you say you do for a living?" I asked. She'd mentioned it in passing, called it boring, and changed the subject. But she had eyes that missed nothing, and I was curious what job would let her hang out in Nowhere, Virginia, for weeks at a time.

"Insurance," she said, slinging the backpack over one shoulder.

Neither one of us retreated. Me because those embers were the only good thing I'd felt in weeks.

"What kind of insurance?"

"Why? Are you in the market for a new policy?" she teased as she started to pull away.

But I wanted her to stay close. Needed her to fan those weak sparks to see if there was anything inside me worth burning.

"Want me to grab that?" I offered, hooking my thumb at the box of files against the door.

The smile disappeared. "I've got it," she said briskly, making a move to step past me.

I blocked her. "Mrs. Tweedy would have my hide if she found out I made you haul that box up those stairs," I insisted.

"Mrs. Tweedy?"

I pointed up. "2C. She's out with her weight-lifting group. But you'll meet her soon enough. She'll make sure of it."

"If she's out, she won't know that you didn't aggravate your bullet wounds by insisting on lugging a box up a flight of stairs," Lina pointed out. "How are they healing?"

"Fine," I lied.

She hummed and raised that eyebrow again. "Really?"

She didn't believe me. But my craving for those tiny slivers of feeling was so strong, so desperate, I didn't care.

"Right as rain," I insisted.

I heard a low ringtone and saw the flash of annoyance as Lina retrieved her phone from some hidden pocket in the waistband of her leggings. It was only a glimpse, but I caught "Mom" on the screen before she hit Ignore. It looked like we both were avoiding family.

I took a chance and used the distraction to retrieve the box, making a point to use my left arm. My shoulder throbbed, and a cold bead of sweat worked its way down my back. But as soon as I locked eyes with her again, the sparks came back.

I didn't know what this was, only that I needed it.

"I see the Morgan stubbornness is just as strong in you as it is in your brother," she observed, tucking the phone back into her pocket. She gave me another assessing look before turning and starting up the stairs.

"Speaking of Knox," I said, fighting to keep my voice sounding natural, "I take it you're in 2B?" My brother owned the building, which included the bar and barbershop on the first floor.

"I am now. I was staying at the motel," she said.

I sent up a prayer of thanks that she was taking the stairs slower than she had on the way down.

"Can't believe you lasted that long there."

"This morning, I saw a rat get into a slap fight with a roach the size of a rat. Last straw," she said.

"Coulda stayed with Knox and Naomi," I said, forcing the words out before I was too out of breath to speak. I was out of condition, and her shapely ass in those leggings wasn't helping my cardiovascular endurance.

"I like my own space," she said.

We made it to the top of the stairs, and I

followed her to the open door next to mine as a river of icy sweat snaked down my back. I really needed to get back to the gym. If I was going to be a walking corpse for the rest of my life, I should at least be one who could handle a conversation on a flight of stairs.

Lina dropped her backpack inside before turning to take the box from me.

Once again, our fingers touched.

Once again, I felt something. And it wasn't just the ache in my shoulder, the emptiness in my chest.

"Thanks for the help," she said, taking the box from me.

"If you need anything, I'm right next door," I said.

Those lips curved ever so slightly. "Good to know. See you around, hotshot."

I stood rooted to the spot even after she shut the door, waiting until every single one of those embers went cold.

2

Avoidance Tactics

Lina

I closed my new front door on all six feet one inches of wounded, broody Nash Morgan.

"Don't even think about it," I muttered to myself.

Usually, I didn't mind taking a risk, playing with a little fire. And that was exactly what getting to know Studly Do-Right, as the ladies of Knockemout had dubbed him, would be. But I had more urgent things to do than flirting away the sadness that Nash wore like a cloak.

Wounded and broody, I thought again as I lugged my files across the room.

I wasn't surprised that I was attracted. While I preferred the enjoy 'em and leave 'em lifestyle, there was nothing I loved more than a challenge. And getting under that facade, digging into what put those shadows in his sad hero eyes would be exactly that.

But Nash struck me as the settling-down type, and I was allergic to relationships.

Once you showed an interest in someone, they started thinking it meant they had the right to tell you what to do and how to do it, two of my least favorite things. I liked good times, the thrill of the chase. I enjoyed playing with the pieces of a puzzle until I had the full picture, then moving on to the next one. And in between, I liked walking into my place, full of my things, and ordering food I liked without having to argue with anyone about what to watch on TV.

I dumped the box on the tiny dining room table and surveyed my new domain.

The apartment had potential. I could see why Knox had invested in the building. He'd never been one to miss potential under the surface of hot mess. High ceilings, battered wood floors, big windows overlooking the street.

The main living space was furnished with a faded floral couch facing an empty brick wall, the small but sturdy round dining table with three chairs, and some kind of shelving system built out of old crates under the front windows.

The kitchen, which was closed off into a tiny, drywalled box, was about two decades out of date. Not a problem since I didn't cook. The counters were a garish yellow laminate that had long outlived their heyday, if they'd ever had one. But there was a microwave and a fridge big enough to store takeout and a six-pack, so it would work just fine for me.

The bedroom was empty, but it had a sizable closet, which unlike the kitchen *was* a requirement for me and my clothes-whorish tendencies. The attached bathroom was charmingly vintage with a claw-foot tub and an absolutely useless pedestal sink that would hold zero percent of my makeup and skincare collection.

I blew out a breath. Depending on how comfortable the couch was, I might be able to hold off on making a decision about a bed. I didn't know how much longer I'd be here, how long it would take me to find what I was looking for.

I hoped to hell it wouldn't be long now.

I flopped down on the couch, praying for it to be comfortable.

It was not.

"Why are you punishing me?" I asked the ceiling. "I'm not a horrible person. I stop for pedestrians. I donate to that farm sanctuary. I eat my vegetables. What more do you want?"

The universe didn't respond.

I heaved a sigh and thought about my town house in Atlanta. I was used to roughing it on the job. Returning from an extended stay in a two-star motel always made me appreciate my expensive sheets, my overstuffed designer couch, and my meticulously organized wardrobe.

This particular extended stay, however, was becoming ridiculous.

And the longer I stayed in town without a break or a clue or a light at the end of the tunnel, the antsier I got. On paper, maybe it looked like I was an impulsive wild child. In reality, I was simply following the plan I'd made a long time ago. I was patient and logical, and the risks I took were—almost always—calculated.

But weeks on end in a tiny town thirty-eight minutes from the closest Sephora without the slightest indication that I was on the right track were starting to wear on me. Hence the conversation with the ceiling.

I was bored and frustrated, a dangerous combination, because it made it impossible to ignore the niggling doubt in my head that maybe I didn't enjoy this line of work as much as I once did. The doubt that had magically sprouted when things had gone south during the last job. Something else I didn't want to think about.

"Okay, universe," I said to the ceiling again. "I need *one thing* to go my way. Just one. Like a shoe sale or, I don't know, how about one break in this case before I lose my mind?"

This time, the universe answered me with a phone call.

The universe was a jerk.

"Hi, Mom," I said with twin pulls of annoyance and affection.

"There you are! I was worried." Bonnie Solavita hadn't been born a worrier, but she'd accepted the mantel that had been thrust upon her with an enthusiastic dedication to the role.

Unable to sit still during these daily conversations, I got off the lumpy couch and headed to the table. "I was carrying something up the stairs," I explained.

"You're not overdoing it, are you?"

"It was one suitcase and one flight of stairs," I said, flicking the lid off the box of files. "What are you all up to?" Redirection was what kept my relationship with my parents intact.

"I'm on my way into a marketing meeting, and your father is somewhere under the hood of that damn car," she said.

Mom had taken a longer-than-necessary hiatus from her job as a marketing executive so she could smother me until I moved three states away to go to college. Since then, she'd reentered the workforce and climbed the ladder as an executive in a national healthcare organization.

My father, Hector, was six months into his retirement from his career as a plumber. "That damn car" was the in-desperate-need-of-some-TLC 1968 Mustang Fastback I'd surprised him with for his birthday two years ago courtesy of a big, fat bonus check from work. He'd had one when he was a young, studly bachelor in Illinois until he'd traded it in on a fancy pickup truck to impress a farmer's daughter. Dad had married the farmer's daughter—my mother—and spent the ensuing decades missing the car.

"Did he get it running yet?" I asked.

"Not yet. He bored me to death with a twenty-minute dissertation on carburetors over dinner last night. So I bored him right back with an explanation of how we're changing our advertising messages based on the demographics of East Coast suburban sprawl," Mom explained smugly.

I laughed. My parents had one of those relationships that no matter how different they were from each other, no matter how long they'd been married, they were still the other's biggest cheerleaders . . . and biggest annoyances.

"That's very on-brand for you both," I said.

"Consistency is key," Mom sang.

I heard someone ask a rapid-fire question on her end.

"Go with the secondary deck for the presentation. I made some tweaks to it last night. Oh, and grab me a Pellegrino before you go in, would you? Thanks." Mom cleared her throat. "Sorry about that, sweetie."

The difference between her boss lady voice and her mom voice was a source of endless entertainment for me.

"No problem. You're a busy boss lady."

But not too busy to check in with her daughter on her designated days.

Yep. Between my mother's iron-fisted itinerary and my parents' desire to make sure I was okay at all times, I spoke to a parent nearly every single day. If I avoided them for too long, they had been known to show up on my doorstep unannounced.

"You're still in DC, aren't you?" she asked.

I winced, knowing what was coming. "Thereabouts. It's a small town north of DC."

"Small towns are where busy professional women get seduced by a rough-around-the-edges local business owner. Ooh! Or a sheriff. Have you met the sheriff yet?"

A coworker had gotten my mother hooked on romance novels a few years back. They took an annual vacation together that always lined up with some book signing somewhere. Now Mom expected my life to turn into the plot of a rom-com at any moment.

"Chief of police," I corrected. "And actually he lives next door."

"That makes me feel a thousand times better knowing you have law enforcement next door. They're trained in CPR, you know."

"And a variety of other special skills," I said dryly, trying not to be annoyed.

"Is he single? Cute? Any red flags?"

"I think so. Definitely. And I haven't gotten to know him well enough to spot any. He's Knox's brother."

"Oh."

Mom managed to pack a lot into one syllable. My parents had never met Knox. They only knew that we'd dated—very briefly—when I was in college and had remained friends ever since. Mom mistakenly blamed him for her thirty-seven-year-old daughter still being single and ready to mingle.

It wasn't that she was desperate for a wedding and grandkids. It was that my parents wouldn't take an easy breath until I had someone in my life who was going to take over the role of worried protector. It didn't matter how self-sufficient I'd become. To my mom and dad, I was still a fifteen-year-old in a hospital bed.

"You know, your father and I were just talking about getting away for the weekend. We could hop on a flight and be there this weekend."

The last thing I needed was either of my parents shadowing me around town while I tried to work.

"I don't know how long I'll be in town," I said diplomatically. "I could be heading home any day now." Unlikely, unless I found something that led the case in a new direction. But still, at least it wasn't an outright lie.

"I don't understand how running corporate trainings can be so open-ended," Mom mused. Fortunately, before I had to craft a plausible answer, I heard another muffled comment on her end. "I have to go, sweetie. Meeting's starting. Anyway, let me know when you're heading back to Atlanta. We'll fly down and visit before you come home for Thanksgiving. If we time it right, we can go to your appointment with you."

Yeah. Because I was going to go to a doctor's appointment with my parents in tow. Sure. "We'll talk about it later," I said.

"I love you, sweetie."

"Love you too."

I disconnected and let out a sigh that ended on a groan. Even from hundreds of miles away, my mother still managed to make me feel like she was holding a pillow over my face.

There was a knock at my door, and I shot a wary look at it, wondering if my mom was waiting to surprise me on the other side.

But then came a thump that sounded like an irritated boot at the base of my door. It was followed by a gruff, "Open up, Lina. This shit is heavy."

I crossed the room and yanked open the door to find Knox Morgan, his pretty fiancée, Naomi, and Naomi's niece, Waylay, standing in the hallway.

Naomi was grinning and holding a potted plant. Knox was scowling and lugging what looked like a hundred pounds of bedding. Waylay looked bored holding two pillows.

"So this is what happens when I move out of the roach motel? People start dropping in unannounced?" I said.

"Move it." Knox muscled his way past me under an off-white duvet.

"Sorry to barge in like this, but we wanted to

Ithaca. He has been gone many months and is now in the Gulf of Mexico. Your ship, as I understand it, plans to hold a gam with it and share news of home. I need this package to be delivered to Henry. Him, and no one else." She fishes in her dress pocket for a coin. Perhaps he will buy some tobacco with it onboard the ship. Instead, he hands it to his young wife. Smart, at least, in one way.

"It would be my honor," the young man says, smiling as he takes the package. He tilts his torso and bows slightly, reminding Eliza of how Henry always made that sweet, formal gesture to her when they were courting. Her heart suddenly aches uncharacteristically. Perhaps this is the true reason she never ventures to the port; it is all too real here. As they stand on the long pier, she pretends to study the ship out in the sparkling blue harbor, the scale and mass of it, the way it rises from the water like a mammal from the depths of the sea.

The bigger the ship, the longer the journey. This leviathan will be gone for over four years, Eliza suspects.

Her parcel will now begin its journey. It is, in many ways, no more or less remarkable than any of the others she sent out to Henry. Like those, this one contains a tiny cake soaked in rum, several detailed letters from the girls, a drawing in pencil made by Mattie (this one of a bluebird), and a long letter from Eliza wrapped together into a loaf of paper and twine.

What's different this time, besides Eliza's slightly chilly tone after being told Henry won't be back as scheduled this summer? Tucked inside her words, folded small and tight, is another warning, bolder than the last two: a third statement from Citizens Bank concerning Henry's impending bankruptcy, should his ship not return profitable, every casket filled to the brim with liquid gold.

The young wife of the greenhand sailor rushes past, head down. She has said her farewell. When this man returns to Nantucket—if this man returns—the wife will be a different person. As, of course, will the husband.

Although not impulsive by nature, Eliza suddenly has the urge to run after the young matron, to call out for her to stop so she can embrace her. Once the tears have dried and the woman's heartbeat settled from its gallop, she will tell her this:

You are married to a soldier gone off to fight an infinite war. You will miss him at first so fiercely that it will feel as if you have reached the brink of madness. The seasons will change and your loneliness will turn to despair, just as winter fog settles over this island.

She will say, *I once became disoriented as a girl, led past the safety of the town's gates and into the moors by an older boy. He charmed me with wondrous stories, but when I refused his kiss, he left me alone as dusk fell. Clouds covered the stars and blocked the moon and I could not find my way back to town and home. I wandered in a silent panic, imagining hungry beasts beyond my vision, until my father came for me, his voice cutting through the syrupy darkness like a beacon.*

The first year without your husband's company will be much like that.

Eliza will press on: *You will miss his birthday, and he yours. Easter will come and go as will the sheep-shearing festival, the Fourth of July. You will spend a summer day at the beach, gazing out across the sea and wondering where he is, if he is. At Christmas, you will not feel the light of the season inside your heart.*

You will give birth, and your child will have his eyes.

You will be wedded to a ghost.

Eliza imagines the woman pulling away from her—who wouldn't, upon hearing such a cataclysmic fate? But Eliza will reach for the stranger's elbow, and tighten her grasp. *Eventually,* she'll say, *the grief will fade. Your heart will toughen and you will grow strong. You will raise your child and teach her well, and control the household as you see fit and celebrate birthdays and make important decisions independently for all of you every day.*

Your marriage will be made up of three beings: a wife, her husband, and the sea between them. And because of that, you will—for better or worse—be free.

But instead of uttering a word, Eliza simply watches the young wife disappear into the crowd.

Now back on Main Street, Eliza enters the cool dark of Citizens Bank and tries not to let the imposing building filled with men intimidate her. Aiming for a calm she doesn't feel, she heads straight to the bank manager's desk.

"Ah, Mrs. Macy," the bank manager Mr. Edmunds says, not at all surprised to see her. "Would you like a seat?"

"No, thank you," Eliza says. The banker merely raises his eyebrows and waits for her to continue. The manager is lanky, his defining feature a protruding Adam's apple. She tries to focus on this. "I'm here to ask for another loan."

"I'm afraid that's impossible, Mrs. Macy. You've taken out three already. The bank won't allow me to approve any more."

Three. *Like her children,* she thinks. Expensive creatures. "Then more time perhaps, to pay off Henry's and my debt?" Darn. She didn't mean for it to come out as a question.

"Need I remind you—which I don't think I do, since we send you new statements every month—

that your line of credit ran out several months back," he says, nodding with false sympathy. "And, to avoid foreclosure and loss of your house, Mrs. Macy, you must begin to repay—at least in part—by the end of the month." He then checks his giant ledger, writes something down, and hands it to her.

The amount scrawled on the piece of paper is enormous. She has an urge to curse at him, say something unkind about his ugly Adam's apple, then storm out past the other bankers' desks and slam the giant wrought-iron door behind her. Instead she turns and quietly leaves.

What now? Eliza slowly skulks away from the bank, the heat of afternoon oppressive, a fierce combination of humiliation and anger building inside. How will she, who has over the years used up all of her own savings from her parents' small dowry, make ends meet until Henry's return? And when will that return come?

Her husband's last trip—from 1839 to '42— was not profitable, thus getting the Macys into this tenuous situation in the first place, and causing Henry to turn right around and head back out to sea. This current voyage needs to be a success. For all of them.

The small piece of parchment with the large sum is crumpled in her damp palm, black ink staining her hands. She crosses town at the corner of Main Street and Federal, stops for a passing horse and buggy, and drops the note in the gutter, right into a steaming pile of dung.

And that's when she notices the new storefront. Well, it's an old storefront, but it is vacant and seems to have a new tenant inside. Right there. On the corner of Main and Federal. In the heart of town. Nantucket's best cobbler—the Black man named Benjamin Wright who has the shoe shop out on Fair Street—stands inside the large glass windows with Mr. Landry from the town council, the pair of them holding up papers as they point around the space and nod at one another like old friends.

This is a terrible development, an unwelcome addition to all the bad news Eliza has already received today. Because Eliza's one last hope in all of this financial mess is to ensure that her daughter Alice and son-in-law Larson's men's shop, Handler's Clothing, only two blocks away from this very location, does well and turns a profit. They are currently the only store on Main Street that sells men's shoes. And right now Alice and Larson aren't making ends meet.

Eliza is doing everything she can to help their business stay afloat. She manages the accounting and purchase orders herself and even works in the shop in her free time whenever Larson allows her to. The last thing they need now is nearby business competition on Main Street. She had tried once before unsuccessfully to stop Benjamin

Wright from encroaching on their territory, but the cobbler keeps turning up.

"Mr. Wright, I shall see you at the town council meeting tonight at seven o'clock," Eliza hears Mr. Landry say as he exits the building with the cobbler. To avoid staring right at them, Eliza glances down. She bends over her skirts and pretends to tie the laces on her left boot, noticing with some irony that the top fastening on the old leather shoe needs replacing. "Bring all of your paperwork, including a bank note and letters of support, and be prepared to explain to the council your plans for buying the property and running your cobbler shop from the first floor."

"With a small inn and grogshop above, don't forget," Mr. Wright added.

"Yes, indeed. A nice little business proposition."

Not just rent, but *own?* Not even her Larson owns his shop. Eliza's neck cramps as she tilts her head up toward the men. She can't possibly stay hunched over her shoe any longer, so she stands and pretends to study the parchment nailed to a wooden pole announcing the time and date of the next abolitionist meeting.

"The councilmen will vote immediately?" Benjamin Wright asks. "Meg and I will have our answer tonight?"

"Yes. You'll know by the end of the evening. We'll open the floor for discussion, let the

39

community speak their piece. Then we'll consider their perspectives and vote."

A new plan begins to form in Eliza's mind. Suddenly, this long, hot Monday is not long enough. So much to do! She must stop at Handler's Clothing and have a little chat with Larson and Alice. See what they are doing later on tonight. Then she must get home to supervise the twins in their afternoon chores and make sure they weed the garden and prune carefully around her few successful tomato plants. Finally, she will prepare a nice supper for her family. One of their favorite dishes. In fact, Eliza should stop in at the butcher's! Splurge on something fresh, writing Henry's name once more in the credit ledger—and then she will get dressed in her finest and prepare some words for tonight's town council meeting.

If anyone in town is gossiping about her, Eliza hardly even notices.

2

MARIA

Maria Mitchell stands in the center of the first-floor lecture hall of the Nantucket Atheneum, this former-church-turned-library and museum, directly under a ray of late afternoon sun shining through the large cathedral windows. Her arms are thrust out in front of her as her fingers pinch the top of a well-preserved creature while the rest of its small body dangles freely as if still alive. Oh, how Maria loves the natural world!

"What is it?" little Joseph Allen whisper-asks behind her, completely entranced. Joseph is one of her Atheneum Boys, who Maria trains in astronomy and map-reading skills in exchange for their help in her library. Although Maria isn't supposed to have favorites, Joseph Allen is a current pet.

"A bat from Madagascar," Maria beams.

"May I touch it?" He is slight for thirteen, giving off the impression of a much younger boy. But he's intelligent and curious, with a pug nose, light brown eyes, and a cowlick like a question mark in his sandy hair. Spunky and wiry, Joseph's body is always in motion, which should serve him well when he goes off to sea in a few years. Although restless by nature, Joseph has a sharp mind and a strong capacity for creating order from chaos, which is exactly what Maria needs in a library volunteer.

"Be gentle," Maria says, letting the boy stroke the bat's mottled fur. He circles the creature to examine its back, something most children wouldn't think of doing. "The scientific name is *Taphozous mauritianus*, or Mauritian Tomb bat. See the all-white ventral surface?"

"You mean like a belly?" Joseph asks, stepping back around to study it from the front.

"Yes, that center region there."

Although Maria, now twenty-seven, has left behind the formal profession of teaching children, educating others will always be a love of hers, as she doles out information all day to volunteers and patrons alike at the Atheneum. Not only did Maria teach at the local grammar school, but she also opened and ran successfully her own school for a year before being offered the position here at the Atheneum. Using her best instructor's voice, she quizzes Joseph about the location of Madagascar, pressing for specifics about the climate. He's ripe for more information, but it's almost closing time, so she shoos him along. "Enough staring for now, Joseph. You still have to shelve the new shipment of books from London. They are stacked on my desk for you upstairs."

"Yes, ma'am," Joseph says. "Thank you for

teaching me about the Taphozous mauritianus!"
And he's off, around the corner and up the stairs
to the library on the second floor.

On the first floor, rows of benches—once
pews—line up neatly behind Maria, awaiting
the next visiting speaker. From Ralph Waldo
Emerson, to Horace Mann and Maria's personal
favorite, Frederick Douglass, who gave his first
speech to a mixed race crowd standing right
here, this space has been graced by the voices
of inspired and inspiring public figures. And, in
the late afternoon, this happens to be the best
spot from which to view a new item for the
museum's collection. Natural light is not good
for preserving unique and splendid curiosities,
certainly, but it works for initial viewing, before
cataloging the artifact and displaying it in the
rear of the hall, where she has set up a small
museum. Maria refers to it as her Cabinet of
Curiosities.

Over the years, whalers and merchants have
brought her incredible treasures, including
minerals and shells from Polynesia, silks from
the Orient, porcelain and onyx figurines, a
variety of spears and other weapons, flora and
fauna from India, ivory and bone carved with
scrimshaw, the jaw of a sperm whale, two sword-
fish swords, and, just last month, the skin of a
python. Maria carefully catalogs each item's
history along with the name of its donor, a task

for which she receives extra compensation from the Atheneum's trustees.

Maria turns her attention back to the winged creature before her. It is a black-and-white mix, with beady eyes, pointy little ears and the furry body of a squirrel. *Fascinating.* She brings it over to a lecture table covered with white cloth and begins to take measurements, first of its wingspan, and then of its body length. She makes other notes about the small mammal on a card, carefully paying attention to every detail. Tonight she'll be presenting an update on the full Cabinet of Curiosities at the town council meeting, and she wants to make certain to highlight all of the best and newest items with accurate and specific descriptions. The more positive attention Maria can bring to this Atheneum and museum, the better. As its reputation grows, Maria hopes to attract even more visitors, both national and international, patrons with deep pockets, and public speakers through its stately doors. Already the Atheneum is the cultural center of the island. Why not the whole world?

Maria is excited for tonight's meeting, reveling in any opportunity to share her mostly solitary work with a wider audience. She carefully wraps up the bat in cloth and returns it to a crate lined with straw by her feet. She seals the top of the box and leaves it there for later. For she's just had the most wonderfully inspired idea: why try to describe this latest curiosity to the town council when she can bring the preserved mammal and display it for everyone to see. Now *that* should garner some attention. The community will be talking about it for days and beyond. She'll become a legend! *Remember the time Maria Mitchell brought a bat from Madagascar to the town council meeting? Oh, Maria, you rabble-rouser.* She can't help but chuckle to herself as she climbs the curved staircase to the second floor and the actual library itself.

She walks past the neat rows of wooden farm tables, straightening piles of books as she goes, and saying hello to patrons bent over small texts. Between the big windows, the walls are lined with floor-to-ceiling mahogany bookshelves, each alcove organized loosely by subject matter, from natural history to encyclopedias and poetry. Maria's most recent catalog of the library's 3000 volumes has just reached 120 pages, and it is growing each week.

"Maria, dear," an old woman named Mrs. Hodges says, looking up from her favorite spot by one of the tall windows. She has a strong, upper-crust Boston accent, putting much emphasis on the middle syllable of Maria's name, Ma-*rye*-ya. At least she pronounces it correctly. "Come sit," Mrs. Hodges says, a glint in her eye. "You work too hard."

Oh no. Maria recognizes that look. Of course

she does, since she receives it several times a week from the married women of this small island town. Their fevered need for matchmaking would almost be humorous if it weren't so cloyingly desperate. She sighs and resigns herself to be patient.

"Yes?" Maria asks.

"I saw you seated next to John Talbot at church Sunday last," Mrs. Hodges says.

"I arrived too late to sit in my usual spot," Maria says.

Her parents and younger siblings are still Quakers, attending church on Fair Street, but Maria left the Friends to join the much more open-minded Unitarians on Orange Street several years ago. She usually sits with her older sister and her husband, both also Unitarians, but by the time she arrived last week, the minister had already begun the service and Maria didn't want to be disruptive. She thought no one would notice her in the back pew, but now she concedes the truth: that everyone notices everything about their neighbors on Nantucket.

"Is that the only reason?" the old woman says, peering at Maria over the top of her spectacles. "Because last I heard, Mr. Talbot stopped courting Winifred Hicks."

Stopped courting! That is certainly a delicate way of presenting the story. "Yes, well, it's hard to court someone once she's run off with a sailor, wouldn't you say?" Maria says, standing and moving some stray books from the table between them. She pictures raven-haired Winnie waving theatrically from the bow of a ship as she and her companion make their way to New Bedford and beyond. Rumor has it they were married once they arrived in that port city, but no one has heard from the couple since.

"However it happened that Mr. Talbot became eligible once again, he is Oxford-educated, tall, and from a family of successful merchants."

Well-bred like a fine horse! Maria thinks. "Quite eligible, yes," she says, stifling a laugh. Not wanting to appear rude, she turns sideways and deposits the books into a pile in need of careful refiling. She will have Joseph put them back where they belong.

And then she spies a small note, wrapped in crisp newsprint and tied with red string, tucked carefully between the piles, and her heart skips a beat.

Linley.

Linley was here.

Maria scans the room for a trace of her friend among the other patrons, between the piles of volumes, but there is none. She smiles softly to herself when she realizes that she missed her yet again.

"Miss Mitchell? Can you assist us, please?" a woman asks, breaking Maria's spell.

Mrs. Jones approaches Maria's desk with her daughter, a girl who dislikes reading because, she says, the words jump on the page. How Maria longs to pore over the letter from Linley right now, unfold it here in the open and laugh and imagine the conversation. But that's impossible. She pockets the note in her full skirt and nods as she walks toward Mrs. Jones to help her daughter find just the right book. She will make time later.

"Can we look at the giant bird book, again, Mother? Like we did yesterday?" a young boy asks as he climbs the steps, and Maria can tell from the excited voice that it is little David Hallett, on his daily visit to the two-hundred-page, fully illustrated Audubon guide, *Birds of America*, bought directly by Maria from the naturalist himself.

She may never get to the note at this rate, although the anticipation is in itself a delight. Maria glances back to her desk and realizes she must finish composing a letter to Horace Mann, the secretary of education for Massachusetts, inviting him to return as a guest speaker. Her hands linger on a newspaper clipping from last month. A local resident wrote another scathing letter to the editor stating that colored children carry diseases like malaria and, therefore, they put white children at risk by attending school together. Nantucket, while progressive in its leanings, still harbors people afraid of change, some of whom are even willing to scapegoat people of color. Should she send the upsetting article along to Mr. Horace Mann to show him the real level of prejudice they are facing here? Or would it scare him off?

During the other seasons of the year, when the island is quiet, Maria pores over the library's academic texts in the sacred silence of this holy building, a cathedral of learning where she is free to study and create her own life's syllabus. She challenges and delights herself by deciphering astronomy textbooks in Latin, struggling through difficult mathematical calculations until night falls and she is needed at home. The Atheneum—with its museum, lecture hall, and compendium of books—is her college.

In summer, however, with the Atheneum abuzz, she must put her personal education (as well as personal relationships) aside for a time. It is a shame since the latest edition of *Silliman's Journal* arrived from Yale yesterday. Maria's meteorological observations on the average cloudiness of Nantucket from 1843 to 1845 were published in that journal just last year. To see her name printed there, in *The American Journal of Science and Arts*, still gives her a jolt of pride, and she looks forward to each new edition, learning about the work of other scientists and hoping someday her work might be once again included. *Ego stadium voluntas cras*, she tells herself. *I will have to wait until tomorrow.*

And always, always there is the matter of discovering a comet. As an amateur astronomer himself, the King of Denmark announced years ago that he would award a prize to the first person to discover a new comet. When the king died in 1839, his son took the throne and kept the contest alive. Originally, Maria was not motivated by competition, but by the joys of discovery for its own sake. But, as the years have marched on without a winner, Maria's competitive spirit has grown along with her astronomical abilities. Maybe this will be the year.

Before she knows it, it's half past five. Maria gently nudges the dozen or so patrons out of their intellectual trances brought on by their collective quiet study. She cannot blame them for getting so lost in thought—this serene building has a mesmerizing quality, one Maria herself helps to cultivate—but she has a busy evening ahead of her. She waves goodbye to them all and almost leaves the premise herself before remembering to take the wooden crate with her.

And then, once everyone exits the building, Maria locks the door behind her and sits on the steps of the Atheneum, her dark dress fanning out around her. She unfolds Linley's note in the fading daylight, her mind soaring toward the heavens.

3

MEG

Meg Wright looks around her kitchen, mostly satisfied. Dinner is cleared away, the dishes are done, and her daughter Lucy has had her bath. Cinnamon buns—a special treat for a special night—are cooling on the butcher block. Meg wipes her sticky hands on a damp rag and dries them on her apron, checking the time on the small clock on the wall by the kitchen table. It's just after six. She and Benjamin have to get going. They can't be late for tonight's town council meeting.

"Hello, Mrs. Wright!" a little voice says. Jenny Cole knocks on the screen door while simultaneously opening it and letting herself in. Her hair is braided in two neat plaits, matching the cloth doll in her hand. "I can smell your baking all the way down the street!"

Meg laughs. "I hope that's a compliment, Jenny! I'd invite you inside, but you're already here."

"Best friends don't have to knock, Mama says," Jenny smiles.

"Yoo-hoo!" a voice sings out.

"And speaking of your mother," Meg says, not needing to finish the rest of the sentence.

The next one through the door is Daniel, Faithful Cole's three-year-old, who dashes in and lets the door slam behind before his mother reaches it. He's got a wide grin and the chubbiest legs sticking out from under his short pants. Meg wishes she could scoop him up into her arms and squeeze him, but she is nine months pregnant and her back is aching and her belly is just too big, so she settles for a pat on the head and asks if he'd like a cinnamon bun.

"Yes, peeze!" Daniel says, clapping his hands together. He scrambles up into a chair and takes the treat with wide-eyed delight, and Meg turns her attention to Faithful, coming toward the door.

"Need help, Faith?" Meg asks.

"No, I'm doing fine. Doesn't hurt. Just slow."

Although Faithful is around Meg's age of twenty-six, she's been plagued with arthritis in her hips since she was a girl, and she grimaces in pain as she climbs the two steps into Meg's shingled house. To add to this, Faithful recently put on quite a bit of weight, which also slows her down, especially in this heat, that hasn't let up even now, at dusk. Faith's hair is tied back in two braids like her daughter Jenny's, her skin a deeper dark than either of her children's. Meg pulls out a chair for her friend and pours her some water from a pewter pitcher on the table. Faithful drinks it down and Meg refills it.

"Thanks for keeping Lucy company tonight,"

Meg says. Although she feels a restlessness to get going, Meg knows that Faithful likes to chat and gossip. Meg doesn't mind indulging her friend for a few minutes while Benjamin changes out of his work clothes.

Faithful makes a gesture with her right hand as if shooing away a fly. "You know I love that little girl like my own. And you know we need your shop to get the town's approval tonight. Now more than ever, especially with everything that's going on in protest of the integration of the schools."

Meg passes her a nicely over-iced warm bun. "I know, believe me. I'm counting the days until school's out." Four more days, to be exact. They have made it through so much; they just need to hold on a little bit longer. On Friday, the island folk can celebrate their victory: that Nantucket made it through its first year of school integration without incident.

Daniel Cole jumps down from the wooden chair, his hands sticky and half the bun uneaten. Meg's baby Elias would have been about the same age as Daniel, had he lived. Would he have been a chubby thing like Daniel, she wonders, or more of a string bean, like Lucy? Would her son have liked raisins in his cinnamon rolls, even though his big sister picks them out? Meg blinks back tears—she's so emotional these days—as she feels the new baby in her belly kick: a good omen. No use in dwelling on the past, on the what-would-have-beens. Time to stay focused on the now and the future. Meg dabs at the corner of her eyes with a knuckle and sits back down at the table beside her friend.

Faithful licks some icing from her thumb and takes another bite of the pastry. "I do not know how you get the dough so flaky! I try for the life of me and mine never come out as good as yours."

Meg laughs good-naturedly but shakes her head no. Faithful's cinnamon buns are identical to her own. The only difference is in having someone else bake for you; that's what makes the food taste better. That act of love is the only special ingredient. Meg has explained her philosophy to Faith, but she won't hear of it. Her friend maintains it's something extraordinary about Meg's butter, or cinnamon, or sugar, when it's really about a friend doing the work so you don't have to.

"Got a letter this morning from Big Daniel, from a ship passing through on its way to Nova Scotia," Faithful says.

"Yes? And?" Faithful is Meg's main source of information, but she doles out her knowledge like she expects a penny for each piece. Meg wants to hand her friend a dime and say, *Out with it!*

"All's the same this trip. Hunt whales and pass the other time carving designs into whalebone as they weigh down the ship with barrels of oil."

"When's he due back?"

"They made it safely back round the horn, so he's inching closer. But he says Captain Macy is making them delay their return. *We got more to do,* the captain says. Daniel said he's been sworn to secrecy, but he said they were docked in the port of New Orleans and I think—"

"What?" Meg asks.

Faithful shuts her mouth, shakes her head no.

"Something bad, then?" Meg adds, a shapeless worry creeping up her spine. The South is not a safe place for any Black man. Even a freeborn person on a Nantucket whaling ship can be kidnapped and sold into slavery, although Meg hasn't ever heard of it happening to someone she knows. "Do you think Daniel and the others are in physical danger? Or is the issue more financial, that they haven't secured enough oil?"

Meg recalls that the last trip wasn't profitable, that something had gone terribly wrong. The men of New Guinea refused to discuss it when they came home, every single one tight-lipped even when plied with liquor at Absalom Boston's alehouse down the street. They stayed in Nantucket for only one month, that crew. Turned right back around and went out with Captain Macy again, no questions asked, Big Daniel included. They all seem to trust and admire that man, but so much can go wrong on a whaling expedition, even when it is in capable hands.

Meg scoots her chair closer to her friend's and takes Faithful's hands in her own. "You can tell me anything, you know that."

"Big Daniel hinted at—well, more like suggested that Captain Macy was trying to—"

But here she stops. Faithful is clearly distressed, so Meg doesn't press her any further. She'll let her know in good time, if there ever is such a time.

"Stop being such a bully!" Lucy calls out from the bedroom.

"I'm not the bully!" Jenny yells back. "You are!"

Meg and Faithful exchange a look, both at first worried a little about the content of their daughters' exchange. But, while the pair of seven-year-olds try to sound menacing, their voices are raised in a playacting tone, eventually dissolving into a fit of giggles.

"They never really argue," Faithful says.

Meg nods. "But Lucy does keep talking about this school bully. Any idea who it might be?"

Faithful shakes her head no. "I keep trying to get Jenny to say, but she won't."

"Maybe we should go by the schoolhouse, ask Mr. Hart if he's witnessed anything."

Faithful raises her eyebrows. "And what would your husband have to say about that?"

Benjamin, so focused on trying to purchase

the cobbler shop, would not be happy if his wife caused trouble at the South Grammar School. But causing trouble is what Meg thinks democracy is supposed to be about. It's her family's legacy. Meg's grandfather, Giddeon Lewis, sued the state of Massachusetts for his freedom in 1775 and won back the money he earned working on a whaling ship. Because of that lawsuit, Meg's father, Captain Wendell Lewis, was born free— becoming wealthy as one of the first Black whaling captains with an all-Black crew—and Meg Lewis was born free. It's a story she tells any and every chance she gets.

Imagine it. Suing your way to freedom.

But that was just the start of what her Lewis family had endured, and had done here on this small island. The battle for school desegregation on Nantucket has been going on since Meg and Faith both were in public school. More precisely, since 1837, when Meg herself passed the high school entrance exam but was denied actual admittance to the high school. Oh, all the studying she did to prepare. Months and months of mathematics and reading, of being quizzed by her father, who hired Quaker tutors like Anna Gardner—an educator and ardent abolitionist besides—to help Meg study for the examinations.

Wendell Lewis's philosophy about his daughter Meg entering the high school was simple, and thus he stated it simply for Nantucketers to understand: Since our whaling ships have been successfully integrated for the past 150 years, why haven't our school buildings in the same port done the same?

Oh yes, Meg is used to watching the tide turn quickly on matters of race on her island; she is, in fact, caught up very much in its current.

Thinking back on her family reminds her of her goals. She wants, needs both her and Benjamin to be the first Black shop owners on Main Street, and to have her daughter Lucy be part of the first integrated class in Nantucket's history.

Four more days, that's it.

She needs a decision in their favor tonight.

And then, if she dares to let herself think it, she needs to deliver a healthy child in a few weeks' time. Her last baby, Elias, didn't survive ten days. Meg isn't sure she could herself survive a loss like that again.

"Ready, my dear?" Benjamin says, coming down the steps from their two-story saltbox, his hair combed back and his beautiful leather shoes shined to a high gloss. He holds a neatly folded stack of papers. Benjamin needs her to be strong.

Meg pushes away her worries and doubts.

"Well," Faithful says, rising from her chair. "Don't the two of you look like important people."

How Meg wants to believe it.

She and Benjamin walk from their home on

Atlantic Avenue toward the main intersection at Prospect Street, the lively center of life in Nantucket's New Guinea neighborhood—comprised of a vibrant mix of cultures, including those of African, Wampanoag, Pacific Islander and Cape Verdean descent—and they pass the barbershop closing up for the night. They give Mr. Thomas a wave, then pass the rope walk, the dance hall and the general store before turning onto York Street, where the gray-shingled African Meeting House stands on the corner. Just past there is the York Street School.

The York Street School was previously the only school on the island for Black children. Lucy attended school there with Jenny Cole for the last two years, and it is where Meg herself was educated, after they moved the school out of the African Meeting House. But now an invisible line has been drawn straight through New Guinea, redistricting some children, including Lucy. Jenny Cole lives on Orange Street, so for her, that newly integrated school is actually closer. For Lucy, it's a bit of a walk, especially on a hot, blustery, or rainy day, which is basically any day on Nantucket.

The couple stop at Absalom Boston's tavern and inn. A horse-drawn, two-wheeled calash is waiting there to take them to the town hall, a large clapboard-fronted building on Orange Street that, during the day, is Lucy's grammar school.

The same structure also serves as the courthouse, not that Meg or Benjamin has ever been there for any legal reason. Like many people on Nantucket who often hold two or more jobs—the barber is also a woodworker, the farmer dabbles in coopering—the buildings also work morning to night to serve different capacities, depending on who needs to use them.

Given Meg's back pain, Benjamin doesn't want Meg to walk, especially at night when she can't quite see the uneven ground beneath her feet. But they must both attend the meeting, so Benjamin was thoughtful enough to ask Absalom to borrow his horse and buggy.

A famous Black whaling captain in his own right, Absalom Boston, who in 1822 was the first Black man to captain an all-Black crew, was friendly with Meg's father and dotes on her like an uncle. Men's laughter punctuates the night along with the glow of candles from inside the first-floor alehouse attached to the inn, and, as the couple prepares to go, Absalom comes to the open door, barrel-chested and full of vitality. He scratches his beard, lifts his eyebrows, and raises the mug in his right hand to them. "Best wishes to you in town tonight. You have every right to own that property on Main Street, Ben and Meggie. Don't let them insinuate otherwise. Stand firm and, if they start to waver, show them your cash."

Benjamin laughs. "I thought you were going

to advise us to show them your letter of recommendation," he says.

"That, too. But on Nantucket, thank goodness, money is king. I have found the dividing line between Black and white can be significantly blurred by green."

Meg smiles and thanks Absalom, who steps forward and plants a small kiss on her cheek. "Your parents are looking out for you, Meg," he whispers. Rum lingers on her skin, which does remind her a bit of her father, and so the scent brings Meg comfort more than the words. "The situation will work out fine, you'll see," he says, waving and heading back into the alehouse.

Oh, how Meg despises that word *fine*. There's nothing fine about this. Every time Meg thinks of walking into that stuffy, dark hall filled with people judging her worth, butterflies of nerves flap their wings under her rib cage. And didn't Absalom run for school committee this year— one of forty-four candidates—and lose? What makes him so sure things will be fine in this town?

Benjamin has readied the horse, and now he helps Meg step up into the open cart. She sits and runs one hand nervously over her dress skirt, which puffs up around her. She wishes she could have worn her best summer dress, a pale yellow frock with lace around the collar, but it doesn't fit her anymore, even after letting the waist out twice, so she has to make do in a flower-print sack hastily stitched together from an extra bolt of fabric she found in the back of Jones's Mercantile on the wharf. After losing Elias, Meg had given away her maternity dress because the sight of it left her bereft. Now she almost wishes she had kept it.

"You look pretty," Benjamin says, putting his foot in a stirrup and settling on the wide brown mare.

He means it as a compliment, but she wants to look fierce. Menacing. Strong. All those daisies and roses dancing around: too much pattern for her liking, and too much like a little girls' dress to be taken seriously as a businesswoman. "I look like a tea cozy," Meg says to the horse's backside, her words lost to her husband. Benjamin clicks his tongue and grabs the reins, and off they go, down Prospect Street and toward town hall as dusk settles over the gray-shingled homes, the air heavy with the scent of roses, which cling and climb up the town's cottages and decorate their roofs like party hats.

Benjamin stops the horse on Orange Street in front of the South Grammar School and Town Hall, dismounts, and hitches the reins to a nearby iron post. A small crowd has gathered on the lawn leading up and into the clapboard building, people milling about trying to enjoy whatever fresh air they can get before entering the cloying humidity of an enclosed space in July. Meg quickly scans the mostly white crowd. Are they a friendly or hostile bunch? Right now, they just seem worn down by the heat.

Benjamin helps Meg out of the calash. It takes a bit of balance and is not the prettiest of exits from a buggy ever seen, although Meg tries to make it look natural. Once she's out, Benjamin squeezes her hand twice. She pumps his hand twice in return. It's their quick signal in a crowd, a way to send a small conversation back and forth between themselves without using words. *You okay? Yes, I am.* Or, *I'm frightened. Me too.* Mostly, it means an echo, of *Here I am. And here am I.*

David Joy, staunch supporter of abolition and Black rights and one of the co-founders of the Atheneum, is here, shaking hands with another man and heading into the meeting hall. Anna Gardner, Meg's former teacher, waves. And William Hadwen and his wife are here, too. They're the ones building that huge white mansion on Upper Main Street. Maria Mitchell, too, who gives Meg a wave hello. Everyone holds lanterns; Meg can see the glow of them from inside the wood building as more and more people enter. Although these are only candles, the smell of so many lanterns in the dense night air reminds Meg of the charred scent hanging over town after the Great Fire of 1838, and she hopes it isn't a precursor of bad news tonight.

And then, some bad news indeed: walking directly toward her down the dusty street is none other than that insufferable Macy woman who tried to prevent Meg and Benjamin from opening their first shop two years ago. She said that it was too close to downtown and her son-in-law's shop, and therefore unfair for business. Mrs. Eliza Macy. Wearing a wide-brimmed blue silk bonnet with colorful rosettes, more appropriate for a formal wedding than a town hall meeting, and on the arm of that very son-in-law, the one who owns that almost-failing men's shop. Beside her on the other arm is a young woman, who must be the man's wife and Eliza's grown daughter, although they look nothing like mother and child. Meg hasn't heard a peep of negativity since opening the shop on Fair Street, though, and had assumed that all of that nastiness was behind them, and, that the woman would have moved on by now to fight other misguided battles against other unsuspecting competitors with stores closer to her son-in-law's.

"Maybe she's here for another reason," Benjamin whispers, as they file into the hall directly behind the woman.

Maybe, Meg concedes. Perhaps Eliza Macy's son-in-law wants to expand his business in some other way. Perhaps they are here about something else entirely, not having to do with them.

mine with our bedrooms and bathrooms sharing a wall. But where mine was an unrenovated blank slate, Nash's apartment had been updated sometime this decade. It had also been trashed.

Nothing about the man struck me as a slob, but the evidence was undeniably strewn everywhere.

The blinds were drawn over the front windows, blocking out the light and view of the street. There was a partially folded mound of laundry on the coffee table. It looked as though he'd given up on the folding and had just been plucking clean clothes off the top for a while. The floor was littered with dirty clothes, resistance bands most likely for physical therapy, and get-well cards. There was a rumpled blanket and pillow on the couch.

The kitchen had new appliances and granite counters and opened to the main living space, which gave me an unobstructed view of dirty dishes, old to-go containers, and at least four dead flower arrangements. His dining room table, like my own, was covered in files and more unopened mail.

The whole place smelled stuffy like it had been closed up, unused. Like there was no life in it.

"It's . . . uh . . . usually not this cluttered. I've been busy lately," he said, sounding embarrassed.

I was now one million percent positive that those wounds of his went deeper than he was letting on.

"Bathroom?" I asked.

"That way," he said, pointing in the direction of the bedroom and looking just a little sheepish.

The bedroom wasn't as much of a disaster as the rest of the place. In fact, it looked like a vacant hotel room. The furniture—a bed, dresser, and pair of nightstands—all matched. Above the neatly made bed was a framed collection of country music prints. Prescription bottles were lined up like a row of soldiers on one of the nightstands. There was a fine layer of dust on the surface.

The man was definitely sleeping on the couch.

The bathroom was typical for a bachelor. Few products and absolutely no attempt at atmosphere. The shower curtain and towels were beige for God's sake.

My bathtub was better, a claw-foot to his more modern tile surround. There was a pile of dirty laundry on the floor next to a perfectly good hamper. If the man hadn't been obviously battling some kind of demons, his hotness would have dropped several points for that infraction.

"Mind closing the door?" I asked.

He still looked a little dazed. There was something about the wounded Nash Morgan that tugged at me. And the temptation to tug back was nearly overwhelming.

"Nash?" I reached out and gave his arm a squeeze.

He jolted, then gave a little head shake. "Yeah. Sorry. What?"

"Mind closing the door so our smelly little pal can't get out?"

"Sure." He closed the door softly, then rubbed that spot between his brows again. "Sorry about the mess."

He looked so lost I had to fight the urge to tackle him and kiss it better. Instead, I hefted the dog into his line of sight. "The only mess I'm concerned with is this one."

I put her down and unwound the T-shirt. She immediately put her nose to the tile and started sniffing. A brave girl scoping out her new environment.

Nash sprang into action like a wooden puppet becoming a real boy. He bent and turned on the water in the tub. The town was not wrong about that very fine ass, I decided as I stripped his sweatshirt off over my head.

I held up the filthy dog T-shirt. "You might have to burn this."

"Might have to burn this bathroom." He nodded at the dog, who was leaving tiny muddy footprints everywhere.

I dragged my stained crop top off and added it to the pile of questionable laundry.

Nash took one long look at my sports bra and then nearly gave himself whiplash spinning around to test the water temperature with his hand and unnecessarily adjusting the shower curtain.

Sweet and gentlemanly.

Definitely not my type. But I had to admit, I liked seeing him riled.

Still avoiding looking directly at me, Nash grabbed a pile of towels from the linen closet and dropped two folded ones on the floor next to the tub before draping a third over the sink.

"Better lose the shirt, hotshot," I advised.

He glanced down at his uniform button-down that was covered in streaks of mud and grass stains. On a grimace, he worked the buttons open and stripped it off, dropping it into the hamper. Then he scooped the pile of dirty laundry from the floor and added it to the hamper.

He had on a white undershirt that hugged his chest. A strip of the colorful adhesive tape athletes used on injuries was visible under the left sleeve.

"Why don't you grab a big cup or something from the kitchen? I don't want to use the sprayer on her if it's gonna scare the hell out of her," he suggested.

"Sure." I left him and the dog and began my quest for a dog-washing vessel.

A quick search of his cabinets proved that most every dish the man owned was either in the sink or the overflowing dishwasher that, judging by the smell, hadn't been run recently. I dumped detergent into the dishwasher, started the cycle, then hand-washed a large, plastic Dino's Pizza cup.

I only felt the smallest splinter of guilt when I wandered past his table to peruse the files.

It was on the way back to the bathroom, so it wasn't like I'd made a special trip. Besides, I had a job to do. And it wasn't *my* fault he'd left them out in the open, I reasoned.

It took me less than thirty seconds to zero in on three folders.

HUGO, DUNCAN.

WITT, TINA.

217.

217 was a police code for assault with attempt to murder. It didn't take a genius to guess that it was probably the police report on Nash's shooting. I was definitely curious. But I only had time for a quick peek, which meant prioritizing. Sending a glance in the direction of the bedroom, I lifted the top of the Hugo file with one finger. The folder felt gritty and I realized that, like the nightstand in his bedroom, it was covered in a fine layer of dust.

I'd barely glanced at the paper on top, an unflattering mug shot from a few years ago, when I heard, "You find something?"

Startled, I dropped the folder closed, my heart kicking into high gear, before realizing Nash was calling from the bathroom.

I took a step back from the table and blew out a breath. "Coming," I yelled back weakly.

When I returned to the bathroom, my heart tripped over itself. Nash was now shirtless, his sopping wet undershirt on the floor next to the tub. And he was smiling. Like full-on hot-guy smile.

Between the half-frontal and the grin, I froze in place and appreciated the view.

"If you don't stop flinging water everywhere, you're gonna flood the barbershop," Nash warned the dog as she raced from one end of the tub to the other. He splashed water from the faucet at her and she let out a series of hoarse yet delighted barks.

I let out a laugh. Both man and dog turned to look at me.

"Figured I'd get her in the tub to make sure she wasn't gonna go all gremlin on us," Nash said.

The man's life might be gathering dust, but that heroism went bone-deep. The splinter of guilt grew into something bigger, sharper, and I counted my lucky stars that he hadn't actually caught me snooping.

There was a fine line between necessary risk and stupidity.

I joined him on the floor, kneeling on one of the folded towels, and handed over the cup. "You two look like you're having fun," I said, trying to sound like a woman who hadn't just invaded Nash's privacy.

The soggy little gremlin set her front paws on the lip of the tub and looked up at us with adoration. Her ratty tail blurred with happiness, sending droplets of dirty water everywhere.

"See if you can hang on to her while I douse her," Nash suggested, filling the cup with clean water.

"Come here, little hairy mermaid."

We worked side by side, scrubbing, sudsing, rinsing, and laughing.

Every time Nash's bare arm brushed mine, goose bumps exploded across my skin. Every time I felt the urge to move closer instead of putting some distance between us, I wondered what the hell was wrong with me. I was close enough to see every wince he made when he moved his shoulder in a way that didn't agree with the damaged muscles. But he never once complained.

It took four water changes and half an hour before the dog was finally clean.

Her wiry fur was mostly white with a scattering of dark patches on her legs. She had one spotted ear and one brown and black one.

"What are you going to call her?" I asked as Nash plucked the dog from the tub. She licked his face with exuberance.

"Me?" He maneuvered his head away from the pink tongue. "Stop licking me."

"Can't blame her. You've got a lickable face."

He gave me one of those smoldering looks before gently setting her down. She shook, sending water in a six-foot radius.

I grabbed the towel and draped it over her. "You found her. You get naming rights."

"She had a collar. She's probably already got a name."

She wiggled under my hands as I rubbed her furry little body dry. "Maybe she deserves a new one. A new name for a fresh start."

He eyed me for a long beat until I wanted to squirm under his perusal. Then he said, "You hungry?"

"Scout? Lucky?" I peered down at the now clean dog as I programmed a pot of coffee.

Nash looked over from the pan of eggs he was scrambling. "Scrappy?"

"Nope. No reaction. Lula?" I sank down to the floor and clapped my hands. She pranced over to me and happily accepted my affectionate petting.

"Gizmo? Splinter?"

"Splinter?" I scoffed.

"Teenage Mutant Ninja Turtles," Nash said, that hint of a smile visible again.

"Splinter was a sewer rat."

"A sewer rat with martial arts skills," he pointed out.

"This young lady needs a debutante name," I insisted. "Like Poppy or Jennifer."

No reaction from the canine, but the man in the room worked his way up to a full smirk of amusement. "How about Buffy?"

I smiled into the dog's fur. "The vampire slayer?"

He pointed the spatula at me. "That's the one."

"*I* like it, but she seems ambivalent to Buffy," I observed.

I could have gone next door to change while Nash made breakfast, but I'd decided instead to pull on his sweatshirt again and hang out. He—unfortunately—had changed, putting on a clean shirt and jeans.

Now we were performing some sort of cozy, domestic scene in the kitchen. Coffee brewed, a gorgeous, barefoot man did breakfasty things at the stove, and the faithful dog danced at our feet.

Nash scooped a portion of the eggs onto one of the three paper plates he'd lined up and set it aside. The little dog sprang out of my lap to paw at Nash's leg.

"Hold your horses. Let it cool off first," he advised her. Her raspy yip said she wasn't interested in holding anyone's horses.

I got up and washed my hands. Nash tossed me the hand towel he wore over his shoulder, then started sprinkling cheese over the eggs. Feeling companionable, I found two dirty mugs on the counter and washed them.

The toaster spit out two pieces of nicely browned bread just as I poured the first cup of coffee.

"We found her in a pipe. So how about Piper?" Nash suggested suddenly.

The dog perked up, then sat, cocking her head.

"She likes that one," I noted. "Don't you, Piper?"

She wiggled her little hind end in acknowledgment.

"Think we've got ourselves a winner," Nash agreed.

I poured the second mug, watching as he deposited the plate of eggs on the floor. "Come and get it, Piper."

The dog pounced, both front paws landing on the plate as she scarfed up her breakfast.

"She's going to need another bath," I said with a laugh.

Nash dropped a piece of toast on each of the remaining plates, then awkwardly used his right hand to top them with the cheesy egg mixture.

"And more breakfast," he observed, handing me a plate.

Nash Morgan was going to make some woman very lucky someday.

We ate standing in the kitchen, which felt safer

and less domestic to me than clearing a spot at the table. Though I wouldn't have minded another look at those files.

I was here to do a job, not complicate things by getting cozy with an unfairly hot neighbor.

Even if he did make really good cheesy eggs. And looked really good with his fresh shirt and soulfully wounded eyes. Every time our gazes connected, I felt . . . something. Like the space between us was charged with energy that kept intensifying.

"What makes you feel alive?" he asked abruptly.

"Huh?" was my witty response, my mouth crammed full of the last bite of toast.

He was holding his mug and staring at me, half of his breakfast abandoned on the plate.

He needed to eat. The body needed fuel to heal.

"It used to be walking into the station for me. Every morning, not knowing what the day would hold but feeling like I was ready for anything," he said almost to himself.

"Doesn't it make you feel the same now?" I asked.

He gave a one-shouldered shrug, but the way his eyes locked on me was anything but casual. "What about you?"

"Driving fast. Loud music. Finding the perfect pair of shoes on sale. Dancing. Running. The chase. Sweaty, desperate sex."

His gaze turned hot and the temperature in the room seemed to rise several degrees.

Need. It was the only word I could think to describe what I saw in those blue eyes of his, and that still didn't do it justice.

He took a step toward me and my breath caught in my throat thanks to a wild mix of anticipation, adrenaline, and fear. *Wow. Wow. Wow.*

My heart was about to explode out of my chest. But in a good way for once.

I needed to get a hold of myself. Wasn't I trying to avoid impulsive leaps?

Before either of us could say or—dear lord—*do* anything, my phone rang shrilly, jolting me out of whatever bad idea I'd been about to jump into.

"I, uh, need to take this," I told him, holding up my phone.

His gaze was still locked on me in a way that made everything inside feel just a little desperate. Okay, fine. *A lot* desperate. And a million degrees of hot.

"Yeah," he said finally. "Thanks for the help."

"Anytime, hotshot," I managed weakly as I tried not to run for the door.

"Hi, Daley," I said, answering the call as I closed Nash's door behind me.

"Lina," my boss said by way of a greeting. Daley Matterhorn was an efficient sort of woman who didn't use two words when one would do. At fifty-two, she oversaw a team of a dozen

76

investigators, held a black belt in karate, and participated in triathlons for fun.

"What's up?" Our line of work didn't respect the Monday through Friday nine-to-five hours, so it wasn't concerning that she'd called on a Saturday morning.

"I know you're in the middle of an investigation, but I'd like you to put that on pause. We could use your help in Miami. Ronald tracked the missing Renaux painting to the home of a recently arrested drug kingpin. We need someone to lead a retrieval team tomorrow night before some officer of the law decides the painting is either evidence or an asset to be frozen. There's only a handful of security on-site. Should be a piece of cake for you."

I felt the familiar quickening of my pulse, excitement rising at the thought of tiptoeing just over the line for another win.

But putting together an operation in twenty-four hours wasn't just risky, it was downright dangerous. And Daley knew it.

Damn it.

"You're asking me to lead a team after what happened on the last job?"

"You got the job done. The client was thrilled. And I didn't hear you complaining when you collected your bonus."

"Someone got hurt," I reminded her. I *got* someone hurt.

"Lewis knew the risks. We're not selling life insurance policies and pushing papers here. This job comes with a certain amount of risk and anyone who doesn't have the balls to face that is welcome to seek employment elsewhere."

"I can't do it." I don't know which one of us was more surprised when the words came out of my mouth. "I'm making progress here and now isn't a good time to leave."

"You're basically doing on-site research. I can send someone else to ask questions and search property records. Literally anyone else."

"I'd prefer to see this through," I said, digging in my heels.

"You know, there's a position opening up in High Net Assets," Daley said, casually dangling my dream job in front of me like it was a pair of sparkly Jimmy Choos.

"I heard rumors," I said, my heart beating a little faster.

The High Net Assets department meant more travel, longer jobs, deeper cover, and bigger bonuses. It also meant more solo assignments. It was my big, scary goal and now here it was.

"Something to keep in mind. It'll take someone with guts, someone who isn't intimidated by dangerous situations, someone who isn't afraid of being the best."

"I understand," I said.

"Good. If you change your mind about tomorrow, call me."

"Will do." I hung up and shoved my hands into the front pocket of Nash's hoodie.

Part of me wanted to say yes. To get on a plane, dig into the intel, and find a way in. But the bigger, louder part of me knew I wasn't prepared to lead a team. I'd proven that resoundingly.

And there was another smaller, barely audible part that was getting tired of shitty motels and endless hours of surveillance. The one that carried the mantel of guilt and frustration for an op gone wrong. The one that might be losing her edge.

5

What Happens in the Shower Stays in the Shower

Nash

S top eatin' the laundry, Pipe," I called wearily from the kitchen floor. I was knee-deep in dead flower petals from the half dozen "sorry you got shot" floral arrangements people had sent during my recovery. It reminded me vaguely of my mom's funeral.

The damn dog zoomed around the island, one of my clean socks hanging out of her mouth.

I was exhausted and exasperated.

I'd called the rescue in Lawlerville to see about dropping Piper off but was told they were full up after taking in a dozen pets displaced by a hurricane that had churned through Texas. I was welcome to try another shelter in DC they'd said. But after another couple of calls, all I'd gotten were more "sorry, we're full" answers or warnings that dogs with medical issues or ones that didn't get adopted out fast enough were at risk of being put down.

So here I was, the reluctant foster dad to a scruffy, anxiety-ridden mutt.

I could barely take care of myself. How in the hell was I supposed to take care of a dog?

We'd taken a field trip to the vet for a checkup, during which Piper had cowered behind me like the nice lady vet with treats was the devil. After her clean bill of health, we hit up Knockemout's pet shop for some basic supplies. But owner and shrewd sales guy, Gael, had seen my dumb ass coming a mile away. One look at Piper's happy little face when she found an entire aisle of stuffed animals and Gael had to put the BACK IN 15 sign in the window to help me haul all my purchases home.

Fancy health food, gourmet treats, leashes with matching collars, toys, an orthopedic dog bed nicer than my own mattress. He'd even thrown in a freaking sweater thing to keep "Princess Piper" warm on walks.

Piper pranced over and gave a muffled bark through the sock and the stuffed lamb she'd managed to cram into her mouth.

"What? I don't know what you want."

She spit the lamb out on top of the pile of dead flowers.

I scrubbed my hands over my face. I wasn't equipped for this. Case in point: My apartment.

It looked like Knox's bedroom as a teenager. Smelled like it too. I hadn't really noticed it until I'd noticed Lina and then Gael noticing.

So instead of plodding through paperwork

at the station like I'd planned, I'd turned on a football game, opened the damn blinds, and got to work cleaning.

The dishwasher was on its third and final load. I had a Mount Everest of clean laundry to put away—if I could get the dog to stop stealing it. I'd attacked the layers of dust and sticky furniture rings, tossed weeks' worth of moldy takeout, and even managed to order a small grocery delivery.

Piper kept me company as I washed, scrubbed, sorted, purged, and put away. She didn't care much for the vacuum cleaner. But then I figured she didn't have room to complain seeing as how up until that morning, she'd been living in a drain pipe.

She cocked her head and danced in place, her newly trimmed toenails tapping on the wood floor.

On an oath, I tossed the lamb in the direction of the living room and watched the dog tear after it in delight.

My shoulder ached. My head pounded. Weariness made my bones feel brittle as if I had a suffered a case of the permanent flu. How easy would it be to just sit here on the floor for the rest of whatever time I had left?

There was a loud *thunk* of the broom handle hitting the floor followed by a pitiful yip and the scrambling of toenails on the floor. Piper reappeared without the sock or the lamb and threw herself in my lap, trembling.

"Fuck me," I muttered. "You think I'm capable of protecting you from anything? I can't even protect myself."

This didn't seem to concern the little dog as she was too busy burrowing deeper into my crotch.

I sighed. "Okay, weirdo. Let's go. I'll save you from the big bad broom."

I tucked her under my arm and creakily got to my feet, feeling like I was a hundred years old. I dumped the rest of the flower carcasses into the overflowing trash can, snagged the last basket of laundry, and trudged into the bedroom.

"There. Happy?" I asked, putting Piper and the basket on the bed.

She trotted to the head of the bed to my pillow, then curled in a tight ball, tail over nose, and let out a snorty sigh.

"Don't get used to it. I just dropped eighty-six bucks on a dog bed for you, not to mention the second I can find a foster family, you're out the door."

She closed her eyes and ignored me.

"Fine. Keep the bed."

It wasn't like I'd been sleeping in it either. Instead, I camped out on the couch, letting the drone of QVC hosts lull me to sleep where the dreams haunted me until I woke again to the dark cloud that never let the light through.

It was a fun and productive cycle.

The mountain of folded laundry—nearly my entire wardrobe—sat there, daring me to ignore it.

"Christ." How many gray T-shirts did I need? And why in the hell did an even number of socks never make it out of the dryer? Just another of life's great mysteries that would never be solved. Like what was the point of it all and why did rabbits wait until you got up to speed before darting out in front of you?

The pill bottles on the nightstand caught my eye.

I hadn't touched the pain pills. But the others, ones for depression, ones for anxiety, had helped in the beginning. Until I'd decided to just embrace that cold, dark emptiness. To wallow in it. To see how long I could survive in its murky depths.

I scraped the bottles into the drawer and shut it.

The dog let out a loud snore and I realized it was dark outside.

I'd made it through another day.

I'd eaten.

I'd cleaned.

I'd talked to people in more than just bad-tempered grunts.

And I hadn't let anyone see the yawning chasm of emptiness that lived in my chest.

If I could squeeze in a shower and a shave, it would be enough.

Piper's legs tensed and she let out a sleepy yip.

She was dreaming and I wondered if it was a good dream or a nightmare. Careful not to wake her, I tucked the lamb next to her to ward off the bad and then headed into the bathroom.

I turned on the now clean shower and cranked the water temperature before stripping out of my clothes. The pink puckered scars caught my eye in the mirror. One on the shoulder, one on my lower abdomen from the shot that had gone clean through.

My body was healing, at least on the outside. But it was my mind I worried about.

Losing one's mind and embracing a downward spiral unfortunately ran in the family.

There was only so far you could run from what was tattooed on your DNA.

The steam beckoned me into the shower. I let the water sluice over me, relaxing coils of tight muscle with its heat. I slapped my palms against the cool tile and ducked my head under the stream.

Lina.

An image of her laughing in a damp sports bra and little else surfaced, followed quickly by the rest of our morning together. Lina wide-eyed and worried. Lina on her hands and knees as I dragged her back against me. Lina grinning at me from my passenger seat as I drove us home.

My cock hung heavy between my legs, stirring to life as thoughts of her blurred into fantasies.

It was a depraved kind of longing. One I almost relished because feeling something, anything was better than nothing. And because that fucked-up need had given me something I was afraid I'd lost.

I hadn't gotten hard since getting myself shot. Not until this morning . . . with *her*.

My cock thickened as arousal kindled in me.

I hadn't let myself think about it. After all, what kind of an asshole prioritized the function of his dick over his mental health? So I'd buried the worry and pretended everything below the belt was just tired or bored or whatever the hell dicks got.

But put Lina Solavita on her knees in front of me and my fantasies came to life. I thought about the feel of her hips under my hands. The curve of her ass as I pulled her into me. Desire had me by the throat and balls. It was dragging me out of the dark and into the fire. Toward her.

I couldn't help myself. I needed more.

Bracing one hand on the tile, I gripped my engorged shaft with the other and bit back an oath. The contact was both a relief and a disappointment. I wanted it to be her hand, her mouth wrapped around me. My hand in her hair guiding her as she got on her knees for me and made me human again.

Her surrender would make me feel powerful, strong, *alive*.

I'd feel guilty about the fantasy later, I promised myself. Just a few strokes to make sure that I was still whole, that everything still worked. A few strokes and I'd turn the water to cold.

Imagining those full lips opening, welcoming me inside, I dragged my tight fist up to the crown as water hit the back of my head. My grip forced moisture to well up and out of the slit. Imagining her eager tongue sweeping out to taste it, I stroked roughly down to the root.

"Fuck," I muttered, fisting my free hand against the tile.

This was wrong. But it felt *so fucking good* and I needed good.

Helpless, I imagined yanking down the scoop neck of that little cropped sweater to find her braless, her nipples hard points begging for my attention even as she worked my dick with her mouth.

My hips jerked forward as if they had a mind of their own, thrusting into my fist.

"One more." Just one more stroke and I'd stop.

Except in my fantasy, Lina wasn't on her knees anymore. She was straddling me. That wet heat from her pussy protected only by a useless strip of silk. My mouth was at her breast. I swallowed hard, thinking about taking one of those dusky pink peaks past my lips and sucking.

My hand had forgotten about the one stroke limit and was moving in swift, mean jerks up and down my shaft. Hips pumping in time, I felt a heaviness in my balls that I knew wasn't going to go away by fucking my hand. But that dark desire was better than the void.

I imagined dragging the silk of her thong to the side, gripping her hips, and thrusting home.

"Fuck yes, angel."

I could almost hear her indrawn breath as I filled her. I slammed my other fist against the tile. Once, twice.

I was way past stopping now, my fist a fucking blur as it serviced my grateful cock.

I'd lick and suck her other nipple to a pebbled point while my hands dragged her hips up and down on my shaft. While she clung to me inside and out. While she needed me to make her come.

"Nash."

I could almost hear her breathe my name as it built between us. As her sweet pussy got tighter and tighter around me.

I could see those brown eyes go glassy, could taste the velvety peak of her nipple against my tongue, could feel the painful clench as her greedy little muscles locked down on every inch of my shaft.

"Angel." I punched the wall again.

She'd come hard and long. The kind of orgasm that would leave her limp enough for me to pick her up and carry her to bed afterward. The kind that would give me no choice but to follow her down, emptying myself inside her. Marking her as mine.

But instead of the release I chased, I found something else.

My vision tunneled, the sound of the shower dulled as blood roared in my ears. My heart thudded wildly in my chest as the band of tension tightened. I released my cock and dragged in a shaky breath, fighting the pressure, fighting the wave of terror that crashed over me.

"Fuck. Fuck," I rasped. "Goddammit."

My knees buckled and I managed to lower myself into the tub.

Still hard. Still wanting. Still afraid. I put my hands on my head and knelt under the stream of water until it went cold.

6

The Middle of a Pissing Contest

Lina

T he Knockemout Public Library was housed across the hall from the police department in the Knox Morgan Municipal Building, a name that was the source of endless entertainment for me.

I snapped a picture of the bold, gold lettering and fired it off in a text to the man, the grump, the legend himself.

Knox's response was immediate. A middle finger emoji.

With a grin, I put my phone away and headed inside.

The building had been largely funded by a hefty "donation" that came from the lottery winnings Knox had tried to force on Nash. It was, in my opinion, an expert-level "fuck you."

Apparently, it had also driven a wedge between the brothers, one that had been reinforced by inherited stubbornness and subpar family communication.

Not that Knox and I had shared any heart-to-hearts in all our years of friendship. We kept things light, didn't burden each other with the heavy stuff. Didn't try to bring things into the light for useless examination.

And that, ladies and gentlemen, was how you made a relationship last.

No burdens. No emotional baggage.

Keep your needs few and your quality time fun.

With this in mind, I made a specific point *not* to peer through the glass into the police station. I wasn't prepared to make small talk with the chief of police mere hours after hearing him bringing himself to climax in the shower one not-so-soundproofed wall away.

Just thinking about it had my cheeks heating, my downtown fluttering.

I'd never stood at a sink brushing my teeth for that long in my life.

One thing was certain, Chief Morgan was a ticking time bomb. And whoever this Angel was, I hoped I wouldn't have to hate her.

I headed into the library. It was busier and louder than I expected. Thanks to Drag Queen Story Hour, the children's section had the energy of a preschool at snack time. Kids and adults alike listened with rapt attention as Cherry Poppa and Martha Stewhot read about diverse families and adopting pets.

I stayed and listened for an entire book before remembering I was on a mission.

I found Sloane Walton, librarian extraordinaire,

on the second floor in the stacks arguing about something bookish with the elderly yet fashionable Hinkel McCord.

Sloane was unlike any librarian I'd known. She was a petite spitfire with lavender-tinted platinum-blond hair. She dressed like a cool teenager, drove a souped-up Jeep Wrangler, and hosted a monthly Booze and Books Happy Hour. From what I had gathered, she had single-handedly turned the failing Knockemout Public Library into the heart of the community through grit, determination, and a number of grants.

There was something about her that reminded me of the nice, cool girls in high school. I'd once been a member of that exclusive club.

"All I'm saying is give Octavia Butler a try. And then come back with apology flowers and tequila because you're dead wrong," she told the man.

Hinkel shook his head. "I'll give it a try. But when I hate it, you need to deliver one of them loaves of sundried tomato bread."

Sloane stuck her hand out. "Deal. Good tequila. Not 'I stole this crap from my parents' liquor cabinet for the high school bonfire' tequila."

Hinkel nodded shrewdly and shook her hand. "Deal."

"Do you always bribe patrons with baked goods?" I asked.

Hinkel flashed me pearly whites and doffed his

straw fedora. "Miss Lina, if you don't mind my saying, you put the autumn leaves to shame with your beauty."

I plucked a paperback off the shelf and fanned myself with it. "Good sir, you certainly know how to turn a lady's head," I said, adopting a southern belle accent.

Sloane crossed her arms, feigning irritation. "Excuse *me,* Mr. McCord. I thought *I* was your Sunday morning flirtation."

He gestured at his pin-striped suit and bow tie. "There is more than enough of Hinkel to go around. Now if you two lovely ladies don't mind, I'm gonna go downstairs and flirt with a queen or two."

We watched the centenarian spryly head for the stairs, cane in one hand, book in the other.

"Knockemout sure grows them charming," I observed.

"We sure do," Sloane agreed, gesturing for me to follow her.

We entered a spacious conference room where Sloane headed straight for the dry erase board and began removing several crude drawings of penises.

"Teenagers?" I guessed.

She shook her head, making her perky ponytail dance. "Northern Virginia urologists. They had their quarterly meeting here yesterday. Figured I'd clean up the evidence before story hour ends."

"I didn't see that one coming."

Sloane flashed me a smirk. "Just wait until the NoVaP host their meetup in January."

I ran the possibilities in my head. "Northern Virginia proctologists?"

"Butts *everywhere*." Sloane dropped the eraser and started organizing the markers by color. "What brings you into my fine establishment today?"

I made myself useful and started stuffing the scattering of penis-centric handouts into the recycling can. "Looking for a book recommendation or two."

And some information, I added silently.

"Came to the right place. What's your poison? Thriller? Time travel? Autobiography? Poetry? Police procedural? Fantasy? Self-help? Small-town romance hot enough to make you blush?"

I thought of Nash in the shower last night. The thump of a fist against wet tile. The strangled oath. I felt a little light-headed. "Something with murders," I decided. "Also, is there any kind of county database I could use to search properties?"

"Looking to make your visit permanent?"

"No," I said quickly. "I have a friend who lives in DC. They're looking to move out of the city and open a business."

It was a lame lie. But Sloane was a busy librarian and people around here were quirky.

She wasn't going to waste time poking holes in my story.

"What kind of business?"

Dammit.

"Custom car garage? I mean, I think it's some kind of custom car garage."

Sloane nudged her glasses up her nose. "I'm sure your friend knows how to use the usual property listing websites."

"He—she, er, they do. But what if the property isn't for sale? They've got deep pockets and have been known to make offers that were hard to refuse."

Technically that part wasn't a lie. Exactly.

She pinned me with a curious look. I was usually much better at spinning an appropriate tale. That whole Nash in the shower thing must have really thrown me. Note to self: Avoid men who make you stupid.

"In that case, you could try a county assessment database. Most have GIS maps of properties, their records, and their tax assessments. I can give you the links."

Twenty minutes later, I did my best to tiptoe past Drag Queen Story Hour with my stack of unsexy murder novels, one book on conquering self-destructive tendencies, and colorful sticky notes with the names of three county property databases.

I made it out the door and into the hall when a familiar voice stopped me. "Investigator Lina Solavita."

I froze, then slowly pivoted on my boot heels.

A ghost from the past smirked at me as the door to the police station closed behind him. He'd grown a mustache since I'd last seen him and added ten or so pounds, but it looked good on him.

"Marshal Nolan Graham. What are you doing—" I didn't need to finish the question. There was only one local case that would require a U.S. marshal's presence.

"Caught a case." He plucked the novel off the top of my stack and peeked under the sticky notes at the cover. "You won't like this one."

"One weekend five or so years ago and you think you know my taste in books?"

He flashed me a grin. "What can I say? You're memorable."

Nolan was a cocky pain in the ass. But he was good at his job, not a misogynistic idiot, and if memory served, he was also a great dancer.

"Wish I could say the same. Nice mustache, by the way," I teased.

He smoothed his finger and thumb over it. "Wanna take it for a spin later?"

"Still an incurable ass, I see."

"It's called confidence. And it's built on years of experience with satisfied women."

I grinned. "You're the worst."

"Yeah. I know. What the hell are you doing here? Somebody steal the *Mona Lisa*?"

"I'm in town visiting friends. Catching up on my reading." I held up the stack of books.

His eyes narrowed. "Bullshit. You don't take vacations. What's Pritzger Insurance after in this place?"

"I don't know what you're talking about."

"Come on. Entertain me. I'm basically sitting on some Podunk chief of police waiting for a dipshit to try to finish the job."

"You think Duncan Hugo is going to try again? Do you have intel on that?"

"Well, aren't we well informed?"

I rolled my eyes. "It's a small town. We're all well informed."

"Then you don't need me to connect the dots."

"Come on. Hugo was taking a run at some list to impress Daddy, but he blew it. Last I heard, he was in the wind. He's got no reason to come back and finish the job."

"Unless Chief Amnesia suddenly remembers the shooting. All we've got is the word of a batshit, pain-in-the-ass, evil twin ex-girlfriend locked up in prison. And the testimony of a twelve-year-old. None of the physical evidence would hold up. Stolen car. Unregistered gun. No prints."

Duncan Hugo had teamed up with Naomi's

twin sister, Tina, to lie, cheat, and steal their way through northern Virginia before he'd made the ghastly mistake of shooting Nash.

"What about the dashcam footage?" I pressed.

Nolan shrugged. "It's dark. Guy had on a hoodie and gloves. You can barely make out a profile. But a half-decent attorney could argue it was literally anyone else."

"Still. Why send you in to babysit? Hugo's small-time, isn't he?"

Nolan raised an eyebrow.

"Ohhh. The feds are after Daddy."

Anthony Hugo was a crime lord whose territory included Washington, DC, and Baltimore. While his son dabbled in stolen electronics and cars, Daddy Dearest had an ugly reputation for racketeering, drugs, and sex trafficking.

"I'm not at liberty to say," he said, jingling the change in his pocket. "Now, spill it. What pretty little treasure are you after?"

My smile was feline. "I'm not at liberty to say."

Nolan put his hand on the wall behind me and leaned in like a high school quarterback with the perky head cheerleader. "Come on, Lina. Maybe we could work together?"

But I was no perky cheerleader. I also wasn't a team player. "Sorry, Marshal. I'm on vacation. And just like work, I do that alone too." It was safer that way.

He shook his head. "The good ones are always stubbornly single."

I cocked my head to study him. In his government-issue black suit and tie, he looked like the top Bible salesperson in the district. "Didn't you get married?" I asked.

He held up his bare left hand. "Didn't take."

Beneath the bravado, I caught a whiff of sad.

"The job?" I guessed.

He shrugged. "What can I say? Not everyone can deal."

I got it. The travel. The long weeks of obsession. The rush of victory when a case came together. Not everyone on the outside could handle it.

I wrinkled my nose in sympathy. "Sorry it didn't work out."

"Yeah. Me too. You could make me feel better. Dinner? Drinks? Heard this place called Honky Tonk a few blocks over has decent scotch. We could go have a few for old time's sake."

I could only imagine Knox's reaction if I wandered into his bar with a U.S. marshal in tow. While his brother was a fan of law and order, Knox had a rebellious streak when it came to rule books.

"Hmm." I needed to take a beat. I needed a plan, a strategy.

The opening of the station door saved me from having to formulate an answer. Then it was the scowl on Nash's face that left me too tongue-tied to spit one out.

"You lost, Marshal?" Nash asked. His voice was deceptively mild with a bit more southern honey layered on top than usual. He was dressed in his uniform of dark-gray Knockemout PD button-down and tactical pants, both of which looked like they'd been washed and ironed. Both of which *also* looked fifty million times hotter than Nolan's suit.

Damn you, thin shower walls. Damn you to hell.

My throat was dry and my brain went stupid, putting Nash's low groan from the night before on repeat in my head.

If broody, wounded Nash was sexy, bossy-pants Chief Morgan was a panty melter.

His gaze flicked to me, then ran from head to toe.

Nolan kept his hand where it was above my head, but he shifted so he could look at Nash. "Just catching up with an old friend, Chief. Have you had the pleasure of meeting Investigator Solavita?"

I now owed Nolan a knee to the balls.

"Investigator?" Nash repeated.

"Insurance investigator," I said quickly before shooting a glare at Nolan. "Chief Morgan and I know each other."

Usually I was good under pressure. No. Not just

good. I was *great* under pressure. I was patient and smart and cunning when necessary. But Nash giving me that hard, authoritarian look like he wanted to drag me into an interview room and yell at me for an hour was definitely screwing with my balance.

"I'm guessing not as well as you and I know each other," Nolan said to me with a wink.

"Seriously?" I demanded. "Get over it."

"Angel and I are close," Nash drawled without looking away from me.

Angel? *I* was the Angel from Nash's shower fantasy? My brain launched into a graphic replay of my nocturnal eavesdropping. I shook myself mentally and decided to deal with that information later.

"We share a wall," I said, not sure why I felt the need to explain. My past with Nolan was none of Nash's business. My present with Nash was none of Nolan's.

"Shared a bath too yesterday," Nash said.

My jaw dropped, and a sound like an accordion getting crushed wheezed out of me.

Both men looked at me. I shut my mouth with a hard snap.

I was going to knee Nolan in the balls and push Nash down the stairs, I decided.

"She always was a sucker for law enforcement," Nolan said, rocking back on his heels and looking like he was enjoying this.

I was fuming, but before I could let the two testosterone-addled idiots have it, the library door opened. Nash moved to hold it.

"Ma'am," he said to Cherry Poppa as she exited.

"Charmer," she cooed.

Nolan bowed.

"It's certainly yummy out here," the drag queen observed as she headed for the door.

"Well, this has been *fun*," I snarled at the idiots clogging the hallway before following the beautiful drag queen outside.

"You know what no one tells you about standing in the middle of a pissing contest?" Cherry said to me with a toss of her blond curls.

"What's that?" I asked.

"You're the one who ends up smelling like pee."

7

We Weren't Dry Humping

Lina

I was still reasonably ragey by the time I got in my car and headed to Knox and Naomi's house for dinner. Sure. What woman hadn't had the stray fantasy about two men fighting over her? But it wasn't nearly as sexy when the fight was actually a jurisdictional pissing match and I was just a pawn.

A little action on the gas pedal had my beefy Charger roaring to life on the open stretch of road. I loved big engines and fast cars. There was something about the open road and the rumble of a V8 that made me feel free.

I eased back to my customary nine miles over the speed limit. Just enough for a little fun but too much hassle for a cop to pull me over.

Angry, kick-ass lady music blasted from the sound system, and wind whipped through my hair.

All too soon, I slowed to make the turn onto the gravel lane that wound through the woods. Part of me was tempted to just keep going. To drive fast and sing loud until all the frustrations that had been building flew right out the window.

But as mad as I was, a cross-country road trip probably wouldn't be enough to clear my head.

So I did the annoying, responsible thing and made the turn.

Even through my pissed-off-ness, I could still appreciate the show autumn was putting on. The woods were alive with color. Leaves of red, gold, and orange clung to branches and rained down to cover the driveway. I had complicated feelings about fall. What had once represented reuniting with friends and starting new adventures had only come to mean missing out on both.

"Man, I am bitchy tonight," I grumbled to Carrie Underwood as she dug her keys into the side of her ex's truck.

I dialed down the volume on the stereo and let the whisper of the creek through the trees fill the car.

Knox and Naomi's house came into view around the next bend. It sprawled out in timber and glass tucked into the trees like it was part of the forest. I pulled in behind Naomi's SUV and got out before I could talk myself into sitting and stewing. The sooner I got in, the sooner I could get out and go home and be bitchy alone.

I headed for the stone walkway that meandered its way through low-growing shrubs and late-season flowers to the wide steps of the front porch.

There was a kid's bike on a patch of lawn and

striped cushions on the rocking chairs. Potted ferns hung from the porch rafters. A trio of hand-carved jack-o'-lanterns were clustered just outside the front door.

I was willing to bet money that Knox's pumpkin was the terrifying ghoulish one vomiting forth its own innards. Naomi's would be the precisely carved, toothy smile one. And Waylay's was the impatient, jagged, lopsided one with scary eyebrows.

The entire place screamed "family." Which was both sweet and entertaining when I thought of the Knox who I'd known forever.

From beyond the screen door came an excited howl immediately followed by a cacophony of barks and yips. Dogs of all shapes and sizes spilled out onto the porch and down the steps, swarming me in a friendly frenzy.

I bent to greet them.

Knox's grandmother's dogs were a petite, one-eyed pit bull named Kitty and a rambunctious beagle named Randy. Naomi's parents, who now resided in the cabin on the property, had brought along their dog, Beeper, a rescued Heinz 57 that resembled a scruffy brick with feet.

Knox's dog, a chunky basset hound named Waylon, landed his pudgy front paws on my thighs to rise above the fray for his fair share of attention.

"Waylon! Knock it off," Knox barked from the

front porch as he pushed open the screen door. He had a dish towel thrown over his shoulder, a pair of grill tongs in his hand, and something close to a smile on his handsome face.

"I'm settin' the table like you told me to!" came the aggrieved cry of a twelve-year-old from inside.

"Way*lon,* not Way*lay,*" Knox yelled back.

"Well, why didn't you say so?" Waylay bellowed.

I grinned.

"Family life agrees with you," I said, wading through the dogs to the front porch.

He shook his head. "I spent an hour googling fuckin' sixth grade math last night and a week listening to women go back and forth over flower arrangements." A chorus of laughter rang out from the house. "It's never quiet. There's always people everywhere."

He might have been standing there complaining, but it was plain as day that Knox Morgan was happier than he'd ever been.

"Sounds like you deserve one of these," I said, holding up the six-pack I'd brought.

"Let's drink in the backyard before someone finds us and needs me to fix the dryer vent or watch another 'hilarious TikTok,'" he said. He tucked the tongs into his back pocket, grabbed two of the beers, then popped the tops on the porch railing. He handed one to me. "Last chance to make a run for it," he offered.

"Oh, I'm not missing the domesticated Knox show for anything," I told him.

He snorted. "Domesticated?"

"Just messing with you. It suits you."

He leaned his forearms on the porch railing. "What does?"

I pointed the neck of my bottle toward the front door. "Those two ladies in there needed you. You stepped up and now the three of you are so blindingly happy the rest of us can't look directly at you."

"You think they're happy?" Knox asked.

Another burst of laughter came from inside the house. The dogs raced around the yard, noses to the ground in search of another adventure.

"Positive," I said.

He cleared his throat. "Something I wanna ask you, and I don't want you makin' a big fuckin' deal out of it."

"I'm intrigued."

"I want you to be a groomsman or whatever."

I blinked. "Me?" Except for my aunt Shirley's wedding to my aunt Janey—I'd rocked my role as an eight-year-old rainbow glitter fairy—I'd never been part of a bridal party. I'd never been close enough to anyone to be asked.

"Naomi's askin' Sloane, Stef, Fi, and Way. I've got Nash, Luce, and Jer. At least I will once I tell them. And you."

Nash. Just the mention of his brother's name

107

had me spiraling further into bitchiness. But the bitchiness was tempered by a bright glow in my chest. "Do you want me to wear a tux?"

"I don't care if you wear beer-stained sweats. Though I'm sure Daisy'll have some opinions. Just be there." He took a pull of his beer. "And don't let me fuck it all up."

I grinned. "I'd be honored to be your grooms-man . . . person?"

"Naomi's calling you a groomsgal, but I'm not saying that shit in public. Stef's a bridesman and I am sayin' that."

We both smirked into the dusk as it settled over the yard.

"Thanks for asking," I said finally. "Even though you didn't ask."

"If you tell people what you want instead of askin' them for it, you're more likely to get what you want," he said.

"Knox the domesticated philosopher."

"Shut up or I'll make you wear tangerine taffeta."

"I'm amazed you know either one of those words."

"Wedding's in three weeks. I'm learning all the words."

"Three *weeks?*"

His grin was lazy. "Feel like I've been waiting for Daze and Way my entire life. I'd go to the courthouse tonight if I could talk them into it."

"Well, if I'm not still in town by then, I'll come back for it," I promised.

He nodded. "Fair warning. There's gonna be a shit ton of hugging."

I grimaced. "I'm out."

Physical affection ranked somewhere between being on hold with the cable company and getting a root canal. There had been a time in my life when my body had belonged more to medical staff than to myself. Since then, I preferred to avoid all surprise touching unless I was the one instigating it. Which only made my reaction to He Who Shall Not Be Named all the more confusing.

"Already got a solution," he said. "I'm puttin' *not a hugger* after your name in the program."

I was still laughing when headlights cut through the trees that lined the lane. Nash's pickup truck, a blue Nissan, pulled into the drive next to my car.

Temper sparked over my skin along with the concern that he'd push the line of questioning on the whole investigator situation. I didn't need him spreading that around.

"I didn't know he was coming," I said.

Knox gave me the side-eye. "Got a problem with my brother?"

"Yeah, actually, I do. You have a problem with me having a problem?"

His lips quirked. "Nope. 'Bout time someone

else gets pissed at him besides me. Just don't let it fuck with the wedding or that'll upset Naomi. And no one upsets Naomi besides me."

The dogs enthusiastically swarmed the vehicle.

My heated gaze met Nash's chilly one through the windshield. He didn't look too happy about the idea of getting out of the car. *Good.*

"I think I'll go inside. See if there's anything I can help with," I decided.

Knox traded me the tongs for a third beer. "Check the chicken on the grill if Lou hasn't already started hovering," he said, then headed in the direction of his brother.

Check on the chicken? My knowledge of cooking poultry was limited to what showed up on my plate in restaurants. I let myself in and followed the noise.

The house was a beauty, rugged and rustic, but with homey touches that made a person want to sit down, put their feet up, and enjoy the chaos.

Family photos that went back a handful of generations decorated the walls and colorful throw rugs softened the scarred hardwood floors.

I found the majority of the noise and people in the kitchen. Knox and Nash's grandmother, Liza J—the home's previous occupant before moving into the cottage down the lane—was supervising Naomi's mother, Amanda, as she constructed a charcuterie board.

Lou, Naomi's father, was—thankfully—already

on the deck peering under the hood of the grill and prodding at the chicken with his own set of tongs.

Naomi and her best friend, the gorgeous and fashionable Stefan Liao, were arguing while he opened wine and she stirred something that smelled pretty great on the stove.

"Tell him, Lina," Naomi said as if I'd been there the entire time.

"Tell who what?" I asked, finding a spot in the fridge for the remainder of the six-pack and the two-liter of Waylay's tooth-rotting soda.

"Tell Stef that he should ask out Jeremiah," she said.

Jeremiah was Knox's partner in Whiskey Clipper, the town barbershop/salon beneath my apartment. As with all the single men in this town, he was also really, *really* good-looking.

"Witty's doing that smug, almost-married lady thing where she tries to pair off all her friends so they can be smug, almost-married jackasses too," Stef complained. He was wearing cashmere and corduroy and looked like he'd stepped off the pages of a men's fashion magazine.

"Do you *want* to be a smug, almost-married jackass?" I asked him.

"I don't even officially live in this town," he said, waving his arms expressively without spilling a drop of the Shiraz. "How should I know if I want to be a jackass?"

"Great. That's three more bucks for the swear jar," Waylay lamented loudly from the dining room.

"Put it on my tab," Stef yelled back.

The swear jar was a gallon-sized pickle jar that lived on the kitchen counter. It was always overflowing with dollar bills thanks to Knox's colorful vocabulary. The money went toward buying fresh produce. The only way Naomi could get Waylay on board with curbing the four-letter words was to keep the family up to their eyeballs in salads.

"Please," Naomi scoffed. "You spend more time in Knockemout than you do at your place in New York *or* with your parents. I know you're not here just because you love the canine chaos."

On cue, all four dogs raced into the kitchen and then charged through the dining room doorway just as Waylay appeared in it. She jumped out of their way, which succeeded in exciting them further.

"Out!" Amanda bellowed, opening the deck door and shooing the blur of fur outside.

Waylay slunk into the kitchen and sneaked a piece of pepperoni off the charcuterie board. "Table's set," she said.

Naomi narrowed her eyes, plucked a piece of broccoli off the veggie tray, and stuffed it into her niece's mouth.

Waylay put up a valiant fight, but her deter-mined aunt won with a suffocating hug.

"Why are you so obsessed with green stuff, Aunt Naomi?" Waylay groaned.

"I'm obsessed with your health and wellness," Naomi said, ruffling her hair.

Waylay rolled her eyes. "You're so weird."

"I'm weird with love for you."

"Let's get back to roasting Uncle Stef for being too chicken to ask out Jeremiah," Waylay suggested.

"Good idea," Naomi agreed.

"Boy like that's not gonna stay single for long," Liza J warned Stef as she slipped a slice of salami to Waylay.

"He's *very* handsome," Amanda agreed.

Everyone turned to look at me expectantly. "He is gorgeous," I agreed. "But only if you're into relationships and monogamy."

"Which I'm not," Stef insisted.

"Neither was Knox," I pointed out. "But look at him now. He's sickeningly happy."

Naomi looped her arm over my shoulder and I barely managed to hide the flinch at the unexpected touch. The engagement ring on her finger glittered in the light. "See, Stef? You too could be sickeningly happy."

"I think I'd rather just be sick."

I slid out of Naomi's affectionate embrace and headed for the meat tray.

Waylay stuffed a pilfered salami into her mouth when Naomi wasn't looking. I could almost hear my mother's voice in my head.

"You're still avoiding processed meats aren't you, Lina?"

"Do you really think it's a good idea to drink alcohol with your condition?"

I took a defiant sip of my beer, sidled up to Waylay, and chose a piece of ring bologna.

"What? I'm hot and gay, so me dating the hot, bisexual barber is a foregone conclusion? Gays and bis have to have more in common than just being gay and bi," Stef sniffed.

"I thought you said he was the most attractive man on the planet with a voice like melted ice cream that made you want to tear your clothes off and listen to him recite his grocery list?" Naomi mused.

"And didn't you also say the whole small business entrepreneurial thing he has going on was intriguing because you're tired of dating fitness models?" Amanda added.

"And aren't you both huge fans of luxury fashion brands, Luke Bryan, and environmentally friendly energy solutions?" I prodded.

"I hate you all."

"Don't date him because he's bisexual, Stef. Date him because he's perfect for you," Naomi said.

Knox and Nash entered, both looking vaguely

114

pissed off. To be fair, that was how they usually looked after a conversation with each other. Nash looked tired too. And hot in his jeans and flannel—yum.

Damn it. I'd forgotten that I wasn't finding him attractive anymore.

I focused on the fact that he'd done his best to humiliate me with Nolan and embraced my inner female rage.

He had a beer in one hand and was holding the shivering Piper in the other. She was wearing a ridiculous pumpkin print sweater. They both looked as if this was the last place on earth they wanted to be.

"Evenin'," he said to the room, but those blue eyes landed on me.

I glared at him. He glared back.

A new wave of pandemonium broke out as the women rushed Nash to get a better look at Piper. Knox waded through it and kissed Naomi on the cheek before making a beeline for the meat tray.

"Hi, pretty girl," Naomi said, gently greeting the dog. "I like your sweater."

"Who is this sweet little thing?" Amanda crooned, gently stroking Piper's head.

The dogs outside, sensing a potential new friend, pressed their noses against the deck door and whimpered pitifully.

"This is Piper. Found her in a storm drain outside town yesterday. Who wants to foster her?"

Nash said, still looking pissily in my direction.

I pointedly ignored him.

"That's not what it looked like you were doing," Stef said in an *I know something you don't* tone.

Nash and I both swung our glares in his direction.

Stef grinned devilishly. "Sorry, kids. Gotta throw someone else under the bus or they'll never move on."

"What did they look like they were doin'?" Liza J demanded.

"Given the compromising position—"

"Why don't we save this story for later?" Naomi said loudly, looking in Waylay's direction.

"You were doin' what?" Knox demanded, tuning in.

"I'm worried that your lack of you-know-what is making you hallucinate, Stef. Maybe you *should* ask Jeremiah out," I suggested.

"Touché, Legs. Touché," he said.

Nash ignored us and put the trembling dog down on the floor. She tried to hide behind his legs, then spotted me when she peeked around his boots.

I waved to her and she took a tentative step in my direction. I crouched down and patted the floor in front of me.

Piper inched her way out from behind Nash's boots and then made a mad dash to me.

I picked her up and submitted to the tongue

bathing. "You smell so much better than you did," I told her.

"Aww! She likes you," Naomi observed.

"Let's get back to this compromising position," Amanda suggested.

Stef topped off the empty wineglass Liza J waved at him. "So I was heading back to town early yesterday morning, and what did I see on the side of the road?"

Knox earmuffed Waylay with his hands.

"A bear?" Liza J guessed.

"Even better. I saw Knockemout's chief of police on his knees in the grass in shall we say 'thrusting position' behind the curvy a-s-s of Miss Solavita."

Nash looked like he was giving serious thought to running for the front door.

"What the f—erret?" Knox snapped.

I sighed. "Seriously, Stef? You say thrusting but you spell ass?"

"Thrusting isn't a swear word," Waylay said knowledgeably.

"Hey! Earmuff her harder," Naomi instructed Knox.

He complied by spinning the girl around and wrapping her in a head-level bear hug.

"I can't breathe!" Her cry was muffled by Knox's chest.

"You can if you're still complaining," Knox insisted.

"Your dumb muscles are breaking my nose!" Waylay whined.

Knox released her and ruffled her hair.

"Waylay, why don't you go see how Grandpa is doing with the chicken?" Naomi suggested.

"You're just sending me away so you can talk about gross grown-up stuff."

"Yep," Stef said. "Now get out of here so we can get to the gross stuff."

Knox put his hand on the top of Waylay's head and steered her toward the back door. "Come on, kid. Neither one of us needs to hear this." Together they trooped out onto the deck and closed the door.

"Back to the thrusting," Amanda insisted. She hopped onto a bar stool and did a little shimmy.

"I pulled over, being a Good Samaritan and all," Stef continued.

"Is that what they call it these days?" Nash said dryly.

"I offered my assistance, but the rosy-cheeked Lina assured me they didn't need any help with their dry humping."

"We weren't dry humping!" I insisted.

"Bet you could be arrested for that," Liza J mused with more than just a hint of pride.

I threw a carrot from the veggie tray at Stef and it bounced off his forehead. "Ow!"

"We were fully clothed and pulling a dog—this

dog—out of the storm drain, idiot." I held Piper up to the crowd *Lion King*–style.

"Speaking of, who's gonna foster her until the rescue finds her a home?" Nash asked.

"I never thought a dog rescue story would disappoint me," Amanda announced after a beat of silence.

"Let's get back to Stef being a chickenshit," I suggested.

A piece of cauliflower bounced off my cheek and landed on the floor.

Lou opened the door, and the flood of dogs rushed in. Liza J's pit bull, Kitty, plopped her butt at my feet and stared up at the pumpkin-sweatered dog in my arms. Waylon gobbled up the floor cauliflower, while Beeper tap-danced at Lou's feet.

"Chicken's ready," he announced. "What did I miss?"

"Nothing," Nash and I said together.

8

Green Beans and Lies

Nash

D inner was as chaotic as a Morgan family gathering usually got. But what I'd once found enjoyable was now plain exhausting.

Conversations flew back and forth across the large table over the country music playing in the background. It went too quickly for me to keep up with let alone participate in, even if I had the energy, which I didn't. I'd spent all day at the station and being shadowed by a U.S. marshal who seemed to take great joy in pissing me the fuck off.

I was bone tired. But I'd come here for one reason, and that was to get answers from Lina "Insurance Is So Boring" Solavita. She'd lied to me and my family, and I was going to find out why.

I'd brought Piper along for company. The dog looked as weary as I felt. She was passed out in a tiny ball against Kitty on a dog bed in the corner. The rest of the canine crew had been too rambunctious to join the party and were banished outside.

Food was passed and drinks were topped off, sometimes without even being asked. I stuck to my one and only beer and forced myself to eat just enough not to draw anyone's attention. We Morgans were plain bad at talking about feelings, which meant I'd get a free pass from my brother and grandmother. But Naomi and her parents were the kind to spot a problem and talk it to death while doing their damnedest to solve it.

When I'd been discharged from the hospital, it had been to a clean apartment, fresh laundry, and a refrigerator stocked with meals. The Witts had made it clear that they'd adopted not just Knox and Waylay but me as well.

After a lifetime with the comfort of Morgan family dysfunction, it was more than a little disconcerting.

Half the table erupted in laughter at something I'd missed. The suddenness of it startled me. Piper too apparently. She let out a worried yip. Unfazed, Kitty put her big head on Piper's body and within seconds both were fast asleep again.

This was more life than this old house had seen since my own childhood, more than I could handle. I'd been prepared to do what I'd learned to do, white knuckle my way through. But Lina's presence on my left gave me a tangle of feelings that knotted themselves up in the middle of the emptiness that now lived full-time in my chest.

That burn of attraction that I didn't understand was still there, along with a sliver of guilt for using her to get a few jabs in at that asshole Nolan. But more than anything, I was pissed.

She'd deliberately misled everyone when it came to her work. And that was as good as a lie to me. I didn't tolerate lies and liars.

Our exchange this morning left me with questions.

I'd done a little digging between slogging through paperwork and helping Animal Control capture one of Bacon Stables' pain-in-the-ass runaway horses after it shit its way down Second Street.

But the dinner table wasn't the place to start the interrogation. So I bided my time and tried to limit the number of times I glanced in her direction.

She was wearing tight jeans and a gray cardigan that looked soft as a cloud. It made me want to reach out and touch it, to rub my face against the fabric. To—

Okay, creeper. Get a hold of yourself. You're depressed and pissed off. Not a sweater-sniffing stalker.

I shook myself out of the fog and made a weak attempt to join the conversation.

"Lou, how's the golf game?" I asked.

On my right, Amanda kicked me under the table. Naomi choked on her dinner coffee.

Lou pointed his fork at me from the foot of the table. "Lemme tell you. There's no way Hole Nine is a par three."

"And now we all have to suffer," Amanda whispered as her husband broke into a discourse on his trials and tribulations on the green.

I made an effort to drag my attention away from Lina while Lou gave us all his top ten reasons why Hole Nine was mislabeled.

Piper was snoring that strangely loud nose whistle that had startled me awake twice the night before. The tip of her tail flicked out a beat or two as if her dreams were happy ones. At least it beat waking to the other noise, the one that lived only in my head.

Naomi's eyes sparkled as Knox slid his hand to the back of her neck and whispered something in her ear. Waylay waited until she was sure her guardians were occupied before slipping two green beans into her napkin. She caught me looking and feigned innocence.

Night had fallen on the other side of the glass, making the woods and creek vanish. Inside, the lights were low and the flicker of candles made it even cozier.

"Pass the chicken, Nash," Liza J called from the head of the table. I picked up the platter and shifted to my left. Lina's fingers got tangled up with mine, and we nearly dropped the dish.

Our eyes met. There was a spark of temper in

those cool brown eyes, most likely carried over from our run-in that morning. But in the overall tally, I had more reasons to be pissed than she did.

She'd added makeup and styled her hair differently. Edgy pixie was what it made me think of. Her earrings were tiny bells that dangled flirtatiously from her lobes. They jingled every time she laughed. But she wasn't laughing now.

"Any day now would be nice," Liza J said pointedly.

I managed to hand off the plate without sending the chicken to the floor. My fingers felt warm from her touch and I balled my hand into a fist in my lap to hold on to the heat.

"Your face looks like shit," Knox announced to me.

"Knox!" Naomi said, exasperated.

"What? If you're gonna grow a beard, grow a damn beard or have the decency to make an appointment and sit in my fuckin' chair. Either way, commit. Don't go walking around town with a half-assed stubble farm all over your face. It's bad advertising for Whiskey Clipper," my brother complained.

Waylay put her head in her hands and muttered something about a jar and vegetables.

I rubbed my hand over my jaw. I'd forgotten to shave again.

"Have some more green beans, Nash," Amanda

insisted on my right, dumping a scoop on top of the one I hadn't touched yet.

Waylay caught my eye from across the table. "This family is obsessed with green things."

My mouth quirked. The kid was still getting used to the whole "family" thing after a short lifetime with a bad influence.

"Waylay, isn't there something you want to ask Knox and Nash?" Naomi prompted.

Waylay looked down at her plate for a second before shrugging in preteen annoyance. "It's just something dumb. You guys don't have to do it." She made a show of spearing a green bean with her fork and scrunching up her face when she took the tiniest bite possible.

"You might be surprised. We like dumb stuff," I told her.

"Well, there's this Girl Dad challenge on Tik-Tok where dads let their daughters put makeup on them. And paint their nails. And some of them do their hair too," she began.

Knox and I shared a frozen look of terror.

We'd do it.

We'd hate every single second of it. But we'd do it if Waylay wanted us to.

Knox swallowed. "Okay. And?" He sounded like he was being strangled.

Naomi sighed. "Waylay Witt!"

The girl's grin was diabolical. "What? I was just priming them with something worse so

125

they'd say yes to what I really wanted them to do."

I relaxed as the threat of lipstick and fake eyelashes dissipated.

Knox rocked back in his chair, rolling his eyes to the ceiling. "What the fuck am I gonna do with her at sixteen?"

"Oh man!" Waylay groaned.

"Jar!" Stef said.

"If you would stop f-bombing every sentence, maybe we could be eatin' potato chips and pepperoni bites instead of dang green beans," Waylay groused.

Lina's earrings jingled as she tried to hold in her laughter.

"What do you really want us to do?" I asked.

"Okay. So my school is doing this dumb Career Day thing and I guess I thought maybe it wouldn't be the most horrible thing if you and Knox came and told my class about your jobs and stuff. You can say no," she added quickly.

"You want me and your uncle Nash to talk to your class?" Knox asked her.

I rubbed my forehead and tried to chase away all the "hell nos" that were echoing in my head. Community relations was a big part of my job, but I'd avoided all public events since . . . before.

"Yeah. But only if you're gonna do a good job, because Ellison Frako's mom is a district court judge and she's going to do like a mock trial thing. So don't, like, show up and talk about paperwork and bank statements."

I smirked. Paperwork and bank statements were ninety percent of my brother's job.

Waylay looked at me. "I thought maybe you could do something cool like shoot one of the annoying boys with a Taser."

Lina choked out a laugh and some of her beer next to me. Wordlessly, I handed her a napkin.

Naomi shot a pleading look my way.

Like I didn't know how much it cost Waylay to ask for what she wanted.

"I might not deploy any weapons in the classroom, but I could probably come up with something," I said. A cold bead of sweat snaked its way down my back. But the happily stunned expression on Waylay's face made it worthwhile.

"Really?"

"Yeah. Really. Fair warning though, my job's way cooler than Knox's."

Knox snorted. "Oh, it's on."

"What are you gonna do? Reenact a lottery win?" I joked.

He threw a chunk of red-skinned potato across the table at me.

I volleyed back with a scoop of green beans.

"Boys," Amanda warned.

Waylay gave me one of those small smiles that I prized. It was one thing to make a happy kid smile, but to pry one out of the girl who had a lot of reasons not to was like winning a gold medal.

"So seriously. Who wants to take Piper home with them?" I asked again.

"Oh, now, Nash. You know that wouldn't be fair to that sweet little girl. She's already obviously bonded with you," Amanda pointed out.

After pie and coffee, the party broke up to a Patsy Cline song, one of my mom's favorites.

Knox started on the dishes while Naomi went upstairs to supervise Waylay's homework. Lou and Amanda volunteered to walk Liza J home. Piper whined pitifully at the front door as Kitty disappeared into the night.

I wanted to disappear too, but good manners wouldn't let me leave without at least lending a hand. I headed back into the dining room and found Lina collecting empty dessert plates.

"Gimme those," I said. "You round up the utensils."

She set the dishes down on the table rather than handing them to me.

"So you and Marshal Graham seemed friendly this morning."

It was the wrong thing to say.

The forks and knives she'd collected clattered as she dropped them on an empty platter. "Seriously?" Her eyes flashed as she crossed her arms. "What's your problem with Nolan?"

My problem was that he was Nolan to her, not U.S. Marshal Graham.

"My problem is your pal *Nolan* is shadowing my ass. He followed me here. Hell, he's probably parked out there in the driveway right now."

She drummed dark red nails against the sleeves of her sweater. Hard and sharp over soft. "He's not my *pal*. And you could have at least invited him in."

The fuck I could have.

There was a crash in the kitchen followed by half a minute of swearing. "Why in the fuck are wet dishes so goddamn slippery? Where the fuck do we keep the broom?" Knox snarled.

"Jar times three," Naomi yelled from upstairs.

"Sit," I said.

Lina's eyes narrowed. "Excuse me?"

I pulled out a chair, pointed to it. "I said sit."

Waylon galloped into the room, plopped his ass on the rug at my feet, and looked around for a treat. Piper joined him, looking hopeful.

"Now you've done it," Lina said.

Muttering under my breath, I dug out two of the treats I had in my pocket and gave one to each dog. Then I pulled out another chair and sat.

"Please s-i-t," I said, gesturing to the empty chair.

She took her sweet time doing it, but she sat. "This isn't an interrogation room, hotshot. And I'm not a suspect. Any relationship past or present between me and Nolan is none of your business."

"Here's where you're wrong, Angelina. See,

I don't believe in coincidences, especially not when there's a whole mess of 'em. You've never visited my brother in his hometown before. All of the sudden, you just up and decide to surprise him with an open-ended visit. Unlikely, but okay. You also show up after I get myself shot and right before Naomi and Waylay get taken. Again, could be just a coincidence."

"But you don't think so," she said, folding her arms.

"Then you just happen to have a history with the marshal in charge of being a pain in my ass."

Lina interlaced her fingers on the table and leaned forward. "Nolan and I had a sweaty, naked forty-eight-hour fling in a motel in Memphis five or six years ago."

"That was right about the time you recovered $150K in stolen jewelry for your bosses at Pritzger, wasn't it? And those fellas you recovered it from just happened to be the subject of an FBI investigation, didn't they?"

She studied me for a long beat. "Where did you get that information?"

"The bust was big news. Made some headlines."

"My name wasn't mentioned in any of them," she said coolly.

"Ah. But it was mentioned in the local PD's incident report."

Okay, so I'd done more than a *little* quiet digging today.

She blew out a breath through her teeth. "What do you want?"

"Why are you here? And don't give me some bullshit about missing your old pal Knox," I warned when she opened her mouth. "I want the truth."

I required the truth.

"I'll say this slowly so you'll be sure to catch it all the first time around. I'm none of your business. My business, including who I am or was 'friendly' with, what I do for a paycheck, and why I'm in town are also none of your damn business."

I leaned in closer until our knees brushed under the table. "All due respect, Angelina? I'm the one with holes in me. And if you're here for any reason relating to that, then it's very fucking clearly my business."

Her phone rang and the caller ID on the screen read "Dad."

She stabbed the Ignore button and pushed the phone away, tension in her movements.

"Talk. Now," I said.

She bared her teeth, her eyes going dark and dangerous. For a second, I thought she was going to lay into me, and I relished the thought of her anger rising up to slam into mine, waking it up and fanning it into an inferno.

But the inferno was interrupted by a shrill beep.

Lina slapped her hand over the watch on her

wrist, but not before I saw the number on the screen next to the red heart.

"Is that a heart rate alert?" I asked.

She came out of her chair abruptly enough to startle the dogs. I got to my feet.

"That, like everything else involving me, is none of your damn business, Chief," she said, then started for the doorway.

She almost made it, but we'd both under-estimated my level of mad. I caught her, my hand clamping around her wrist and drawing her back.

She spun. I stepped. And that was how I found myself standing flush against her with her back to the wall.

We were both breathing heavily, our chests moving against each other with every inhale. She was a tall, long-legged woman, but I still had enough inches on her that she had to tilt her head to look up at me. I could see the pulse at the base of her throat.

Yes. It was a whisper in my blood. The closer I got to her, the louder it grew.

With control, I ran my hand down her opposite arm to her wrist and lifted it. She watched me without pulling away. I broke eye contact to glance at her watch. "That's a pretty high heart rate for sitting around talking," I observed.

She tried to pull free, but I held on.

"I wasn't sitting around talking. I was sitting around trying not to break a cop's nose."

I still had her hand in mine. Her other one was fisted in my shirt. But she wasn't pushing me away. She was holding me where I stood.

"Let's both calm down," I said mildly.

"Calm down? You want *me* to calm down? Gee. Why didn't I think of that?"

I'd scaled the volcano and now I was looking down into pure, molten lava. All I wanted to do was jump into that glorious heat.

"Tell me what we're dealing with here," I insisted. "Do you need a doctor?"

"Oh my God, Nash. If you don't let me go right now, no jury on earth will hold me accountable for the damage I do to your testicles with my knee."

That threat combined with the way she was moving against me had me going from halfway hard to flag-flying, pitch-a-tent, that's-the-ball-game-folks fully aroused.

Fuck.

Then we were both moving.

I had her fully pinned against the wall, one hand at her waist just under her breast, the other flat on the wall next to her head. Meanwhile, her hands were white knuckled in my shirt, holding me to her.

I could follow her breath as she sucked it in, expanding her chest, before the exhale warmed my face and neck. I breathed her in and shifted against her.

I needed to back off. Not only was it a shitty idea to get involved with a woman I knew was lying to me, there was the fact that my head was messing with my dick.

"You want me to back off?" I said, running my nose along her jawline.

"Yes," she hissed. But her hands pulled me tighter to her.

"You want me to stop touching you, Angel?" I prayed to every religious deity I could think of, then threw in a few celebrities and musicians for good measure. Sweet Dolly Parton, please don't let her say yes.

Her lashes flickered. Surprise and something else sparked to life in those beautiful brown eyes.

"No." It was a whisper. A smoky plea that started my blood simmering.

Our gazes met and held as I skimmed my hand an inch higher until my fingers brushed the underside of her breast. My dick throbbed painfully behind my fly. Little licks of flames warmed my muscles.

Lina let out a sexy little whimper, and I swear to Dolly, I almost came then and there. I committed the sound to memory, knowing I'd pull it out over and over again. Knowing even if my dick never worked again, I'd still wrap my fist around it remembering that sound coming out of those parted lips.

She bucked her hips against me and nearly

broke me. Maybe it would have. Maybe I would have dragged her to the floor and used my teeth and tongue and fingers on her until she was naked and begging for me.

But maybes weren't in the cards.

"What in the fucking fuck are you doing?" Knox snarled. He was holding a broom in one hand and a beer in the other and looked as though he wanted to break both over my head.

"We're havin' a private discussion," I snapped.

"The hell you are," my brother growled.

"Actually, I was just leaving," Lina said, her cheeks flushed a tantalizing pink. "If you want to have another private interrogation, Chief, I'll make sure I have my lawyer present."

"Swear to God, Nash, if you don't back the fuck up, I'm gonna break this bottle over your head and then make you clean it up with this fuckin' broom."

Being happily engaged was definitely affecting my idiot brother's ability to craft threats.

Still, it wasn't smart for me to keep my back to him. I removed my hand from Lina's waist and tried to take a step back. But she was still clinging to my shirt.

"You're the one who's gotta let go, baby," I whispered.

She glanced down at her hands clamped on my shirt and slowly released her grip.

"Are you okay to drive?" I asked her.

"She had one fucking beer. You gonna run a sobriety checkpoint in my dining room?" Knox demanded.

"I wasn't talking about the beer," I said to him through clenched teeth.

"I'm fine. Thanks for dinner, Knox. I'll see you around." She slipped past me and headed out the front door.

"What. The. Fuck. Was. That?" Knox punctuated each word with a jab from the broom handle into my ribs.

"Ow."

"No," he said.

"No what?"

Using the broom handle, Knox pointed to the door Lina had exited through, then back at me. "That. It's not happening."

I ignored his comment. "How much do you know about Lina?"

"What the hell do you mean? I've known her forever."

"Do you know what she does for a living?"

"She works in insurance."

"Wrong. She's an insurance investigator for Pritzger Insurance."

"Not seeing a difference."

"She's basically a bounty hunter for personal property."

"So what?"

"So she shows up in town right after I take a

136

couple of bullets. She lies about what she does for a living, and she knows the U.S. marshal who's up my ass. You don't think those are some interesting coincidences?"

"Why does everyone in my fuckin' life wanna talk shit to death?" Knox muttered.

"Why does she wear a watch that monitors her heart rate?"

"How the fuck should I know? Don't all those idiots who run for fun do that? I'm more concerned with why my brother had one of my best friends pinned up against a wall."

"You got a problem with that?"

"Yeah. A big one."

"Care to elaborate?" I asked.

"Fuck no. You and Lina ain't happenin'. End of story. No elaboration necessary."

"That strategy ever work with your girls?"

Wearily Knox pulled out one of the chairs and sat. "Not so far, but I'm hopin' one of these times they'll let me take the win. Sit your ass down." He indicated the chair Lina had vacated.

As soon as I sat, Piper scrabbled at my shins and I picked her up. She cuddled up against my chest and let out a sigh. As if I made her feel safe. Damn dog.

"You wanna talk. Fine. Shut the hell up and listen. Trust me when I say Lina's the kind of friend you want on your side. Not just cause she's hell on wheels when you've pissed her off, but because she's one of the good ones. If she ain't runnin' her mouth about job descriptions and stupid smart watches, she's got a reason for not sharing. Maybe that reason is you haven't earned her trust. Or maybe that shit's because it's none of your damn business."

But there was something in me that knew it was my business.

"I know—"

Knox cut me off. "Shut it. She's one of the best people I know. So are you. Fix things with her and then leave her alone. I'm not lettin' you two play games with each other. And stop pinning her to goddamn walls. The woman hates to be touched. I can't believe she didn't detach your balls on her way out."

Lina hated being touched? This was news.

"We're goin' out tomorrow night. You, me, and Lucy," my brother continued.

I shook my head. "I've got a lot on my plate—"

"We're goin' out tomorrow night," he repeated. "Honky Tonk, 9:00 p.m. It's your day off, and if you try and cancel, Lucy and I are gonna show up at your place and drag you out. We've got shit to discuss."

9

A Neighborly Cockblocking

Nash

I flipped the bird to my federal shadow in the parking lot, dropped Piper off at my place, and then grudgingly headed next door. Lina's door loomed in front of me like a castle wall. There was music coming from inside. Something with a driving beat. Something that said "Beware: Angry Woman." I hesitated for a second, then knocked hard.

The door swung open almost immediately, and I blinked in surprise when Mrs. Tweedy appeared in the doorway. She was holding her usual evening glass of bourbon on the rocks and dressed in her usual uniform of workout tights, tunic, and frosty pink lipstick. Her white hair was tall and poufy, adding another four inches to her five foot even frame.

I checked the apartment number, wondering how in the hell I'd knocked on the wrong door.

"Well, if it isn't Studly Do-Right," she said in her southern twang. The ice in her glass clinked merrily.

2B. Right next door to my place. I hadn't gotten the wrong place. Mrs. Tweedy was answering the wrong door.

"Lina here?" I asked.

"Nope. I'm breaking and entering. Wanna cuff me?" She held up her hands, wrists together, and wiggled her eyebrows suggestively.

January Tweedy was feisty enough at 76 that I shuddered to think what she'd been like as a teenager.

Lina appeared in the doorway behind her and I breathed a sigh of relief.

"What can I do for you, Chief?" Lina asked. Her tone was icy. "Do you need to know what I had for lunch today? A list of every person I've spoken to since I got here?"

"I'm on that list. We're BFFFs," Mrs. Tweedy piped up.

"BFFFs?" I repeated.

"Best fuckin' friends forever," she said. "You got a problem with Lina here? You've got a bigger problem with me. Oh, also I need you to stop by and fish my watch out of the garbage disposal again."

Lina's lips quirked. But all amusement vanished when she caught me looking at her.

"Mrs. Tweedy, if you let me speak to Lina in private, I'll stop by after to get your watch out of the sink."

"And hang my new shower curtain."

140

"Another new shower curtain? What the hell happened to the last one?"

She took a rebellious sip of bourbon. "That sounds like a no to me, don't it, Lina?"

"It sure wasn't a yes," she agreed.

"Fine. Watch and shower curtain. Now go away," I said.

Mrs. Tweedy patted me on the cheek. "You're a good boy, Nash. Try not to leave your head up your ass for too long. Sooner or later, the condition's permanent." She turned to Lina. "See you at the gym tomorrow morning. Bright and early!"

"It was nice meeting you," Lina called after her.

All amusement disappeared the second the door closed across the hall.

"If you came here to continue your interrogation—"

I rested my forearm on her doorframe. "No, ma'am."

"Don't you 'ma'am' me. This is northern Virginia. Y'all barely say y'all here. You can't 'aw shucks' your way out of this."

Mrs. Tweedy's door cracked open behind me.

"I came to apologize," I said, ignoring the eavesdropping audience.

Lina crossed her arms.

"Not gonna make it easy on me, are you?"

"Why should I?"

I decided to push my luck. I put a hand on her

141

shoulder and gently but firmly backed her inside, then shut the door behind me.

"Sure. Come on in. Make yourself at home," she said dryly.

It didn't look as though she'd done much on that front.

The only personal belongings I spotted were a houseplant hanging out in one of the front windows and that box of files on her table.

I backed her up another step and then removed my hand. "Turn down the music. Please," I added when she shot me eye daggers.

She made me wait long enough that I thought I was going to have to do it myself before she finally walked over to the table and picked up her phone. The music lowered to a dull roar.

It didn't escape me that she took a detour to put the lid back on the files.

"You ever have a near-death experience?" I asked her.

She went still.

"As a matter of fact, I have," she said evenly.

"I'm gonna want some answers on that later," I warned her after a beat. "But for now, I'll assume that you know better than most what it's like to wake up and realize you're still here when you almost weren't."

She didn't give me anything other than a level stare from those whiskey-colored eyes.

I blew out a restless breath. "Angel, I almost

bled out in a ditch. Most of me is still here, but part of me didn't make it out. If you're here because of any part of that, I deserve to know."

She closed her eyes for a beat, long lashes fringing tan skin.

When she opened her eyes, she held my gaze. "I'm not here for you."

It rang like the truth.

"Is that all you're willing to give me?" I pressed.

She pursed her lips. "We'll see how the apology part of your presentation goes. And it better include an 'I'm sorry I'm a dumbass and let a U.S. marshal think we'd had sex.'"

"I'm sorry for the interrogation. I don't have my feet under me, and I'm just doin' the best I can in a shit situation. It felt like you were hiding something, especially when I saw Pain in My Ass Mustache making a move on you this morning. I'm used to trusting my gut. Still getting used to the fact that I can't anymore."

Her eyes narrowed. "Why can't you?"

"Because I walked right on up to that car."

Lina dropped her arms to her sides and let out a sound of aggravation. "Now, how's a girl supposed to hold a grudge against the whole broody, wounded hero routine?"

"I'm hopin' she can't," I admitted.

She drew in a breath and let it out. "Fine. I *am* in town looking for something." She held up a finger in my direction when I opened my mouth. "I didn't come here because someone put a bullet or two in you. I'm looking for something someone stole from a client. A couple of leads pointed me in this direction. Nolan and I crossed paths years ago on a different job. I didn't know he was in town and vice versa."

"Are you planning to cross paths with him while you're both here?"

There was about two feet of space between us and I swear I felt the air crackle like lightning was about to strike.

"I'm wondering why you would think that was your business," she said.

"I'll tell you if you say you accept my apology."

"Fine. Apology accepted."

"You're quick," I observed.

"Quit stalling," she ordered.

"I'm gonna be honest here and you're probably not gonna like it."

"Only one way to find out."

"I like stirring you up. I provoked you, and for that I'm mostly sorry," I admitted.

"Why?"

"Why am I sorry?"

"No. Much as you acted like it this morning and tonight, you're not an idiot. You know I could be a scary neighbor to piss off. Why did you provoke me?" she asked.

"You make me feel things. And after going

long enough without feeling anything, feeling something—even if it's anger or adrenaline—is better than the nothing."

The spark of light in her eyes turned to a smolder.

I took a slow step toward her. "Every time I'm near you, every time you laugh or look at me like you're looking right now or get pissed off, I feel something."

"What kind of something?"

I took another step and closed the distance between us.

"Good," I said, taking a chance and cupping my hands loosely around her biceps. She didn't pull away. "Though to be honest, good is pretty much anything other than what I've been feeling. I might be working up the courage to fight for the right to stay close. I can't do that if you've got another man in your bed."

She pursed her lips and considered. "There's no one occupying that space at the moment," she said finally.

"Does it bother you when I touch you?" I asked.

She rolled her eyes. "I take it Knox opened his big mouth?"

"He may have mentioned you had a problem."

"Yet here you are with your hands on me," she pointed out. "Pretty ballsy of you."

"My brother was surprised you'd let me get

145

this close to you with said balls attached. It got me wondering. What if?"

"What if what?"

"What if you like me touching you as much as I like touching you?"

I was close enough to kiss her. It would be easy enough to lean down and close the distance. To feel that smart mouth under mine and taste those secrets. Something about this felt so right. So fucking inevitable.

"All right. I'll play. What if I do?" She had flecks of gold and topaz in those brown eyes that were sizing me up.

"What if you let me get closer?"

She quirked an eyebrow. "Exactly how much closer?"

I took half a step into her, bringing my body flush with hers. Every nerve in my body fired to life at the contact as if she were jumper cables and I was a dead battery.

"As close as you'll let me. I don't just want this, Angelina. I need this."

"Are you saying you want me to be some kind of emotional support fuck?"

"I'm sayin' I want to get as close to you as you'll let me. The closer I get to you, the better I feel. Like right now," I said softly. "I feel like I can finally breathe easy."

She brought a hand to my chest and pressed it there. "That's . . . a lot of pressure."

"I know it," I admitted. This wasn't looking for a one-night stand. This was a quest for an anchor. Something I could hang on to in the storm. "Cards on the table?"

"Why stop now?"

"There's a whole lot of reasons why you should say no. Not the least of which is I'm damaged enough to know there's a chance I might not ever be right again."

"Nobody's perfect," she said with a quirk of those soft, full lips.

I skimmed my hands up her arms and then back down just to feel the softness of her sweater, the warmth of her body. "Knox doesn't want us anywhere near each other."

"Too bad for him I hate being told what to do," she said, bringing her other hand to my chest. She pressed it there and I leaned into the touch.

"I hate surprises and I don't tolerate lies. Not even the little ones."

"I despise boredom and routine. Some would even say I invite drama."

"Until this summer, I was pretty set on finding a wife. Starting a family," I confessed.

She let out a nervous laugh. "Okay. That one scared me a little. Now what are you set on?"

"Feeling alive."

Her gaze locked on mine and it felt like the midday sun warming me down to my core.

"And you think I can help with that?" she asked.

My heart was beating strong against my sternum. An answering pulse echoed throughout my body, warming my blood, stirring my cock. "Angel, you already have."

Her eyes went wide and I wondered if I'd gone too far.

"You're not my type," she said finally.

"I know."

"I'm not planning on sticking around."

"Got that too."

"You just said you were looking for a wife, Nash."

"I was. Now I'm just looking to get through the day."

She blew out a breath that I could feel.

We kept getting closer and closer. Standing in the middle of her mostly empty apartment, we filled the space around us with heat. Her breasts brushed my chest, bare feet skimming the toes of my boots. My breath stirred her hair.

"Need to ask you something else," I said.

"If it's my mother's maiden name and the last four digits of my social security number, I'm going to realize this is a really elaborate scam."

I ran a finger down her sharp jaw. "Do you like it when I touch you?"

A shiver ran through her. "Why?"

"You know why. But I want you to say it. Cards on the table."

Her face softened. "I don't seem to mind when it's your hands doing the touching, hotshot."

"If that changes, I need to know. Immediately."

She hesitated before nodding.

"Yeah?" I pressed.

She nodded again. "Yeah."

I took one of her hands from my chest and slid it over my shoulder. Then I did the same with the other. She felt warm, alive, and so fucking soft against me. I shifted my weight to one foot, swaying us to the side.

"We can't slow dance to the Struts," she pointed out as the driving beat of "Could Have Been Me" thumped.

"Looks like that's exactly what we're doing."

She let out a shaky breath. I brushed a fingertip to the pulse in her neck. Despite her calm exterior, her pulse fluttered under my touch.

"Is you monitoring your heart rate part of that near-death story?" I asked her.

She paused midsway, then bit her lip, looking uncertain for the first time I could remember. "I think maybe we've had enough honesty for one night," she said.

I didn't agree. But I was a patient man. I'd unravel every one of those secrets she held back until she was laid as bare as I was. I tucked her head under my chin, then slid my hands under the hem of her cardigan to touch the skin of her back. Breathing in the scents of shampoo and

149

laundry detergent, I held her to me like she was precious cargo and swayed.

I was hard again. One thing was for sure, Lina Solavita knew how to make a man feel alive.

I was so focused on absorbing all the soft and warm she had to offer that Lina reacted to the knock at the door first.

"This shower curtain ain't gonna hang itself, Chief," Mrs. Tweedy bellowed.

"Fuck," I muttered.

"I guess you'd better go," Lina said, her arms slipping free of my neck.

"Guess so. Think about what I said?"

"I might not think about anything else," she confessed with a wry smile.

Gently, I cupped her face in my hands and moved in. But instead of going for those full lips that parted when I was just a breath away, I pressed a kiss to her forehead.

"Thanks for the dance, Angel."

10

Sweating with the Oldies

Lina

K nockemout's gym was like the rest of town: a little rough around the edges and a lot interesting. It was a long, low metal building with a gravel parking lot. At 7:00 a.m., it was respectably full of motorcycles, minivans, and luxury SUVs.

I'd spent a good portion of the night tossing and turning, thinking about Nash's proposition. I wasn't used to a man getting under my skin or into my head like that. I hoped a good workout would help me shake out the obsessive rumination about exactly how close Nash wanted to get to me. Or how close I was willing to let him.

I was tempted. *Very* tempted. It was exactly the kind of rush the old me would have jumped at. But wasn't it time to break old patterns? To learn to make better choices?

Besides, if I let the man into my bed, he'd want to get close. And close meant I'd run the risk of Nash discovering my practically insignificant omission of the truth, which he would definitely view as an act of war. And this was why I didn't do things that remotely resembled relationships.

So what if his hands on me made me feel melty and decadent like a gourmet grilled cheese? This was one challenge I didn't need to meet. One mystery that didn't need solving. The smart thing would be to avoid him. Just stay out of his way, get the job done, and be on my way.

Inside, the music was hard-driving classic rock instead of the usual peppy pop mix most gyms preferred. There were no tanning beds or massage chairs, just rows of machines, free weights, and sweaty people.

"You new?" The girl behind the corrugated metal front desk had a nose piercing, a neck tattoo, and the body of a yoga goddess.

"Yeah. I'm meeting Mrs. Tweedy and her friends."

She flashed a quick grin. "Have fun with that. And definitely sign this." She slid a clipboard with a waiver toward me.

Wondering just how bad a workout with septuagenarians could possibly be, I scrawled my name at the bottom and handed it back.

"Try not to hurt yourself keeping up," she warned. "Locker rooms are behind me. Your crew is down there." She pointed toward the far end of the gym.

"Thanks," I said and headed in that direction.

The center of the space was occupied by a few

dozen cardio machines. Treadmills, ellipticals, rowing machines, bikes. There was a large studio in the back where some kind of boot camp class was in progress. Someone was throwing up in a trash can and another person was lying flat on their back with a towel over their face while the instructor led the rest of the class through an excessive number of burpees.

The crowd was a melting pot of horse people in their Lululemon and high-tech gadget watches mixed with the biker crowd flexing their tattoos in ripped tank tops and bandannas. Running full out on neighboring treadmills were a lean twentysomething white guy in head-to-toe Under Armour and a Black woman with silver box braids and a Harley tank top that had seen its own mileage. His face was contorted from effort. She was grinning.

Agatha and Blaze, middle-aged biker babe lesbians who frequented Knox's Honky Tonk, threw me a salute from their side-by-side stair-climbers.

"Lina!"

Mrs. Tweedy waved from the free weights section. The half dozen elderly folks in matching track suits behind her eyed me as I approached.

"Morning," I said.

"Gang, this is my new neighbor and bestie, Lina. Lina, this is the gang," she said.

"Hi, Lina," they said as one.

"Hi, gang." They were a motley crew if I'd ever seen one. Best guess, their ages ranged from midsixties to eighties. There were wrinkles and gray hair but also muscles and top-of-the-line athletic shoes.

"You ready to work?" Mrs. Tweedy twanged.

"Sure." I'd stuck mostly to running since arriving in town. A nice, easy weight workout would be a good way to ease back into strength training.

"Don't start without me!" Stef jogged up in designer gym threads.

"We meet again," I said to him.

"About time, Steffy," the woman on Mrs. Tweedy's right said. Her jet-black hair was streaked with silver, and her T-shirt said MY WARM-UP IS YOUR WORKOUT.

"I was in the parking lot giving myself a pep talk," he said. He looked at me. "You sure you're up for this?"

I scoffed. "I run five miles a day. I think I can keep up."

Mrs. Tweedy clapped her hands. "Let's get these old bones warmed up, y'all."

"Oh God. I'm dying. Save yourself. Go on without me," I begged Stef.

He reached down and hauled me off the long strip of mat that ran along one wall of the gym. My knees buckled. I was a dehydrated husk of a human being. My muscles were too weak to hold me up. Miraculously, my heart had stayed in the safe zone through the workout from hell, but the rest of my body had given up.

"Pull yourself together, woman. If you quit now, they'll never let you forget it," Stef wheezed. Sweat dripped off his chin. His usually perfectly styled hair stood up in damp black tufts all over his head.

I sucked in a breath. "I don't understand how a seventy-year-old can go so hard on the battle ropes. Does that mustache give him super-powers?"

Stef squeezed his water bottle over his face. "Vernon was a Marine. Retirement bored him so he took up training for Iron Man events. He's not human."

I leaned against the wall next to the water fountain and used the hem of my tank to wipe the sweat out of my eyes. "What about Mrs. Bannerjee? She just dead-lifted two hundred pounds. *Eight* times."

"Aditi started lifting weights in her fifties. She has three decades of experience."

"Let's go! You can rest when you're dead," Mrs. Tweedy bellowed.

"I can't do it," I moaned.

Stef put his hands on my shoulders, but the sweat made me too slippery too hold on to. He gave up and leaned against the wall next to me.

"Listen to me. We *can* do this. We *will* do this. And when we're done, we'll go to Café Rev, order Red Line Lattes, and eat our weight in pastry."

"I need more motivation than pastry."

"Shit." He pushed away from the wall and faced me, looking ill.

"Shit what? Did they just add more wall balls? I hit myself in the face last round." Wall balls were a special kind of hell that involved squatting with a heavy exercise ball and then explosively launching out of the squat to throw the ball several feet above your head. They were worse than burpees. I hated them.

Stef shoved both hands through his hair, then with a grimace wiped his palms on his shorts. "How do I look?"

"Like you were just dragged into the deep end of the pool by handsy mermen."

"Damn it!"

"But in a totally handsome, Henry Golding kind of way," I amended.

"Maybe I should take off my shirt?"

"What's happening right now?" I demanded, snatching the water bottle out of his hands and aiming for my mouth.

"Jeremiah just strutted his fine ass in here to do bicep curls."

I didn't stop sucking down water, but I did peer over Stef's shoulder. The gorgeous barber wasn't hard to spot, curling forty-fives in front of the mirror . . . next to Nash Morgan.

I choked and nearly drowned.

"Shit!" I yanked off my headband and soaked it with water before putting it back on.

Stef elbowed me. "Excuse me! You can't have him. He's mine. If I ever get up the nerve to actually ask him out."

"I'm not 'shitting' about Jeremiah, dummy. I'm shitting about Nash 'Dat Ass' Morgan," I hissed.

A flutter in my chest had me glancing down at my watch. My heart was steadily thumping along. Now the flutter was moving into my stomach. Apparently this wasn't a structural defect. This was worse.

Stef glanced over his shoulder, then whipped his head back in my direction, sending a shower of sweat in all directions. "Somebody's got a crush," he sang.

"First of all, gross. I have your sweat in my eyes. Second, it's not a crush," I argued. "It's . . . an awareness."

My awareness went into roller-coaster-plummet mode when Nash's gaze locked on me as he stood over a bar loaded with weight plates. There was nothing friendly about the way his eyes roamed me. It was all hunger.

This time, my knees buckling had nothing to do with muscle fatigue.

"No offense, but aren't you supposed to be some kind of edgy badass?" Stef asked.

I tore my eyeballs away from the smoldering chief of police. "Huh?"

"I'll admit, Studly Do-Right looks like he wants to walk over here, strip you naked, and bend you over a weight bench."

My core clenched in involuntarily need.

"But I thought you were a play-it-cool-make-'em-beg type."

There was nothing cool about the way I reacted to Nash Morgan. It was molten hot need laced with icy licks of fear. "I can't believe I'm saying this, but apparently some men make playing it cool impossible," I admitted.

"You two gonna run your mouths all day or you gonna finish this set?" Mrs. Tweedy hollered. "Don't make me add more wall balls!"

"And now everyone's looking at us," Stef muttered.

Everyone including Jeremiah and Nash.

I squared my shoulders. "We have to do this."

"And we have to do it sexy."

"You might as well take your shirt off then," I said.

"Same goes. Maybe they'll be so hypnotized by my pecs and your tits they won't notice when we go into cardiac arrest."

"Let's try to avoid that part," I suggested.

"I can't promise anything."

"Let's go, kids!" Vernon called.

"Last set, best set," Mrs. Tweedy shouted.

Stef gritted his teeth. "Come on. Let's strip and sexy walk."

"Drink."

My eyes fluttered open and I found myself staring up into the startling blue of Nash's. A water bottle dangled in front of my face.

I was too tired and thirsty to take offense to being ordered about.

I worked my way into a seated position. Nash was crouched down next to me, a sheen of sweat glistening on his skin and sucking his T-shirt fast to his chest. Jeremiah stood behind him looking amused.

I kicked Stef's leg.

"Leave me alone to die, woman," he said. He was facedown on the mat next to me.

I kicked him again harder this time. "We can't die in front of *witnesses*."

He peeled his upper body off the rubber and blinked at our audience.

"Need a hand?" Jeremiah asked Stef.

I scraped up enough energy to smirk as my workout buddy's crush hauled him to his feet.

"I'm impressed," Nash said as I finally gulped down the proffered water. "No one survives their first Sweating with the Oldies workout."

"I wouldn't say I survived," I croaked.

"You got that last rep in," he insisted. "It counts."

"And had to dry heave into the trash can."

His mouth was softened by one of those almost smiles that fired up the wild swooping in my belly. "Still counts."

"They're superhuman. Every single one of them."

"That they are," he agreed.

I noticed some of the gym goers noticing us. "Either I'm topless or you're walking around bottomless to warrant this kind of attention."

He glanced up and around, then grimaced. "Small town. There hasn't been much to gossip about lately."

"Besides their chief getting shot, two citizens being abducted and rescued, and a U.S. marshal lurking around town. Where is your shadow with a badge anyway?"

Nash hooked a thumb over his shoulder to where Nolan was sweating all over a stationary bike, looking both pissed off and bored.

"Just another day in Knockemout," Nash said, offering me his hand.

I took it and let him pull me to my feet.

My muscles sang with a mix of post-workout exhaustion and elation.

"If you're wanting an answer about your offer—" I began.

But he cut me off with a shake of his head. "I'd

rather you think about it a little longer than one night. It's a big ask. I've got a smaller ask I need you to say yes to first."

"What's that?"

"Mind watching Piper for me tonight? I haven't left her alone for longer than a few minutes."

"Sure."

"I won't be too late," he promised.

I would *not* ask him what his plans were. And I *definitely* wouldn't ask him if it was a date.

"I'm going for drinks with Knox and Lucian," he said, reading my mind.

The ladies of town would be aflutter over that kind of sexy sandwich of hotness, I guessed.

"Yeah. No problem," I assured him, pretending that I didn't feel the stupid wash of relief that it was only a guys' night out.

He dipped his head toward me in that sexy, intimate way of his. My pulse tripped. So did the woman on the treadmill behind us. She shot me a rueful grin and a shrug when she recovered.

Nash Morgan was a danger to women everywhere.

"Appreciate it. I'll drop her off a little before nine," he said.

I vowed to be showered, made up, and wearing something not soaked in sweat. If I could make my legs work by then. "Okay."

He checked his watch. "I've gotta go. I

promised Liza J I'd clean the gutters today."

"Here." I held out his tumbler.

"Hang on to it. I know where you live."

"Thanks," I croaked.

"See you later, Angelina." He gave me a goose bump–inducing once-over before turning to leave.

"Nash?"

He stopped and turned.

Glancing around at our not-so-subtle audience, I closed the distance between us with the sexiest limp I could muster. "Exactly how much of me do you want?"

Those blue eyes changed to icy fire. "The gentlemanly answer would be as much as you're willing to give."

"And you're a gentleman?"

"I used to be." Then he lifted his chin. "Drink more water and don't forget to stretch or you'll regret it tomorrow."

It was a good thing my face was already on fire from exertion.

He flashed me a wink and the ghost of a grin before heading for the locker room. I watched him go. So did the rest of the female population of the gym and a handful of the men too.

Nolan got up and wiped down his bike. He threw me a little salute before following Nash.

Stef appeared next to me. "Still up for coffee and carbs?" He had a goofy grin on his face.

"God, yes. Why do you look so happy? Are you delirious?"

"I think so. Jeremiah gave me a sweat towel."

"Nash gave me his water. Are we as pathetic as I think we are?"

"Oh, much worse," Stef insisted.

Vernon clapped me on the shoulder on his way to the treadmills. "Way not to suck too bad out there."

"Thanks," I said.

"You did well," Aditi said.

"If you're up for it, tomorrow is chest and back day," Mrs. Tweedy offered.

"Don't you dare say yes or I'll have to come too. And I need three days to recover," Stef whispered.

My laugh was a barely audible wheeze.

11

Panicking Never Helps

Nash

My hands clenched into fists when I heard the thump of country music outside Honky Tonk's front door. I'd taken a walk around the block just to hype myself up into going inside. There was laughter and life on the other side of the front door. I was supposed to participate in it when all I wanted to do was stay home, in the dark. In the quiet.

The day had started out better than most. I'd gone to the gym with the express purpose of seeing Lina. Between watching her move that beautiful body and me actually moving mine, I'd gotten a boost. But somewhere in the middle of Liza J's mile-long list of chores, that cold, dark wave had crashed over me again without warning. It dragged me under, and even the antidepressant I'd remembered to take that morning couldn't help me fight my way back to the surface.

I'd started half a dozen texts to Knox making up excuses for why I couldn't make it tonight, but I knew he'd keep his word. He'd just appear at my door and try to drag me out.

It was easier to show up, go through the motions.

Upstairs, I'd managed a dozen stilted words before shoving Piper into Lina's arms. I'd use the dog as an excuse to get back within the hour.

I could fake it for sixty minutes. Fifty-six now, seeing as how I was already four minutes late.

Steeling myself, I opened the front door and stepped into the world of the living.

It was a Monday night, which meant a smaller crowd and country classics on the jukebox rather than a live band.

Out of habit, I scanned the thin crowd. Tallulah and Justice St. John occupied a table with pet shop owner Gael and his husband, Isaac, for their monthly double date. Sherry Fiasco, Jeremiah's sister and Knox's right-hand person, was shrugging into a coat behind the bar next to Silver, the edgy blond bartender.

My brother clocked me before I made it two steps inside. He was in his standard uniform of jeans, battered motorcycle boots, beard, and an air of "fuck around and find out."

Knox always appeared to be looking for a fight.

Beside him stood Lucian Rollins in a suit that probably cost more than my first car. He was tall, dark, and also dangerous, but in a different way.

Where Knox was more likely to punch you in the face if you pissed him off, Lucian was the type to methodically and creatively destroy your life.

Lucky for me they mostly kept their powers in check.

There was an empty stool between the two, which told me I was about to be the unwilling center of attention.

The door opened behind me, and my U.S. marshal shadow strolled inside. "You know this would be a hell of a lot easier if you told me where you were going and how long you planned to be there," he groused.

"Yeah, well, my life would be a hell of a lot easier if I didn't have you up my ass all day."

"Long as we're both miserable," he said before peeling off to grab an empty two-top facing the door.

Knox straightened away from the bar.

Fuck me.

Fifty-six minutes. Drink a beer. Shoot the shit. Keep my brother from assaulting a fed. Then I could go home and hide from the world.

I made my way through the tables, nodding as people called out greetings.

"Evening, boys," I said when I reached them.

Lucian offered me his hand and pulled me in for a one-armed hug.

"Good to see you."

"You too, Lucy."

Knox was glaring over my shoulder at Nolan

Graham. "Think I might go kick your shadow's ass," he said over the rim of his glass.

"Appreciate the sentiment, but I really don't wanna help bury a body tonight," I told him.

Knox's attention shifted away from the marshal and back to me. "You look like shit. You shave with a butter knife?"

"Nice to see you too, dick," I said, sliding onto the stool between them. I didn't have the energy to stand.

"You've been avoiding my calls," Lucian said, taking his seat and shooting me one of those piercing looks that had women's underwear falling down to their ankles for over two decades now.

"Been busy," I said, signaling Silver for a drink.

She winked a smoky eye at me. "Comin' up, Chief."

One benefit to still living in the small town you'd grown up in, you never had to tell anyone what your drink order was. They remembered.

"Better not be busy with your new neighbor," Knox said, straddling his stool and angling toward me.

"If that's why we're doin' this, I'll save you an hour and say what Lina and I do or don't do is none of your damn business."

"You're my brother. She's my friend. That makes it my business."

"Save your breath. Nothing's happened . . . yet," I added on a smirk.

"Yeah? Well, it better stay that way. You two don't work. She's all wanderlust and adrenaline and you break out into hives if you venture out of the county. You've got nothin' in common."

"Said the expert whose been engaged what? A handful of weeks? To a woman who is way too good for you, I might add. Thanks, Silver," I said when she slid me a draft beer.

"Gentlemen, I suggest we table this discussion," Lucian said. "We have other matters to discuss."

The faster they spilled it, the sooner I could go home.

Lucian put his scotch down on the bar and nodded at my brother.

"Where does the investigation stand? Lucian thinks the feds are ignoring Duncan Hugo because they're more interested in landing his fuckface father," Knox said.

Okay, maybe I'd rather go a few rounds about me seeing Lina if the alternative was talking about Duncan Hugo. "It's an ongoing investigation. No comment," I said.

Knox snorted. "You can't tell me you're not running your own investigation. If the feds are focused on Daddy, then we'll go after Junior. Only problem is, Junior's so far underground no one knows where he is."

"Our most likely theory is that Anthony helped his son leave the country," Lucian said.

If the junior Hugo had split the country, that

meant the odds of him coming back to finish the job were slim.

The relief I felt was immediately replaced with a wave of shame. As an officer of the law, I was programmed to fight for justice. As a Morgan, I was destined to just plain fight. Yet here I was, too depressed to spur myself into action.

"I'd have bet my brokerage balance that asshole doesn't have two brain cells to rub together. But Naomi and Way insist he's smarter than he's given credit. Says when he had 'em . . ." Knox trailed off, his knuckles going white on the bar.

I realized that Hugo hadn't just taken something from me, he'd taken from my family. And that still wasn't enough to bring me to the surface of the dark.

My brother cleared his throat while Lucian and I did the polite, manly thing and ignored him.

"Way said he was sly like a fox with rabies," Knox said finally.

The corner of my mouth lifted. Waylay would make a fine cop someday, but I doubted Knox would want to hear that about his little girl.

"He better hope for his sake his ass is in South America getting eaten alive by mosquitos," Knox said.

"I don't see a scenario where it would make sense for him to stick around. He's most likely living it up somewhere far away from here."

"But in case he isn't," Lucian said, "you need

to be vigilant. You're a loose end regardless of where he is. You're the only one who can identify him as the shooter."

"And how would you know that?" I demanded.

Lucian held up his palms, the picture of innocence. "I can't help it if information falls into my lap."

"What kind of information?"

"The kind that summarizes your dashcam footage."

My jaw clenched. It was more of a reflex than any real emotion. "That leak better not have come from my end."

"It didn't," he assured me.

"You remember anything yet?" Knox demanded.

I stared at the bottles behind the bar. People drowned themselves in those bottles daily to numb the pain, the fear, the discomfort that life doled out. Some numbed themselves in even more dangerous ways. Some never surfaced.

But I was already numb. I needed to feel. And no amount of alcohol was going to help me dig my way out of this all-consuming emptiness. There was only one thing that could. One woman that could.

"No," I said finally.

I could feel Knox and Lucian communicating silently.

"You think about talking to one of those, uh . . . therapists?" Knox choked out.

Lucian and I both swung our heads in his direction and stared.

"Oh, fuck you both. Naomi suggested it. I'm man enough to admit it's not a horrible idea . . . if you don't mind spilling your guts to a complete stranger. It's not like Dad gave us any kind of healthy coping tools."

"I did see a shrink. Department requirement," I reminded him.

"Trauma has a way of damaging memory," she'd said. *"In some cases victims never get those memories back."*

Trauma. Victims. They were labels I'd spent an entire career applying to others. My own label, "hero," had been peeled off and replaced with "victim." And I didn't know if I could stomach it.

"I see a therapist," Lucian announced.

Knox straightened. "See? As in present tense?"

"Occasionally. I was much younger and less . . . interested in the law when I started seeing him to get access to his patient records."

I glanced over my shoulder. Nolan lifted his bottle of beer in a silent toast.

"Can we not talk about this or any other hypothetical crimes with a U.S. marshal twenty feet away? You two can't be playing goddamn Scooby-Doo in the middle of a federal investigation."

"I'm offended," Lucian announced.

"You be offended. I'll be pissed the fuck off," Knox decided.

I picked up my beer even though I didn't want it. "And what do you find so offensive?"

"That you doubt my abilities."

To be fair, Lucian was practically a corporate 007. Except for the fact that he was American, preferred bourbon to martinis, and worked in the cutthroat world of political consulting, which probably did bear certain similarities to international espionage.

He was tight-lipped on the specifics of exactly what his company did for its clients, but I didn't have to be a genius to guess that it wasn't all aboveboard.

"I don't know about your abilities. But I do know that out of the three of us, you're the only one to do actual jail time."

It was a low fucking blow and we all knew it. Hell, I wanted to punch myself in the face for it.

"I'm sorry, man," I said, digging my thumb into the spot between my eyebrows. "I've got a short fuse these days."

My patience had most likely bled out of me along with that pool of O negative on the side of the road. This was why I didn't want to be around people.

He held up a hand dismissively. "It's fine."

"No. It's not. You've always been there for me, Lucy, and I'm being a petty asshole taking a swipe at you. I'm sorry."

"If you two start hugging it out, I'm leavin'," Knox threatened.

To spite him, I wrapped Lucian in a bear hug. My shoulder sang, but in almost a good way.

Lucian thumped me on the back twice. I knew we were just fucking around with my brother. But there was something steadying about my oldest friend's instant forgiveness. It paled in comparison to the anchoring heat Lina's touch stirred in me. But it still meant something.

We turned back to Knox, grinning.

"You takin' your beer to go?" I asked him.

"Assholes," Knox muttered.

"I am sorry, Lucy," I said again.

"You're forgiven. You've been through a lot."

"Is that why you're hanging around in town on a Monday night instead of running your evil corporate empire?"

My friend's lips quirked.

"Seriously, man, if you're in town just to keep an eye on me, I've already got an armed mustache up my ass," I said, nodding in the direction of Nolan. "You don't need to camp out here and lose all your money."

"Running an evil corporate empire means having a team in place to pick up the slack when I'm otherwise engaged."

"You're not making that commute up here every day are you?" Traffic in northern Virginia was its own special ring of hell.

173

Knox snorted. "Don't get all teary-eyed over the gesture. The empire has a helicopter. Luce is just using you as an excuse to play with his toy."

"Just don't land it on the roof of the elementary school. I don't need the feds, the U.S. marshals, *and* the FAA up my ass."

"How are the wedding plans going?" Lucian asked, changing the subject.

"Can you believe Daze was thinking white linen on the tables? I mean, for fuck's sake, it's a Knockemout party, we're gonna be spillin' shit all night long. I don't want our reception lookin' like the tables are covered in some murdered bed wetter's sheets."

My brother certainly knew how to paint a picture.

"So what did you decide to go with?" Lucian asked.

"Navy blue," Knox said proudly.

"Nice," Lucian said with an approving nod.

"By the way. You both are groomsmen." My brother looked at me. "I guess you can be my best man."

I made it an hour and fifteen minutes and was damn proud of myself. I'd nursed the second beer, made mostly the right responses, and said my goodbyes when Naomi called Knox to tell him Waylon had chased after the skunk he had a crush on and gotten sprayed. Again.

We said our goodbyes and I tried not to make it look like I was bolting for the door.

I even paused at Nolan's table where he was shrugging back into his coat.

"I'm walking the ten feet to my door. I think I can survive it on my own," I told him.

"Your call, Chief. Try not to end up in the gutter full of holes."

"I'll do my best," I lied.

I ducked out into the crisp night, the door closing behind me on the light and the music. Something didn't feel right. Standing here under the streetlight, mere feet from my front door, I felt exposed, vulnerable, on edge. Something or someone was out there.

Was it him? Had Duncan Hugo come back to finish the job? Or was it all in my imagination?

I cast a glance up and down the street, looking for the source of the doom that settled over me.

My hands began to tingle. It started in my palms and rolled into my fingers.

"Fuck. Not now," I whispered under my breath. "Not here."

There was no shooter lurking in the dark. The only villain here was the malfunction in my brain.

The tingling turned to a burn. I closed my hands into tight fists, trying to force the sensation away. I'd stopped it before. But I knew I was already too far gone.

A light sweat broke over my body, while inside, I felt chilled to the bone.

"Come on, man. Keep it together," I said through gritted teeth.

But the band around my chest was tightening, tightening. The breath I held began to leave my lungs. The sound vanished from my ears, replaced with the muffled thud of my own heartbeat.

My breath was a thin wheeze.

There was no stopping it. No talking myself down. Cold sweat coursed down my back.

"Fuck me."

My hands clenched into fists as the band around my chest got tighter and tighter. My heart raced under my ribs as the ache spread. I made it through the door to the foot of the stairs before my legs gave out. I crashed into the wall and slid down to the cold tile.

"Not real. It's not fucking real," I repeated between thready inhales.

Panic was never the solution. It would never serve you in times of crisis. As a cop, that had been drilled into my head. I'd been trained to stay calm, to follow procedure, to operate on instinct. Yet no procedure, no training had prepared me for these kind of attacks.

I was burning up and freezing at the same time. Pain radiated through my chest and my vision started to go dark around the edges. Spots of light danced in front of my eyes.

I hated myself. Hated the weakness. The lack of control. Hated the thought that this was all in my head. That it could happen anywhere. I couldn't do my job if I was curled into a fucking ball on the ground. Couldn't protect this town if I couldn't even protect myself from the monsters in my own fucking head.

12

Welcome to the Danger Zone

Lina

G reat job pooping on the grass and not the sidewalk," I told Piper as we scurried toward the entrance to the apartments. She pranced confidently toward the door like it had been her home for more than three days.

It was a cold, quiet night in Knockemout. The air was crisp and still.

I slid my key in the lock, opened the heavy door, and froze.

"Nash?" I ushered Piper inside, let the door slam shut behind us, and raced to his side.

He sat on the floor, his back to the wall at the foot of the stairs, his knees drawn up to his chest, arms wrapped around them, hands fisted.

"Are you all right? Are you hurt?"

I ran my hands over his shoulders, down his arms. He caught my hand with one of his own and squeezed hard.

"Just . . . catching . . . my breath," he managed.

I held on tight to his hand and used my free one to push his hair back from his forehead. He was sweating and shivering at the same time. Either the man was down with the flu or he was on the tail end of a panic attack.

"You okay?" he asked me.

"I'm fine. So are you," I insisted. "You have enough air."

Grimly, he clenched his jaw and nodded.

With a whimper, Piper shoved her face under Nash's arm and crawled into his lap.

"We were out for a walk. I thought I'd take her out one last time so you wouldn't have to when you got back. She did her business and we took a stroll around the block. I think her limp is a little better. Did the vet say anything about PT? I read this article about acupuncture for dogs."

I was babbling. The man had scared the shit out of me *again*.

"Relax, Angel," he rasped, his grip on my hand starting to loosen. "It's okay." His other hand came up and stroked down Piper's back.

Still holding his hand, I sat next to him on the floor. My shoulder and arm pressed against his. His body's fading tremors rolled through mine and I absorbed them.

"I'll relax when you stop scaring the hell out of me." I bumped my shoulder into his. "Starting to fade?"

He nodded slowly. "Yeah."

"Then let's get you upstairs before you crash," I said. I got to my feet, plucked Piper out of his lap, and set her on the ground. Then I held out a hand.

He stared at it, head cocked, thumb pressing into the spot between his eyebrows.

"Come on. You know as well as I do that the crash sucks almost as much. You can either lean on me or I'll call your brother."

"Mean," he said before taking my hand. It took effort from both of us, but I managed to get him on his feet at the foot of the stairs.

"Kids in elementary school used to call me Meana because I was so bossy," I confessed. I ducked under his arm and wrapped my own around his waist.

"Kids are assholes," he wheezed.

We tackled the first step together. Piper dashed ahead of us, tail wagging. Nash was holding back, trying not to put too much of his weight on me. But there was a long flight of stairs between us and his apartment.

"It started with these twins in elementary school, Darla and Marla. Pretty, popular, and they wore matching, name-brand outfits," I told him.

"They sound horrible," Nash joked. "Want me to do a run on them? See how many times they've been arrested?"

I laughed and felt him give me just a little bit more of his weight.

My legs were trembling from my workout that

morning. I was not looking forward to sitting down to pee tomorrow.

"So what are the odds that you'll magically forget this ever happened tomorrow?" Nash asked as we took a break halfway up the stairs.

Piper returned to us, sniffed anxiously first at Nash's shoes, then mine, before running back to the top.

"I can be bribed."

"Name your price," he said, taking the next step.

"Cheese sticks," I decided.

"The cold, peeling kind or the clog-your-arteries kind?"

He still sounded winded as we trudged along, but not like he was fighting for every molecule of oxygen.

"No contest," I scoffed. "Give me all the deep-fried goodness."

"I'll keep you in fried mozzarella for the rest of your days if you never tell anyone about this."

"Unlike *some* people, I respect the privacy of others," I said pointedly as we finally hit the top step. Piper danced in front of us like she was proud of our accomplishment.

He sighed. "There you go again, Meana. Kickin' a man when he's down."

I angled us toward his door. "Keys, hotshot."

He didn't quite manage to hide the wince when he used his left hand to dig into his pocket.

Bullet wounds and panic attacks. Nash Morgan was a hot mess. Emphasis on the hot.

I took the keys from him and unlocked his door. Piper darted across the threshold into the dark apartment.

Nash pulled me along with him as he reached for the light switch and flicked it on.

"Wow. Someone got their act together," I said, noting the transformation inside. It even smelled clean.

"Yeah. Right," he said through gritted teeth.

"Let's go, big guy," I said, kicking the door closed and guiding him over to the couch.

He collapsed onto it, eyes closed. His face was pale and sweat still dotted his brow. Piper hopped up next to him and put a tiny paw on his thigh.

"It's time for the Lina Special," I decided, depositing the dog leash on the coffee table.

"Please tell me that's code for some kind of sex," he said without opening his eyes.

"Very funny. I'll be back in a minute."

"Don't go." The easygoing humor vanished and those blue eyes pleaded with me to stay. "It feels better when you're close."

Now it was my turn to have trouble catching my breath. I'd never been with a man who needed me. Wanted me? Yes. Enjoyed me? Of course. But needed me? That was brand-new, terrifying territory.

"I'm going next door and I'll be back in less than a minute," I promised.

The subtle clench of his jaw was nearly my undoing. But he finally nodded.

I ducked back into the hall, leaving his door open, and made the two-second journey to my apartment. Inside, I quickly found what I needed. When I returned, Nash was still in the same position, watching the door.

"Fifty-seven seconds," he said.

Juggling my haul, I closed the door again.

"Get ready to relax your ass off," I said, switching off the overhead lights. I turned on the lamp next to Nash, then took everything else into the kitchen and deposited it on the counter. "I assume your phone connects to this manly looking speaker over here."

"You assume correctly," he said, still watching me. "Coat pocket."

He was still wearing his jacket, a slim-fitting field coat in army green.

"Two birds," I decided. "Lean forward."

With my help, Nash slid his arms free. He was wearing one of those sexy thermal shirts that hugged a lot of muscle. It was an unnecessary observation given the current circumstances. Unnecessary yet somehow unavoidable. I could have been on my death bed and I still would have paused to appreciate the man's form.

I found his phone and used his face to unlock it.

"Oh, come on! You have a playlist called Country Slow Dance," I complained, pushing play.

"Got a problem with that?" he asked as George Strait's voice crooned low.

"How are you not married with a pack of kids?"

He waved his right hand down his body. "Honey, in case you haven't noticed, I'm a brittle husk of a man."

I sat on the coffee table in front of him. "The husk thing is temporary. You're the marry-your-high-school-sweetheart type. How did some Knockemout cheerleader not tie you down?"

"I had some wild oats to sow first. Had fun sowing 'em for a while. Then fell in love with the job. Had a lot to clean up before I felt like I could give someone the attention they'd deserve."

"You thought that someone might be Naomi," I guessed. And why not? She was pretty, kind, loyal, and sweet. She didn't have any of the rough edges that I did.

"For about five seconds. It was pretty clear she was it for Knox."

I pointed at his feet. "Boots," I ordered.

He glanced down wearily as if the task were too monumental.

I pulled one of his feet in my lap and worked the laces loose on his boot.

"I know this is supposed to be humiliating and all, but is it weird I'm also turned on?" he asked, head back, eyes closed.

"You're a charmer, hotshot. I'll give you that."
I took off the other boot and scooted off my perch
to replace my butt with a pillow. "Feet up."

"Bossy."

"Feet up *please*." I smiled when he complied.
"Good boy." I gave him a pat on the leg and
returned to the kitchen with Piper on my heels.

While the coffee maker spat out a mug of hot
water over a tea bag, I opened Nash's freezer
and found a bag of frozen broccoli.

I brought both the mug and the broccoli back to
the couch. "The tea is some hippie concoction for
relaxation. Tastes like you're chewing up a bridal
bouquet, but it does the trick. The broccoli is for
your chest."

"Why am I wearing frozen florets?" he asked
as I positioned the bag. Piper wasn't a fan of the
bag of veggies and hopped down to inspect her
toy basket.

"Thanks to science I learned from social media.
Cold pressure applied to your sternum stimulates
the vagus nerve."

"And we want my vagus nerve stimulated?"

I took a seat on the opposite end of the couch.
"It tells your brain to calm your body down."

He tilted his head on the cushion to look at me.
"Mind sitting a little closer?" he asked.

I couldn't come up with a good enough reason
not to besides the fact that I was scared to death
I was going to let him sweep me off my feet with

his sexy vulnerability. So I eased toward him across the cushion into the danger zone until our shoulders touched again.

His sigh was one of relief.

"Try the tea," I said.

He picked up the mug, sniffed, then blanched. "This smells like Liza J's flower beds after the fertilizer."

"Drink it. *Please.*"

"The things I do for you," he muttered, then took a sip. "Oh God. It tastes like someone stomped on rose petals with their damn feet. Why can't I have a beer?"

"Because as you've probably surmised, alcohol isn't great for panic attacks."

Squeaka-squeaka-squeak squeak.

Piper pranced up to the couch with a toy in her mouth. I took it from her and threw it across the room. She looked nonplussed and then headed back to the toy bin.

"She doesn't understand the concept of fetch yet. How are you such an expert on the subject? Panic attacks, not fetch," Nash clarified, hazarding another sip of tea and wincing again.

"I used to have them," I said simply.

We sat in silence, staring straight ahead at the blank TV screen. I knew he was waiting for me to speak up and fill the gap with answers. But I was comfortable with uncomfortable silences.

"Anyone ever tell you you talk too much?" he teased.

I smiled. "Where did Nash come from?"

"Silence *and* a subject change," he observed.

I reached over and flipped the bag of broccoli. "Humor me."

"Mom was a country fan. Everything from Patsy Cline to Garth Brooks. She and Dad spent their honeymoon in Tennessee."

"And then along came Knoxville and Nash-ville," I guessed.

"You got it. Now it's my turn for some answers."

"You know, it's getting pretty late. I should go," I said. But before my sore muscles could contract to get me into a standing position, Nash gripped my thigh with his hand.

"Nope. You can't leave me alone with thawing broccoli and this god-awful tea. You'll be too worried about me to sleep."

"You're awfully confident for someone who claims to be a husk of a man."

"Tell me why you know all the right things to do."

I wanted to throw a quippy answer at him, to keep my own secrets. But for some strange reason, I didn't want him to feel like he was the only one laid bare.

I blew out a breath.

"That sounds like the beginning of a long story," he said.

"A long, boring story. There's still time to send me home," I reminded him hopefully.

He put the tea down and then carefully slid his arm around me.

"That's your bad shoulder," I reminded him as he used his other hand to press my head to his chest next to the broccoli.

"Honey, I know. You're giving me a place to rest it."

I didn't know what to do with the fact that I didn't hate the way his arm felt around me. Warm and solid. Protective. As a rule, I didn't cuddle or snuggle or any other verbs that applied to platonic canoodling. That kind of touching was unnecessary. Worse, it gave men ideas about the future.

Yet here I was, cozied up in the danger zone with my head on the chest of a man who wanted a wife and kids. Clearly I had learned nothing.

Come on, Lina "I Make Bad Choices" Solavita. Sit up and get the hell out, I warned myself.

But I didn't move a muscle.

"That's better," he said, sounding like he meant it. "Now talk."

"The abbreviated version is I went into cardiac arrest at fifteen on the soccer field and had to be revived."

He was silent for a beat and then said, "Yeah, Angel. I'm gonna need the extended director's cut with commentary version."

"You're ridiculous."

"Angelina," he said with just a hint of grumpy cop in his tone.

"Ugh, fine. It was district finals on a cold, fall night during my sophomore year. The stadium was packed. It was the first time the team had made it that far in the tournament. Two minutes left in the game, and we were all tied up at 2–2. I'd just intercepted a pass and was sprinting with teenage confidence and energy toward the goal."

I could practically reach out and touch that moment. Feel the sharp edge of the cold air as it hit my lungs, the warm looseness of my muscles. Hear the distant roar of the crowd.

Nash's thumb brushed my arm, back and forth, and for once touch felt comforting.

"And then there was . . . nothing. It was like I blinked and the next thing I know, I'm flat on my back in a hospital room surrounded by strangers. I asked if I scored, because *that* was the most important thing to me. I didn't know my parents were in the waiting room wondering if I'd ever wake up again. I didn't know that an entire stadium of people—including my teammates— watched me go into cardiac arrest."

"Jesus, baby," Nash murmured, his chin brushing the top of my head.

"Yeah. My coach started CPR until the paramedics got on the field. My parents were in the stands. Dad jumped the fence. The other

189

moms just made a circle around my mom and held on to her."

Tears pricked my eyes at the memory and I cleared my throat to dislodge the annoying lump of emotion.

"They revived me in the ambulance on the way to the hospital. But information didn't travel quite as quickly as it does today," I said lightly.

"So everyone left behind thought you hadn't made it," Nash filled in the blank I'd left.

"Yeah. It was a big game. There were cameras and press there. I watched the footage . . . after. No matter how long I live, I'll never forget the noise my mom made when Coach dropped to his knees and started CPR. It was . . . primal."

I carried an echo of that scream with me wherever I went. Along with it was the image of my dad kneeling next to my lifeless body as paramedics tried to bring me back.

Nash brushed his mouth over my hair and murmured, "It's official. You win our near-death contest."

"I appreciate you conceding."

"What caused it?" he asked.

I blew out a restless breath. "That's a separate long story."

"Honey, you picked my sweaty, pathetic ass up off the floor. We're nowhere near even yet."

There was nothing pathetic about his ass, but now was not the time to discuss that. His thumb was gliding along my arm again. The heat from his chest warmed the side of my face and the steady thump of his heartbeat soothed me. Piper, finished with her chew toy, hopped up on the couch next to me and curled up against my feet.

"Fine. But just like your escapades tonight, we're never speaking of this again. Deal?"

"Deal."

"Myxomatous mitral valve disease with prolapse and regurgitation."

"You gonna dumb that down for me or am I gonna have to go find my dictionary?"

I smiled against his chest. "I had a defect in one of the valves of my heart. They're not sure what caused it, but it might have been from strep throat infections I had when I was a kid. Basically, the valve didn't close right, so blood was allowed to flow backward. Something in the electrical system shorted out, blood went the wrong way, and I essentially died in front of a few hundred people."

"Is it still a problem? Is that why you monitor your heart rate?"

"It's not still a problem. I had surgery—valve replacement—when I was sixteen. I still see a cardiologist, still monitor things. But it's mostly to remind myself to be careful how I handle stress. I still get these flutters. Premature ventricular contractions. PVCs."

I brought my hand to my chest and rubbed absently over the small scars.

"They feel like your heart is tripping or limping. Like it's out of sync and can't get back in the rhythm. They're harmless. More just annoying, really. But . . ."

"But they remind you of what happened."

"Yeah. I'd been stressing out over school and boys and normal hormonal things leading up to that game. Pushing myself too hard, not sleeping enough, living off Mountain Dew and pizza rolls. I hadn't mentioned the flutters or the fatigue to my parents. Maybe if I had, I wouldn't have keeled over in front of my entire school."

"How long were you in the hospital?" Nash asked.

The man had an uncanny knack for digging up what I wanted to keep buried.

"Off and on for about eighteen months." I suppressed a shudder.

That was when touch had stopped equaling comfort. My body wasn't my own anymore. It had become a science experiment.

"A lot of tests. A lot of needles. A lot of machines." I gave Nash's thigh a cheerful pat. "And *that's* how I became an expert on panic attacks. I started having my own. The nice thing about having them around medical staff is they can give you some pretty decent advice."

Nash didn't respond to my attempt at playfulness. Instead he continued to stroke my arm.

"Your parents call you every day," he noted.

"You don't miss much, do you?" I complained.

"Not when it counts."

My heart gave a flutter and not the PVC kind. No. It was the much more dangerous kind caused by handsome, wounded men with broody eyes.

"I should go. You should get some sleep," I said.

"That's a lot of shoulds. Tell me about your parents."

"There's not much to tell. They're great. Good people. Kind, generous, smart, supportive." *Smothering,* I added silently.

"The kind of people who call their daughter every day," he prompted.

"I moved on, but my parents didn't. I guess there's something about seeing your only child nearly die in front of your eyes that changes a parent. So they worry. Still. Chalk that one up in the Things We Never Got Over column."

They'd never gotten over seeing me die in front of them. And I'd never gotten over the suffocating prison sentence the rest of my teenage years had been.

Because after figuring out the problem, fixing it, and recovering from the fixing, my parents weren't open to letting me take any chances.

They still weren't. Which was why they thought I pushed papers for an insurance company and went to a lot of trainings. White lies kept the peace and let me live my life.

"Does Knox know any of this?" Nash asked, his voice a low rumble against my ear.

I frowned. "No. Why would he?"

"Seein' as you two have been friends for knockin' on two decades, I would have thought you'd share some stories."

"Uh, have you met your brother? Knox isn't the talk-about-anything type. And judging from the way you're pretending to be just fine right now, I'm guessing you're not much of an open book yourself."

"It's the Morgan way. Why shine the light on things when you can pretend they don't exist?"

"I'm all for that. Keeps things simple. But just so you know, that's probably something you should work on before you catch yourself a wife."

"Good to know."

I sat up and slid out from under his arm. "It's unsolicited advice time."

"Who invited Mrs. Tweedy over?" he quipped.

"Ha. It's your life and none of my business, but do yourself a favor. Instead of using up your energy trying to hide this from everyone, maybe try working your way through it. Both ways take a hell of a lot of energy, but only one of them gets you through to the other side."

He nodded but didn't say anything.

I gave his thigh another friendly pat. "I'm going to go home and you're going to go to bed. And when I say bed, I mean you're going to sleep *in* your bed *under* the covers. Not out here on the couch with the TV on."

I felt the weight of his gaze, the hot caress of his need as if they were physical sensations.

"I'll do all that on one condition," he said.

"What?"

"You stay the night."

13

Bed Buddies

Lina

O kay, even "daredevil, throw caution to the wind" me knew this was a terrible idea. I knew it just like I knew mozzarella sticks were bad for me. But just like mozzarella sticks, the temptation was real. "Nash, that's not a good idea."

"Hear me out," he said, tightening his hold on my hand. "I'm too tired to make a move on you."

"I've heard that one before," I said dryly.

"Fair. How about this? Whenever you're close, everything is better. The closer you are, the easier I breathe, the less I feel like life is just a never-ending pour of lemon juice into an open wound that won't heal. You take away the dark, the cold. And you remind me what it's like to want to be here."

"Damn it, Nash! How am I supposed to be responsible and say no to that?"

That tired half smile was my undoing. I believed him. Because he was the kind of man who told the truth. And right now, he was telling it to me.

"I'm so fucking tired, Angel. I just want to close my eyes next to you. Can we worry about the consequences after?"

The man knew how to get to me in the best possible way.

"Fine. But no one is sleeping naked. There will be *no sex* or running of any bases. There will be no snuggling or cuddling or canoodling. And I'm not cooking you breakfast. Not because it's a rule but because I don't know what I'm doing in the kitchen and I'd end up poisoning you."

"If you stay, breakfast is on me."

I chewed on my bottom lip, considering. "One more thing."

"Name your price."

"We keep this between the two of us."

Piper's head popped up at my feet. Nash leaned over and gave her ears a half-hearted ruffle, and I swear I saw hearts appear in her little doggy eyes.

"My apologies. The three of us," I amended.

"I agree to the terms. But if you want it notarized, we're gonna have to bring Nancy Fetterheim in, and she's not known for keepin' secrets."

"High-five?" I held up my hand.

That ghost of a smile got a little more pronounced. "You high-five to close deals?"

High fives were less intimate. There wasn't a lingering pressing of palms, a knowing grip of fingers. It was easy, casual, and absolutely not sexy.

"Don't leave me hanging, hotshot."

He slapped my palm.

"Now that that's settled, you're going to shower and I'm going to go change."

"Don't go. Please. I'll give you something to sleep in. Just . . . don't leave."

For a second, the facade of charming confidence disappeared and I caught another glimpse of the man beneath it all.

I sighed. I'd already brushed my teeth and performed my five-step skincare routine, so technically, I didn't need anything from my place.

"I'm sorry for putting you in this position, Angelina. I get that it's not fair. And I want you to know that under normal circumstances, I'd absolutely be trying to get you into my bed. But I'd be doin' it with flowers and dinner and a different aim."

"Are you always this honest?"

"No point in being otherwise," he said, putting his hands into the cushion and slowly getting to his feet. Exhaustion was evident in the hunch of his shoulders.

I rose with him and slipped an arm around his waist. His arm fell heavily over my shoulders. He was too tired to hide the fact that he really did need to lean on me.

"Oh, so you've talked to your brother and Liza J about what's going on?" I pried as we headed toward Very Bad Idea Town, a.k.a. his bedroom.

"There's a difference between bein' honest and keepin' private matters private."

I was glad to hear him say that. For me, of course. Not for him, because obviously *he* should be truthful with the people who cared about him. *My* situation was entirely different.

"I'm not here to tell you what to do. You're a big boy. You know what's best for you."

He paused at the dresser and opened a drawer. It was full of neatly folded shirts. "Long sleeve or short?"

"Short." Truth be told, I preferred to sleep naked. But this wasn't the kind of situation in which to divulge that information.

Nash handed me a soft gray T-shirt that said KNOCKEMOUT BOOK OR TREAT 2015.

"Thanks," I said.

I'd been in this man's clothes twice in the past three days. I'd flirted with him, fought with him. I'd done him a favor and had his back when he needed me. Now I was about to climb into bed with him. Things seemed to be accelerating awfully fast, even for me.

"You can take the bathroom first," he said solicitously.

"Thanks, bed buddy."

"Bed buddy?" I mouthed in the mirror after I closed the door between us. What was wrong with me?

I did my final bathroom break business, then stripped out of my clothes. His T-shirt hit me at midthigh, but the fact that I wasn't wearing underwear made the ensemble feel less modest and more risqué. I would just have to not flail around in bed like I usually did to keep the hemline in place. I probably wouldn't sleep anyway. Being fiercely independent was only one of the reasons I didn't usually let men spend the night. I was a light sleeper, which meant any noise or movement that happened within a hundred-foot radius woke me up.

I gathered my clothes and returned to the bedroom where I was temporarily rendered speechless. Nash was shirtless and barefoot, and his jeans were unbuttoned.

"Be out in five," he said.

I nodded, still unable to form words.

The bedroom hadn't escaped the cleaning frenzy, I noted. The fine layer of dust was gone, as were the prescription bottles. The curtains were drawn over the windows and he'd turned down the covers on the bed. Piper lay curled in a tiny ball in the exact center of the pillows.

The water kicked on in the bathroom and I briefly entertained the idea of tiptoeing out to his table and taking another snoop through his files. But I immediately discarded that. It would be a betrayal to use the opportunity for personal gain.

Instead, I got myself settled on the right side of

the bed and scrolled through some work emails until the bathroom door opened again.

Sweet baby cheeses. His hair was damp, making it look darker than usual. His scars, one on the shoulder and one on the torso, were a puckered, pink reminder of what he'd been through. He was wearing only a pair of boxer briefs. Dark-blue ones.

His thighs and calves were muscular. A fine layer of chest hair that tapered down into a V disappeared under the waistband.

Piper's tail tapped out a happy beat on the bedspread. If I had a tail, it would have done the same.

"That's my side," Nash said.

I had to look away before I managed to form words. "You have a side of the bed?"

"Don't you?"

"I sleep alone."

He raised an eyebrow in question and rounded the foot of the bed to approach me.

I shrugged. "What?"

Nash gave my hip a nudge and signaled for me to slide over. "You don't share your bed? Ever?" he asked.

"I'm no virgin," I scoffed as I scooted past Piper to the opposite side of the mattress. "But I don't usually do sleepovers. I like sleeping alone. And since I don't *have* to share, I sleep in the middle and use all the pillows. Do you always sleep on the right?"

He shook his head. "I sleep on whatever side's closest to the door."

I flopped back against his pillows. "Ugh. You're good guy hero down to the bone, aren't you?"

"What makes you say that?" Those cool blue eyes searched mine as he pulled back the covers and got into bed.

"You sleep closest to the door so anyone who gets in has to get through you to get to Mrs. Hotshot."

"There is no Mrs. Hotshot."

"Yet. But seems like you've given her a lot of thought."

The dip of the mattress under his weight did something funny to my heart. So did the weary look on his handsome face when he turned his head to look at me.

Piper snuggled closer to him and rested her head on his injured shoulder. I was not the swooning type. But if I was, I would have melted into a puddle on that mattress.

"Maybe I used to," he said finally. "But right now, all I can think about is goin' to sleep and waking up next to you."

"Don't be sweet. This is a platonic arrangement," I reminded him.

"Then I won't tell you how much I like seein' you in my shirt in my bed."

"Shut up and go to sleep, Nash."

"Night, Angel."

"Night, hotshot."

Piper let out a whiny little yip.

I grinned and gave her a pat. "Good night to you too, Piper."

Nash reached out and turned off the lamp on the nightstand, plunging the room into darkness.

Somehow this was worse. Now instead of seeing him mostly naked and adorably snuggled up to a dog, my senses were dialed in to pick up on every breath, every shift of his body.

In the dark, he reached for me, his hand linking with mine on top of the covers.

Yep. There would be no sleep for me tonight.

I was jerked awake from an absolutely delicious sex dream by something. Something warm and hard.

My eyelids flew open so fast I worried I'd sprained them. I found a strong, male arm snaked around my waist, up my torso, and under my shirt where the attached strong, male hand gripped my bare breast.

Nash.

I was about to demand he unhand me when his body went rigid against mine. Like he was bracing to meet a threat. The hand on my breast tightened and I realized that I wasn't mad. I was turned on.

The tension drained out of him just as suddenly

as it had appeared and when his hips gave a little involuntary buck, I realized why I was feeling like Lady Horndog of the Northern Virginia Horndogs.

My back, every inch of it, was glued to Nash's front. My heels were against his shins. The backs of my thighs rested flush against his quads. The useless T-shirt barrier was gathered around my waist, leaving my entire downtown exposed. I was also pretty sure he had his face buried in my hair.

Last but definitely not least, there was another warm, rigid, male appendage making itself known against my naked rear end. Wait. One quick Kegel check and I realized my situation was far more dangerous. Said appendage had tunneled its way between the apex of my thighs.

My lady parts were in full-blown throb. Nash's extraordinary hard-on was nuzzled *right up against me.* As in his shaft had parted the lips of my sex and the tip rested just beneath my needy, needy clitoris. One of us was very, very wet.

What the hell had happened to his underwear? Had his penis just hulked its way to freedom?

I needed to move, but I couldn't decide between wriggling away or rolling over, mounting him, and putting myself out of my misery.

No sex. No snuggling, I reminded myself. He'd been through a lot and damn it, I was turning over a new leaf. Besides, *Nash* was the one who'd broken our bargain. He'd crossed the center line of the mattress and . . . Oh shit.

I was on *his* side. *I* had *my* arms locked around the one against my chest. He couldn't have dragged me across the bed. Manhandling would have woken me and I would have at least elbowed him in the face.

Oh God.

Had I flailed my way over here? Had I put my own *ass* on Nash's *crotch* in my *sleep?*

This was very, very, very bad.

Okay. I needed a plan. I always had a plan and a backup plan, plus two or three contingencies.

I just needed to block out that insane desire for Nash to angle those hips up. Yep. Just block out the needy little throbs and focus on how to get out of this situation without humiliating myself.

Dear Lord.

It was an ocean of wetness down there. Which was worse, my hot neighbor thinking I'd wet the bed or my hot neighbor realizing I'd put us in a compromising position, gotten turned on, and then leaked sex juice everywhere?

Maybe I could blame it on the dog?

I was mulling over my options along with potential solutions on how to mop us both up without waking him when Nash gave a little groan behind me.

I was confident I could have dealt with the inherent sexiness of that raspy moan had it not also been accompanied by the gentlest shift of his hips. That tiny thrust set off an explosive chain reaction.

The crown of his cock slid forward and nudged that demanding bundle of nerves. At the same time, the hand clamped around my breast flexed, brushing pebbled nipple to rough palm.

And that was all it took.

I came against the hot head of his erection, muffling a moan with my hand. My hips bucked involuntarily as the orgasm fluttered through me, curling my toes and contracting every muscle in my body.

Congratulations, me. It was a new low. Orgasming on a sleeping man's cock. It was basically assault.

"Mmm. You okay, Angel?" Nash asked sleepily, his face buried in my hair, lips brushing my neck.

Well, hell. He was awake. There was no way I could just casually mop up his crotch now.

"Yep," I squeaked. "Totally fine. Just a . . . charley horse." *In my vagina,* I added silently.

It took a beat, but Nash tensed behind me again. Which caused that talented erection to poke me in the clit again.

The whimper clawed its way up my throat.

"Oh shit. I'm sorry," Nash said, scrambling away from me under the covers. "I didn't mean—"

"You know what? I think I'll take a rain check

on breakfast," I said in a high-pitched voice that sounded like my mother's I'm-pretending-I'm-not-upset-even-though-it's-clear-I-am-upset tone. I rolled twice to get to the edge of the bed and tried to sit up.

But I didn't make it that far.

Nash grabbed a fistful of T-shirt and pulled me back.

"Baby, are you okay?"

Mortified, I hooked my fingers over the edge of the mattress and hung on. "I'm totally fine. I just really need to go away now."

"Angel, please look at me," Nash begged. "I'm so sorry. I didn't mean to touch you like that."

He rolled me onto my back and pinned me with one hand. I saw the moment he realized his dick was out. His spectacular, girthy, ten out of ten dick.

"Jesus, what the fuck?" His other hand slipped down between us and yanked the waistband of his underwear up over his erection.

My cheeks were so hot I could have fried eggs on them if I knew how to.

"Oh my God. What are you sorry for?" I said, slapping my hands to my flaming cheeks.

"I promised I wouldn't do . . . that," he said. He was so angry, so horrified, I couldn't let him take the blame.

His mouth was apologizing—unnecessarily—to me, but I was paying more attention to his cock and the fact that it seemed to be having a tough time getting interested in going soft.

I moved my hands from my cheeks to his. "Nash. I was the one who invaded your side. You were a sleep gentleman. I promise. I woke up a few minutes ago and I was the one who didn't immediately remove my body from your body's vicinity."

His muscles lost some of their rigidity. "You came to me? In your sleep?"

I'd also come *on* him in his sleep.

"Where's Piper?" I asked, desperate to change the subject.

"In her dog bed with one of my socks," he said without looking. "Back to you turning into a cuddler in my bed."

"I didn't turn into a cuddler! I was probably just trying to claim my usual spot in the middle and maybe we got tangled up or whatever. I don't know. Let's not overthink this. Or discuss it ever again. Just let me slink away in embarrassment and we'll forget the whole thing ever happened."

He shifted his weight over me, careful to keep his morning wood from touching me. Which if he'd known what had happened two minutes ago, he'd realize was a moot point.

He brushed my cheek lightly with his knuckles, forcing me to question my status as a non-swooner.

"Are you sure you're okay?"

God, early-morning Nash was cute. His hair was a mess and his stubble gave him just a hint of rakish charm to offset the good guy vibe. He had a pillow crease under his left eye. Not to mention that sleepy, earnest look on his gorgeous face.

"Besides being embarrassed at my dreamland defilement of you, I'm fine," I assured him.

"You slept?" he pressed.

"I did. How about you?"

He nodded. "I did."

"How do you feel?" I asked.

The curve of his lips was undeniably sexy. "Pretty fucking great."

"Really?"

"Yeah. Really. Thanks to you." In a lightning-quick move, he dropped a kiss to my forehead, then hopped out of bed. "Omelets in ten," he said, heading toward the bathroom. "Oh, and, Angel?"

I rolled to my elbow. "Yeah?"

"If you try to leave, I'll personally deliver it. Loudly."

14

Snack Cake Heists and Bad Apples

Nash

T he thieves looked even more pitiful than their haul of crushed snack cakes and potato chips.

Three boys under the age of fourteen in varying painful stages of puberty sat on cold metal chairs outside the store manager's office, looking like they were ready to puke. Beyond them, Nolan Graham hovered in the cookie aisle.

After that morning's three-vehicle fender bender on the highway, the hardware store's "stolen" string trimmer display that turned up in the storeroom, and Mr. and Mrs. Wheeler nearly getting scammed over the phone by someone claiming to be their grandson, I'd had a busy damn day already.

It was a good thing I'd had my first full night's sleep in weeks.

Thanks to Lina.

I usually woke with a start to the sound that haunted my brain. And while I did remember it in my dreams, this morning I'd woken to Lina in my arms. She'd sought me out in her sleep. That fact—and my reaction to it—made me think that just maybe I was still alive, still worth trusting.

I owed her, the woman who was taking up every available brain cell that wasn't occupied with work and breathing. Thanks to the talk and the sleep, I was feeling more hopeful than I had in a long time. She'd opened up just a crack, and what I'd seen beyond her sexy exterior had me wanting a longer, deeper look.

"Hate to call you in here for a couple of Little Debbie's, Chief, but I gotta set an example," Big Nicky said. Manager of Grover's Groceries for nearly as long as I'd been alive, the man took his job seriously.

"I understand your predicament, Big Nicky. All I'm sayin' is I think there's a way around this that doesn't involve pressing charges. We all do stupid things. Especially at that age."

He huffed out a breath and glanced over my shoulder at the kids. "Hell, when I was that age, I was stealin' my daddy's cigarettes and cutting class to go fishing."

"And you made it out of childhood without a record," I pointed out.

He nodded thoughtfully. "My mama scared me straight. Guess not all of us are lucky enough to have parents who care enough to scare the shit out of us."

I knew what that was like. Could still feel the tilting of my axis after Mom—the glue, the fun, the love of our family—left this world, and us, behind.

"Toby and Kyle, their parents are gonna ground them until it comes time for learner's permits," I predicted.

"But Lonnie . . ." Big Nicky let that hang there. But Lonnie.

Knockemout wasn't good at keeping secrets. That was how I knew Lonnie Potter was a tall, tough kid who had a mom that skipped out on him and his siblings two years ago. His dad worked third shift, which left little time for raising kids. I also knew that Lonnie had quietly joined the Drama Club at school. First, probably to have a place to go when no one was home, and then because he'd taken a liking to trying on other people's lives. He was good at it, according to Waylay. But no family members ever showed in the audience on opening night.

"Noticed the paint's peeling outside," I mused.

"That's what I get for hiring that yahoo's crew outta Lawlerville. Did a shit job with shit paint because they don't give a shit. Pardon my French. None of them live here to be embarrassed by watching their half-assed work flake away."

"Bet some motivated young labor could get the job done for you for the cost of materials." I nodded toward the hallway.

Big Nicky's smile was slow. "Huh. You might be right, Chief. Nothing like a little manual labor to keep you out of trouble."

I hooked my thumbs in my belt. "That option

sits well with you, I'll talk it over with their parents. I have a feelin' they'll be amenable."

"I'm feelin' pretty amenable myself," he said.

"Then I'll get 'em out of your hair and we'll work it out with the parents."

"Appreciate that, Chief."

I found Grave standing guard over the boys, frowning like a terrifying specter.

"All right, gang. I've got a one-time offer for you that's gonna save you from a lifetime of grounding and me an acre of paperwork . . ."

Grave and I trooped the boys out the back and into my SUV to keep the gossip mill from getting any hotter. Piper greeted the troublemakers with nervous peeks between the seats.

We ran through the situation with Toby's and then Kyle's parents. Punishments were doled out, community service and official apologies agreed upon.

"My dad ain't home," said Lonnie, the remaining member of the felonious trio in the back seat. "He's workin' a double."

Piper wagged her tail from her perch on Grave's lap.

"I'll get a hold of your dad at work," I told him.

Logan stared out the back window, looking mournful. "He's gonna kill me."

That crust of tough wasn't as thick as he thought it was.

"He's gonna be mad. But mad means he cares," I told him.

"I fucked up." The kid winced. "Sorry. I mean screwed up."

Grave and I exchanged a look.

"You ever set fire to your daddy's shed with fireworks you stole from your drunk neighbor?" Grave asked him.

"No! Why? Someone say I did?"

"You ever get busted for fighting four guys on the playground just because they said your brother was an asshole when they weren't wrong and your brother was an asshole?" I asked.

"No. I only have sisters."

"Point is, kid, we all fuck up," Grave said.

I met Logan's gaze in the rearview mirror. "What matters is how we handle things post-fuckup."

"Wait. *You guys* did all that?"

Grave smirked. "And more."

"But we learned that raisin' hell gets old and the consequences of bad decisions last a hell of a long time." Lucian came to mind. I'd wondered over the years what path he would have followed if he'd had it easier in the beginning. One thing was for sure, he never would have ended up behind bars at seventeen if someone had given him a chance. "That goes for life and women and everything in between."

"You should be writin' this down, kid. This shit's gold," Grave told our passenger.

• • •

After dropping Logan off at home and calling his father at work, I sprang for sodas at the Pop 'N Stop. I parked in the school zone to scare the shit out of speeders . . . and to annoy Nolan, who stuck to my ass like glue in his black Tahoe.

Grave took off his KPD cap and rubbed a hand over his bare scalp. "Got a minute?"

That was never a good sign.

"Problem?" There was a reason he hadn't wanted to have this talk at the station, I guessed.

"Dilton."

And there was the reason. Tate Dilton had been a rookie patrol cop when I'd taken the helm from longtime chief Wylie Ogden whose decades of good-ol'-boy "leadership" had left a stain on the department.

Dilton was what I labeled a "jock" in the profession. He wanted the adrenaline, the pursuits, the confrontations. He enjoyed showing off his authority. His takedowns were more aggressive than necessary. His citations were lopsided with him coming down harder on people who rubbed him the wrong way personally. He also spent more time in the gym and at the bar than he did at home with his wife and kids.

I just plain didn't like him.

Clearing out the entire department when I took over hadn't been an option, so I'd kept him on, invested time trying to mold him into the kind of cop we needed behind the badge. I partnered him with a solid, experienced cop, but training, oversight, and discipline only went so far.

"What about him?" I asked, reaching for my drink so my hands had something to do.

"Had a few issues with him when you were laid up."

"Such as?"

"He was a dog off the leash while you were on leave. Roughed up Jeremy Trent for public intoxication in the parking lot after the high school football game couple of weeks ago. Unprovoked. In front of the guy's kid—defensive tackle—who got in Dilton's face along with half the team. Rightfully so. Things woulda gotten real messy if Harvey and a couple of his biker buddies hadn't stepped in."

Fuck.

"Jeremy okay? He press charges?"

"Laughed it off. Paid his fine. Pair of bruised knees and some road rash as souvenir. Didn't remember a damn thing after sleepin' it off. But there would have been a hell of a lot more to remember if it had gone any further."

Jeremy Trent had been captain of the baseball team and beat out Dilton for homecoming king their senior year of high school. They'd had more than a handful of run-ins over the years ever since. Jeremy was an affable guy who worked for the sewer authority and drank too much on the weekends. He thought he and Dilton were friends. But Dilton still seemed to think they were in some kind of competition.

Grave's mouth was tight as he stared through the windshield.

"What else?"

"Tried to take a traffic stop too far. Real nice Mercedes SUV goin' just a hair over the speed limit on the highway. Just got passed by a souped-up pickup going about twenty over the limit. Dilton ignores the truck driven by his drinkin' buddy Titus and pulls over the Mercedes instead. Black driver."

"Goddammit."

"Dispatch flagged me as soon as Dilton called it in. Had a bad feeling about it so I headed out with Bannerjee. Good thing too. He had the driver out of the car and cuffed, was yellin' at the wife who was recording him on her phone."

"Why's this the first I'm hearing about it?"

"Like I said, you were laid up. And you're hearin' about it now cause last night he was overheard running his mouth at that shithole bar Hellhound talkin' bout how he's gunnin' for chief since you can't do the job."

Grave pulled no punches.

"I'll take care of it," I said, putting the car in gear and scaring the hell out of seventeen-year-old Tausha Wood when I pulled out behind her pickup truck.

"Now?" Grave asked.

"Now," I said grimly.

A day ago, I wouldn't have had the energy for this shit, but I'd woken up with a mostly naked Lina pressed up against a mostly naked me. It was more powerful than any prescription I'd tried.

I ran a small, solid department that served a small, solid community. A few thousand people who had more history between them than most families. Sure, we were a rough-and-tumble community maybe a little more likely to solve an argument with fists and alcohol. But we were tight-knit. Loyal.

That didn't mean that we didn't see trouble. Being this close to Baltimore and DC meant it occasionally spilled into town limits. But having trouble come from a badge in my department? That wouldn't stand.

We were good men and women dedicated to serving and protecting. And we were getting better with every response, every training.

There were a thousand ways beyond our control a call could go south. A thousand ways we could make a dangerous mistake. There was no room or reason to add attitude and prejudice to the list.

So we trained and drilled and debriefed and analyzed.

But a department was only as good as its weakest officer. And Dilton was ours.

"Here he comes," Grave said, giving the heads-up.

Tate Dilton didn't bother knocking. He strolled into my office like he owned the place. He was a reasonably good-looking guy despite the receding hairline and beer belly. His mustache pissed me off, probably because it reminded me of Marshal Graham, who had helped himself to an empty workstation and was doing a goddamn sudoku.

"What can I do ya for, Chief?" Dilton said as he took a seat, ignoring the rest of the room's occupants.

I closed the case folder I'd been reading, added it to the stack on my desk.

"Shut the door."

Dilton blinked before getting to his feet and closing the door.

"Have a seat," I said, indicating the chair he'd just vacated.

He dropped down again, kicking back and lacing his fingers over his belly like he was on his buddy's couch watching the game.

"Officer Dilton, this is Laurie Farver," I said, introducing the woman he'd yet to acknowledge standing by the window.

"Ma'am," he said, giving her a dismissive nod.

"You know, Tate, growing up, my neighbor had this dog that he kept on a leash. From a distance, that dog looked nice. Soft, yellow fur. Big, fluffy tail. As long as he was on that leash, he was fine. But the second that leash slipped, it was game over. You couldn't trust him. He started gettin' loose. Chasin' kids. Bitin' people. My neighbor didn't shore up that hole in his fence. Didn't tighten up the leash. Eventually, one day, that dog attacked two kids out ridin' their bikes. Dog had to be put down. And his owner got sued."

Dilton sneered around the gum he was chewing. "No offense, Chief, but I don't really give a flying fuck about no neighbor and no neighbor's dog."

Beneath my desk, Piper let out a low growl from her dog bed.

"Here's the thing, Officer Dilton. *You're* that dog. I'm not always gonna be here to keep that leash on tight. Bottom line is, if I can't trust you in the field on your own, I can't trust you period. Your recent actions have made it clear that you aren't prepared to serve, much less protect. And if I can't depend on you to do your job to the best of your ability, then we've got a serious problem."

Dilton's eyes narrowed and I saw a glint of mean in them. "Maybe you don't get it since you're basically riding a desk these days, but I got shit to do out there. Someone's gotta maintain order."

I sat with that for a second. I had been slipping. And that had consequences. Dilton had taken advantage of the loose leash, which meant not only were his actions on me, it was also up to me to make it right.

"I'm glad you brought that up. Let's talk about that shit you've been doin'. Like tripping Jeremy Trent outside a football game, kneeing him in the back, and cuffing him in front of his kid and half the stadium when all he did was remind you that you owed him twenty bucks on the Ravens game. Or shit like letting your buddy Titus drive twenty miles an hour over the speed limit while you pull over a Black aerospace engineer and his civil rights attorney wife in a Mercedes for going five over. You then proceeded to remove the driver from his car under the probable cause of . . . let me check your report to make sure I get this right . . ." I glanced down at the paperwork in front of me and read. "The wanted poster of a prison escapee that's been hangin' on our bulletin board for three years."

Dilton's face twisted into an ugly mask. "I had the situation handled until your lap dogs showed up."

"You had the driver handcuffed, bruised, and lying facedown on the road in a tuxedo while his wife recorded your actions on her cell phone when Sergeant Hopper and Officer Bannerjee arrived on scene. According to their report, they could smell alcohol on your breath."

"That's bullshit. Hop and that bitch are out to

get me. I observed the suspect driving erratically above the posted speed limit and I—"

It felt as though someone had switched a light on inside me. Gone was the icy numbness, the dark void. In its place, a simmering anger bubbled to life, warming me from within.

"You fucked up. You put ego and prejudice ahead of your job, and in doing so you put your job at risk. You put this department at risk. Worse, you put *lives* at risk."

"This is bullshit," Dilton muttered. "Is that bitch wife waving her law degree around, makin' threats?"

"Officer Dilton, you are hereby suspended with pay, but only because that's procedure. Pending a full investigation of your conduct as an officer. I wouldn't get used to that paycheck."

"You can't fuckin' do that."

"We're opening an official investigation. We'll be talking to witnesses, victims, suspects. And if I find *anything* that looks like a pattern of abuse, I'll have your badge permanently."

"This wouldn't be happening if Wylie was still here. You stole this office from a good man and—"

"I *earned* this office and I've worked damn hard to make sure men like you don't fucking abuse it."

"You can't do this. Ain't no union rep here. You can't throw some bullshit suspension at me without my rep."

"Ms. Farver is your union rep. Though I'm guessing she's not as enthusiastic about repping you after hearing your bullshit. Mr. Peters? Mayor Swanson, are you still with us?" I asked.

"Still here, Chief Morgan."

"Yep. Heard it all," came the replies from my speakerphone.

"Officer Dilton, Mr. Peters is Knockemout's solicitor. That means lawyer who represents the town in case you need the definition. Mr. Peters, does Knockemout need me to cover anything else with suspended Officer Tate Dilton?" I asked.

"No, Chief. I believe you covered everything. We'll be in touch, Officer Dilton," the lawyer said ominously.

"Thank you, Eddie. How about you, Mayor Swanson? You want to say your piece?"

"I've got a lot pieces I'd like to say of the four-letter variety," she said. "Y'all are lucky I've got my grandkids in the car with me. Suffice it to say I am looking forward to a thorough investigation and if, like Chief Morgan says, we find a pattern of a-b-u-s-e, I will not hesitate to kick your a-s-s."

"Thank you, ma'am. Message received." I looked at Dilton, who was turning a shade of lobster. "I'll take that badge and service weapon now."

He came out of his chair like he was on a spring. His hands curled into tight fists at his sides, fury flashing in his eyes.

"You wanna take a swing at me, do it. But understand that that's got its own consequences and you're about up to your ears in them already," I warned. "Think on it."

"This won't stand," he snarled, throwing his badge and gun on my desk, knocking over my nameplate in the process. "This is supposed to be a brotherhood. You're supposed to have my back, not take the word of a couple of asshole outsiders or some pathetic drunk who peaked in high school."

"You can run your mouth about brotherhood all you want, but the bottom line is you're in this work for yourself. For the power trips you think you can get out of it. That's not a brotherhood. That's one pathetic kid trying to make himself feel like a big man. And you're right, I'm not gonna stand for it. Neither are any of them."

I pointed to the window where the rest of Knockemout's officers stood—even the ones who had the day off. Arms crossed, legs braced. Behind Dilton, Grave grunted in satisfaction.

"Now get out of my station."

Dilton yanked the door open so hard it bounced off the wall. He stormed out into the bullpen and laid a glare on the rest of the department.

Zeroing in on Tashi, he got in her face, looming over her. "You got a problem, little girl?"

I was halfway out of my seat and Grave was

already in the doorway when Tashi smiled up at him. "Not anymore, asshole."

Bertle and Winslow stepped up behind her, smirking.

Dilton raised a finger, shoved it in her face. "Fuck you." He glared down the other officers and pointed at them. "Fuck you too."

With that, he stormed out of the station.

" 'Not anymore, asshole?' Bannerjee, that's some *G.I. Jane*–level shit there," Winslow said, slapping her on the shoulder.

She beamed like the teacher had just handed over a gold star. Even I couldn't help but smile.

"Guess I'll be on my way," the union rep said with a marked lack of enthusiasm.

"Good luck," I said.

She rolled her eyes. "Thanks."

"Good to have you back, Chief," Grave said to me before following her out of my office.

Piper scrabbled at my legs. I leaned down and put her in my lap. "Well, that went well," I said to the dog.

She gave me an enthusiastic slurp with her tongue before hopping down onto the floor again.

I picked up my nameplate and ran my fingers over the letters. Chief of Police Nash Morgan.

I wasn't back. Not all the way yet. But it felt like I'd finally taken a step in the right direction.

Maybe it was time to take another.

15

Satan in a Suit

Lina

Naomi: Don't forget! We shop for brides-maid dresses Wednesday. I'm thinking all the fs. Fall, fun, and flattering!
Sloane: Lina, I think this means she's going to dress us up like pumpkins.
Me: Pumpkin is not my color . . . or shape.

I didn't enjoy wasting my entire morning fruit-lessly checking potential properties off my list. Not when it felt like there was a ticking clock hanging over my head. I needed progress. I needed a break. I needed to stop thinking about Nash Morgan.

That meant banishing all thoughts of his offer, his confessions, and his hot, hard cock. Okay, that last one had already taken up permanent residency in my head. But the rest needed to vacate my brain immediately.

I was mechanically chewing my way through a Cobb salad at a diner forty minutes outside Knockemout when six feet four inches of sin in a suit slid into the booth opposite me.

Lucian Rollins wore danger like it was custom tailored for him.

"Lucian."

"Lina." That low timbre, those piercing eyes. Everything about the man was vaguely threatening . . . and therefore a reasonable distraction from my obsessing over all things Nash.

"What brings you to my booth?"

He stretched one arm across the back of the vinyl cushion, taking up even more space. "You do."

The perky twentysomething server who'd brought me my food and chatted about my leather biker jacket for five straight minutes hustled up to the table holding a coffeepot at a precarious angle. Her eyes and mouth were wide. "C-coffee?"

"Yes. Thank you," he said, looping a finger through the handle of the upside-down mug in front of him and flipping it over.

Her eyes got even wider and I wondered if they were about to pop out of her head. Just in case, I moved my salad out of the pop and splatter zone.

"Could I get some extra dressing, please?" I asked when she finally managed to pour the coffee.

"Extra creamer. Got it," she whispered dreamily and wandered away.

"Great. Now I'm never going to get my extra dressing."

Lucian's smile had the bite of frost to it. "I'd hoped this conversation wasn't going to be necessary."

"I love it when men track me down and open with that line."

"Nash Morgan," he said.

I raised an eyebrow but said nothing.

"He's going through a difficult time. I'd hate to see anyone take advantage of that."

I pointed to myself. "Me?"

"Anyone," Lucian repeated.

"Good to know." Not about to make this chat easier on him, I speared another bite of salad with my fork. I chewed thoroughly, not breaking eye contact with Lucian, who didn't move a muscle.

We stared each other down, willing the other to break first.

These were the kinds of social situations I excelled in. Making small talk about normal girly things? Nope. But going head-to-head with a cagey man when there was important information on the line? This was my Olympics and I was a goddamn gold medalist.

I took a theatrical sip of iced tea. "Ahhhh."

His lips quirked.

"Are there any other vague statements you'd like to make or are you just going table to table issuing warnings?" I asked.

"We both know you've got ulterior motives for being here. I am aware of your employer just as I'm aware of the interesting timing of your arrival in town."

I feigned shock. "Is there some town ordinance that makes it illegal to work in insurance?"

"Must we play games?"

"Listen, pal. You're the one who decided to play cat and mouse, hunting me down out of town just to prove you can. I don't like being toyed with any more than you do. So cut to the chase or you're going to piss me off," I said with a mean smile.

Lucian leaned in and interlaced his fingers on the table. "Fine. I know who you are, who you work for, and what happened on your last job."

I kept my expression one of marked boredom even though that last bit impressed and unnerved me.

"Despite your low profile," he continued, "you've built an impressive reputation for finding things that others couldn't. You're known for being fearless to the point of recklessness, a trait rewarded by your employer. You're not in town for a weeks-long visit with your old pal Knox. You're here looking for something . . . or someone."

He let the accusation hang between us. I took another casual bite of dry salad.

"Why are we having this conversation now? Why not when I first came to town?"

"Because there's the damage a bullet wound

does and the damage a broken heart does."

I pointed my fork at him. "Speaking from experience?"

He ignored my question. "Not only do you arrive in town just before Naomi and Waylay were abducted, now you just so happen to move in next door to Nash."

"You don't look like the kind of man who's spent any significant time in roach motels, so I won't waste time trying to explain the move. Though given the fact that you've got more money than some state budgets, you should really think about buying the motel and fixing it up . . . or maybe just burning it down."

"I'll take that under advisement," he said dryly. "Now assure me Nash won't come to further harm because of you."

Feeling oddly protective of the man in question, I put my fork down.

"For the record, I had nothing to do with Nash's shooting or Naomi and Waylay's abduction. If I *am* in town looking for something, it's none of your damn business or anyone else's. And finally, Nash is a big boy. He can handle himself."

"Is that what you told Lewis Levy?"

I was officially pissed off.

I smiled. "You're like a little kid showing off the terrible finger painting you did at school expecting me to be impressed. If I hang it on the refrigerator, will you go away?"

"Sooner or later, someone else in your circle is going to get hurt and it better not be Nash."

"What are you going to do about it? Give him a bodyguard to go with his U.S. marshal?" I suggested flippantly.

"If that's what it takes. I know you spent the night at his place."

"Don't worry, *Dad*. We're both consenting adults. I'll have him home before curfew."

Lucian slammed a palm down on the table, rattling the spoon on his saucer and sloshing coffee over the rim. "Do *not* make light of this," he said coldly.

"Finally. Geez, how far under the ice do you hide the human in you? I thought I was going to have to threaten an 'accidental' pregnancy to get you to crack."

He swiped my napkin and mopped up the spill with it before returning it to me. "Congratulations. If my team was here, you'd have won someone a lot of money."

"A how-long-before-he-cracks pool? Don't tell me Lucian Rollins has a sense of humor."

"I do not."

I leaned back in the booth. "Here's what I'm seeing. You either think that I'd be the easier target to manipulate, *or* you're afraid to have an open, honest conversation with your friend. Either way, your bad judgment is showing, Lucian."

He let out what sounded like a low growl. But the man knew I was right.

"Look. You're right to be worried about your friend. He's not telling you or anyone everything about what he's going through. That includes me, because we barely know each other. And what he *has* told me stays between me and him, because unlike some others at this table, I know how to respect the privacy of others. Yes, I spent the night at his place last night. No, we didn't have sex. I'm not telling you that because I think it's your business. Because it's not."

"Why are you telling me?"

"Because I know what it's like to have people so worried about you they do stupid things behind your back."

The muscles in his jaw flexed and I wonder what sore spot I'd just prodded.

"Nash is a good guy, which automatically makes him not my type. But that doesn't mean I won't make an exception."

"You're not helping your case."

"I'm not building a case," I told him. "I don't give a shit what you think about me. You think I'm the problem in the situation but it's not me. It's you."

"I'm not the one positioning myself to take advantage—"

"I'll stop you there before you make me angry. If you think that I'm taking advantage of your friend or that he's keeping things from you, you have two choices."

"And what might those be?"

"You either trust your friend to handle himself or you have this conversation with him. At the very least, have the decency to have his back to his face."

Lucian's frown was downright chilling, but I had the heat of temper to protect me.

"You couldn't possibly understand our history," he said coolly.

"Oh, but I could. You're good at collecting information? Well, I'm good at reading people. You three grew up together without ever really growing all the way up. Knox tried to hide from love so he'd never get hurt again. Nash doesn't trust either one of you enough to have his back so he's not going to talk to you about what's going on in his head. And you . . . Well, let's save that for another day."

"Let's not."

I shrugged. "Fine. You asked for it. You're a shadowy political consultant who has been linked to the downfall of several prominent men and women in our nation's capital, not to mention the force behind the rise of several others. 'Machiavellian' is the word most often whispered in your direction. And you like it. You like that people fear you. I'm guessing because you had the taste of fear once and it made you feel powerless. So now you've got the power to pull all the strings you want. But you're still not happy."

His eyes narrowed.

"You allow yourself one cigarette a day probably just to prove that nothing has a hold on you. You're loyal to your friends and I get the sense that you'd do anything for them. And that 'anything' definitely doesn't end on this side of the law. But would you want Knox or Nash 'handling' things for you behind your back?"

"This is different," he insisted.

"You'd like to think it is, but it's not," I said. "Let me put it in terms that I think you'll appreciate. The amount of time and energy you've wasted going behind your friend's back trying to 'fix' things for him could have been saved with a ten-minute conversation. Imagine how many politicians you could ruin or city blocks you could buy if you didn't have to hunt down innocent women to vaguely threaten them."

His stony expression changed not one iota, but I still caught it. A flicker of something like amusement in his icy eyes. "I'd never apply the term 'innocent' to you, and my threats were more overt than vague," he said.

"Semantics," I said breezily.

He watched me finish my salad. "I suggest we keep this conversation between the two of us."

Keeping secrets. It was what I did. Only I'd

been in Nash's shoes before. My parents hadn't trusted me to handle anything bad. I hated how it felt to have people discussing my well-being behind my back as if I weren't strong enough to take part in my own life. I guessed Nash would feel the same.

"Which one of us are you trying to protect, Luce? Can I call you Luce?"

"I hope you're not out to hurt my friend, Lina. Because I'd hate to have to destroy your life."

"Looking forward to seeing you try. Now go annoy someone else."

16

A Pair of Thank-Yous

Nash

I looped Piper's leash around my hand and grabbed one of the two bouquets out of my vehicle's cup holder.

"Come on, Pipe. Quick stop."

We got out on the street just as Nolan pulled up to the curb behind me. I threw him a sarcastic salute, which he returned with a half-hearted middle finger.

I was actually almost starting to like the guy.

Piper led the way up the walk to the duplex. It was a two-story brick-and-vinyl building. Both units had a small front porch and flower boxes.

I headed up the three steps to the door on the left. There was a gray-and-white cat crammed up against the screen in the front window. Classical music filtered out to me. I gave the skeptical cat a wave, then I stabbed the doorbell.

Piper sat at my feet, her tail wagging with enthusiasm. It wasn't as annoying as I thought it would be, having her at work with me. Her routine demands for attention kept me from spacing out over paperwork. And while she wasn't comfortable enough to let any of the other officers pet her yet, she had started taking hourly trips around the bullpen once she figured out they had treats for her in their pockets.

Footsteps sounded on the other side of the door along with an annoyed, "I'm coming. I'm coming. Hold your damn horses."

The door opened and there she was. My guardian angel.

Xandra Rempalski had thick, curly hair. It was black with strands of violet woven throughout. She wore it half up in a lopsided topknot while the rest cascaded past her shoulders. She had tan skin and brown eyes that went from annoyed to curious to recognition.

Instead of scrubs, she was wearing a denim apron with hand tools and loops of wire stuffed in the pockets. Long, silver earrings made up of dozens of interconnected hoops dangled from her ears. Her necklace dripped with tiny chains that formed a V between her collarbones. It reminded me of chain mail.

"Hi," I said, suddenly feeling stupid I hadn't done this a long time ago.

"Hi yourself," she replied, leaning against the doorframe.

The cat lazily threaded its way between her bare feet. Piper cowered behind my boots and pretended she was invisible.

"I don't know if you remember me—"

"Chief Nash Morgan, age forty-one, two gunshot wounds to the shoulder and torso, O negative," she rattled off.

"I guess you do remember me."

"It's not every night a girl finds the chief of police bleeding out on the side of the road," she said, flashing me a quick grin.

Piper chanced a peek around my boots. The tubby tabby hissed, then plopped its ass down in the doorway and started licking its butthole.

"Don't mind Gertrude the Rude," Xandra said. "She's got attitude for days and no sense of propriety."

"These are for you," I said, shoving the bouquet of sunflowers at her. "I should have come by earlier to thank you. But things have been . . ."

She looked up from the flowers, the smile fading to a sympathetic grimace. "It's tough. Seeing it on shift isn't easy. I'm sure living through it is no picnic."

"Feel like I should be kind of immune to it," I confessed, looking down at Piper, who had once again glued herself to the back of my legs.

Xandra shook her head. "When you start being immune to it, that's when it's time to get out. It's the hurt, the caring that makes us good at our jobs."

"How long have you been in the emergency department?"

"Since I graduated with my RN. Eight years. Never a dull moment."

"Ever wonder how long you can afford to care?"

Her smile was back. "I don't worry about things like that. It's one day at a time. As long as the good balances out the bad, I'm ready for the next day. It's never gonna be easy. But we aren't doing this for ease. We're doing it to make a difference. Things like this? A thank-you from one of the ones who made it? That goes a long way."

I should have gotten her a card.

Or something that would last longer than a pile of sunflowers.

But I had nothing but words. So I gave her those. "Thank you for saving my life, Xandra. I'm never gonna be able to pay you back for that."

She hitched the bouquet up on her hip. Her earrings caught the light and glittered. "That's why you just keep payin' it forward, Chief. One day at a time. Keep doing good. Keep balancing those scales."

I hoped to hell removing Dilton from duty was a step in that direction. Because right now, like everything else I did, it felt like not nearly enough.

"I'll do my best."

"You know, having something besides the job

helps. Something good. Me? I date inappropriate men and make jewelry," she said, sweeping a hand over her apron full of tools.

Right now, I felt like I didn't have a damn thing besides a needy foster dog and a hole or two that would never be healed.

There was a resounding crash next door followed by a loud, long wail. I jolted, my hand automatically moving to my service weapon.

"Don't," Xandra cautioned briskly. She stowed the flowers and the cat inside and made a move to push past me.

"You need to get inside," I insisted, nearly tripping over Piper as I hurried down the steps. Nolan was hustling up the walk, his holster unsnapped.

"Wait! It's my nephew. He's nonverbal," Xandra explained, following me next door.

The details of her statement came back to me. She'd been running late to work because she'd stayed to help her sister calm her nephew.

I paused and shared a look with Nolan. I let her pass me on the steps.

"He has autism," she said, letting herself in her sister's front door.

"Keep the dog," I said, tossing Piper's leash to Nolan and following her inside.

My blood was still pumping, focus still narrowed. In the middle of the gray living room carpet was a man—no, a boy—curled on his side, hands covering his ears as he rocked and howled with a pain only he could feel. Next to him were the splintered remains of a toy brick castle.

"The cops? Really, Xan?" A woman bearing a striking resemblance to Xandra knelt just out of range of the violent kicks from the boy's long, gangly legs.

"Very funny," Xandra said dryly. "I'll get the blinds."

"Can I do anything?" I asked cautiously as Xandra quietly closed the curtains on the front windows.

"Not yet," Xandra's sister said over her son's plaintive screams. "We have a doctor's appointment in an hour. His headphones are charging."

I stood inside the door feeling helpless while the two women worked in tandem to make the room darker, quieter. A protocol, I realized.

The wails soon quieted and the boy's mother slid a weighted kind of cape over his shoulders.

Before long, he sat up. He was tall for his age, with dark skin and the spindly limbs of early puberty.

He glanced at the ruined castle and let out a low moan.

"I know, buddy," his mother said, carefully sliding an arm around his shoulders. "It's okay. We'll fix it."

"Amy, this is Chief Morgan," Xandra said.

"Chief, this is my sister Amy and my nephew Alex."

"Chief," Amy said as she rocked Alex in her arms.

"Hi. I just came by to thank Xandra for . . ."

"Saving your life?" she prompted with a small smile.

"Yeah. That."

"Sorry for the disturbance," she said, accepting the book Xandra handed to her.

"No apologies necessary."

"And you were worried how well your first interaction with the cops would go," Xandra teased her sister.

Amy's lips quirked again before she pressed a kiss to the top of her son's head and began to read.

"That's another strategy. Laugh even when things aren't funny," Xandra said, handing me a fabric tote.

With Alex shooting looks of concern in my direction, I did my job and helped restore order, brick by brick.

When the room was clean and the story was over, I nodded to Amy and followed Xandra to the door. Alex got to his feet and slowly crossed to us. He was tall and broad-shouldered, and the grip of his hand on my arm was strong. But there was a sweet, little-boy smile on his face as he looked at my chest.

"He doesn't believe in personal space," Xandra warned in amusement.

Alex reached out and traced a finger over my badge, point to point to point. After he'd traced the star twice, he nodded and released me.

"Nice to meet you too, Alex," I told him softly.

With my arms full, I gave the door two light kicks and waited.

It opened seconds later and everything in me went warm when I saw her. Lina wore leggings in a dark purple. Her sweater was a fleecy ivory that stopped an inch above the waist of her pants. A wide tie-dye headband held her hair back. She was barefoot.

"Evenin'," I said, strolling across the threshold and dropping a kiss on her cheek. Piper followed me in and made a beeline for the couch.

"Well, hello. Uh, what's all this?" she asked, closing the door behind me.

I ducked into the kitchen and dumped the bags on the counter. "Dinner," I said.

She appeared in the doorway. "That doesn't look like the Thai takeout I was going to order."

"Not only beautiful but smart." I plucked the wildflowers out of one of the grocery totes. "Vase?"

She gestured at the bare countertops. "Do I look like I have a vase lying around?"

"We'll make do." I started opening cabinet

doors until I found an ugly plastic pitcher. I filled it with water, then shredded the plastic around the flowers. "Wildflowers because they reminded me of you," I explained. And because the lily of the valley reminded me of my mom.

Lina shot me one of those complicated woman looks before giving in and burying her face in the flowers.

"This is very sweet of you. Sweet but unnecessary," she said.

I noticed she was giving me a wide berth in the tiny space. It was cute that she thought she could rebuild those walls that had come down the night before.

"Mind gettin' Pipe a bowl of water while I start the prep?"

She hesitated for a second, then opened a cabinet and found an empty takeout bowl. "You really don't have to cook me dinner. I was a minute away from ordering food," she said as she turned the water on in the sink.

"I had a long day," I said conversationally as I pulled a bottle of wine, a corkscrew, and two glasses out of one of the bags. "And thanks to you, for the first time in a long while, I had the energy to deal with it." I opened the wine with a pop and set the bottle aside.

"I heard something went down with one of your officers," she admitted, setting the water dish on the floor. "Mrs. Tweedy said you caught one of your guys stealing counterfeit bills out of evidence after they spent it at a strip club."

"I wish," I said.

Piper appeared in the doorway with a sports bra in her mouth. She spit the bra out in the bowl and drank around it.

"Come on, Pipe. Stop eatin' laundry." I snatched up the bra. "I believe this is yours."

Lina took the bra and threw it on the counter next to the broccoli.

"Then Neecey all but tackled me on the sidewalk in front of Dino's," Lina said, hopping up to perch on the counter. "She told me you headbutted that no-good Tate Dilton in the candy aisle of the grocery store."

"I worry about this town's language comprehension sometimes."

She smirked. "Neecey also said she heard that you two wrestled into a canned soup pyramid and that the store manager found two cans of minestrone all the way over in the freezer section."

"If you pour, I'll tell you the real, much less eventful story."

"Deal."

I filled her in on my day. All of it. It felt good. To share a kitchen. To share my day. Lina seemed genuinely interested. She sat on the counter and we talked as I sautéed chicken, peppers, and onions. Piper joined us with an endless parade of toys and laundry.

I had to stop myself over a dozen times from moving between Lina's legs, sending my hands sliding up her thighs, and going in for those pretty, red lips.

This connection I felt was real, tangible, and deep, but I didn't know how deep it went for her. And I wasn't about to scare her off with the level of my need for her.

"Why are there pajama pants in this bag? Is this some new age dessert I don't know about?" she asked, poking around in the last tote.

"Yeah, about that," I began.

"Nash." My name was a gentle warning on those lips.

"I know last night was supposed to be a one-time thing. I know you took pity on me because I was a fucking mess." I turned the burner off under the chicken and popped the lid on the pan before turning to her. "I also know I haven't slept that well in . . . maybe ever."

"We can't keep doing this," she said softly.

I wiped my hand on the dish towel I'd brought and then did what I'd been dying to do. I stepped between her knees and slid my hands up her thighs to rest on her hips.

Her hands planted on my shoulders and stayed there. Not pushing. Not pulling.

It was an intimate position. And I wanted *more* as my blood went from warm to simmering in a heartbeat.

"Look, I know it's not fair to ask you. To make you responsible for this piece of my well-being. But I'm desperate. I need you, Angelina."

"Why do you call me Angelina?"

I gave her hips a squeeze. "It's your name."

"I know that. But no one calls me Angelina."

"It's a beautiful name for a beautiful, complicated woman."

"You're quite the charmer. I'll give you that. Flowers. Dinner. Sweetness. But how long are we going to play this game?"

"Baby, it's not a game to me. This is my life. You are the only thing in my entire existence that makes me feel like I've got a shot at finding my way back. I don't understand it. And frankly I don't need to. All I know is I feel better when I'm touching you. When I woke up this morning, I didn't feel like a ghost or a shadow. I felt *good*."

"I felt . . . uh . . . good too," she confessed, not quite meeting my eyes. "But we're playing with fire here. I mean, sooner or later, you're going to get overly attached and I'll have to destroy your fragile man heart. Not to mention the fact that we basically woke up dry humping."

I grinned. "That's why I brought pants. With a drawstring."

"This is not the kind of peer pressure TV movies prepared me for. 'Hey, Lina. Sleep snuggle with me so I can feel alive again,' " she said, faking a deep baritone.

I gave her hips another squeeze and pulled her an inch closer to me. " 'There's nothing I'd rather do than go to bed and not have sex with you, Nash,' " I said in a breathy, Marilyn Monroe imitation.

She blew out an aggrieved sigh. "It's annoying how cute you are."

"Annoying enough that you're gonna let me sleep with you tonight?"

She squeezed my shoulders and brought her forehead to mine. "I'm really trying to make better decisions, but you are not making that easy."

I gave in to temptation and kissed her nose.

"Ugh. You're impossible!" she complained.

"What was wrong with your previous decisions?"

She bit her lip.

"Need I remind you that I've been disgustingly vulnerable with you for, what, forty-eight hours now? I just spent twenty minutes tellin' you all about my day. It's your turn. Give and take. Talk, Angel."

She wrinkled her nose. "I don't like sharing. Especially not when I don't come out looking good."

"I repeat. Fetal position at the foot of the stairs."

"I was leading a team during an operation. We had to make a quick, unplanned exit off a roof when our thief came home early. I didn't know the guy I was with was afraid of heights. I made the jump and landed in the canal. When I looked back, he was still standing there frozen. I yelled, and he panicked and landed on his ass on the hood of a car."

"Ouch," I said, deciding I didn't need to know exactly what danger required an escape by roof.

"He broke his tailbone, so he was lucky. But I should have known better. At the very least, I shouldn't have forced him to take the risk."

Her fingers traced tiny circles on my chest.

"The thing is, there are rewards for doing my job well. Bonuses, status, the thrill of the chase. Being the hero and bringing home the win. In my company, aggressive tactics are praised. I got a bonus and Lewis got a busted ass. I realized that as good as I am, sometimes it just comes down to luck. And I don't want to count on that forever."

"Minus the money part, I get that." It galled me that I was here in this kitchen because of luck.

"It's more heroic to be a hero for something other than a big, fat paycheck," she said.

"How big and fat are we talkin'?" I teased.

Her smile was feline. "Why? You have a problem making a lot less than your emotional support bed buddy?"

"No, ma'am. I do not. Just curious how much 'a lot less' is."

"I have a brokerage account and a walk-in

closet full of very nice designer duds. That sexy Charger out there in the parking lot? I paid for it in cash with last year's bonus."

I let out a low whistle. "Can't wait to see what you get me for my birthday."

"If memory serves, you and your brother barely spoke for years because he gave you money."

"Now that's a dirty lie," I said, picking up my wine. "We barely spoke for years because he forced money on me, told me what to do with it, then didn't like what I chose to do instead."

"Well, in that case, Team Nash," she said.

"Figured I'd get you there."

"What exactly did Knox want you to do with the money?"

"Retire."

Her eyebrows skyrocketed. "Retire? Why?"

"He hates that I grew up and became a cop. We had our fair share of brushes with the law growing up. Knox never outgrew his distrust of authority. He's mellowed some. But he still likes to dabble in the gray area. Like those illegal poker games I'm not supposed to know about."

"What about you? Why aren't you still dabbling in the gray?"

"If you ask my brother, it was a 'fuck you' to him and our childhood. Us against the man."

"But that's not the truth."

I shook my head. "I thought, instead of operating outside the system, why not make changes within it? Our scrapes with the law were pretty minor. But Lucian? No one was there to protect or serve him. He was thrown in jail at seventeen and sat there for a week, which never shoulda happened. That's what changed for me. No amount of hell-raising and lawbreaking was going to help him out of that jam. And all it would have taken was for one good cop to do the right thing."

"So you're out there doing your job for all the future Lucians," she said.

I shrugged, feeling a little embarrassed. "And the free uniform. Rumor has it the pants make my butt look good."

Lina grinned and I felt that warm campfire-like glow in my chest. "Oh, Studly Do-Right, that rumor has been substantiated. It is official fact."

"Studly Do-Right?"

"Something around town you don't already know?" she teased.

I closed my eyes. "Tell me that's not my nickname."

She fluttered those long lashes at me. "But, Nash, I know how important honesty is to you."

"Christ."

17

Pillow Talk

Lina

S o you went from a high-profile, roof-jumping assignment with a team and now you're here?" Nash asked.

We were in my bed staring up at the ceiling. Nash was on the left side, closest to my bedroom door. Piper was curled up snoring in his armpit. I'd shoved a pillow between us to prevent any repeat performances of last night.

I hesitated, surprised by the desire I had to confess the whole truth, to tell him why we were both looking for the same man. But I squashed it. I'd already committed to the plan. I didn't need to waste energy second-guessing myself. "I needed some breathing room to think things through. There's a new job opening up. More travel. Longer jobs. It's my dream job. But . . ." I trailed off.

"Does your family know what you do?"

"They think I travel the country providing corporate trainings. I prefer to live my life without carrying the responsibility of other people's opinions. Especially opinions about how I should find a safer, easier way to make a paycheck."

"Fair enough. What's in the box of files?"

"Nash, this sleeping together thing only works if you shut up and go to sleep."

"Just turning things over in my head."

I didn't like where this conversation was going. It felt like he was forcing me into little white lie after little white lie. And I was getting more uncomfortable by the minute. So I dug into my arsenal and deployed my favorite weapon: misdirection.

"I ran into Lucian today," I announced, rolling to my side to face him in the dark.

"Here?"

Interesting. So the overprotective pain in my ass really hadn't wanted Nash to know about our chat.

"No. Down in Lawlerville at a diner."

"Lucian was eating in a diner? Are you sure it was him and not some doppelgänger?"

"He didn't actually eat. He had coffee while I ate," I told him.

"What did you two talk about?"

"Don't tell me Studly Do-Right is jealous," I teased, reaching over the pillow to tickle him. Nash captured my hand and brought it to his mouth.

"Damn right I am." He nipped at the pad of my index finger.

"We talked about you. I think he's worried about you."

He was silent for a beat and I could feel his worry building in the dark. "You didn't tell him anything, did you?"

"Of course not. You asked me not to. I assumed there's a reason you told the stranger next door about your panic attacks rather than your oldest friend or your brother."

"We're not strangers," he insisted, placing my hand over his chest and holding it there.

"Are we . . . friends then?" I asked. His chest was warm beneath my touch.

He was quiet for a long beat. "Feels like more than that," he admitted.

"But what *kind* of more?"

Let's see how you like annoying, uncomfortable questions, Mister.

"The kind of more that if I were in better shape, you'd be naked and there sure as hell wouldn't be a pillow between us."

"Oh."

"Oh? That's all you've got to say?"

"For now."

An alarm rang shrilly, yanking me from a yummy dream about me, Nash, and some tasteful nudity that definitely seemed to be leading somewhere hot.

A low growl came from beneath me and for a second I worried I'd rolled over on the dog in my sleep.

But Piper was a lot furrier and much smaller than whatever my head was resting on. The alarm stopped and the growl turned to a yawn. A warm hand stroked up my outer thigh to my hip. Meanwhile, my inner thigh was cuddling the hell out of an erection.

"You've *got* to be kidding me," I groaned.

"You jumped the fence, Angel," Nash said, smug and sleepy.

I was lying *on top* of the pillow I'd shoved between us. My head and hand rested on Nash's broad chest. My leg was thrown across his . . . er . . . penile area.

"This is getting downright embarrassing," I muttered.

I tried to pull away, to do the roll of shame back to my side of the bed. But his arms banded around me. With one quick tug, I was sprawled on top of him chest to chest, groin to groin.

Holy hallelujah hotness.

"Least my pants stayed on," he said cheerfully.

"It's not funny," I groused. I was *not* a cuddler, and no man, especially not one depending on me to be his emotional support whatever, was going to change that.

"Oh, honey, I agree. There's nothing funny about where you're sitting." His hard-on twitched against me, causing my vagina to throw a temper tantrum at being denied by the shorts I'd insisted on wearing to bed.

I made a respectable attempt to get off him, but the ensuing flailing and friction only turned me on more.

Nash's hands came to my hips. "Calm down, Angel." His voice was gruff, and he sounded much less sleepy and much more aroused as those hands held me in place.

Meanwhile, I wedged my hands and arms between us to get as much distance as possible. My orgasm was on a hair trigger, and if he gave so much as one little thrust in that direction, there would be no hiding it.

"God, you're gorgeous in the morning," he said, pushing a piece of hair off my forehead. "Best way I ever woke up."

It was the second-best way for me, yesterday being the best. But I sure as hell wasn't going to share that nugget with him.

"Stop being sweet," I said.

But those blue eyes, soft and dreamy, drew me in. I wasn't fighting for my freedom anymore. I was hovering over him, eyes locked, mouths too close to make good decisions.

He brought his other hand up. His fingers danced along my jawline and skimmed into my hair. "Gonna kiss you now, Angelina."

"Hell no." That was what I should have said. Or *"I think this is a bad idea and we should take some time to consider the consequences."* At the very least I could have said I needed to brush my

teeth and then I could have locked myself in the bathroom until my lady parts wised up.

Instead I nodded stupidly and said, "Yeah. Okay."

But just as he surged up, just when all I could see were those blue eyes coming in hot, just when my lips parted, the pounding at my front door started.

Piper startled at the foot of the bed and let out several shrill yips.

Nash frowned. "You expectin' someone at 6:00 a.m.?"

"No. You don't think it's Mrs. Tweedy trying to get me to go to the gym, do you?" I wasn't above hiding under the bed.

The pounding started again.

"She's short. She knocks lower on the door."

Not going to lie, I felt a twinge of relief that it probably wasn't my elderly neighbor looking to kick my ass at the gym again.

"Stay here," Nash ordered, sliding me off him and onto the bed.

"Like hell. This is my place. Whoever's knocking is looking for me."

"Then won't it be a fun surprise for them when they find me instead?" he said, sounding less like a sleepy lover and more like a hard-edged cop.

I grabbed my robe and hurried after him. "Nash!" I hissed. "Maybe I don't want whoever's on the other side of that door to know that we spent the night together again."

257

"Too late," came the deep, annoyed baritone from the other side of the door.

Nash yanked the door open and Lucian, looking like he'd been up for hours already, strolled inside in another one of those bespoke suits.

"You've got to be kidding me," I muttered.

"Do you sleep in a suit?" Nash asked him.

"I don't sleep," he quipped.

My vagina hated Lucian Rollins.

"What are you doing here?" I demanded.

"Taking your advice," he said with a little sizzle to his tone. "Come on, Nash. We're going to breakfast."

"No offense, Lucy, but I was in the middle of something that I'd much rather be doing than grabbing eggs with you."

Lucian shot me a look that would have incinerated a weaker woman. "You're free to get back to it after I've said my piece."

"I need coffee," I muttered and headed for the kitchen.

"I warned you," Lucian called after me.

"Yeah? And I warned you back." I tossed him a middle finger over my shoulder.

"Warned her? What the hell is this, Lucy?" Nash demanded.

"We need to talk," Lucian said. "Get dressed."

"I'll handle the dog," I called. "You handle your pain-in-the-ass friend."

18

Eggs Benedict for Assholes

Nash

I was not in the mood for breakfast food or the cheerful pop music on the diner's speakers. For the second day in a row, I hadn't woken up with that horrible crunching sound echoing in my head.

Instead, I'd woken up to Lina. And my asshole friend had ruined it.

"Where's your marshal shadow?" my asshole friend asked.

"Probably still in bed. Where *I* should be. You interrupted something."

"You should be thanking me."

"Have you lost your fucking mind?" I said just as the server approached.

"I can give you another minute," he said hesitantly.

"Coffee. Black. Please," I added as I slid my menu to the edge of the table and glared at Lucian.

"We'll both have the smoked salmon eggs Benedict with yogurt and berries," my cockblocking friend said.

"Sure thing," the kid said before he hustled away.

Lucian had a way of intimidating and impressing people. Often both at the same time. Today, however, he was only pissing me off.

I scrubbed a hand over my face. "What the hell is going on with you?"

"I'm here to ask you that very question," he said, frowning down at his phone before tucking it into his suit jacket.

"You're like a vampire who stays up plotting how to cockblock his best friends."

"You've spent two nights in bed with her and—"

"How do you know I spent two nights in bed with her?" I interrupted.

"Two nights in bed with who?" My brother slid into the booth next to me looking pissed off and like he'd just rolled out of bed.

"What are you doing here?" I demanded.

He yawned and signaled for coffee. "Lucy called. Said it was important. Two nights in bed with who?"

"I'm not talking about it. And how in the fuck do you know what my sleeping arrangements are?" I asked, turning back to Lucian.

"Information finds its way to me."

"I swear to God, if Mrs. Tweedy is listening at my door with a drinking glass—"

"What the hell is going on with you two?" my brother cut in.

The server returned with coffee for all.

"Can I get you anything for breakfast?" he asked Knox.

"Maybe after I find out who my brother's taking to bed."

"Jesus. It's nobody's business who I'm taking to bed. What I want to know is why in the hell Lucian showed up at Lina's door at six in the morning and dragged me out of bed for fucking breakfast."

"You were at Lina's at six in the morning?" Knox didn't sound happy about that.

"Frankly, I wouldn't have had to be there if my lunch with your bedmate had gone better yesterday," Lucian said, sounding annoyed.

I was considering lunging across the table and grabbing him by the lapels of his fancy-ass suit when the server wisely decided to disappear.

"Why are we here? What are you doing having lunch with Lina? And what the fuck does that have to do with you suddenly having a hankering for eggs Benedict?"

"Why the fuck were you at Lina's at 6:00 a.m.? And the answer better not be that she's the one you're banging," Knox snarled.

Lucian cocked an eyebrow at me and picked up his mug. "She told you we had lunch, but she didn't tell you why? Interesting."

"None of this is interesting to me. Either get to the point or get out of my way," I said.

"If someone doesn't start answering questions,

261

I'm gonna start throwin' punches," Knox warned.

"Things aren't right with him," Lucian said, pointing to me. "They haven't been since the shooting."

"No fucking shit, Sherlock. Some asshole put two holes in me. It takes a while to come back from that."

"You say that as if you're trying."

A white-hot anger clawed its way to life under my skin. Next to me, my brother tensed.

"Fuck you, Lucy," I said. "I am trying. I'm doing my PT. I'm going to the gym. I'm going to work."

He shook his head. "Physically, you're healing. But mentally? You're not the same. You hide it. But the cracks are starting to show."

"I'm gonna need something stronger than coffee if we're having this conversation," Knox muttered.

I picked up my coffee and considered whipping it at him. "Get to the point, Lucy."

"You don't need distractions. You need closure. You need to remember. You need to find Hugo. And you need to get him off the street."

"Getting Hugo off the street doesn't change a damn thing about what's already happened. And *how the hell* is remembering what happened going to put me back together again?"

Did that blank spot in my memory hold the key? If I finally remembered how it felt to face death, would I be ready to live again? Wasn't that part of what I was struggling with? I could put criminals behind bars, but that didn't undo what they'd already done. I could stop them from doing it again, but I couldn't prevent the first.

I must have raised my voice because the couple at the table next to us turned to look at me.

"I can't believe you got me out of bed with Naomi for this," Knox complained.

"Same here."

"Your brother was in bed with Lina," Lucian tattled.

"The fuck he was. The fuck you were," Knox said, swinging my way.

"Don't you fucking start," I warned.

"I told you to stay away from her."

"I told her the same," Lucian said.

"What? Why?" Knox and I snapped together.

"Same team, Knox," Lucian reminded him.

"Did you threaten her?" I asked, my voice low and dangerous.

"You're damn right I did."

"What the fuck is wrong with you? Both of you," my brother demanded.

"She's taking advantage of you," Lucian insisted.

"You're really starting to piss me off, Lucy," I warned.

"Good. That's a start."

"You are not to go near Lina again," I told him.

"You can't fucking threaten people on my behalf. Especially not her."

"I can't believe you're sleeping with Lina after I told you not to," Knox growled.

"And you can't bury your head in the sand hoping things will get better. Your father spent the last few decades numbing himself to life. What you're doing isn't much different," Lucian said.

A charged silence fell over our table as we glared at each other.

"I'm depressed. Okay, you fucking assholes? My life has been one big black hole since I woke up in that hospital bed. Happy now?" It was the first time I'd admitted it out loud. I didn't much care for it.

"Do I look happy?"

To his credit, Lucian looked miserable.

"Tell me what any of this has to do with Lina," my brother said, his face in his hands.

"I don't believe she's being truthful. I have concerns she could take advantage of you when you're . . . like this. She shows up in town a day before Hugo made a move on Naomi and Waylay. She didn't tell you about her real job. She moves in next door. And she just so happens to have a history with the marshal assigned to you."

"She also picked my ass up off the floor, got me upstairs, and helped me through a fucking panic attack two nights ago. I don't know what the fuck it is about her but the closer I am to her, the better I feel. The easier it is to get out of bed and force myself to go through the motions. So while I *appreciate* your concern, I'll point out that she's been there for me in a way no one else has been. Not you. Not Knox. No one."

Lina made me feel like a man, not like the broken shell of one.

Lucian's jaw tightened beneath his neatly trimmed beard.

"Two smoked salmon eggs Benedicts." The server appeared with our breakfast.

"Thanks," I said flatly when it became clear Lucian wasn't going to.

"Can I get you anything else right now? More coffee? Napkins to mop up any future bloodshed? No? Okay then."

"She's lying to you," Lucian insisted. "She's here because of you."

"You both need to shut your damn mouths now," Knox ordered. "Lina is one of the fucking good ones."

"You don't trust her with your brother either," Lucian pointed out.

"Because he's gonna get his stupid heart broken, that's why," my brother said in exasperation. "Not because she's taking advantage or whatever bullshit you made up in that suspicious-ass mind of yours. She isn't gonna settle down and be a cop's wife and chase after a bunch of kids. So if you go fallin' head over heels for her and she kicks you in the gut on the way out the door, I'm the one who's gonna have to deal with your bitching and moaning about it."

I was oddly touched, but still mostly pissed off.

I faced them both. My brother and my best friend thought I was too weak to survive this.

"Go near her again and I will make you regret it," I said, my knuckles going white on the handle of my mug.

"I'm sayin' the same thing to you," Knox said to me.

"Not your call to make," I reminded him.

"I don't trust her," Lucian said stubbornly.

"Yeah? And I didn't trust that dental hygienist you dated for a month three years ago."

"You were right not to. She stole my watch and my bathrobe," my friend admitted.

"Lina isn't after me for my watch and I don't have a bathrobe."

"No. But she's after something. A liar can smell a lie."

"Stop looking into her."

"If you get your head on straight, I'll stop keeping tabs," Lucian said.

When Lucian Rollins kept tabs, that meant he knew what was in your garbage before it went out to the curb. It meant he knew what you were going to have for dinner before you did. The man had a gift for information gathering, and I shouldn't have been surprised that he'd wield it against me. Especially if he thought it was for my own good.

"I don't need to be hearing this."

"Yes, you do," he insisted. "I'm hearing more rumors that Duncan Hugo didn't run off with his tail between his legs."

"So what?" I shot back.

"You're a loose end. A direct threat to him. You can't hide in the blanks in your memory forever. I need you to be operating at one hundred percent. Because if he does get to you again, if he does manage to take you out . . . that leaves me with only Knox as a friend."

"Hilarious."

"Fuck you," Knox muttered.

"You're too good to let this end you. You need to claw your way out of this darkness if necessary and beat him. And you're not going to accomplish that by distracting yourself with a woman you can't trust."

"There's a simple solution to this. Both of you stay the hell away from Lina," Knox said.

"Fuck you both."

19

Khaki Is Not Her Color

Lina

T he usual, lovely Lina?" Justice called from behind Café Rev's counter when I walked in.

"Yes, please. Mind if my furry friend joins me?" I asked, holding up Piper in her pumpkin sweater. The dog sniffed the coffee-scented air and trembled at the excitement of the early morning rush.

Justice grinned. "Not a problem. I'll make something extra special for Miss Piper."

Of course the beloved barista already knew the dog's name. And of course he knew my usual. I'd been going to the same café around the block from my town house for the past two years, and they still got my order and name wrong.

"Everything okay?" he asked me over the buzz of the busy café as I paid for my coffee.

I blinked. That *definitely* never happened in my coffee shop.

"Yeah. Sure. Totally fine," I said.

It was a big, fat lie.

But I wasn't about to explain to Justice that I was freaked out because there was something so irresistible about Nash Morgan that I was acting completely out of character around him. Snuggling. Confiding. Emotionally supportive. And I certainly wasn't about to voice my concern that Lucian was about to ruin it all even though I wasn't sure I wanted "it all" in the first place.

They had been friends for years, and if Lucian said I was bad news, Nash would listen.

I should be happy. Lucian's interference would extricate me from a situation I didn't know how to handle and let me focus on what I came here to do. I should be ecstatic. Instead, I felt like that time I'd insisted on going on that roller coaster after four shots of tequila in college.

"You sure? Because your face doesn't say totally fine," Justice pressed.

"My face and I are fine," I promised. "I'm just . . . trying to work a few things out in my head."

He grabbed a mug and twirled it around his finger by the handle. "Sometimes the best thing you can do is distract yourself and let the answer come to you."

I threw a twenty in the tip jar. "Thanks, Justice."

He winked. "Grab a seat. I'll yell for you when it's ready."

I grabbed the first vacant table I saw and plopped down in the chair.

Justice was right. Nash wasn't some operation to plan out and execute. He was a grown-ass man and he could make his own decisions.

But he should probably make them with all the information. If I told him the truth and he still wanted to believe that I was bad news, then it was his loss. Not mine.

Then why did it feel like mine? The tiny voice niggled in my head. I wasn't actually falling for the guy. Was I? Prior to this weekend, I'd drunk at a bar with him and patched him up after a shootout. We barely knew each other. This was just a crush. Nothing more.

"You look like you're a million miles away," Naomi said, appearing with several beverages.

"How much coffee do you drink in the morning?" I asked as she took the seat next to me.

"Two of these are yours," she said. She slid a latte and a paper cup of whipped cream with Piper's name written on it my way. "You didn't hear Justice calling."

Piper forgot to be terrified and stuck her snout into the whipped cream.

"How did you know Knox was the one?" I blurted out the question without even consciously thinking it.

But if Naomi was surprised by the question, she didn't let on. "It was a feeling. Some kind of magic. A rightness, I guess. It definitely didn't make any logical sense. On paper we couldn't be more ill-suited to each other. But there was something so *right* about how it felt to be with him."

Shit. That sounded . . . familiar.

I busied myself with a hit of caffeine.

"But you can't just fall for someone over the course of a few days, can you?"

"Of course you can," she scoffed.

I wished I'd gone to a bar instead of a café.

"But there are layers to it. You can fall head over heels for someone on the surface. You can find them attractive and exciting or, in Knox's case, infuriating. And it can stop there. But the deeper you dig, the more pieces you see of that person, the further you can fall. That can happen fast too."

I thought about our late-night confessions, the strange, fragile intimacy we'd built between us by trusting the other with things no one else knew. I wondered if it would shatter if I told him the full truth. Or was there an invisible strength in that kind of honesty?

"Or if you're like me and Knox, it can take a chisel and a hammer before you get past the 'You're hot. Let's have sex' layer," Naomi added.

"I like that layer," I admitted.

"What's not to like about that layer?" she teased.

"Can the deeper layers even compare to that?" I was only half joking.

She hit me with her full wattage grin. "Oh, honey. It just keeps getting better. The more you know and love and respect your partner, the more vulnerable you are together, the better *everything* gets. And I do mean *everything*."

"That sounds . . . terrifying," I decided.

"You're not wrong," she agreed. "Have I waited the appropriate amount of time before demanding to know who is making you feel these feelings?"

"This is all hypothetical."

"Right. Because you're not sitting there with Nash's dog. And you and Nash didn't almost set fire to my dining room table with the sparks flying between you two at dinner. And Knox didn't throw a fit about Nash cornering you afterward."

"Nothing wrong with your communication as a couple," I said.

She stared me down, willing me to break, but I held fast. "Ugh. Fine," she said. "But just know that if you do need to talk, hypothetically or otherwise, I'm here. And I'm rooting for you."

"Thank you," I said, stroking a hand over Piper's wiry fur. "I appreciate that."

"That's what friends are for," she said before glancing at her watch. "If you'll excuse me, it's time for me to go let Sloane talk me into using the money from the sale of my house for the good of the community since my husband-to-be absolutely refuses to let me pay for the wedding, the honeymoon, or Waylay's college."

"Why not save it?"

"I'm saving some of it. But I used an inheritance from my grandma for the down payment on that house, and it just feels right to invest that in the future of something I care about. Sloane says she has the perfect cause." She picked up her gallon-sized coffee and stood. "Don't forget about dress shopping!"

We said our goodbyes and I watched Naomi glide out the door into the chilly autumn morning.

I looked down at Piper. She had whipped cream on her doggy mustache. "I think I need to tell your dad the truth," I said.

The dog cocked her head and made an uncomfortable amount of eye contact.

"Have any advice for me?" I asked.

Her pink tongue darted out and snagged the whipped cream on her snout.

If Lucian hadn't managed to convince Nash that I was a scheming, manipulative femme fatale over breakfast, maybe I could tell him why I was there and that I was kinda, sorta into him over lunch.

"You know, even if he's initially mad at me, I still have you," I said to the dog. "Maybe I can hold you hostage and ransom you for his forgiveness."

Piper sneezed whipped cream on the table. I took that as an affirmative sign, and as soon as I finished mopping up the mess, I fired off a text to him.

> **Me:** Have time to grab lunch today? I
> have something I want to tell you.

I put the phone down and stared at the screen, willing three dots to appear. But none did.

He was probably busy. Or he'd already made up his mind that I was bad news and no amount of belated honesty would fix that. What was I even doing? I was here to do my damn job and figure out a way to stop making risky decisions.

"Damn it," I muttered under my breath.

I picked up the phone again.

> **Me:** Just realized I don't have time for
> lunch so forget I said anything about it.
> I have some errands to run so I'll drop
> Piper off with Mrs. Tweedy.

There. Good.

It was the smart move to end it all now. It didn't matter what Nash thought of me. I wouldn't be here long enough to deal with the consequences.

"Hello, lovely." Tallulah, Justice's wife, appeared holding a large tumbler of coffee and a pastry bag. "Just wanted to tell you if that sexy car of yours needs an oil change, bring it my way. I love American muscle."

"I wouldn't trust anyone else," I assured her.

She winked and left.

I froze with the mug halfway to my mouth.

Tallulah knew what kind of car I drove. I was part of a group text with fun, friendly women who seemed to be hell-bent on pulling me into their friend circle. The local café owner knew my name and how I liked my coffee. I had gym buddies, granted they were all members of AARP, but that wasn't slowing them down on the dead lifts.

I glanced around me and recognized half a dozen faces.

I knew where to find all my favorite foods at the local grocery store and remembered to avoid Fourth Street between three and three thirty when school let out. I was in someone's wedding. I was dog-sitting someone's dog. I'd woken up two mornings in a row in bed with Nash.

Without me noticing it, Knockemout had sucked me into its gravitational field. And it was up to me to decide whether I wanted to break free. Whether I was brave enough to see what those other layers were like.

"Well, hell," I muttered and picked up my phone again.

> **Me:** Me again. Lunch is back on the table. Literally and metaphorically. I mean, if you're available. Hope to talk soon.

"Oh my God. Hope to talk soon?" I dropped the phone and swiped both hands over my face.

"What is wrong with me? What is this guy doing to me?"

Piper let out a little whimper. I looked at her. "Thank you for your feedback. I'm going to drop you off at Mrs. Tweedy's so I can go talk to someone horrible."

"Well, look who's back." Tina Witt looked awfully smug for a woman in a khaki prison jumpsuit.

The first time I'd met the woman, her resemblance to her twin sister, Naomi, was uncanny. It felt like I was meeting a literal evil twin. Only instead of a diabolical goatee, Tina sported the entitled attitude of a not-so-mastermind criminal.

"Tina," I said, sitting across from her on the metal folding chair.

I'd been here twice before and left both times with big, fat nothing. Either Tina was holding on to some strange loyalty toward Duncan Hugo or she really didn't know anything about, well . . . anything. Seeing as how she'd rolled on her ex to the feds, I was guessing it was the latter.

"I told you and your fed buddies fifty million times, I don't know where Dunc is."

It was time to try a new tactic. "I don't work for the feds," I told her.

Her eyes narrowed. "You said—"

"I said I was an investigator."

"What the hell are you investigating if it ain't where that deadbeat, brain-dead moron went?"

"I work for an insurance agency," I explained.

"You trying to sell me some bullshit car warranty? I'm behind bars, bitch. You see me driving?"

It was clear who'd gotten all the brains in the womb. "I don't *sell* insurance, Tina. I find insured things when they go missing."

"Huh?"

"I'm like a bounty hunter, only instead of finding people, I find the things they stole. I think Duncan stole something that's valuable to my client, and I think he stole it while he was plotting criminal world domination with you."

"How valuable?"

It was on-brand for Tina not to care about the details, just the bottom line.

"To my client? Priceless. Market value? Half a million."

Tina snorted. "Priceless as in a sentimental bullshit baggie of baby teeth? Never did understand that shit. The tooth fairy. Elf on the stool."

I felt a twinge of sadness for Waylay and the way she'd been brought up. At least my parents had smothered me with love. An active disinterest would have done much more damage. Thank God for Naomi and Knox and their extended families. Waylay now had an army of loved ones at her back.

"Priceless as in a 1948 Porsche 356 convertible that's been in the family three generations."

"So you're saying not only did this dickweasel leave me high and dry to get blamed for the whole damn thing, he also cut me out of some windfall?"

"Pretty much."

"That son of a bitch!"

"No yelling, Tina," the guard outside the door called.

"I'll yell if I wanna fucking yell, Irving!"

"Did you remember if Duncan was with you on this weekend in August?" I asked, showing her the calendar on my phone.

Last time I was here and asked, she'd suggested I ask her "social secretary," then told me to fuck off.

"That when your expensive-ass car got stolen?"

I nodded.

"I did some remembering since last time. Dunc and his buddies went on a spree that weekend. Came back with six cars. No old-ass Porsche though. But Dunc came back later than everyone else did. I remember 'cause I laid into him because his douchebags showed up without him and drank all my goddamn beer. Then here comes Dunc, struttin' like one of those birds with the big, fancy tail."

"A turkey?"

Tina rolled her eyes. "Jesus. No. With the blue

feathers and the screaming." She tilted her head back and let out a warbly scream.

Irving the guard opened the door. "One more warning and you're going back to your cell, Tina."

"A peacock!" I cut in.

Tina pointed at me. "Yeah! That one. What were we talking about again?"

Irving closed the door on a long-suffering sigh.

"Duncan coming home late after stealing six cars," I prompted. "How late was he?"

She shrugged. "Long enough for those dick-heads to drink a whole case of Natty Light. 'Bout an hour or two?"

I clamped down on my rising sense of triumph. I knew it. I was right. He'd stashed the Porsche somewhere within an hour of that original shop location. It might not still be there, but if I could find that first bread crumb, I could find the second.

"And you never saw a vintage Porsche at the shop?" I asked.

She shook her head. "Nah. He stuck with new *Fast and Furious* shit."

"Did Duncan ever take you to meet his father?" I asked.

"Anthony?" She screwed her face up in derision. "Me 'n Dunc were more at the fuck-in-an-alley than meet-the-parents stage before he screwed me over."

"But he talked about him," I prodded.

"Shit yeah, he talked about him. The guy was obsessed with gettin' Daddy's approval. At least, up until Dunc fucked up that hit."

My body tensed at the way she so casually mentioned Nash's shooting. I did my best to keep my expression blank, but on the inside, my heart was thundering against my sternum.

Some people didn't understand that their actions had consequences. Others simply didn't care.

"You know, I didn't even know he was gonna try to take out that Morgan guy. I woulda talked him out of it," Tina said, lighting a cigarette.

"Why?"

"Well, for one thing, them cop pants looked mighty fine on that man's ass."

Tina Witt might have been a horrible human being, but she was not wrong on that particular point.

"For another, he was a decent guy. And not just to look at. He never once treated me like his piece-of-shit brother and everyone else did. Even when he arrested me that one time, he put my head in the car real gentle like." Her hard-lined face had gone dreamy.

"He's a good guy. Good-looking too," I prompted.

"You ain't wrong there. Given how much I avoid cops in general, you know the guy's gotta be hot if I don't run in the opposite direction at the grocery store even with chipped turkey I ain't paid for stuffed in my bra. Bet he's got a huge dick too," she said wistfully.

Great. Now I was thinking about Nash and his incredible morning erections and how I might never get to experience one again. "Back to Duncan," I said desperately.

Tina waved a dismissive hand. "Oh, he just had a medium-sized one. Didn't really know how to use it. He was kind of a poker instead of a thruster, if you know what I mean."

I did not. My face must have said as much because Tina stood and began a lewd thrusting demonstration with the cigarette dangling from her mouth.

"Do you think Anthony Hugo would help hide his son?" I asked, interrupting the show.

Tina snorted and sat back down. "Are you shittin' me? After as bad as Dunc fucked up?"

"Parents forgive all kinds of mistakes," I pointed out. Case in point, Tina's own parents.

Tina shook her head. "Not Anthony Hugo. Dunc came home all pissed off and freaked out. Told me he tried to take out a cop and it didn't go as planned. I was layin' into him good when two of Anthony's goons showed up to bring Dunc in for a 'chat.' And I was there when he dragged his ass home beat to hell and bloody."

"What happened during that chat?"

281

"Oh, you know. Screaming. Humiliation. Threats. Anthony was pissed off that Dunc had brought 'unwanted attention' to their business. Dunc said his dad called him names, roughed him up. Which was a real slap in the face, pun intended. Word is Anthony hasn't gotten his hands dirty roughing up anybody in a long time. He's got guys for that. But he made an exception for Dunc."

"How did Duncan feel about that?"

She looked at me like I was stupid. "He felt it moved their relationship into a healthier place. How the hell do you think he felt about it?"

"So you don't think there's any way that Duncan's dad would have helped him go to ground?" I pressed.

"I'd be surprised if the old man isn't hunting for him to take him out before the cops find him," she said.

This was news. I filed it away. "Really?"

"I mean, Dunc was an idiot. Way too impulsive. But his dad is downright scary. After Anthony came down on him all high and mighty about how he'd ruined his plans and endangered the family business, I knew what was gonna happen next. The old man would send someone out to clean up the mess. And by 'clean up the mess,' I mean he woulda put a couple of bullets in Dunc's head. Probably mine too."

"So what happened?"

282

"Well, lemme tell you, ain't nothin' sexy about a man who's sad Daddy didn't love him enough. I told him it was time to move on. To make a name for himself. So I convinced him we needed to go into hiding. He made some calls, and we moved into that warehouse in Lawlerville and started to make a plan. We needed money and fast. Dunc figured the best way to do that was to resell a copy of the list. Lotta people between here and DC would be interested in a list of hard-ass cops and their snitches."

"So that's when you abducted your daughter and your sister."

Tina Witt's bad decisions made my own look like tiny lapses in judgment by comparison. I'd been there to see the immediate fallout. A trail of bleeding bad guys. Knox on the floor with Naomi and Way. Nash, heroically leaning against the wall, gun in hand, shoulder bleeding, looking exhausted and pissed off. My heart gave a pathetic little pitter-patter.

"That was another clusterfuck that dipwad got me into. It was never supposed to be a kidnapping thing, you know? He was just supposed to scare them a little. Get 'em to cough up the list. Then we'd send 'em on their way. But noooo, he had to do things *his* way. Dunc was an idiot, but he wasn't stupid. He could be sneaky smart when he wanted to be, but he was impulsive. One second, he'd be planning some heist, and the next, he'd be zoned out playing video games until 4:00 a.m."

"So once you two struck out on your own, who worked with him? There were men at the warehouse the night you were arrested. Were they Anthony's? Other family members? Friends?"

That's what friends are for. Naomi's words from earlier that morning resurfaced in my head. No one was truly alone in this world. There was always someone a person would turn to when they needed help.

"Oh. Like his known associates, right? I'm picking up all the cop speak by watching *NCIS* and shit in case Chief Morgan ever comes to pay me a visit," she said proudly.

I wondered how Nash would feel knowing that Tina Witt had a raging crush on him. I also wondered if that meant he'd never come to see her in jail.

"Yes. Known associates," I agreed.

"Heard most of 'em were picked up by the cops," Tina said.

"Most, but not all. Someone had to help him get away."

"There were a couple of goons he had working for him in his chop shop. Then there was Face Tattoo Guy and Chubby Goatee Guy. That dude could eat a twelve-inch cheesesteak in under ten minutes. They were Dunc's buddies from high school before he dropped out. They all started working for the old man around the same time, but they were Dunc's friends first."

Dutifully, I made notes and hoped the descriptions would be enough to lead me in a direction.

"Is there anyone else you can think of?"

She pursed her lips and stubbed out her cigarette. "He had a guy I never met. Burner Phone Guy. I don't think they were buddies. Least, they didn't talk like they were. But he was the one Dunc called when we needed to get the hell outta Dodge after his dumb ass shot Chief Morgan."

"How did Burner Phone Guy help?" I asked.

Tina shrugged. "Dunno. I was too busy yelling at Dunc for bein' a dumbass to pay attention."

I closed my notebook and stowed it in the pocket of my jacket. "One more question. What made Duncan start with Chief Morgan?"

Tina shrugged. "Maybe it was that I mentioned how fine the chief's ass looked one day or that I told him that the chief hadn't done me wrong like every other fucking resident of Knockemout. He never looked at me like I was a nobody."

She twirled a piece of straw-textured hair around her fingers. She'd cut and dyed her hair to look more like her sister for the abduction. Now, gray roots were visible at her part and she was in desperate need of a deep condition.

"Course, it coulda been the double asterisks next to his name that caught Dunc's eye."

I fought the urge to drum my fingers on the tabletop. "He say what the asterisks were for?"

Tina shrugged. "Dunno. You'd have to ask Dunc."

"Well, thanks for your time, Tina," I said, getting to my feet.

"I got nothin' but time thanks to that asshat. You find him, tell him I sent you."

I stepped outside into the bright autumn sun feeling like I always did after leaving the prison. Like I needed a shower.

But at least this time, I *finally* had a few leads to tug on.

I held my breath as I checked my phone. There were no messages or missed calls from Nash. I blew out a sigh and dialed the office as I crossed the parking lot, leaving barbed wire and high fences behind me.

My favorite researcher, Zelda, answered on the second ring. "Yello?"

"Hey, it's me. I need you to dig up everything you can on Duncan Hugo's known associates. Concentrate on ones he's known the longest. Specifically anyone with a face tattoo and anyone on the heftier side."

I heard the crinkle of a potato chip bag.

"On it," Zelda said, crunching noisily into my ear. "How's life in Knockemup? You ready to run screaming to the closest metropolitan area yet?"

"Knockemout," I corrected, heading in the direction of my vehicle.

"Whatevs. Hey, you hear about Lew?"

I stopped in the middle of the parking lot. "What about him?"

"He's back on desk duty starting tomorrow."

"He's doing okay?" I asked.

"He's fine. Said it would take more than a broken ass to keep him down. Besides, Daley told him he better get his busted ass back out there if he wants to keep earning."

I waited for the relief to come, but it was only guilt that lingered.

20

Carpool Confessions

Nash

I was still pissed off over the breakfast ambush by the time I made it to the station. I didn't know who I was more angry with: Lucian for overstepping, Knox for being a stubborn asshole, or Lina for still holding back on me when I'd been nothing but honest with her.

She'd texted three times saying she wanted to talk.

My guess was she was worried about what Lucian told me. Right now, I was in the mood to let her worry.

Or maybe this roiling inner rage was directed at myself.

At this point, it didn't really matter. Everyone was pissing me off.

"You're supposed to tell me where you're gonna be, Morgan."

I turned around and found an equally irate-looking U.S. marshal storming up the sidewalk toward the station's side door.

I was not in the mood. "I'm already pissed off at two assholes who dragged me out of bed this morning. I were you? I wouldn't be in a hurry to add your name to that list."

"Look, shithead. I'm not happy about this assignment either. You think I *like* camping out in *Deliverance* banjo territory watching your ungrateful back for some threat that probably doesn't even exist?" Nolan snapped back.

"Gee, I'm sorry you're bored, Graham. Do you want a coloring book and some crayons? I'll pick some up when I go get you a thank-you card and fucking balloons."

Nolan shook his head. "Christ, you're a dick. If I hadn't seen you dealing with those kids yesterday and making that fuckhead cop piss his pants, I'd think the condition was permanent."

"Yeah, well, maybe it is."

To illustrate my point, I didn't hold the door for him.

I acknowledged the round of "Mornin', Chief," with a curt nod as I headed straight for my office where I could shut the damn door on the whole damn world.

No one said anything to Nolan when he stomped in after me.

"Where's Piper?" Grave asked, holding up a bag of the pet shop's gourmet doggie treats.

Fuck.

Lina had the dog. I might not have wanted the damn dog, but I sure as hell wasn't going to let Lina keep her.

"She's with a neighbor," I said.

Officer Will Bertle stopped me just shy of my door. He was the first Black officer I'd hired as chief. Soft-spoken and unflappable, he was well-liked in the community and respected in the department. "You've got a visitor, Chief. He's waiting for you in your office," he said.

"Thanks, Will," I said, trying to tamp down my exasperation. The world did not seem inclined to leave me the hell alone today.

I headed into my office and stopped short when I spotted my visitor.

"Dad?"

"Nash. It's good to see you."

Duke Morgan had once been the strongest, funniest man I'd known. But the years had all but erased that man.

You didn't have to look far past the clean, baggy clothes, the neatly trimmed hair and beard, before seeing the truth of the man in my visitors chair.

He looked older than his sixty-five years. His skin was weathered and lined from years of neglect and exposure to the elements. He was too thin, a shadow of the man who had once carried me on his shoulders and tossed me effortlessly into the creek. His blue eyes, the same shade as mine, had bags under them, slashes of purple so dark they almost looked like bruises.

His fingers nervously traced the stitching on

his pants over and over again. It was a tell I'd learned to recognize as a kid.

Despite my best efforts to save him, my father was a homeless addict. That failure never got easier for me to stomach.

I was tempted to turn around and walk out the door. But just as I recognized the tell, I also recognized the need to confront the bad. It was part of my job, part of who I was.

I unhooked my belt and hung it and my jacket on the coatrack behind my desk before sitting. We Morgans weren't huggers and for good reason. Years of disappointments and trauma had made physical affection between us a foreign language. I'd always promised myself that when I had my own family, it would be different.

"How are you doing?" I asked.

Duke rubbed absentmindedly at the spot between his eyebrows. "Good. That's kind of why I'm here."

I braced for the ask. For the no I'd have to deliver. I'd stopped giving him money a long time ago. Clean clothes, food, hotel rooms, treatment, yes. But I'd learned early on exactly where cash went as soon as he got his hands on it.

It didn't make me angry anymore. Hadn't in a long time. My dad was who he was. There was nothing I could do to change that. Not getting better grades. Not performing on the football field. Not graduating with honors. And definitely not handing him money.

"I'm going away for a little while," he said finally, stroking a hand over his beard.

I frowned. "You in trouble?" I asked, already jiggling my computer mouse. I had an alert set for if and when his name popped up in the system.

He shook his head. "No. Nothin' like that, son. I'm, uh, starting a rehab program down south."

"Really?"

"Yeah." He ran his palms over his knees and back up his thighs. "Been thinkin' about it for a while. Haven't used in a bit and I'm feelin' pretty good."

"How long is a bit?" I asked.

"Three weeks, five days, and nine hours."

I blinked. "On your own?"

He nodded. "Yeah. Felt like time for a change."

"Good for you." I knew better than to be hopeful. But I also knew what effort it took for an addict to get to this mental space.

"Thanks. Anyway, it's a different kind of place than the ones I did before. Comes with some counseling, medical treatment plans. Even get a social worker to help with after. They've got outpatient support programs, job placement."

"That sounds like it's got potential," I said.

I wasn't optimistic. Not with him and not with rehab. Too many disappointments over the years. I'd learned that having expectations where he was concerned only guaranteed my own disappointment. So I made it a point to always meet him where he was, not where I wanted him to be. Not where he'd once been.

It helped me in my job too. Treating victims and suspects with respect, not judgment. Despite the fact that he'd turned into a toxic father figure, Duke Morgan had made me a better cop. And for that, I was grateful.

"You need anything before you go?"

He shook his head slowly. "Nope. I'm all set. Got my bus ticket here," he said, patting his front pocket. "I leave this afternoon."

"I hope it's a good experience for you," I said and meant it.

"It will be." He reached into the same pocket and pulled out a business card. "Here's the number and address of the place. They'll limit phone calls to emergencies for the first few weeks, but you can send letters . . . if you want."

He put the card faceup on my desk and slid it toward me.

I picked up the card, looked at it, then pocketed it. "Thanks, Dad."

"Well, I'd best be gettin' on," he said, getting to his feet. "Gotta see your brother before I hit the road."

I rose. "I'll walk you out."

"Not necessary. I don't wanna embarrass you in front of your department."

"You're not an embarrassment, Dad."

"Maybe in a few months I won't be."

I didn't know what to do with that. So I clapped him on the shoulder and squeezed.

"You healing up okay?" he asked.

"Yeah. It's gonna take more than a couple of bullets to keep me down," I said with feigned confidence.

"Some things are tougher than others to get over," he insisted, those blue eyes locking on to mine.

"Some things are," I agreed.

Bullet holes and broken hearts.

"I didn't do right by you and your brother."

"Dad, we don't have to get into this. I understand why things happened the way they did."

"I just wish I woulda kept trying to look to the light instead of sinking into the dark," he said. "A man can learn to live in that dark, but it's no life."

I spent the next hour reviewing case reports, time-off requests, and budgets with my father's words echoing around in my head.

Maybe the dark was an empty, meaningless existence, but it was the light that could burn you. I needed something from Lina that she didn't seem willing to give. Something that was as essential to me as oxygen. *Honesty.*

Sure, she'd shared bits and pieces. But what she

did share was shaded and spun to tell the kind of story she wanted. She'd made it seem like she'd run into Lucian and had a benign conversation with him. She hadn't told me that my oldest friend had hunted her down and threatened her over the time she'd been spending with me.

I was almost as pissed off about the fact that she'd decided to handle it on her own as I was over Lucian's overprotective, asinine actions.

But despite the fact that I knew for sure that Lina wasn't telling me the whole truth, I felt something I couldn't identify, something a hell of a lot like need. And the scales wouldn't be balanced unless she needed me back.

Something Lina Solavita wasn't programmed to do.

Something I wasn't prepared to deliver on. Who would need me in this state? I was a fucking mess.

Hell, I'd just spelled my name wrong signing a PTO request.

"Fuck," I muttered and shoved away from my desk.

I was too restless to hide from the world. I needed to do something that felt productive.

I grabbed my jacket and belt off the hook and headed out into the bullpen.

"Headed out," I said to the room in general. "I'll bring back lunch from Dino's if y'all text me your orders. My treat."

There was a flutter of excitement that all cops got at the thought of free food.

I paused at Nolan's desk. "Feel like takin' a ride?"

"Depends. You gonna take me out to the woods and leave me for the banjos?"

"Probably not today. Thinkin' about paying an inmate a visit."

"I'll get my coat."

"What's with the change of heart?" Nolan asked as I hit the highway.

"Maybe I just want to save the environment by carpooling."

"Or maybe you're in the mood to have a chat with Tina Witt and you don't want to get any of your officers in trouble with the feds."

"You're not as dumb as that mustache makes you look," I said.

"My wife—ex-wife—was really into *Top Gun*," he said, running his finger and thumb over the 'stache.

"The things we do for women."

"Speaking of—"

"You mention Lina's name and I will leave you for the banjos," I warned.

"Noted. What about her friend? The blond librarian?"

"Sloane?" I asked.

"She single?"

I thought about Lucian this morning at breakfast. A slow, vengeful smile spread over my face. "You should ask her out."

We rode in silence until I took the exit for the prison.

"Those kids yesterday," Nolan said. "You talked the manager out of pressing charges."

"I did."

"Then you kicked the ass of Officer Fuckhead."

"You got a point rattlin' around in there somewhere, Graham?"

He shrugged. "Just saying you don't suck at your job. Some local lawmen would have thrown the book at the kids and let that officer slide."

"My town saw enough of the good ol' boy style of leadership. They deserve better."

"Guess you're smarter than those bullet holes make you look."

The Bannion Women's Correctional Facility was typical for a medium-security prison. Out in the middle of nowhere, the perimeter was protected by tall fences, miles of barbed wire, and guard towers.

"You gonna run and tattle to the feds about this?" I asked, swinging into a parking space near the entrance.

"Guess that depends on how it goes down." Nolan released his seat belt. "I'm comin' in."

"Less problematic for you if you don't know what I'm doin' in there."

"I got nothing to do but wonder how many assholes are lined up to make a move on my ex since she moved to DC and wait for some low-level criminal to ask you to dance again. I'm comin' in."

"Suit yourself."

"Get anything useful out of her yet?" he asked.

"Dunno. This is my first visit."

He shot me a look. "Guess Studly Do-Right takes orders seriously."

"Was really hopin' that nickname would die."

"Not likely. But seriously, Idler tells you let the big girls and boys handle it and you just sit on your hands? If I were in your shoes, I'd sure as hell be running my own investigation. Hell, these are local players. They'd be more likely to talk to you than to a bunch of feds."

"Speaking of," I said, looking pointedly at his department-issue suit. "Lose the jacket and tie."

Nolan had just thrown his jacket between the seats and was rolling up his sleeves when a leggy brunette strolled out of the prison and into the parking lot.

"You've got to be fucking kidding me."

"Well, well, well. Looks like Investigator Sola-vita is up to something after all," my passenger mused. "What are the odds—"

"Zero in a million," I said as I glared at her reflection in my rearview mirror. I watched her hang up her phone and get into her car.

I called up Lina's last text on my phone.

"Aren't you gonna bust her?" Nolan asked.

"Nope," I said as my thumbs moved across the screen.

Me: Lunch sounds good. Meet at Dino's in ten?

My phone rang a few seconds later. Lina.

"Hey," I said, fighting to keep my tone neutral.

"Hi," Lina said.

"Is Dino's in ten good?" I asked, knowing full well it wasn't. Nolan snickered from the passenger seat.

"Actually, I'm out running errands. Can I meet you in an hour?"

She was lying to my face . . . well, my ear. My blood pressure spiked. "I don't think I'm gonna be free then," I lied. "What kind of errands are you running?"

"Oh, you know, just typical errand stuff. Groceries. Pharmacy."

A visit to a women's correctional facility.

"How did breakfast go this morning?" she asked, changing the subject.

"Breakfast was fine," I lied. "Piper with Mrs. Tweedy?"

"Yeah. She's sleeping off her puppyccino on Mrs. Tweedy's couch."

The woman had taken my dog for a treat and now she was lying to me. Lina Solavita was maddening.

"Hey, listen. If you haven't hit the pharmacy yet, mind grabbing me a bottle of ibuprofen?" I asked.

We were both going to need it later.

"Sure! I can do that. No problem. Is everything okay?" She sounded nervous. *Good.*

"Yep. Fine. Gotta go do cop stuff. See you later." I hung up.

Thirty seconds later, the cherry-red Charger zipped past us before flying out of the parking lot with a chirp of tires.

I got out and slammed my door harder than necessary.

Nolan got out and jogged to keep up.

"That was cold, my friend," he said with just a hint of glee.

I grunted and stabbed the intercom button outside the main entrance.

When the heavy door buzzed open, we stepped into a squeaky-clean lobby. Guards waved us through the metal detector and directed us to the front desk behind its protective glass. I'd been here before for hearings and interviews, but this time, it was personal.

"Well, hello, gentlemen. What brings you to

my fine establishment today?" Minnie had been working the desk at this prison for as long as I could remember. She'd been threatening to retire for the past five years but claimed her marriage wouldn't survive retirement.

The truth was, the prison would probably fall apart without her. She was a grandmotherly figure to inmates, visitors, and law enforcement alike.

I produced my badge. "Good to see you again, Minnie. I need to see a list of all the visitors Tina Witt has had."

"Ms. Witt sure is popular today," Minnie said, giving us the eyes. "Lemme talk to the boss lady and I'll see what I can get you."

21

Fan, Meet Shit

Nash

I gave Lina's door an official-sounding knock and waited.

Finally, the door opened a crack and she peered out at me, then smiled and opened the door a little wider. "Hey. I was just taking a bath."

I brushed past her and stepped inside.

"Uh, come on in," she said, sounding nonplussed. She was wearing nothing but a towel and a pair of fuzzy flip-flops. Her skin glistened with water droplets. I had to look away because I didn't trust myself. I felt like a volcano ready to blow. Betrayal and need. Those two opposing forces mixed in my blood, fanning the need to explode.

I shouldn't have come when I was this keyed up.

"Your ibuprofen is on the counter," Lina said, her voice more tentative now.

The box of files caught my eye. It was open and there were papers lined up in neat stacks around it.

I headed for it.

"Nash. Wait!"

She caught up to me just as I picked up the first folder. Her front met my back and she reached around me, but I shrugged her off and flipped it open. My gut rolled in on itself. I absorbed it like I would a blow.

"I can explain," she said quietly.

I slammed the folder down on the table with Duncan Hugo's face staring up at me. "Talk. Now."

"Nash."

"You can start with what you were doing visiting Tina Witt in prison today. Or maybe you should start with why you've got the guy who shot me in your files. Your choice." I wanted the cold, the dark. But she'd unlocked something in me, and instead of the nothingness I'd gotten used to, I was burning alive with rage.

She crossed her arms in front of her defiantly. "This has nothing to do with you."

Wrong move.

"Don't fucking lie to me, Angelina. This has *everything* to do with me. And I'm not leaving until you tell me why."

"Is this an interrogation, Chief? Do I need a lawyer?"

My stare was hard, unyielding. "You tell me," I said. I was spoiling for a fight. I needed it more than my next breath.

She met my gaze with her own anger.

I gave in to the need and wrapped my fingers around her elbow. Hating the way I reacted to the feel of her against my palm, I pulled out a chair and pushed her into it. "Sit. Talk."

Her chin came up defiantly.

"If the next words aren't an explanation of why the fuck you've been paying Tina Witt visits and looking for Duncan Hugo, then I swear to God I will haul you down to the station right now and you can sit in a cell in nothing but that bath towel for the rest of the night."

"You're making a big deal out of—"

"I *trusted* you, Angelina. I opened up to you and you played me."

I saw the wince before she smoothed it over with indignant anger. "I didn't *play* you. I'm sorry your feelings got hurt. It wasn't my intention."

"God, you're worse at apologies than Knox," I observed.

"I'm just doing my job! It's not a crime."

I slammed my hand down on the table. "Damn it! Why are you looking for Hugo?"

She should have been scared, but she wasn't. She looked ready to deck me.

"What are you after that made you come here? That had you cozying up to me asking me about the shooting. That put you in *my* bed talking to you about fucking panic attacks and memory loss."

"You're gonna want to walk that back," she said with an icy calm.

"Do *not* try to tell me what I can and can't do right now, Lina. I've had a long fucking day and you're making it longer."

"I was going to tell you."

I swept her from head to toe and willed myself not to be affected by the way her chest heaved with every breath she took. "That's how you're gonna play this?"

"I'm not playing. That's why I texted you today, you idiot."

"Oh, so you weren't worried that Lucian was going to poison me against you with the truth?"

"He didn't know the truth. And I stupidly felt like I should be the one to tell you."

I shoved the paper with Duncan Hugo's face at her. "Talk. Now."

She was silent and I could practically hear her calculating her options.

"Have it your way." I moved fast so she wouldn't see me coming. I ducked my shoulder low, wrapped my good arm around her waist, and hauled her over my shoulder. Her furry slippers went flying in opposite directions.

"Nash!"

"I gave you the chance to do this here," I said as I headed toward the door.

"Don't you *dare!*" she shrieked. She struggled against me and I slapped a hand to her ass to hold her still. My other hand locked around her bare thigh. I was instantly hard, and that pissed me

305

off even more. But my dick didn't seem to care about things like betrayal.

I made it all the way to the door before I heard what I wanted. "Okay! Jesus. You win, you gigantic asshole."

"How's that heart rate?" I asked her. I barely dodged the kick she aimed at my groin.

"I swear to *God* I'm going to have you singing soprano," she said through what sounded like gritted teeth.

I started for the door again. "You're gonna have to ride in the back and I'm definitely gonna have to cuff you," I said conversationally. "I hope that towel holds up. Word'll probably spread real fast. I can't promise your mug shot won't make it into the papers."

"Okay! Oh my God!" She went limp against me. "Just put me down and I'll tell you everything."

"That's all I wanted, Angel."

I bent at the waist and let her slide off my shoulder until her feet hit the floor.

Her towel was barely hanging on at this point. One good breath or the lightest tug from me and it would be around her ankles. Her eyes sparking with fire didn't do anything to alleviate the pressure building in my balls. "Fuck. Go put on a robe," I ordered, looking away.

She spun on her heel and stormed toward her bedroom.

"It takes you longer than thirty seconds, I'm comin' in there after you," I called after her.

I looked back in time to see the middle finger she held over her shoulder.

For the twenty-eight seconds it took her to reappear, I fantasized about marching into that room, pinning her to the bed, and throwing that towel on the floor.

The robe wasn't much better than the towel. It covered more skin, but the silky fabric didn't do a damn thing to hide those insolent nipples that begged for my attention.

Eyes flashing, she returned to the table and sat.

I took the next chair and picked up Hugo's file. "Talk."

"Are you asking in an official capacity?"

"I'm sure as hell not asking as a friend. How many times have you visited Tina Witt, keepin' in mind that I have her list of visitors, so don't bother lying."

She blew her breath out through her teeth. "Three."

"What did you two talk about?"

"I was trying to get information on Duncan Hugo's whereabouts," she said to the brick wall across the table.

I plucked another folder off the pile and opened it. She reached for it, but I pulled it back.

"You can't look at those without a warrant," she insisted.

I raised an eyebrow. "You want me to go get one? 'Cause I will. Your old pal Marshal Graham might even help me. He wasn't any happier than I was to see your name on that visitation list. In fact, why don't the three of us meet up down at the station and clear this whole thing up while the judge approves a warrant?"

"*Damn it,* Nash!"

"Why are you looking for Hugo?"

"I'm not looking for him. I'm looking for something he took," she said.

I leaned back in the chair. "I'm listening."

The glare she shot me would have incinerated someone with thinner skin. "I'm never going to forgive you for this."

"Back at you, baby. Now talk."

I could all but see the steam whistling out of her ears. "You already know my company insures things for wealthy clients. When insured assets are stolen, we run parallel investigations with law enforcement. One of our clients lives in a DC suburb. His car was stolen a few days before you were shot. I was assigned the case and started digging."

"A car. You're hunting down an attempted murderer over a fucking car."

"You'd be doing the same thing as a cop."

"I'd be doing it to protect and serve. You're doing it to save your company an insurance payout and to earn a bonus."

"I guess we can't all be heroes, can we?" There was fire beneath all the ice she was throwing at me.

"What makes you think Hugo took the car?"

"Process of elimination. There was a spike of grand theft auto cases within a ten-mile radius of Hugo's warehouse. Six other cars were stolen the same day, two from the same neighborhood as my client's. All those cars, or at least pieces of them, were found in Hugo's warehouse after he got away."

"So you show up to a hostage situation unarmed with a civilian to find a fucking car?" She'd arrived on scene with Sloane. I could still see her walking in the door in slow motion. She came straight to me. And the second she'd put her hands on me, I *knew* I wanted to keep them there.

Wasn't that a fucking kick in the goddamn teeth?

It was official. My instincts were gone. I couldn't see through a leggy temptress with secrets in her eyes.

"First of all, I didn't know Duncan Dumbass Hugo was into kidnapping in addition to running chop shops. But I've been in high-stakes situations with and without law enforcement. And if I hadn't gotten in Sloane's car, she would have driven there herself and probably put herself in danger."

"You didn't just come here and coincidentally end up in the middle of Hugo's crime spree."

"The thefts happened less than an hour from here. The plan was to swing through town and see my old friend on my way. I was going to stay in town long enough to catch up, and then everything went to hell the next day when they took Naomi and Way."

"Why should I believe that?" I asked.

"I don't care what you believe," she snapped.

"Yeah, I got that too, sweetheart. You get all your sources to tell you things the way you did with me?" I asked.

"Subtlety doesn't become you, Chief."

I leaned forward. "I trusted you, Lina."

She crossed her arms defiantly. "You're acting like a scorned lover when the only thing we are is . . ."

"What? What are we, Angelina? You want to say neighbors? Acquaintances?" I slapped the file down on the table in a display of temper. "You know my darkest fucking secret. You let me tell you."

She threw her arms up in the air. "You think anyone besides my family knows about my history? You weren't the only one opening your-self up, Nash."

"Then you're either a cold piece of work or at the very least that made us friends."

"Made?"

"I told you I don't tolerate liars. Anything that we had or could have had is gone now."

Her jaw ticked.

"You deliberately lied to me," I said.

"I didn't lie. I omitted part of the truth."

"You used me being vulnerable against me."

"Oh please," she snapped. "I was walking *your* dog when I found you on the floor. I didn't give you a panic attack."

"No, but you sure as hell took advantage of it."

"How?" she sputtered. "Did I pump you for law enforcement secrets? Am I blackmailing you with your secrets?"

"Maybe not. But you made sure to get access to me, my place. You started pushing me about what happened that night," I pointed out, fitting the pieces together.

"For your own good, *ass*. If you want to block it out forever, it's none of my business. But you'll just keep ending up on the floor if you don't eventually work your way through it."

I shook my head. "I've got a hunch of my own. I think the only reason you pretended to care was you thought you could get something out of me. Something that would lead you to Hugo and that damn car." I picked up another folder and opened it, but my gaze was on her. "I bet you couldn't help but take a look at those files I have on my table, could you?"

Her face turned to stone, but not before I saw the flicker of guilt.

"Yeah. That's why you agreed to our little sleepovers. The more access you had to me, the more time you'd be able to spend at my place."

Lina stared at me with fire in her eyes. She laughed bitterly. "And here I thought Knox was the asshole brother."

"Guess it runs in the family. You're gonna want to stay away from all of them from now on," I warned her.

"That's gonna be a little tricky since Knox asked me to be in the wedding party," she shot back.

"I don't trust you and I don't want you anywhere near my family. You're reckless and you use people to get what you want. You're going to get someone hurt."

She blanched but covered immediately.

"My brother might be an asshole," I continued when she said nothing. "And we might not get along all the time. But do you really wanna go up against me when it comes to testing his loyalty? Because I won't hesitate to make sure you lose your oldest friend."

"Get out," she said on a whisper.

"I'm not done with you," I warned.

She slammed her palm down on the table. "Get. Out. Now."

I sat for a beat and studied her. "I catch wind

of you hounding my family for information or interfering with an official investigation, I won't hesitate to throw your ass behind bars."

She said nothing but stared at me stonily until I rose.

"I mean it, Lina."

"Go home, Nash. Leave me alone."

I went, but only because looking at her made my chest hurt. Like she'd managed to do more damage than the two bullets I'd taken.

When I opened the door, Piper wasn't waiting for me. She was under the table, looking at me like it was all my fault somehow.

22

Soccer Game Showdown

Lina

Naomi: Emergency meeting of the wedding brain trust. Can everyone make it to Waylay's soccer game tomorrow morning?

Stef: Why can't she play an evening sport? These early-morning Saturdays are messing with my Friday night social life.

Naomi: What social life? You still haven't asked Jer out yet. *chicken emoji*

Stef: Nobody likes a bridezilla, Witty.

Sloane: I can make it as long as we're hiding Bloody Marys in our cups.

Me: Sorry guys. I can't make it.

Naomi: *frowny face* Lina, you were too busy for lunch and you backed out of bridesmaid dress shopping this week. I'm afraid I have to enforce my bridal reign and insist that you join us . . . unless you really are doing something more important than discussing wedding party attire and traditional wedding cake versus a pastry table. Then I totally understand

and you should forget that I tried to make any demands on you.

Stef: Forgive Witty. She's been honored with a lifetime achievement award in people-pleasing.

Sloane: Can confirm that Lina did not have plans for Saturday morning as of last night when we picked up our Dino's to-go orders at the same time.

Naomi: It's official. Lina's avoiding us.

Stef: Let's kidnap her and find out why. Wait. Too soon for kidnapping jokes?

Me: Oh, THIS Saturday. I thought you meant some other Saturday. Who else is going?

Sloane: I second this question. I'm tired of showing up to places and running into Tall Dark and Pissy.

Stef: She means Sinful Suit Daddy.

Naomi: My parents, Liza J, and Knox will all be there. No other family members or friends are on the agenda.

Me: I guess I can make it. As long as you weren't kidding about the Bloody Marys.

"These leaves," my dad's voice boomed through the speakers of my SUV. "Never seen so many colors before. You should fly up for the weekend and check 'em out."

I made the turn into the gravel parking lot of

315

the soccer fields and inched my way through throngs of players and families.

"Fall is in full swing here too," I told him. "You'll never guess what I'm doing right now."

"Winning an award at work? No, wait. Taking ballroom dance lessons? Oh! I know, eating sushi while booking a plane ticket home to surprise me for my birthday?"

I winced. "Good guesses, but no. I'm going to a kid's soccer game."

"No kidding?"

"Bet you don't miss those early Saturday mornings in the cold," I said lightly. I watched a family of five, bundled up in layers of clothing, jog toward the fields.

Dad had always loved soccer. He'd lobbied a local sports bar in our neighborhood to air UK football matches long before David Beckham had set one golden boot in America. His love of the game was the reason I'd started playing as a kid. We'd drilled for hours in the backyard. He'd known every one of my teammates by name and was the team dad who made sure everyone got home safely from games and practices.

After the "incident," we'd all been affected in different ways.

Mom fluttered around me convinced I was one heartbeat away from death.

My return to "normal" had taken long enough I no longer had a place to belong to. So I'd focused all my energy on catching up academically with the aim of starting over someplace new.

As for my dad, I'd never seen him watch another soccer game.

"Apparently social occasions here are often paired with children's sporting events. My friend Knox asked me to be in his wedding, and I'm meeting with the bride to talk cake on the sidelines."

"A wedding? How long are you planning to stay there?"

"I'm not sure. This project work has me on is really dragging out."

"Well, if you can't come to us, we can always come to you."

"Everything is up in the air at the moment, but I might be heading home soon. I'll let you know."

"You doing okay? You sound a little down."

"I'm fine," I told him, unwilling to do a deep dive into why I'd spent the last several days swinging back and forth between mad and sad. "I've got to get going. It looks like the game's about to start."

"Okay, sweetheart. Oh, and one more thing. Your mom would kill me if I didn't ask. Everything good with the ticker?"

"Everything is fine," I said, forcing my exasperation into the box with my mad and sad.

Just a few emotional dings from a wounded, pissed-off officer of the law.

"I love you, Dad."

"Love you too, Leens."

I disconnected the call and slumped back on my heated seat. I'd preemptively called him to get it out of the way for the day. It was a constant balancing act of assuring my parents that I was alive and capable of taking care of myself while still giving myself the actual freedom to be an independent adult.

Having overly loving parents wasn't something that I could take for granted, but it also wasn't something I was thrilled about.

Reluctantly, I got out of the car and headed in the direction of the field, scanning the crowd for the man I hoped I'd never see again.

I'd successfully avoided Nash since he'd threatened to arrest me. My research team was running down Hugo's known associates and keeping an eye on vintage car auctions. I was still crossing properties off my list. In my downtime, I managed to survive another workout with Mrs. Tweedy and consulted on two other investigations at work.

Something needed to break and it needed to break soon or else I was going to have to do something I'd never done before: quit.

I found Naomi and Sloane in folding camp chairs under blankets on the sideline.

"There she is," Naomi said when I approached. She was holding a huge coffee in one hand and

318

an innocuous-looking tumbler in the other. "We brought you a chair."

"And alcohol," Sloane said, holding up a short red tumbler for me.

"Thanks." I took the offered drink and the chair. "Where's Stef?"

"He's getting, and I quote, 'all the coffee in the world.' He had a conference call with investors in Hong Kong about who knows what," Naomi said.

"What does Stef do for a living?" I asked, studying the crowd. Naomi's dad and Knox stood next to Wraith, a scary biker dude and dubious choice for a girls' soccer coach. The only tattoos visible on the silver fox today were poking out of the neck of his leather jacket. He stood on the sidelines, legs braced apart like he was ready to battle it out with a rival motorcycle club.

Knox, I noted, didn't bother to say hi. He merely glared at me before looking away.

Stupid Nash and his big, stupid mouth.

"No one really knows. He's like Chandler from *Friends*," Naomi said.

Sloane studied me from under her pom-pomed hat. It was black to match her mittens. "You always look like a badass video game heroine ready to kick down a door or grab a sexy gun-toting guy and bang him into oblivion."

Naomi sprayed a fine mist of coffee into the chilly air while I laughed.

"Uh, thanks? I think."

"Tell her about the dress," Sloane insisted.

"We put you in scarlet," Naomi told me. "It's very bombshell."

"You'll definitely get laid at the wedding in it," Sloane insisted.

"Is everything okay with you?" I asked her.

The librarian groaned dramatically and threw her head back. Which gave me an unobstructed view of Lucian Rollins approaching from behind her. His cashmere coat flapped in the wind like some kind of vampire cape. His gaze wasn't friendly. Especially not when it landed on me.

"Ugh. I need sex," Sloane announced, unaware that her nemesis was nearly within earshot. "Everywhere I look, I see potential sex. Naomi has this annoying, permanent orgasmic glow, and you look like you could walk into any room and leave with a guy in under five minutes."

"Then why aren't you hate-banging him?" I pointed and we all turned to stare at Lucian, who looked like a model in jeans, a sweater, and a ball cap.

"Damn it! Naomi, you said he wasn't coming!" Sloane hissed.

"He didn't tell me he was. I have no idea why he's here," she insisted.

"The man spends so much time next door and around town I'm starting to doubt that he has an actual job," Sloane complained.

"Next door?" I asked.

"Apparently Sloane and Lucian grew up next door to each other. Sloane bought her house from her parents when they moved, and Lucian kept his mom's place," Naomi explained.

"God knows why," Sloane muttered.

"Maybe he's here to have sex with you. Like some kind of dark sexy fairy granting dirty wishes," I teased.

I noticed Knox didn't bother greeting Lucian when he joined him. Looked like the pissed-off-ness was contagious.

"I'd rather go to the gynecologist *and* the dentist on the same day," Sloane said. "Besides, I have a date."

"You have a date?" Naomi shouted the question loud enough that all the men turned and stared at us.

Lucian looked like he was about to set the world on fire with his dark smolder.

"Thanks, mega mouth," Sloane muttered. "Yes. I have a date."

"A date or a hookup?" I asked at normal volume.

Lucian's hand closed into a fist, crushing his to-go cup and exploding coffee everywhere.

I grinned as he settled that dark and dangerous gaze on me. *Oops,* I mouthed smugly.

"Nothing to see here," Naomi said, making shooing motions with her hands. At least that was what I think she was trying to do. It was hard to tell with her double-fisting beverages. "Go about your business, gentlemen."

Knox shot his fiancée a wicked wink, then gave me a chilly look before turning his attention back to the field where the team was warming up.

"Uh, what's up with the silent treatment and steely stares?" Sloane asked.

"You're just trying to change the subject. Who are you hooking up with?"

Sloane looked over both shoulders and then gestured for us to lean closer. When we'd formed a vodka-breathed huddle, she cracked a smile. "I'll give you a hint. He's got a mustache and a badge."

"You're going out with Nolan? Nolan Graham? U.S. Marshal Nolan Graham?" I demanded.

"He's really cute," Naomi said.

"He's a great guy," I added.

"You two dated, right? Any red flags I need to know about before letting him go for the gold after the third date?" Sloane asked me.

"We had a very brief fling a few years back. He's a genuinely nice guy and he's a good dancer."

"Maybe he'll be my date to the wedding," Sloane mused.

The men were staring at us again. Make that glaring. Lucian looked like he couldn't decide if he hated me or Sloane more. Knox's expression was best described as resting pissed face.

"Okay, I get that Sloane and Lucian have this

hate fest going on, but what's with you and Knox?" Naomi asked, frowning at her husband. "He didn't say something mean and offensive to you, did he? He's supposed to be trying to get better at that."

I looked down at my drink. "As far as I know, everything is fine."

"Oh, look. Here comes Nash. I thought he had to work."

I nearly fell out of my chair and spilled my Bloody Mary whipping my head around.

"Damn it," I muttered and slumped lower in the chair when I spotted him. He was dressed in his uniform, towing Piper on a pink leash, and looking even more furious than Knox and Lucian combined. Nolan strolled along a few yards behind him, his phone to his ear.

"Ladies," Nash growled. His gaze landed on me and I made zero attempt to cover the fury he inspired in me.

"Morning, Nash," Naomi chirped.

"Hey, Chief," Sloane said.

"Thought I told you not to come around my family," Nash said to me.

Oh, goody. We were gonna go there. In public. With witnesses.

"I'd think long and hard about starting that conversation right now. Unless of course you want to air *all* the dirty laundry," I said, firing poisoned eyeball daggers at him.

Everyone stared at us as if Nash and I had just turned into a live-action telenovela in front of them.

"I said leave her alone, not be a dick to her," Knox snapped.

"I don't need you to defend me. Especially when you're not even speaking to me," I reminded him.

"Yeah, I'm gonna need an explanation immediately," Sloane said.

"I'm glad you came to your senses," Lucian said to Nash.

"Fuck off, Lucy," Nash snarled. "And fuck you too, Knox."

Amanda sidled over. "I smell drama. What's happening?"

"Everyone is mad at everyone else," Sloane said. "Will someone *please* explain what crawled up y'all's butts so I can choose a side? Spoiler alert: Team Not Lucian."

Lucian turned his steely eyed gaze on her. "I don't have the energy for you today, Sloane."

Naomi put her hand out to keep Sloane from launching herself out of her chair. "Listen, I can only handle one pair of feuding friends at a time." She turned to me. "What's going on with you and Nash? And you and Knox. And Lucian and, well, everyone."

They all turned to look at me. The women eyed me expectantly. The men looked at me with varying degrees of scowling faces. One of the team moms was aiming her phone in our direction, probably recording the whole thing.

Stef chose that moment to wander up with a coffee cup the size of a bucket. He stopped short when he sensed the standoff. "What'd I miss?"

"Lina's been lying to everyone," Nash announced.

It was go time. I was really good at go time. I wasn't one of those people who came up with their best zingers in the shower days after a confrontation. I was someone who fired back hard.

The only problem was, I didn't feel good about deploying his secret. Nash might be acting like a gigantic asshole, but I'd seen real pain beneath the surface, and I couldn't in good conscience break that trust. Unless of course he pushed me too far, in which case he only had himself to blame.

Naomi put one of her drinks down and reached over to squeeze my wrist. "If Lina's been less than truthful, then I'm guessing it's because she has a good reason for it."

It was such a Naomi thing to say. And she meant it. At least right now, before she heard the truth. But if anyone was going to share my truth, it should be me.

"I'm here looking for Duncan Hugo," I said.

Naomi's mom, Amanda, gasped theatrically.

Knox's nostrils flared as he swore under his breath. Lucian, of course, showed no outward reaction.

Sloane was the first to recover. "Why? What are you into, Lina?"

"It's work. I don't sell insurance. I recover stolen assets. Hugo stole something from a client and I tracked him to the area, not knowing that he was also wrapped up in other situations. I came to town just to see Knox for a day. But then everything happened."

"What did he steal?" Amanda asked. "I bet it was jewels. Was it jewels?"

"It was a car," I admitted.

"What kind of car?" Knox wanted to know.

"A 1948 Porsche 356 convertible."

He let out a low whistle. "Nice ride."

"She lied to all of us," Nash said, his words striking like a hammer. "She got you to put her up next door to me so she could get access to me and my files."

I could feel the adrenaline dumping into my system. My heart immediately fluttered over a beat, then another one. I brought the heel of my hand to my sternum and willed myself not to open my mouth to release the torrent of insults clogging my throat.

"What the fuck?" Knox said.

I braced for the end of my longest-running friendship. But he was looking at his brother.

"She didn't *make* me put her up in that apartment. I swung by the motel to pick her up for breakfast and found her hair spraying a roach the size of a fuckin' beaver," he continued. "I told her to pack her shit and she refused. We yelled at each other for a good half an hour while stompin' on a multigenerational roach fest before she agreed to move."

"Time out," Naomi said to her soon-to-be husband. "Viking, if that's not why you're mad at Nash and Lina, what got your boxer briefs in a twist?"

Knox smoothed a hand over her hair, the gentle gesture at odds with his stormy expression.

"I'm pissed because these two idiots didn't listen to the sense I was talkin'."

I took three healthy gulps of my Bloody Mary and began to plot my escape.

"What sense?" Stef asked, pulling up a chair and setting it as close to the action as possible.

"Seriously? Come on!" Knox gestured back and forth between me and Nash.

"You're gonna have to be more communicative than that, dear," Amanda told him.

"For fuck's sake. They can't get together." He pointed at Nash. "This idiot practically has 'put a fuckin' ring on it' tattooed on his fucking ass." Then he jerked his chin in my direction. "And that pain in the ass has 'love 'em and leave 'em' tattooed on hers."

Naomi leaned in and whispered, "Is he being literal or metaphorical?"

"Metaphorical. But I do have a sun tattooed on my shoulder blade."

Nash's eyes narrowed on me.

"They get together and it's time for her to go, he's gonna get his stupid heart broken and she's gonna feel bad about it. Then they'll both end up taking it out on me. So I told Nash to leave it be and then I find out he's climbing into bed with her."

"Everyone is having sex but me," Sloane muttered under her breath.

"Now things are getting good," Amanda said. She held out a hand to Stef.

"Agreed," he said, handing over his Bloody Mary.

"We weren't having sex and we definitely never will. You could have talked to me about it," I said to Knox.

He grimaced as if I'd just suggested he rip his toenails out and throw them around like confetti.

"Yeah, right, Leen," he scoffed. "Then we could have a heart-to-heart about our feelings and shit."

He had a point.

"Bad time?" Nolan wandered up in a windbreaker, holding a normal-sized coffee.

"Yes," Nash and I said in unison, which resulted in more glaring at each other.

He winked at Sloane. "Hey, cupcake. Looking forward to dinner."

The librarian gave him a flirty grin. Lucian growled.

"So if Lina and Nash aren't"—Naomi paused as part of Waylay's team jogged past the side-lines—"enjoying adult tickle time, which we are definitely going to revisit, by the way, why are you still mad at them?"

"Because *he's* acting like it's none of my business and *she* wasn't being honest with me. You coulda told me why you were here," Knox said to me.

I nodded. "I could have. Probably should have. Opening up doesn't come easy," I admitted.

"Sure don't mind when you're on the receiving end," Nash said.

"Keep pushing, Chief. They still haven't dug deep enough on you yet," I warned.

His glare would have incinerated me if I'd used more hair spray that morning.

"What the hell's that supposed to mean?" Sloane asked in a stage whisper.

"Hold on. We're not done yet. We haven't gotten to why Suit Daddy, I mean Lucian, is involved in such immature, emotional shenanigans," Stef pointed out.

"Come on in, Lucian. The water's warm," I said to him.

"Well, now you have to," Naomi said encouragingly.

"I knew there was something off with Lina's

329

story. And when Knox voiced his concerns about her, I did some digging. Then I tracked her down and threatened her."

He said it as casually as someone describing an amusing encounter at Target.

"Unbelievable," Sloane muttered under her breath.

"Lucian, that's not how we solve things," Amanda chided like he was a six-year-old mid temper tantrum.

"So Lucian was technically right and you're still mad at him?" Naomi asked.

Nash's answer was an irritated shrug.

She turned to Knox. "And you were right about Nash getting hurt and now you're both mad at each other for that."

"Well, breakfast didn't help," Knox admitted.

Naomi closed her eyes. "Is that why you were such a bridezilla with the florist yesterday?"

"Baby's breath is stupid. Fight me," he said.

"What happened at breakfast?" Stef asked.

"I invited Knox and Nash to breakfast to talk things out like mature adults," Lucian explained.

"You showed up unannounced and dragged me out of bed at six in the morning," Nash corrected.

"You're welcome," he shot back.

"Wait," Sloane interrupted. "You, Lucian Rollins, willingly tried to talk things out?"

His gaze was icy when it locked on to her. "I do when it's something that matters."

330

She got to her feet, vibrating so hard the pom-pom on her hat trembled. "You are the *worst* person I've ever met," she hissed. Sloane was usually much sharper with her insults.

Sensing impending violence, I jumped out of my chair and stepped between them before Sloane could charge. "He's got a lot of lawyers," I reminded her. "And as satisfying as it would be to punch the smirk off his face, I'd hate to see his legal team bankrupt you."

Sloane growled. Lucian showed his teeth in what was definitely not a smile.

"A little help here, Marshal?"

Nolan looped an arm around Sloane's waist and pulled her back. "How do you feel about standing all the way over here?" he asked her conversationally.

Lucian let out what sounded like a feral snarl and slammed his chest into my waiting hand. Even after I dug my heels in, he still managed to move me back nearly a foot before Nash pushed his way between us.

"Back the fuck off," Nash snapped, getting into Lucian's face.

"We're about to get thrown out of a kids' soccer game," I said to no one in particular.

"So how was the sex?" Stef asked me with a wicked grin.

"For the love of God! We *didn't have sex*. We never even kissed," I snapped.

"So you were just sleeping together?" Amanda asked. "Is that a new thing with you youngsters? Friends with partial benefits? Netflix and cuddle?"

"Definitely not friends," I said, glaring at Nash. "And unlike some others, I respect people's privacy, especially when it comes to things they've shared in confidence."

Damn, it felt good to take the high road. Especially knowing Nash's family was about to pry the truth out of him with a crowbar. That made it even more satisfying.

A barrage of questions was immediately volleyed at the man.

"You seriously just slept? What's up with that?"

"Does this have somethin' to do with you bein' depressed?"

"You're depressed? Why didn't you say something?"

"Was it naked sleeping or were there pajamas?"

"Excuse me, people!"

Everyone turned to find Waylay standing on the sidelines, hands on hips. Her team was lined up behind her, trying and mostly failing to stifle giggles.

"We're tryin' to play a game out here but you guys are distracting everyone!" she said.

We all managed to mumble a chorus of apologies.

"If I have to come over here again, you're all in

trouble," Waylay said, making eye contact with each of us.

"Jeez, when did she get scary?" Sloane whispered when Waylay and the rest of the team returned to the field.

"I blame you," Knox and Naomi said at the same time. They grinned at each other.

My heart tripped unevenly again and I took a deep breath, blowing it out slowly until the fluttering in my chest dissipated.

"You okay?" Nash asked, not sounding like he cared that much. "Or was that a lie too?"

"Don't. Start," I warned him.

"What's happening now?" Naomi whispered.

I needed to get out of here. I needed to go someplace where I could breathe and think and not want to punch stupid sexy men in their stupid sexy faces. I needed to call my boss and quit this investigation. Not only was I basically compromised, the thought of sticking around Knockemout, now just another place I didn't belong, actually hurt.

"Sit down, Angelina," Nash ordered. He was still pissed, but his tone was a degree or two gentler.

"What's wrong?" Knox demanded.

"I'm sure Nash will be happy to fill you in," I said, then turned to Naomi and Sloane. "You two have been nothing but wonderful since I got here and I'll always be grateful for that. You deserve better from me and for that I'm sorry. Thank you for the friendship and good luck with the wedding." I handed Sloane my Bloody Mary.

My heart tripped again and then again. My vision went spotty for the moment it took to resume a normal beat.

No more caffeine. Or red meat. Or man-induced stress, I promised myself. I'd open my meditation app and do yoga after every run. I would practice breathing exercises every hour on the hour and take nature walks. I would get the hell out of Knockemout and never look back.

I didn't trust myself to say a more official goodbye, so I just started walking toward the parking lot.

"Lina," Nash called after me. Not Angelina. Not Angel. Now it was just Lina.

I ignored him. The sooner I forgot Nash Morgan existed, the better.

I increased my speed and cut across a now empty soccer field. I didn't quite make it to half field before a hand closed around my elbow.

"Lina, stop," Nash ordered.

I jerked free. "We have nothing left to say to each other and we have no reason left to concern ourselves with each other."

"Your heart—"

"Is *none* of your damn business," I hissed.

A series of flutters had my vision going dark

around the edges and I willed myself not to let it show.

"Okay. I'm inserting myself in here with great reluctance," Nolan said, jogging up.

"Butt out, Graham," Nash snapped.

Nolan took off his sunglasses. "My job is to protect you, dumbass. And you are one point five seconds away from having your face punched in by a very angry woman."

"I'm not letting you get behind the wheel if you're not okay," Nash said to me, ignoring the U.S. marshal standing between us.

"I've never been better," I lied.

He tried to take another step toward me, but Nolan put a hand to his chest.

I turned and headed for the parking lot. I was halfway to my car when I felt attention on me. I spotted a guy with a mustache and a KPD ball cap leaning against a set of bleachers, arms crossed, mean in his eyes.

23

Team Lina

Lina

I was trying to stuff the last sweater into my overflowing suitcase when there was a knock at my door. I would have ignored it as I had all the other knocks on my door since yesterday's soccer game truth bomb if it hadn't also been accompanied by a barrage of text messages.

> **Sloane:** It's us. Let us in.
> **Naomi:** We come in peace.
> **Sloane:** Hurry up before we make enough noise to alert your grumpy neighbor.

I was not up for company, emotional blackmail, or another round of apologizing.

> **Naomi:** I should add that Knox gave me the master key so we're coming in no matter what. You might as well make it your choice.

Damn it.

I threw the sweater on the bed and headed for the door.

"Hi," they said cheerfully when I opened it.

"Hi."

"Thanks, we *will* come in," Sloane announced, giving the door a shove.

"If you've come to do battle, I'm all out of energy," I warned.

I'd spent the half the night defrosting frozen vegetables on my chest while listening to guided meditations and trying to will the stress from my body.

"We're here to tell you that we picked a side," Naomi said. She was wearing tight-fitting jeans and a silk blouse the color of emeralds. Her hair was curled in loose waves that framed her pretty face.

"A side of what?"

"We've given it a lot of thought and we're Team Lina," Sloane said. She too was nicely dressed for a casual Sunday afternoon. She was wearing distressed jeans, heels, and a damn good smoky eye. "I wanted to make T-shirts, but Naomi thought it would be better if we just showed up and took you out."

"Took me out?" I repeated. "Like to murder me?"

"No homicides, I promise," Naomi said, heading toward my bedroom. "Why is there a packed suitcase in here?"

"Because I can't carry all my clothes in my hands."

"You were right not to wait on the T-shirts," Sloane said, following Naomi into my room.

Naomi started pawing through my suitcase. "This is cute. Oh, and definitely these jeans."

"Are you robbing me?" I knew Knockemout was a little rough around the edges but this seemed excessive.

"You're getting dressed and we're going out for a girls' plus Stef afternoon, possibly night, depending on how much alcohol and fried food is consumed," Sloane said, handing me a pair of jeans and a red sweater with a plunging neckline.

"We're still working on the name," Naomi added.

"But I wasn't honest with you. I kept things from you," I pointed out, wondering if perhaps they'd forgotten my treason.

"Friends give friends the benefit of the doubt. Maybe you had a good reason for not being honest. Or maybe you've never had awesome friends like Sloane and me," Naomi said, tossing me my gigantic cosmetic bag. "Either way, what kind of friends would we be if we left you when you needed us most?"

"So you're not mad at me?" I asked slowly.

"We're concerned," Naomi corrected.

"And we really want more details on you sleeping with Nash," Sloane added with a playful eyebrow wriggle.

"He's miserable, by the way," Naomi said, pointing in the direction of the bathroom.

"His state of misery is none of my business," I insisted.

He'd knocked on my door twice yesterday after the disaster at the soccer game. The third time, he'd threatened to break it in if I didn't at least confirm that I was okay.

To save the expense of replacing the door, I'd texted him a succinct *I'm fine. Fuck off.*

"Hurry up and get ready. We can't drink all day if we don't start now," Sloane said, examining another sweater. "Hey, can I borrow this for my date with Nolan?"

And that was how I ended up at Hellhound, a dingy biker bar, on a Sunday afternoon with Team Lina.

The music was loud. The floor was sticky. The pool tables were all taken. And there were more wallets on chains than off.

"This place still makes me want to use a bucket of Pine-Sol and a pallet of Lysol before sitting down," Naomi complained as we bellied up to the bar.

Stef grimaced and rolled up the sleeves of his Alexander McQueen sweater before resting his forearms gingerly on the wood. "Well, hello, hot bartender," he said under his breath.

Joel, the gentlemanly bartender, was tall,

muscly, facial hair-y, and decked out in head to toe black. His hair was a mane of silver swept back from his tanned face. "Welcome back, ladies," he said with a smirk of recognition. "I see you brought a new friend along."

Naomi introduced Stef.

"What'll it be? Shots? Liquor? Wine?"

"Shots," Sloane said.

"Wine?" Naomi asked.

"Definitely wine," Stef agreed.

Joel's gray eyes came to me. "I'll have water."

"Booooooo!" Naomi and Sloane said together.

Stef frowned at me. "Do you have a head injury?"

"I'll get started on those drinks. Try not to punch anyone in the meantime," Joel cautioned mostly me.

"You're not drinking," Sloane said.

"Water is a drink."

"What Sloane means is why are you hydrating instead of being irresponsible and ordering adult beverages?" Naomi said.

"One of us has to drive," I pointed out.

"One of us has a sexy as hell fiancé ready and waiting to pick up our charmingly intoxicated selves," Naomi explained.

"Knox didn't give you shit about coming back here?" I asked.

The last and, well, only time we'd been here had been the day I arrived in town. Knox and Naomi were in the midst of a breakup that neither knucklehead actually wanted. I'd whisked Naomi away from her shift at Honky Tonk and brought her here to the diviest of dive bars.

Sloane had joined us and the day almost ended in a bar fight when some of the dumber, drunker patrons thought they had an actual chance with us.

"That's why Stef's here," Naomi explained.

"He made me promise to send an update every thirty minutes," Stef said, holding up his phone.

"Is he still mad at me?" I asked, trying to sound like I didn't care.

"He will be if he finds out you were planning on leaving town without telling any of us," Naomi said.

This was why I didn't have friends. Relationships of all kinds were too sticky. Everyone felt they had a right to tell you what you were doing was wrong and give you instructions on how to fix it to their liking.

"I wasn't leaving town. I was going to move back to the motel and *then* leave town."

"As your friend, I can't in good conscience let you get a roach-borne disease when there's a perfectly nice, clean apartment available to you," Naomi insisted.

"I'd rather live with roaches than next door to Nash."

Joel returned with our drinks. Two shots of God knows what for Sloane, two wineglasses filled to the brim, and a water with a lemon garnish.

Sloane made grabby hands at the shots.

"Thanks, Joel," I said as he set the water down in front of me.

"You doin' okay?" he asked me.

"I'm fine."

"Errrrr!" Sloane, already one shot down, made a loud buzzer noise. "It's against the law to lie during girls plus Stef afternoon."

Naomi nodded. "Agreed. Rule number one: No lying. We aren't here to pretend everything is fine. We're here to be here for each other. I said here too many times. Now it doesn't sound like a word. Here. Here?"

"Here." Sloane tried frowning.

"They been drinking already?" Joel asked me with the arch of a sexy silver eyebrow.

I shook my head. "Nope."

He wisely filled two more glasses with water and set them in front of my friends before disappearing down the bar.

"Heeeeeere," Naomi enunciated.

"Oh my God. Fine! I'm *not* fine," I admitted.

"It's about damn time. I was afraid you were going to make us keep going," Sloane said, picking up her second shot and downing it.

"The first step is admitting you're a disaster," Stef said sagely.

"I'm not fine. I am a disaster. Even my family doesn't know what I do for a living because they

342

can't handle the thought of me anywhere near even the slightest whiff of danger. If they had any idea how dangerous my job is, they would fly out here, form a protective shield around me, and force me to move home with them."

My tiny personal audience all watched me over the rims of their glasses.

"And I'm drinking water because I had a heart condition that almost killed me when I was fifteen. I missed out on all the normal teenage things thanks to surgeries and being the weird girl who died in front of an entire stadium of people. It's fixed now, but I still get PVCs when I'm stressed. And I'm stressed as hell now. Every stupid flutter reminds me what it was like to almost die and then live a suffocating half-life of homeschooling, medical appointments, and overbearing parents who I couldn't blame for being overbearing because they watched me essentially die on a soccer field."

"Whoa," Sloane said.

"More alcohol, Joel," Naomi begged, holding up her now empty wineglass.

"So excuse me if I don't tell everyone I meet all the details of my life. I spent enough of it being micromanaged and reminded that I'm not normal and I won't ever have normal. Until I got here and I met Nashhole."

"Good one," Sloane said with an approving nod.

"What happened when you got here and met Nash? Sorry. I mean Nashhole?" Naomi asked, hanging on my every word.

"I took one look at him and his whole wounded, broody *thing*—"

"By 'thing,' do you mean penis?" Stef asked.

"I do not."

"Stop interrupting her," Naomi hissed. "You took one look at his wounded, broody not-penis and what?"

"I *liked* him," I confessed. "I really liked him. He made me feel like I was special and not in the weird cardiac-arrest-in-front-of-everyone way. He made me feel like he needed me. No one's ever needed me. They've always protected me or babied me or avoided me. God, my parents are trying to book plane tickets just to bully their way into my next cardiology appointment so they can hear my doctor say I'm still fine."

More drinks appeared in front of Naomi and Sloane. Joel slid a bowl of nuts my way. "Those are fresh out of the bag. No one fingered them up yet," he assured me.

"Thank you for the unfingered nuts," I said.

"So Nash came clean—after some berating—about the panic attacks he's been having and how you helped him," Naomi said.

"I didn't take advantage of him," I insisted.

"Honey, we know. No one thinks that. Not even Nash. He's a Morgan. They say stupid things when they're mad. But I have to tell you, it's nice to see him mad," Naomi confessed.

"Why?"

"Before you, he wasn't mad or happy or anything. He was like a photocopy of himself. Just flat, lifeless. And then along came you and you gave him something to care enough about to get mad."

"I lied to him. I lied to all of you."

"And now you'll do better," Naomi said, as if it were that simple.

"I will?"

"If you want to stay friends you will," Sloane said. Three shots in and she was already listing to one side like she was on the deck of a ship.

"Friends make friends better. We accept the bad parts, celebrate the good parts, and we don't torture you for your mistakes," Naomi said.

"I'm sorry I wasn't honest with you," I said softly.

"It kind of makes sense now at least," Sloane pointed out. "If I had to lie to my parents about everything just to lead a somewhat normal life, I can see how easily that would turn into a habit."

"I get it," Naomi said sympathetically. "I did lie to my parents about everything when I first got here because I was trying to protect them from my mess and Tina's mess."

"I know the feeling." I stirred my straw around

the water. "I actually let myself start to ask 'what if?' "

"What if what?" Stef asked.

"What if it worked out with him? What if I stayed here? What if this was the sign I'd been looking for to quit my job and try something new? What if I could actually have normal?"

Naomi and Sloane were staring at me with wide, watery eyes.

"Don't," I warned.

"Oh, Lina," Naomi whispered.

"I know you don't like to be touched, and I respect that," Sloane said. "But I think you should know that I'm hugging you in my mind."

"Okay. No more shots for you," I decided.

They both continued to stare at me like big doe-eyed, needy cartoon characters. "Make it stop," I begged Stef.

He shook his head. "There's only one way to make it stop."

I rolled my eyes. "Ugh, fine. You can hug me. But don't spill anything on me."

"Yay!" Sloane said.

They hugged me from both sides. There, sandwiched between a drunk librarian and a tipsy community relations director, I felt just a little bit better. Stef patted me awkwardly on the head.

"You deserve to be happy and have normal," Naomi said, pulling back.

"I don't know what I deserve. Nash hit pretty much every shame and guilt button I have."

"He dropped a truth bomb on me at one of Waylay's games earlier this season," Naomi sympathized.

"Thank God the season's almost over," Stef joked.

"You know why honesty is so important to him, don't you?" Naomi asked me.

I shrugged. "I guess it's important to everyone."

"Knox and Nash's dad is an addict. Duke started using drugs—mostly opioids—after their mom died. Knox said every day with their dad felt like a lie. He'd swear he was sober or promise he'd never use again. He'd commit to picking them up after school or tell them he'd be at their football games. But he just kept letting them down. Over and over again. One lie after another."

"That sucks," I admitted. My upbringing had its challenges . . . you know, like dying in front of all my friends and their families. But that didn't compare to how Knox and Nash had grown up. "However, unpopular opinion here. You're not responsible for how you were brought up, but you *are* responsible for your actions and reactions once you're an adult."

"That's true," Naomi admitted before guzzling more wine.

"The beautiful woman with the very long legs

has a point," Sloane said. "How tall are you anyway? Let's measure!"

I nudged her glass of water closer. "Maybe you should give the shots a break."

"Let's follow this train of thought," Stef announced. "You went through a shit time as a teenager, which thanks to puberty is already horrible."

"Fair."

"Stick with me here," he continued. "So you grow up, move away, become fiercely independent, and take a dangerous job. Why?"

"Why?" I repeated. "I guess to prove that I'm strong. That I'm not the same weak, helpless girl I used to be."

"You are a badass," Stef agreed.

"To badasses," Naomi said, hefting her nearly empty wineglass.

"Save the toast, Witty. I'm about to blow your minds," Stef insisted.

"Blow away," Sloane said, resting her chin in her hands.

"Who are you proving yourself to?" Stef asked me.

I shrugged. "Everyone?"

Stef pointed at Sloane. "Make the buzzer noise again."

"Errrrrrrr!"

Half the bar turned to look at us.

"I take it you don't agree?" I prompted Stef.

"Here comes my brilliance. If your family doesn't know what you do for a living, they are unaware of your professional badassery. And if your colleagues don't know about your history, they have no idea how impressive you really are because they don't know what you had to overcome to get here."

"What's your point?"

"The only one left to prove anything to is you. And if you don't realize what a strong, capable badass you are, you haven't been paying attention."

"That felt a little anticlimactic. But he's not wrong," Naomi said.

"Not done yet," Stef said. "I think you aren't actually trying to prove that you're a badass. I think you spend all your energy trying to smother any hint of vulnerability."

"Ooooooh! And Nash makes you feel vulnerable," Sloane guessed gleefully.

"So you sabotage any chance at real intimacy because you don't want to be vulnerable again," Naomi added. "Okay. *That* was climactic."

Stef gave a mock bow. "Thank you for appreciating my genius."

I'd been vulnerable before. Flat on my back on that soccer field. In all those hospital beds. In that operating room. I couldn't protect myself or save myself. I was at the mercy of other people, my life in their hands.

I shook my head. "Hang on. Vulnerability is

weakness. Why would I ever want to be weak again? Back me up here, Joel."

The bartender's gaze flicked to me as he sent two shot glasses sliding down the bar to a customer with a pink mohawk.

"Being vulnerable doesn't mean you're weak. It means you trust yourself to be strong enough to handle the hurt. It's actually the purest form of strength."

Sloane wiggled her fingers at her temples and made an exploding sound. "Mind officially blown," she slurred.

"That was fuckin' beautiful, Joel," the biker with the mohawk said. The man mopped at his eyes with a drink napkin.

I'd spent my entire adult life proving I was invincible, capable, independent. I lived alone, worked alone, took vacations alone. The only way I could get more independent was if I entered into a monogamous relationship with my vibrator. To be told I was taking the coward's way out didn't sit well with me.

"Look, I appreciate the super fun game of 'let's analyze what's wrong with Lina.' But the fact is, every time I have to operate within the bounds of a relationship, whether it's personal or professional, people get hurt."

"That doesn't mean you can't be in a relationship. It just means you're not good at it," Naomi said, gesturing with her wine.

"Gee, thanks," I said dryly.

Naomi held up a finger and drained her glass. "*Nobody* is good at it at first. No one has a natural talent for being in a relationship. Everyone has to learn how to be good at it. It takes a lot of practice and forgiveness and vulnerability."

"Shit," Stef muttered. He stood and squared his shoulders. "If you ladies will excuse me, I need to make a phone call. Mind keeping an eye on them, Joel?"

The bartender threw him a salute.

"It's not just that I'm bad at relationships," I said, returning to the original point. "I don't want to be tied down. I want to be free to do what I want. To pursue a life that suits me."

"I don't think those things have to be mutually exclusive."

"Boom!" Sloane said, slapping a hand to the bar. The more she drank, the louder the librarian's sound effects got.

"I'm not going to find a man out there who's going to be content following me around, working remotely in shitty motels while I track down stolen goods. And if I did, I probably wouldn't want him."

Naomi hiccupped.

"Seriously? You too? Did you guys pregame before you came to get me?" I asked.

She shrugged and grinned. "I made a wrap for lunch and Waylon stole it off my plate when I wasn't looking. I'm an empty stomach lightweight."

I slid the bowl of nuts in her direction. "Soak up that alcohol."

A tall biker with an eye patch and a bandanna sauntered up.

"No," I said when he opened his mouth.

"You didn't even know what I was going to say," he complained.

"No we don't want a date, a ride, or for you to tell us your penis's nickname," I said.

Sloane raised her hand. "Actually, I'd like to know the penis nickname."

The biker puffed out his chest and hiked up his pants. "It's Long John Silver . . . cause it's pierced. Now, who wants a personal introduction?"

"Happy now?" I asked Sloane.

"I'm both happy and disgusted."

I turned back to the biker. "Go away unless you want to become part of a therapy session."

"Hit the road, Spider," Joel said from behind the bar.

"Try to get a little action and everybody gets pissy," Spider muttered as he stomped away.

"Wait, I think I was about to make a super smart point," Naomi said. She scrunched up her nose and, deep in thought, mainlined the rest of her wine. "Aha!"

"Aha!" Sloane echoed.

Naomi wiggled on her stool and cleared her

throat. "As I was saying, you're comparing what you're doing now to what you could be doing in the future."

"Um, isn't that what *everyone* does?"

"There's a subtle difference," she insisted, slurring a little on the word *subtle*. "But I forget what it is."

Sloane leaned in on my other side. Well, more like fell into the bar. "What my esteemed colleague is trying to say is that just because you want the freedom to make your own choices doesn't mean you have to be alone."

Naomi snapped her fingers in Sloane's face. "Yes! That! That's what I forgot. What you do or have and how you *feel* are two separate constructs. For instance, people will say 'I want a million dollars,' but what they really want is to feel financially secure."

"Okaaaaaaay." I drew out the word.

"You want to feel like you have the power to make your own decisions. That doesn't mean that you have to stay an independent bounty hunter lady forever. Or that you have to not find a great guy to have hot sex and takeout dinners in bed with. It just means that you have to find a relationship where you can be yourself and make sure your needs are met."

"I'm glad you remembered, because that's a very smart point and you're very pretty," Sloane said to Naomi.

"Thank you. I think you make smart pretty too!"

"Aww! Group hug!"

"You guys are abusing your hug privileges," I complained as they both fell on me again.

"We can't help it. We're really proud of you," Naomi said.

"Want me to spray them down?" Joel offered, holding up the soda hose.

I sighed. "Let them have their moment."

24

Pecan Pie Punch and Pointy Elbows

Lina

I don't wanna go home," Sloane whined as I steered her toward my car in the parking lot.

"I'm hungry," Naomi sang.

"Where do you think you're going?" I asked Stef as he began to peel off from us.

He looked guilty and nervous. "I, uh, called Jeremiah and asked him if he wanted to grab dinner. And he said yes. So . . . I'm going to dinner with a hot barber."

Naomi pounced on him. "I'm. So. Proud. Of. You," she said, slapping him in the chest on each word.

He rubbed his pectorals. "Ow."

"Text us every thirty seconds. Better yet, live-stream your date!" Sloane said, bouncing on her toes.

"Oooh! Yes! We'll comment and let you know if we think it's going well," Naomi chimed in.

"You sure you can handle the tipsy twins?" Stef asked me.

"No. But—"

"I'm pretending you said yes," he said, backing away with a wicked grin.

"Have fun and try not to scare him off," I called after him.

Maybe Stef was ready to get crushed like a spotted lantern fly, but I still wasn't convinced that vulnerability was the ultimate strength. It sounded to me more like the ultimate way to get your heart trampled.

Sloane grabbed Naomi's arm and they both almost went down. "Oh my God. We forgot to tell her the other thing."

"Tell who what? Am I her?" I asked, steadying them on their feet.

Naomi gasped, releasing a cloud of chardonnay-scented breath. "I totally forgot! We had an idea on who you could talk to about where Duncan Hugo might hide a car."

"Really? Who?"

"Grim," Naomi said.

"What's a grim?"

"He's a motorcycle club leader . . . er, boss? Maybe prime minister? Anyway, he knows everything that happens," Naomi said.

"He knew where Naomi was when she got kidnapped because he was watching Duncan Hugo," Sloane filled in.

"Also, he's super nice and taught me how to play poker," Naomi added.

"How do I reach this motorcycle club prime minister Grim?" I asked.

"I have his number. Or a number. I never called

it, but he gave it to me," Naomi explained.

Sloane's eyes lit up as if inspiration had just struck. "You guys! I know this place with the best pecan pie in the universe."

Naomi squealed. "I *love* pie."

"Is it within the tristate area?" I asked.

I returned to the table just as the server delivered three slices of what admittedly looked like a pretty damn good pecan pie.

"Did you talk to sexy, dangerous biker guy?" Sloane asked.

"I did not." I'd called the number Naomi gave me, but after three rings, there was a beep. I'd left a vague message requesting a call back, not even knowing if it was recording what I said.

"Ohmygoodness," Naomi said with her fork still in her mouth. "This is the *best* pie ever."

I sat down and was just picking up my fork when my phone rang. I looked at the screen.

"Shit."

"Is it him?" my friends demanded in high-pitched unison.

"It's not," I assured them and slid out of my chair again.

"Hey, Lewis," I answered, heading past the host station to the vestibule. "How's it going?"

"Great. Good. Okay. Well, kind of shit actually," my coworker said.

Guilt manifested itself as an instant tension headache. "I heard you were back to work."

"Desk duty," he clarified. "Which is part of the problem. I have a situation here and need your help."

Yet another reason why I didn't do relationships.

"What do you need, Lew?"

"Yeah, so remember that time I jumped off a roof and broke my ass?"

I winced. "I remember." Vividly.

"And remember how you said if you could do anything to help me, you would?"

"Vaguely," I said through clenched teeth. Behind me, Naomi and Sloane had struck up a conversation with an elderly couple wearing matching sweatshirts.

"Today's your lucky day," Lewis announced.

I sighed. "What do you need?"

"I got an FTA who just popped up on the grid in your neck of the woods."

FTA was bounty hunter speak for "failure to appear," a label slapped on people who skipped out on court dates, endangering the money bail bonds companies coughed up for their freedom. "You know I switched to assets for a reason," I reminded him.

I'd paid my dues for one very long year as a bail enforcement agent before making the switch to asset recovery investigations.

"Yeah, but you're so good at it. More importantly, you're right there. I can't get anyone else there before tomorrow."

"I'm in charge of two intoxicated women right now. I can't just leave them to fend for themselves. They'll end up with matching tattooed eye shadow."

"Take them along. This guy isn't dangerous. He's just stupid. Well, technically he's crazy smart, which makes him stupid."

I was familiar with the type.

"Show your friends how Legs Solavita runs down a bad guy."

"What did he skip on?"

"A two-million-dollar bond."

"Two million? What the hell did he do?"

"Hacked into the state's DMV, created a bunch of fake IDs, then sold them online."

Computer nerds were generally less dangerous to apprehend than, say, murderers or other violent offenders. All you had to do was grab their laptop and then use it to lure them into the back seat of your car. But I still wasn't taking chances with my very new, very drunk friends.

"I don't think it's a good idea, Lew."

"Look. I hate to play this card, but you owe me. I'll split the payout with you."

"I hate you and your busted ass." I groaned. "I'll do it tomorrow."

"Actually, it's gotta be in the next hour. He's

skipping town and I don't know where he'll land next. I need him in custody."

"Damn it, Lew." I peered through the glass at Naomi and Sloane. "You swear he's not dangerous?"

"I'd send my own grandma to pick him up if she lived closer."

I sighed. "Fine. But this means we're even."

"Even Steven," he promised.

"And no more jokes about me busting your ass," I added.

"I'll text you the address and a pic. Thank you. You're the best. I'm hanging up now before you change your mind. Bye!" he said quickly before disconnecting the call.

Swearing under my breath, I headed back inside, my headache blooming like a damn rose.

"Hey, Lina Bo-Bina! Want some fries?" Sloane asked.

I looked at the table. Naomi and Sloane had eaten their pie and my pie and then moved on to the French fries the elderly couple left behind.

I flagged down the server. "Can I give you a hundred-dollar tip to babysit these two while I go run an errand?"

She blew her auburn bangs out of her face. "Sorry, honey. I'm not falling for that one again." She pointed to a sign on the wall. It read, UNATTENDED DRUNKS WILL BE ARRESTED.

Crap.

"What's wrong, Lina Weena?" Naomi asked. "You look sad."

"Or constipated," Sloane added. "Do you need more fiber in your diet?"

"I need to go to work for an hour or so and I don't know what to do with you two. How do you feel about checking into a hotel and sitting quietly in a room until I get back?"

Sloane gave me a thumbs-up, then flipped it upside down and blew a raspberry.

"I'll take that as a no."

"Did you find Huncan Dugo?" she asked. Her glasses were askew.

"No. I have to find another person for a coworker."

"Let us help! I'm so good at finding stuff. Yesterday, Knox looked for the ketchup for ten minutes in the refrigerator and I found it in half a second!" Naomi announced.

"Thanks, but I don't want your help. I want you two to stay out of the way while I go catch a bail jumper. Do you think you could pretend to be sober for as long as it takes Knox to drive down here and pick you up?"

They exchanged glances, then shook their heads and dissolved into giggles.

"I'll take that as a no."

"We're coming with you," Naomi said firmly.

"No, you're not," I said just as firmly and without slurring.

"I *told* you to stay in the car," I said as I muscled my FTA down the sidewalk. My face hurt, my hip ached, I was sweating profusely, and my favorite sweater was ruined.

"Sorry," Naomi said, trying to look contrite.

"We helped you catch him," Sloane said defiantly. Naomi elbowed her. "Oh, I mean, sorry."

"I should have left town when I had the chance," I muttered as I limped around the block.

"Ow! These zip ties hurt!"

Melvin Murtaugh, a.k.a. ShadowReaper, was no violent criminal. The second he'd seen me reach for my restraints, he'd bolted out of the kegger his cousin was hosting. I'd followed him out the back, off the rickety porch, and down the alley.

The kid was wearing sneakers and I was in heeled boots, but my athletic prowess and cardio endurance were way more effective in a footrace than his keyboard skills.

He'd also made the monumental mistake of pausing at the alley entrance, distracted by something.

That "something" turned out to be Naomi and Sloane playing drunken sidekicks.

It had given me enough time to tackle him to the ground. I was getting rusty. I used to know exactly how to execute a tackle while using the tacklee as a cushion for landing. This time, my hip and shoulder had made direct, painful contact with the asphalt while my face had bounced off Melvin's sharp elbow.

This was why I'd switched from bounties to asset recovery. People were too much a pain in the ass . . . and face.

"Where are my glasses? I can't see anything without my glasses!"

"You should have thought of that before you ran when I told you not to," I told him, sounding like an annoyed mother dealing with a teenage son who never bothered to pick his underwear up off the floor.

I hooked my hand in the back of his shirt and marched us all back to the car. Thank goodness it wasn't a neighborhood overrun with car thieves, because my two drunken charges had left the Charger's doors wide open.

"Oops," Naomi said when she spotted the car. "I guess we forgot to close the doors."

"It was the thrill of the chase," Sloane said.

"You weren't supposed to be part of the chase. You were supposed to wait in the car. And you," I said, tightening my grip on the squirmy hacker, "were supposed to make your court date."

"If I go to court, they're going to send me to jail," he whined.

"Uh, yeah. That's what's supposed to happen when you commit a felony."

He groaned. "My mom is gonna kill me."

"That was so badass the way you flying tackled him," Sloane said, entering the conversation. "Can you teach me how to do that?"

"No," I said tersely and shoved Melvin into the back seat by his head. "Stay." I shut the door and turned back to my friends, who did not look nearly contrite enough. "This is a dangerous job. You're not trained to handle these kinds of situations. So when I tell you to stay in the car, you *stay in the car*."

"Friends don't let friends be in danger alone," Naomi said sternly. "When Waylay and I were abducted, you and Sloane showed up for us. Sloane and I just showed up for you."

"The difference is, I wasn't abducted, Naomi. I was doing my job. Well, I was doing Lewis's job. But I've been trained for this. I have experience in these situations. Neither of you do."

Sloane pouted. "Don't you even want to know how we distracted him?"

"I threw a bag of dog poop I found on the sidewalk at him." Naomi preened.

That explained the smell. I was definitely going to need to have my car detailed.

"And I yelled and flashed him my boobs," Sloane announced proudly.

If it had been any two other civilians, I would have been impressed. But all I could think of was the fact that Naomi and Sloane willingly put themselves in danger for me. And that I now had to make a phone call I really didn't want to make.

I sighed. "I have to make a call. Stay here and keep an eye on Melvin. Do not get in the car. Do not wander away. Do not befriend any homicidal maniacs roaming the streets."

"She's just mad because she didn't get any pie," Sloane whispered to Naomi as I dialed.

Knox picked up on the first ring.

"What's wrong? Why isn't Stef sending updates anymore, and why isn't my fiancée answering my texts?"

"Nothing's wrong. Stef had to leave early, and as for Naomi"—I glanced over my shoulder to where Naomi and Sloane were posing for selfies—"she's not answering your texts because she and Sloane are busy trying out all the Snapchat filters."

"Why are you calling? Aren't we pissed at each other?"

"I'm not sure. I can't keep up."

"Good. Then if we were fighting, let's call it over."

This is why I liked being friends with men. It was just easier.

"Agreed. I need a favor. Two actually. I need you to not get justifiably pissed off, and I need a ride for two intoxicated women who refuse to listen to me."

"What's wrong with your car?"

"It's currently occupied by a criminal master-mind in zip ties."

"Fuck."

"If you let me go, I'll hack into the IRS so you never have to pay taxes again," Melvin offered from the back seat.

"Don't talk," I growled.

With the windows down, wind buffeted us from all sides at highway speeds. It helped with the smell of dog shit.

"That beardy tattoo guy looked like he was going to rip my arms off and beat me to death with them. I thought he was going to break the glass just to get to me."

As predicted, Knox had not been happy. First with me for allowing Naomi and Sloane to talk me into bringing them along, then with Naomi and Sloane for deliberately putting themselves in harm's way, and finally with Melvin for smashing my face.

I hadn't taken a good look in the mirror yet, but judging from Knox's reaction and the hot, swollen feeling under my eye, I guessed I didn't look so great.

"That's how he usually looks," I assured him.

"He blamed me for your face. Can you believe that? I didn't hit you," Melvin scoffed.

"Your flailing elbow did."

"Your face hit my flailing elbow. I'm probably going to have a bruise too."

I pushed down on the accelerator and hoped the responding roar of rpms would drown out my passenger. The sooner I could turn this guy in, the sooner I could go ice my entire body.

"I'll be sure to send a doctor to your cell," I said dryly.

"Where are you taking me?"

"The Knockemout Police Department." It wasn't ideal, but FTAs needed to be handed over to police custody, and Knockemout was the closest fully staffed department. Also, I may have called ahead to give them a heads-up . . . and to make sure that Nash was off tonight.

The last thing I needed was a run-in with him.

"Can we at least listen to some music?" Melvin grumbled.

"Yes, we can." I turned up the stereo and took the exit for Knockemout.

We were two miles from town limits when red and blue lights lit up my rearview mirror.

I glanced down at the speedometer and winced.

"Ha! Busted," my passenger snickered.

"Shut up, Melvin."

I pulled over onto the shoulder of the road, put my hazard lights on, and dug out my registration by the time the officer got to my window.

When Nash Morgan shined his flashlight in my eyes, I knew this was not my night.

25

Speeding Ticket

Nash

G et out of the car."

"You're not supposed to be working tonight," she muttered, gripping the wheel.

"Get. Out. Of. The. Car. Angelina," I ordered through gritted teeth.

"Help! This woman kidnapped me!" the idiot in the back seat shouted.

"Shut up, Melvin," Lina snapped.

I yanked open her door. "Don't fuck with me, Angel."

She released her seat belt and stepped out of the car and into my body. I knew better. Knew I couldn't trust myself this close to her. But hadn't it already been a foregone conclusion when Grave had filled me in on the situation?

Somehow I'd known it would end like this.

"Are you gonna back up or just stand here and crowd me all night?" she hissed, doing her best to stand defiantly in front of me and still shrink away from making any physical contact. That killed me.

Her jeans were torn on one knee. There was dirt

all over her sweater and jacket. And I thought I caught a hint of a limp. But it was her face that sent my blood pressure skyrocketing.

"He do this?" I demanded, gripping her chin and tilting her head so I could see the bruising. Anger was a living thing under my skin. It ate at me and took every ounce of control not to unleash.

She reached up and gripped the wrist of the hand that held her face, but I didn't let go. "The only thing he's guilty of besides hacking into state databases is having pointy elbows."

"Why are you bringing in an FTA?"

She rolled her eyes insolently. "Can we skip over the part where you pretend to care so I can be on my way? I've had a long day."

"Don't listen to her! I didn't skip out on bail! I was innocently walking home from reading to shelter dogs when she tackled me in an alley and threatened me," her passenger whined.

"Shut up, Melvin," Lina and I said in unison.

I pulled her around the trunk of her car and took inventory of her in my headlights. "Are you hurt anywhere else?" The bruising under her cheek was ugly and swollen. I hated it with every fiber of my being.

She batted my hands away. "Is this part of all traffic stops now?"

Having her this close wasn't just frying my circuits. It was destroying them.

The anger that bubbled up inside wanted to claw its way out of my throat and let itself loose on the world. I wasn't cold now. I wasn't empty now. I was a volcano about to erupt.

"It was an accident." Lina's tone was calm, almost bored. Her voice was a beautiful poison in my veins.

"You said you recovered assets, not hunted down people," I reminded her.

"I do. So before you call me a liar again, someone called in a favor. Not that it's any of your business."

She kept saying things like that. Things that were technically true.

But despite the fact that I was furious with her, that I'd insisted I was done with her, I needed to know she was okay. I needed to know what had happened. I needed to fucking take care of it.

She was my business and I wasn't done with her. I was just getting started. I accepted the truth, pretending that I had a choice.

"Who called in a favor? Who asked you to do this?"

"Jesus, Nash. Relax. No laws were broken and your sister-in-law and friend—despite being drunken pains in the ass who refused to follow orders—are safe. Knox picked them up and drove them home."

"I realize that." The fact that my brother thought it wise to leave Lina alone to handle a criminal on her own was another issue that was going to have to be raised. Most likely with fists.

Fuck.

The emotions she raised in me were dangerous. Gone was the even-keeled lawman with a badge. Gone was the empty shell of a man. In his place was a fire-breathing dragon that wanted to lay waste to everything.

I wondered if this was how Knox felt most of the time.

I reached out and cupped her chin again, angling her beautiful face so I could examine the bruising. Touching her, even just like this, lit something inside me.

"You need ice."

"I'd get to it faster if you weren't holding me up."

I blew out a bad-tempered breath. "Get him out of the car."

"What?"

"Get him out of the car," I said, enunciating slowly.

"Oh no. I'm not falling for that. I'm driving this ass's ass to the station and getting a receipt. Then he's all yours."

"I don't want you transporting him," I said. A wave of possessiveness washed away all rational thought. I didn't care. I just needed her safe and close.

"I don't give a shit what you want," she snarled.

"I'll give a shit enough for the two of us. Get his ass out of your car."

She crossed her arms. "No."

"Fine." I stepped back and started to round the car. "I'll do it."

She grabbed my arm and I reveled in the touch. "You take another step near my FTA and I'll . . ."

"You'll what?" I challenged when she trailed off. I wanted her to push back. Wanted to meet in the middle in a tangle of anger and lust.

"Why are you doing this?" she hissed, shoving her fingers into her hair.

"Wish I knew, sweetheart." But I did know. She could lie to me. She could put herself in danger. She could avoid me or hate me. But I still wouldn't be able to leave her alone. Because I wasn't done with her.

I hated myself for how much I wanted her.

"I don't belong to you. I didn't break the law. The only thing I was in danger of was bruising my ego taking this idiot down. So unless you want to abuse your authority and detain me, I suggest you let me do my job."

"I don't want to care, you know."

"Poor Nash. Are you being forced to play the hero for the villain?"

I pinned her against the car with my hips. Her eyes dilated. Her delicate nostrils flared like a doe scenting danger. But her hands had a mind of their own. They gripped me by the shirt and held on tight.

"You're playing a dangerous game, Angel."

"From where I'm standing, it looks like you're the only one who's going to get hurt," she shot back.

I was standing on the side of the road caging an angry woman against a fast car. My heartbeat hammered in my head, a steady thrumming that matched the throb in my cock. She wasn't the safe choice, the smart choice. But for some electrifyingly stupid reason, my body thought this woman who lived her life in the gray area was the right choice.

I cupped her jaw and ran my thumb over her lower lip. The light in her eyes changed from fury to something just as dangerous. I was vibrating with need. I couldn't trust myself to be this close to her.

But just when I'd nearly talked myself into pulling back, she nipped the pad of my thumb with her teeth.

The tiny zing of pain shot through me, down my spine, and zeroed in on my balls.

I could feel her heart racing against my chest.

We both moved at the same time. I dipped at the knees just as she spread her legs, making room for me.

This. Now. Her.

My blood demanded more. Any performance fears I had evaporated into the night, burned off by the heat of lust. I needed to make her mine. To prove to her she belonged to only me. Sliding my hands under her knees, I yanked up and out, spreading her legs until my erection nestled at the juncture of her thighs. Even fully clothed, the feel of her body welcoming mine was almost too much to bear.

"I need you—"

"I don't want to need you, but I do," I said, nuzzling my face into the silky smooth skin of her neck.

"Damn it, Nash," she breathed. "I need you to back up and let me breathe."

I stilled against her but didn't move back. I couldn't. The pulse in her throat fluttered just beneath my lips.

"Nash. Please? Just back up and let me breathe."

It was the please that damned me. I would give her anything, as long as she gave me everything.

I bit out a curse and stepped back, letting her slide to the ground.

"If I'm not going to be your emotional support fuck, I sure as hell won't be your hate fuck."

"Angel."

She held up a hand. "We've already proved we can't trust each other. And I'm pretty sure we just proved we can't trust ourselves to be anywhere near each other."

"I don't know how long I can fight this," I confessed.

She leveled me with a look. "Try harder."

"I am trying. I'm furious with you. You betrayed my trust."

"Oh please," she scoffed. "I was more honest with you than I have been with anyone. You just refuse to acknowledge that there's a whole world out there beyond the black and white."

"As I was saying, I can't stop thinking about how mad I am at you. But all I want to do is get down on my knees and bury my face between your—"

She slapped a hand over my mouth.

"Don't finish that sentence. We're dangerous to each other. I can't keep my head on straight when you're touching me. We're the worst decision we could make. And if *I'm* the one saying that, it means something."

But for once in my life, I wasn't worried about consequences. I wasn't thinking six steps down the road. All I knew for certain was that I wanted her. Even though she'd lied. Even though she'd hurt me. Even though she wanted to fight me on everything.

I wanted Angelina Solavita.

"Excuse me? I know you two are in the middle of a fight, but I really have to pee."

"Shut up, Melvin!"

I rode the ass of the red Charger the entire way to the station, not giving her an inch of breathing room. When we arrived, I was out of my SUV, opening the door of her car before she'd even shut off the engine.

"Back off, hotshot," Lina warned.

But I was already hauling the scrawny felon out of the back seat. "Let's go, asshole," I said.

"I feel like the name-calling is uncalled for," he complained.

"What's uncalled for are bruises on her face," I said, spinning him around to look at Lina. Seeing her hurt unleashed something ugly inside me. Something that wanted to sweep all her infractions under the rug. Something that wanted to keep her close so no one else could get near her.

"I told you, she's the one who tackled me after the brunette hit me with dog poop and the blond showed me her boobs. It's not my fault she got banged up."

I shot a look at Lina. She shrugged. "Naomi and Sloane," she said by way of explanation.

"Listen, I'm really hungry," Melvin whined. "I ran out of my cousin's place before dinner. You think I could get some crispy nuggies or maybe some of those smiley face mashed potato things? You know, comfort food. I'm feeling pretty stressed out."

Christ. Did his mom still cut the crusts off his bread too?

"If you apologize to the lady for assaulting her, I'll feed you."

"I'm sorry your face ran into my elbow, Lina. Honest. My mom would kick my ass if I even thought about hurting a lady."

"Apology accepted," Lina said. She turned to me. "Now give me the receipt."

"Let's go," I muttered, pushing Melvin ahead of us.

"Damn, gorgeous. What the hell happened to you?" Grave asked Lina when we trooped inside.

"Pointy elbows," she explained.

"I got them from my dad. Most of his body parts are sharp and pointy," Melvin announced. "So about those nuggies . . ."

I shoved Melvin at Grave before I was tempted to jam one of my elbows into his face. "Do me a favor and take care of this. I'll deal with the paperwork."

Lina looked like she was about to laser me in half with her eyes.

"I have to make a call," she said and stalked out into the hallway.

"Got a pretty good limp," Grave observed as if I hadn't already cataloged her every move.

By the time Lina came inside, hiding her limp as best she could, I had her paperwork ready.

"This is for Murtaugh," I said handing the first slip over. "And this is for you."

She took the second slip of paper and then gave me the heated death stare. "A speeding ticket? You're joking."

"Pulled you over going fourteen over the limit," I reminded her.

She was so mad she sputtered. "You . . . you . . ."

"You've got two weeks to pay it or contest it. Though, if you're thinkin' about fightin' it, I wouldn't. Seein' as how I was the one who pulled you over and I'd have no qualms about taking a day off to sit in traffic court."

She took a deep breath and, when that didn't seem to calm her down, sucked in another one. Fury radiating off her, she pointed at me and shook her head before backing through the door.

"You sure you know what you're doing there, Chief?" Grave asked.

"No fucking clue, Hopper."

Instead of going home where I didn't trust myself to leave Lina alone, I took my bad mood out of town. My tires kicked up a cloud of dust into the night sky as I sped down the dirt lane. The lights were on in the big house, so I slammed on the brakes and got out of my vehicle.

I stomped up onto the porch and pounded on the front door until it opened.

"Christ. What the hell is—?"

I didn't give my brother the chance to finish his sentence. My fist connected with his jaw and snapped his head back.

"You fucking fuck!" he snarled.

One punch didn't feel like enough. I was happier than a pig in shit when he barreled into my gut with his shoulder. We went flying, smashing through the porch railing and landing on a leafy bush.

I kneed him in the general vicinity of the crotch and flipped over to get on top of him.

He let me land another punch to his face before sneaking one past my defenses. I tasted blood and anger and frustration in a delirious cocktail.

"What the fuck is your problem?" he demanded as I smashed his face into the shrubbery.

"You left her alone to handle a criminal."

"Jesus Christ, you idiot. Did you get a look at him? Lina eats guys like that for breakfast."

"He fucking hurt her."

I landed a jab to his ribs. My brother grunted, then rolled me off him with some fancy leg sweep move.

He grabbed me by the hair and bounced my face off the mulch. "He *bruised* her. You're the asshole who hurt her."

I threw an elbow over my shoulder and felt it connect with his jaw.

Knox grunted, then spit. "If anyone should be kickin' anyone's ass, it's me kickin' your ass for messin' with her head. She's my friend."

"And I'm your fuckin' brother," I reminded him.

"Then what are we doin' fightin'?"

"How the fuck should I know?" The mad was still in me. The helplessness. The need to touch her when I knew I didn't have the right anymore.

"Knoxy?" Naomi sang drunkenly from somewhere inside the house.

"He's outside fightin' with Uncle Nash in the yard. They broke the porch," Waylay reported.

"Great. Now you're gettin' me in trouble," he complained.

We both flopped over onto our backs on top of the crushed greenery. The stars were brilliant pinpoints in the inky black sky.

"You left her alone," I said again.

"She can handle herself."

"Doesn't mean she has to."

"Look, man, what do you want me to say? She needed me to take Daisy and Sloane, who were both three sheets to the damn wind. If I don't ever hear another Spice Girls karaoke song in my life, it'll be too soon."

Lina needed Knox. I let that fact rattle around in my head.

When she'd gotten into trouble, she'd called Knox and not me. For good reason. I wasn't stupid enough that I didn't see that. Yet here I was, lying in the dirt, pissed off that I'd created a world where Lina went to someone else when she needed help.

"How did you fuck it up?" Knox asked.

"What makes you think I fucked anything up?"

"You're here rolling around in the landscaping with me instead of giving her hell. What did you do?"

"What do you think I did? I pulled her ass over and gave her a speeding ticket and a ration of shit."

He was silent for a long beat and then said, "You're usually better with women than this."

"Fuck you."

"If you want my advice—"

"Why the hell would I? You couldn't tell Naomi you loved her until she got abducted in sex handcuffs by her sister and that asshole."

"I was working through some shit, okay?"

"Yeah, well, so am I."

"My advice is work through it faster if you want a shot with her. She was packin' a suitcase today. Naomi said she and Sloane had to practically twist her arm to agree to stay long enough for them to go out."

"Packing?"

"Said she was gonna move back into the motel until someone else could replace her on the case. Then she was going home."

Leaving?

Absolutely fucking not.

Lina wasn't going anywhere. Not until we'd hashed this out. Not until I figured out why she was under my skin and in my blood. Not until

I found a way to either get her out or keep her close.

But these were not things Morgan men said out loud.

Instead I stuck with our comfort zone. "So now you're fine if I hook up with your friend? Christ, man, you're fuckin' mercurial."

"Bite me, asshole. Accordin' to Naomi, Lina feels something real for you. Something you didn't fully fuck up yet. Unless that speeding ticket put the final nail in that coffin. And since you're over here makin' a fool of yourself over her, I'm thinkin' maybe there's something there worth exploring."

I scraped a leaf off my face. "Lina feels something? What did she say?"

"I don't fuckin' know," Knox said, irritated. "Daze and Sloane were singin' it with British accents between verses of 'Wannabe.' Ask them once they sober up and leave me the hell out of it."

We were quiet for a while. Just two grown men lying in a ruined flower bed staring up at the night sky.

"Heard Naomi threw dog shit at the guy Lina was chasin' and then Sloane distracted him by flashin' him her tits," I said.

Knox snorted next to me. "Jesus. No more girls' nights out. From now on, the three of them go out together, it's with a goddamn escort."

"Agreed."

We heard the creak of the screen door but never saw the bucket of cold water coming. It hit us both in the face.

Sputtering and swearing, we got to our feet to face the enemy only to find Naomi, Waylay, and Waylon on the porch looking down at us.

"No more fighting," Naomi said regally. Then she hiccupped.

Waylay snickered as she turned the hose on us.

26

Nash Who?

Lina

Nash Morgan no longer existed to me. That was the mantra I chanted as I powered my way through the last set of back squats. I could focus entirely on my workout and not the sweat-slicked chief of police who, from the tingle at the base of my spine, hadn't stopped glaring at me since he got here.

The physical pull of the man was overwhelming and quite frankly pissed me the hell off.

"Drop that booty lower," Vernon barked, bringing me back to my present suffering.

"You . . . drop . . . your . . . booty," I wheezed as I dug deep, preparing to exploit the last remaining molecules of energy in my legs.

"Bring it home, Solavita," Nolan called from the weight bench behind me. Apparently he and Nash had reached some sort of peace accord and were working out together now.

I managed to raise both middle fingers off the bar and then muscle my way back to standing.

The whoops of approval from my elderly workout buddies echoed in my ears as I parked

384

the bar back on the rack and hinged at the waist to catch my breath.

Unfortunately, I forgot to close my eyes and caught a glimpse of the Man Who Didn't Exist full-on staring hungrily at my ass.

Knox, sweaty and grumpy from his morning workout, walked up to his brother, noticed the direction of Nash's gaze, and slammed an elbow into his gut.

They both had fading bruises on their faces, but I was so over Nash, I had zero interest in finding out what happened.

Okay, maybe, like, ten percent interest. Fine. Forty percent tops.

Not that I'd ask either one of them. Knox and I had maintained our tentative truce as long as neither of us brought up Nash. And Nash seemed to have finally gotten the message that he didn't exist. After three days of me refusing to answer my door or my phone, he'd stopped knocking and calling.

It was better this way. We'd proved on multiple occasions that we couldn't be trusted in any kind of proximity to each other.

It wasn't cowardly of me to time my own comings and goings to make sure we didn't run into each other on the stairs. I was not a big, giant chicken for tiptoeing past his door. For once, *I* was making the safe, smart decision.

I straightened and took a long hit from my

water bottle, pretending I couldn't physically feel Nash's attention on me.

Just like I chose to ignore the low-level buzz of awareness that sparked in my veins when I knew he was next door, only one wall away.

Well, I still found myself straining to hear the sound of his shower.

But I was only human, okay?

I was committed to the new and improved, healthier, slightly more boring but definitely in a better head space Lina. I'd cut back on caffeine and alcohol, upped my vegetables, and was on a four-day meditation streak. My PVCs had stopped for the most part. And now there was nothing else distracting me from the investigation.

I'd left three more messages on Grim's weird answering service but had yet to get a response.

Thankfully, my research team had come through for me. Zelda managed to work her nerd magic and identify the two henchmen from Tina's vague descriptions. Face Tattoo Guy was Stewie Crabb, a two-time felon with a dagger tattooed under his left eye. Chubby Goatee was Wendell Baker, a beefy white guy with a shaved head and a Fu Manchu mustache that connected to a goatee. He had only done time once for an assault charge.

Both had been in Anthony Hugo's employ since they were teenagers thanks to their friendship with Duncan. Zelda hadn't had any luck identifying the mysterious Burner Phone Guy yet, but at least I had leads on Crabb and Baker.

I'd set aside my property search in favor of surveillance. Unfortunately for me, watching low-level criminal henchmen who knew the feds were probably keeping an eye on them mostly involved sitting in a lot of strip club parking lots.

"Nice job," Stef wheezed. His T-shirt was soaked from neck to hem and his black hair was spiked down the middle in a sweaty faux hawk.

"Thanks," I said, sucking down more water. "I keep waiting for it to get easier, but every time I still feel like I'm going to die."

Stef grunted.

"So are you ever going to tell me how your date went Sunday after you abandoned me with the tipsy twins?"

He closed his eyes and doused himself with water, but I still caught the curve of his lips.

"It was . . . fine."

"Fine?" I repeated.

"Nice." The curve was becoming more pronounced despite his best efforts. "I didn't have a horrible time."

I elbowed him. "You liiiiiike him. You wanna make ooooout with him."

"Don't be a third grader."

"Did you end up in a tree k-i-s-s-i-n-g?" I teased.

"He did the hand on the lower back thing when we walked into the restaurant."

"That's hot."

"So hot," he said, taking a swig of water. The ghost of a smile still played on his mouth.

"Are you going to see him again?"

"Maybe," he said smugly.

"So that little barstool therapy session was actually meant for you, not me."

Stef shot the scowling police chief a glance. "I figured one of us had to man up and take the leap."

"Excuse me, *jerk*. The man pulled me over, yelled at me, and gave me a speeding ticket for *doing my job*."

"I'm sure you were driving the speed limit."

"That's not the point."

Stef looked at Nash again, then back to me. He smirked. "Like it or not, there's something volcanic between you two. And I can't wait to see which one of you explodes first."

"You went on one date. You don't get to pull the smug committed relationship thing on me."

"Two dates. We had lunch yesterday. I'd love to stay here while you pretend you aren't dying to get in Nash Morgan's pants, but I'm meeting Jer for coffee. Don't fight it too long. You might miss out on something pretty great."

"Bite me, heart eyes."

He headed off to the locker room and left me brooding by myself.

"Yo, BFFF!" Mrs. Tweedy sauntered up to me, a sweat towel slung around her neck. "Your face looks better."

"Thanks," I said dryly. My black eye was slowly fading to a sickly yellow green. In a few more days, I wouldn't have to cover it with makeup anymore.

"You're takin' me grocery shopping today," Mrs. Tweedy announced.

"I am?"

"Yep! Be ready in ten." She slid the towel off her neck and snapped me in the butt with it.

Rubbing my abused ass cheek, I gathered my things. It was a good thing bad guys didn't bother getting out of bed before noon, I supposed.

"Lina." Nolan gave a head jerk, signaling for me to swing by.

I gave Nash a wide berth and joined Nolan in front of the mirror.

"What's up?"

Nash walked past me to rerack his dumbbells, and I felt the disturbance of his proximity.

Our eyes met in the mirror and I deliberately looked away, not wanting to see what those troubled blue eyes held.

"Wanna go for a drink tonight after I put the kid to bed?" He hooked his thumb in Nash's direction.

"That depends."

"On what?"

"Whether a drink is just a drink, seeing as how you just took my friend on a date."

He rolled his eyes. "I'm not trying to get in your pants, Solavita."

A drink with a friend who was a guy sounded like the only kind of social interaction I was up for. That meant no talking about feelings. No dealing with sexual tension. And no drunken gal pals to babysit.

"Then I'll see you tonight."

"It's a date," he said, then smirked.

"You're such an ass," I said with affection.

The temperature in the gym suddenly dropped twenty degrees. I realized that it wasn't a problem with the HVAC. It was Nash standing next to me. We didn't look at each other, didn't touch, but my brain was sending out danger warnings like I'd just stumbled into the gorilla enclosure at the zoo.

"You gonna work something besides that mouth today?" he asked Nolan.

"Look, pal. You don't need to get all pissy because I kicked your ass in the shoulder press," Nolan said.

I had better things to do with my time than watch a bromance bloom. Like take an elderly bodybuilder to the grocery store.

"I'll see you around," I said to Nolan, pointedly ignoring Nash.

I made it all the way to the water fountain

before I again felt the dark presence of Chief Nashhole. "You can't ignore me forever," he said, stepping in front of me. I stopped short so as not to plow into his sweaty chest. I couldn't afford the fantasies.

"I don't have to ignore you forever," I said sweetly. "Once I wrap this investigation, we'll never have to see each other again."

"What about the wedding?"

Crap. The wedding.

"I can't speak for you, but I'm an adult. Just because the sight of you makes me want to hit you in the face with a folding chair doesn't mean I can't pretend to tolerate you for one day."

He bared his teeth and I wondered if I imagined the low, dangerous growl. "You just keep pushing my buttons."

"And you just keep pissing me off." The stare down lasted a good thirty seconds before I finally asked, "What happened to your face?"

"It ran into my fists. Repeatedly," Knox said as he stomped past us on his way to the water fountain.

"Seriously? When are you two gonna outgrow that?"

"Never," they said together.

I didn't know which one of us had edged closer, but Nash and I were now standing toe-to-toe. I was close enough to reach out and trail my fingers over his sweaty torso, a thought that should have been revolting. But of course it wasn't. I was starting to think there was something very, very wrong with me.

"We need to talk," Nash said. His glare was giving me a sunburn.

"Sorry, Chief. I'm all talked out. You're just going to have to find someone else to piss off."

"Goddammit, Angelina."

This time I very definitely did *not* imagine the growl. Or the hot, hard hand that splayed across my stomach and backed me into the dark, empty studio. It smelled like sweat and industrial disinfectant.

"What are you doing?" I hissed as he shut the door behind him and stood in front of it.

There were weapons in here, five-pound dumbbells and large exercise balls. Both could be bounced off thick skulls.

"Stop giving me the cold shoulder," he ordered.

I wasn't sure what I was expecting but it sure as hell hadn't been *that*. I was definitely going for the dumbbells.

Temper burned like fire under my skin. "You have two options. Cold shoulder or hellfire. And let me tell you, Chief, I would be *so happy* if you chose hellfire."

"What the fuck am I supposed to do?" he demanded. "You take advantage of my trust, betray me, and I'm just supposed to be fine with it?"

This time, it was me who closed the distance between us. "Are you even listening to yourself? I took advantage of you? I betrayed you? We barely know each other. Certainly not well enough for me to do either of those things. And much as it pains me to admit, you're not dumb enough to let someone you just met take advantage of you. You came with that baggage packed and you were itching to unload it on me. Well, guess what, assface? I was more honest with you than I had been with anybody and you made me immediately regret it."

I slapped a hand to his sweaty chest and gave a shove. He didn't budge. Not even an inch. But his hand clamped over my wrist and then he was yanking me into him.

He was a wall of heat and muscle and anger. My own fury melded with his and everything went molten inside me.

"I *hate* how much I still want to be near you." His voice was a low, angry rasp, like the bite of gravel on bare feet. Just what every girl dreamed of hearing.

"And *I* hate that I ever opened up to you," I hissed.

It was the truth. I hated that I'd shared any part of myself with him. That he now owned a piece of my story. One that I hadn't trusted anyone with in a very long time. I hated that as angry as I was, as hurt as I was, I still just wanted him

393

to touch me. It was like my lactose-intolerant roommate in college who had a toxic relationship with cheesecake.

We were both panting, breathing the same air, inhaling the same anger, fueling the same blaze. The music and cacophony of gym sounds seemed so far away.

I wanted to punch him. To kiss him. To bite his lip until he lost control.

He dipped his head, then stopped just shy of my mouth, his nose brushing my cheek.

His hands circled my biceps and slid all the way down to my wrists. "Then why does it feel so right to touch you?" he rasped.

I almost melted against him. Almost threw every principle out the window and jumped into his spiteful arms. I didn't understand it any better than he did. There was a flaw in my DNA that made his touch feel like home.

My heart was pounding against my ribs. Fight or flight. I wanted to choose fight. I wanted to give myself over to the anger and let it come spilling out. I wanted to see what would happen if we erupted together.

But that wasn't who I wanted to be anymore.

As much as my body wanted the seething, angry man before me, my head knew it was a mistake.

"Stay away from me, Nash," I said, mustering the frost of Antarctica in my tone.

"I've tried." The admission was like an illicit caress.

"Try harder." I yanked my hands free. In a moment of petty spite that felt damn good, I shoulder checked him on my way out the door.

"Couldn't help but notice you and Nash haven't been enjoying any sleepovers lately," Mrs. Tweedy announced as she tossed a box of wine into the cart next to the value pack of canned tuna and the baker's dozen of almost expired donuts.

You could tell a lot about a person by the contents of their grocery cart. Mrs. Tweedy's cart screamed "chaos."

"You certainly see a lot from that peephole," I said. I was still feeling hot, bothered, and ragey from my run-in with Nash at the gym. I wasn't sure five minutes in the ice cream freezer would be enough to cool me off.

"Don't dodge me. My nose is already fully invested in your business. Y'all stand next to each other in a room and suddenly it feels like something's about to explode. In a sexy way." She added a six-pack of light beer to her grocery haul.

"Yeah, well. We're not the kind of people who should even dabble at being together," I said. We couldn't even stand next to each other without it spiraling out of control.

The physical draw I felt to Nash was like a

gravitational field. Inevitable. It had the power to overcome all the very excellent reasons why I should stay away from him, the number one reason being he was an order-giving, emotionally damaged dick.

"What's not to like? He's got a good head on his shoulders, he can shoot like a cowboy, he rescues dogs, *and* he's got a butt that don't quit in those uniform pants. My pal Gladys drops her purse every time she sees him just so he'll bend down to pick it up."

"He also sees everything in black and white, acts like he has the right to tell me what to do, and manhandles me."

"I know this is not politically correct, but I love me a good consensual manhandling," Mrs. Tweedy said with a suggestive eyebrow wiggle.

Okay, I didn't hate it either. If anyone other than Nash had dragged me into that room at the gym, they'd be breathing through a straw in the waiting room of a plastic surgeon. But I didn't feel like thinking about that. Instead, I grabbed a jar of peanut butter and threw it into the cart.

"He's also got that whole broody thing going right now. Like the man's got storm clouds in his head and he's just lookin' for a little sunshine."

"Yeah, well, he can go find his vitamin D someplace else."

And so would I. Ha. Solid inner monologue dick joke.

My elderly shopping partner tut-tutted. "Two people who keep gettin' drawn together like magnets can't be wrong. It's a law of nature."

"Nature made a mistake this time around," I assured her and added a carton of sparkling water to our cart.

Mrs. Tweedy shook her head. "You're looking at it all wrong. Sometimes the body recognizes what the head and heart are too stupid to see. That right there is real truth. The body don't lie. Huh. Maybe I should put that on a bumper sticker?" she mused.

"I'd much rather trust my head than my body." Especially since my body seemed to be set on self-destruct mode. I'd never been so attracted to a man so infuriating before.

It was disorienting, frustrating, and borderline sadomasochistic. Yet another sign that I needed to commit to changing my ways. That was the message the universe was sending me, not *Hey, here's a hot guy. Get naked with him and everything will work out.*

Mrs. Tweedy snorted indelicately. "If I had your body, I'd be listening to every damn thing it said."

"I seem to recall your body kicking my body's ass at the gym half an hour ago," I reminded her.

She fluffed her hair as we turned into the cereal aisle. "I do look pretty good for my age."

There was a man at the opposite end of the aisle pushing a cart in our direction.

"If you're dead set against Nash, how about I reel this one in for you?" Mrs. Tweedy offered.

He was a buff-looking guy in his thirties with glasses and short, dark hair.

"Don't you dare," I whispered out of the side of my mouth.

But it was too late. Mrs. Tweedy came to a halt in front of the marshmallow and cartoon character cereal section and made a show of stretching for the top shelf. A shelf I could have easily reached.

"Excuse me, young man. Would you mind fetching me a box of Marshmallow Munchies?" Mrs. Tweedy asked, batting her lashes at him.

I pretended to be fascinated by the lack of nutritional value in a box of Sparkle Pinkie O's.

"No problem, ma'am," he said.

"That is so sweet of you," she said. "Isn't that sweet, Lina?"

"Very," I said through clenched teeth.

The man grabbed the box and flashed me a knowing grin.

He was close to a foot and a half taller than Mrs. Tweedy. Up close, he looked like an accountant who went to the gym a lot. According to his cart, Big Guy looked like he took his nutrition seriously. He had a rotisserie chicken, all the fixings for a couple of salads, a six-pack of protein shakes, and . . . a large bag of gummy candy. Well, no one was perfect.

"Are you married?" Mrs. Tweedy demanded.

"No, ma'am," he said.

"What a coincidence. Neither is my neighbor Lina," she said, giving me a shove forward.

"Okay, Mrs. Tweedy. Let's leave the nice man with the long arms alone," I said.

"Party pooper," she muttered.

"Sorry," I mouthed to the man as I dragged my meddling neighbor and our cart down the aisle.

"Happens all the time," he said with a wink.

"Is there something wrong with your libido?" Mrs. Tweedy demanded when we were probably still within earshot.

I thought of waking up with Nash with his hard-on between my legs. "Very definitely. Now, come on. I need to stick my head in the ice cream cooler."

27

Snakes and Shakes

Nash

I'm gonna burn this house to the ground,"
Mayor Hilly Swanson griped as I emptied her
coat closet of boots and gardening clogs.

"Probably shouldn't be sayin' that in front of
the law," I said as I shook out a snow boot and
tossed it aside.

She was standing behind me on a step stool in
the foyer, wringing her hands.

Officer Troy Winslow was backed up against
the front door holding the twelve-gauge shotgun
we'd relieved the mayor of upon our arrival. He
was looking like he wanted to bolt.

"I should sue that dang real estate agent. If she
woulda said 'snake migration' at any point during
the buying process, my ass woulda said no thank
you," Hilly said.

She'd lived in this house for twenty years, and
the Knockemout PD went through this ritual
twice a year. In the spring, snakes slithered their
way down from the limestone bluffs toward a
swampy area of nearby state park lands for the
summer. In the fall, they slithered their way back
to the bluffs to wait out the long winter.

Hilly Swanson's house was smack-dab in the middle of the migration path. Over the years, she'd spent a small fortune to snake-proof the foundation, but one or two always managed to find their way in.

I shoved the now empty shoe rack aside and checked behind it.

"This is just like waitin' for those refrigerator biscuits to pop," Winslow said. "You know it's comin' but that don't mean you're ready for it." Winslow was not a snake person. The guy had no problem chasing bears out of campgrounds, but if it slithered, he wasn't going near it.

I, on the other hand, had grown up on and in the creek, which had given me a hell of a lot of experience with snakes.

"I told Mickey not to leave the door open when he was cartin' groceries inside. But he said I was crazy. And then he took his butt off to the golf course and *I'm* the one who has to deal with the consequences. If I was a braver soul who wasn't about to pee her pants, I'd put that damn snake on his side of the bed to teach him a lesson."

I reached for the trench coat belt in the corner only to realize it was moving. "Gotcha."

"Oh my God. I'm gonna kill Mickey."

I aimed the beam of my flashlight at the reptile and reached out lightning-quick to grab it just behind the head. It was cold and eerily slick under my hand, like no matter how tight I held on, the muscles under all that smooth would just slide right out.

"It's practically a baby," I said, stuffing all five feet of pissed-off rat snake into the pillowcase I kept in my cruiser for such occasions.

I backed out of the closet and got to my feet.

Hilly recoiled. "Lord have mercy."

Winslow looked like he was trying real hard to back through the front door without opening it.

"I think we're done here," I said, holding the wriggling pillowcase in one hand.

"Thank you, thank you, thank you," Hilly chanted. She followed us out onto the front porch, still wringing her hands. "You got a second to talk about another snake-related matter?"

"Sure. Mind gettin' our new friend settled in the car, Winslow?" I handed over the snake in the bag to him, mostly to mess with him. "Watch where you step. The ground's slithering this time of year," I warned.

He swallowed hard, held the pillowcase gingerly at arm's length, and tiptoed toward the SUV.

"What's the latest on Dilton?" Hilly asked, sliding back into her usual tough broad role now that the snake was no longer in her vicinity.

"Investigation is ongoing," I said.

"That's the standard line," she complained.

"That's what's on record."

"Well, then gimme off the record so I can start preparing what the hell I'm gonna say to the town council."

"Off the record, so far we've only dug back a few months into his cases, interviewing victims and suspects."

"But?"

"But there's a pattern on the calls he handled solo since I got myself shot. Being a man down opened a window for him and he took advantage. He's not comin' back from this."

"What's the town's responsibility in all this? How do we make this right?"

I expected the first question and respected the hell out of her for the second.

I blew out a breath. "We're going by the book, crossing t's and dottin' i's. He's not getting off on a technicality. But here's the part you're not gonna like."

"Knew it was comin'."

"I reached out to the Kennedys, the husband and wife Dilton harassed during the traffic stop. I spoke with both, without counsel."

She raised her auburn eyebrows. "And how did that go?"

"It was a judgment call. I'll tell you the same thing I told them. Dilton was my responsibility. It happened on my watch. Husband was more understanding that he needed to be. The wife was understandably less so. But we talked it out. I apologized profusely and took full responsibility."

"Solicitor's gonna love that," Hilly said.

"Yeah, well. Sometimes sayin' you're sorry is more important than coverin' your ass. Either way, it was the right thing to do. Mrs. Kennedy called me back yesterday and gave me the contact info of a training organization that works with departments on de-escalation and diversity training. Expensive, but in my opinion, necessary. And cheaper than the lawsuit we'd settle."

"How much are we talkin'?"

I nodded toward the car where Piper's head was hanging out the driver's side window. "Let's just say that's gonna be the only K-9 officer we can afford for a while."

She shook her head. "Fuckin' Dilton. One bad cop is all it takes."

"I know. It's one hundred percent my fault for keepin' him on. For thinkin' I could change him."

She put her hands on her hips and stared out through the forest. "Yeah, well, now you know how it feels to be a woman in love with a dumbass with potential. Ninety-nine percent of the time, that potential never gets realized."

"Mickey have potential?" I teased.

Her smirk was quick. "Hell yeah, he did. And I didn't give him a choice about the realizing part of it."

"Been thinking," I began.

"Anytime an official says that, things are about to get expensive."

"Not necessarily. Since we're already adding on some education, what would you think of bringing in Social Services caseworkers to do a training for us?"

"What kind of training?"

"Mental health calls. You know Xandra Rempalski?"

She shot me a look that said I was tiptoeing into dumbass territory. "The nurse who saved my chief of police's life? Nope. Never heard of her. Nor do I own four necklaces and three pairs of her earrings."

"Okay. All right. Her nephew has autism."

"Sure, yeah. I know Alex."

"He's nonverbal, six feet tall, and Black," I said, rocking back on my heels.

Hilly blew out a sigh. "I'm pickin' up what you're puttin' down. Moms with Black babies have a lot of conversations with those babies on how to interact with cops."

"And I wanna make sure that we cops are having conversations on how to safely and respectfully interact with those babies. All of them. Especially the ones who can't talk back. Doesn't sit well with me that some of our people still don't feel safe here. That's exactly why I took this job, and I've still got a lot of learning and a lot of work to do."

"Don't we all, Chief? So how do we go about that?"

"I'd like to talk it over with Yolanda Suarez. She's been a caseworker a long time and she'll have some ideas. Right now, I'm thinking some kind of combination of ongoing department training and tag teaming mental health calls with social workers. Other departments in bigger cities have rolled out programs like that and they're seein' results. Maybe we could bring Naomi Witt into it since she's community outreach coordinator."

"It's a damn good idea."

"I think so too."

"Why don't you set up a meet with you, me, and Yolanda first? Then we'll go from there."

"Appreciate it. Guess I'd better get your slithering roommate to his new home."

Hilly shuddered. "Chief, after I'm done burning this place to the ground and murdering my husband, I'm putting you up for a raise."

I paused. If there was one thing Hilly guarded with her life, it was Knockemout's purse strings. "I wouldn't feel right about that. Not with what's gone down the past few months."

She reached out and patted me on my cheek. "That's exactly why you're gettin' one, son. You care. You take responsibility. And you create solutions. This town is lucky to have you. I'm damn proud of the man you've grown up to be."

I wasn't one to get choked up about a few compliments, but growing up without the mom who'd sprinkled them so liberally through my childhood left a void. A deep one that I was only just beginning to recognize.

It had been a long time since anyone I loved had been proud of me.

I surprised us both by leaning down and brushing a kiss to her cheek. "Thanks, Mayor."

She turned bright red. "Go on now. Get that damn snake off my property and get back to work. We've got people to serve."

I threw her a little salute and headed for the car. "Make sure you alibi up before you go on your arson-murder spree."

"Will do, Chief."

28

Shark Week Crappy Hour

Lina

I was early for my nondate drinks with Nolan. It was more in an effort to avoid Nash when he and Piper came home from work than any actual enthusiasm. But after a long day of sitting in a car watching a low-level henchman hit the gym, the Chinese buffet, and the strip club, I was actually looking forward to talking shop with the marshal.

The crowd was mostly female in Honky Tonk, and the tables had little signs on them that said WARNING: SHARK WEEK. I smirked. Leave it to Nolan to pick a night when the female bar staff's menstruation cycles synced.

Knowing the drill, I grabbed an empty two-top and did not attempt to flag down Max, the server, who was busy adjusting the peel-and-stick heating pad on her abdomen with one hand while stuffing a chocolate cupcake into her mouth with the other.

Max would take my order when she was good and ready, and I would get my drink when Silver the bartender was done shocking the shit out of the burly biker dude's abs with the mini electrotherapy machine.

It was a new addition to Shark Week's Crappy Hour. Electrical impulses from the electrodes simulated period pain. Knockemout's residents weren't ones to back down from a challenge, and I had to admit, it was pretty entertaining to watch tatted bikers and buff farmer types line up for their turn to try to walk with level 10 period cramps.

It took a hot minute or five, but Max finally ambled over and flopped down in the chair across from me. She had icing on her chin. "Lina."

"Max."

"Your eye looks better."

"Thanks."

"Heard you got it wrestling two murderers who tried to attack Sloane and Naomi while filming the pilot of a bounty hunter TV show."

So much for my professional anonymity . . . and pesky things like the truth.

"Nothing that exciting," I assured her.

"What'll it be? Feel like tryin' a Crappy Hour special? We got half-priced Bloody Marys and a cocktail Silver came up with called Red Death. It tastes like shit and it'll fuck you up."

"I think I'll stick with bourbon." It was one and done for me until I was sure I'd gotten my stress level under control.

"Suit yourself." Max sighed and heaved herself

to her feet. "I'll be back after the Midol kicks in."

She shuffled back to the bar and I used the opportunity to wade through some work emails on my phone until raucous male laughter erupted in the corner.

I'd spent a lot of time in a lot of bars watching people interact. I knew when the vibe wasn't right. And there was no doubt in my mind something ugly was brewing from the four men. Their table was littered with empty beer bottles and shot glasses. Their body language was rowdy and borderline aggressive, like sharks deciding whether to attack.

Max arrived at their table and started stacking empties on her tray. One of the men, an older guy with a beer gut and a white, bushy mustache nowhere near as nice as Vernon's, said something that Max didn't like. It caused the table to burst into laughter again.

Max tipped her tray, rolling the empties back on to the table, and—with a parting middle finger—stomped back to the bar.

I recognized one of the younger troublemakers as the man who'd stared at me when I was leaving Waylay's soccer game. "Come on, Maxi Pad, don't be so sensitive. We're just teasin'," he yelled after her.

The foursome put their heads together for what was most likely an off-color joke and busted up laughing again.

"Keep it down, Tate," warned Tallulah from the next table. She was sitting with three other regulars who didn't look any more entertained by the men's shenanigans than I was.

So that was Tate Dilton, disgraced bad cop and good ol' boy.

"It's awful *hard* to keep it *down* around you, pretty," one of Dilton's pals said, gesturing lewdly at his crotch.

The men around the table erupted once again and the tension in the room rose.

I stared hard at Dilton from across the room and waited. It didn't take long. As long as they were sober enough, people could usually sense a threat.

He took a long look back and then said something to the rest of his cronies. They all turned to look at me. I kicked my legs out and crossed them at the ankles.

He stood and headed in my direction, using his best intimidation glare. He walked with the confidence of a man who had peaked in high school and didn't realize the glory days were over.

When he got to my table, he stopped and stared some more. "You got a problem, sweetheart? Maybe an itch I can scratch for you?"

He had a short, Hitler-esque mustache that twitched every time his jaw opened and closed on a piece of gum.

"I doubt there's anything you could do for me."

"You're Morgan's bitch, ain't ya?" He was wearing a Knockemout PD shirt and that pissed me off even more than the insult.

"No. Are you?" I asked sweetly.

His eyes narrowed, nearly disappearing behind his ruddy cheeks as he pulled out the chair opposite me. He spun it around backward in a move that should never impress a woman of any age and sat uninvited. "Saw you at the soccer fields fighting. You tell your cop boyfriend there are plenty of us round here who don't like the shit he's forcing down our throats. Maybe let him know that if he ain't careful, we might just have to take him down a peg or two."

"Have you considered taking your aversion to the social requirement of regular bathing up the chain of command?"

"Huh?" He blinked, then chewed furiously for a few seconds.

"Oh. Maybe your cause is more public affairs related. Let me guess. You don't think you should have to wear pants inside the Piggly Wiggly when you buy your six-pack of cheap-ass beer."

He leaned in and I could smell the liquor on his breath. "That's some smart mouth you're runnin'."

"Are all these multisyllabic words making it hard for you to keep up?"

"Keep it up and your bitch ass will be leaving

here with serious regrets." His gaze flicked to my eye. "Looks like someone already taught you some manners."

"They tried. Now, why don't you and your friends go on home before one of you does something stupider than usual?"

"You want me to take you down to the station for runnin' that pretty mouth at a cop?" He popped the *p* on cop and I nearly rolled my eyes.

"Does Chief Morgan know you're running around impersonating a police officer? Because I'm fairly certain in order for you to be a cop, you gotta have a badge. And I heard a rumor that your badge is locked up in a drawer in Nash's desk."

He jumped to his feet and slammed meaty palms on the table in front of me. I didn't move a muscle as he leaned into my space, filling my nostrils with the smell of cheap liquor.

Fi, Max, and Silver were heading in our direction looking like they were ready to go to war. But they didn't need to make themselves targets. Not when I was the one who was only in town for the short term.

I held up a hand. "I got this," I assured them and slowly got to my feet to face the bloated bully.

"Go home, Tate," Fi said, taking the lollipop out of her mouth to use her scary mom voice.

Silver's jaw flexed as she kept one hand

clamped over her uterus and the other curled into a fist. Max was holding her tray on her shoulder like it was a baseball bat.

"You wanna take a swing at me, Dilton?" I whispered softly.

He bared his teeth . . . and his chewing gum.

I gave him a mean little smile. "I dare you. Because you do and you're not making it out of here intact. Not only am I itching to add 'broken nose' to your physical catalog of 'beer belly' and 'receding hairline,' but the entire female population of Knockemout is riding the crimson tide right now, and I'm betting there're more than a few local ladies you did wrong over the years."

He sneered, his face turning harder and uglier with the effort.

"So go ahead, asshole. Take your free shot, but it's the only one you're gonna get. Once we're done with you, there won't be anything left to pin a badge on," I said.

He straightened and balled both hands into fists at his sides. I could see him weighing the options in his tiny, inebriated brain. But before he could make my day by making the wrong move, a large hand landed on his shoulder.

"Think it's time you went home, pal."

I looked up and then up some more at the man who'd stepped in. Cereal Aisle Guy to the rescue.

Dilton turned to face him. "Why don't you mind your own damn . . ."

The rest of his sentence disappeared a split second after Dilton realized he was talking to the man's Adam's apple, not his face.

I smirked, and a twitter of nervous laughter rose up around us.

"You wanna finish that thought?" Cereal Aisle Guy asked.

Dilton glowered at him. "Fuck you," he spat.

"I were you, I wouldn't want to be making a spectacle of myself. It draws unnecessary attention," Cereal Aisle Guy said.

Dilton looked like he wanted to say something else, but he was interrupted by his asshole posse.

"Let's hit up another bar. One with less bitches," one of his idiot friends suggested.

I kid you not, the women at the tables closest to us started hissing.

Someone threw the remains of their fry basket, hitting Dilton square in the chest.

"Now ain't the time, Tate," the older man with the mustache called. "Be smart."

There was something ominous about the way he said it.

"If you don't get him out of here, Wylie, I'm callin' the cops. The real ones," Fi snarled.

"Already here." The entire bar turned to see U.S. Marshal Nolan Graham at my back, his badge and gun on full display. "We got a problem here?"

"I think that's your cue to leave, *sweetheart*," I said to the ketchup-covered Dilton.

"Why don't we step outside?" Nolan suggested. His tone was almost amicable, but his eyes were cold steel.

"I'll be seein' you again," Dilton promised me as his friends each took an arm and followed Nolan out the door. The older man with the mustache stopped in front of me, looked me over from head to toe, snorted, and then strolled outside with a smirk.

The ladies who weren't too busy pressing both hands to their cramped abdomens erupted in cheers as the door swung shut behind them.

I produced my credit card and held it aloft. "Fi, this round's on me."

The pandemonium reached hysteria levels and then someone plugged Shania Twain's "Man! I Feel Like a Woman!" into the jukebox.

I turned back to the man who had white knighted me twice now. "Cereal aisle guy," I said.

His lips curved in an almost smile. "Unmarried friend of the old lady."

"Your nickname is better."

"I could call you Trouble."

"You wouldn't be the first."

He nodded toward the door. "You shouldn't go around antagonizing men like that."

Even Cereal Aisle Guy had an opinion on my life choices.

"He started it."

"Sounded like he's got an issue with the local cops. Wasn't the chief of police here shot a couple weeks back?" he asked.

"He was."

The guy shook his head ruefully. "And I thought small-town life would be quiet."

"If you want quiet, Knockemout probably isn't the place to find it."

"Guess not. They find the guy who shot the cop? Cause the one they just hauled out of here looks like he wouldn't mind putting a bullet or two in someone," he said.

"The FBI is investigating but they haven't made any arrests. I'm sure the guy who did it is long gone. At least, he is if he has half a brain."

"I heard the chief doesn't even remember what happened. That's gotta be weird."

I didn't really feel like talking about Nash to anyone. Especially not a stranger, so I simply raised my eyebrow.

He flashed an embarrassed smile. "Sorry. The gossip here runs fast and deep. Back home, I didn't even know my neighbors' first names. Here everybody seems like they already know your social security number and great-grandmother's maiden name."

"Welcome to Knockemout. Can I buy you a drink for your heroics?" I offered.

He shook his head. "I've gotta get going."

"Well, thanks for stepping in. Even if I totally had the situation handled."

"No problem. But maybe be more careful next time. You don't wanna go making yourself a target."

"I'm sure that creep has bigger problems than worrying about me. For instance, he'll probably be having nightmares about you tonight."

The grin was back. "Rain check on that drink."

"You got it," I said and watched him leave.

"On the house," Max said, appearing next to me with the bourbon I'd ordered.

"Thanks. And thanks for not telling me I should have minded my own business."

Max snorted. "Please. You're the shero of Honky Tonk. Tate has no idea how lucky he is. We woulda tore his ass up tonight. Then Knox woulda been pissed at all the property damage. And Studly Do-Right woulda been mad about the blood and paperwork."

"The Morgan brothers owe us one," I agreed.

Nolan came back inside, stroking his finger and thumb over his mustache and frowning.

"What's wrong?" I asked.

"I think I might have to shave."

My lips twitched. "I think you should keep it. Reclaim the 'stache."

He took the chair Dilton had vacated and waved Fi over.

"I wouldn't do that if I were you," I warned, pointing to the Shark Week signage.

"Shark Week's in the summer, isn't it?"

"Not that kind of Shark Week. This one's scarier."

Fi appeared with a fresh lollipop. She tossed my credit card on the table in front of me and then dug the heels of her hands into her lower back. "God. It feels like my kidneys are trying to tunnel their way out of my flesh. Why is nature such a bitch?"

"Oh, *that* kind of Shark Week," Nolan said, catching on.

"Yeah. So whatever you're about to say better be worth my time and suffering coming over here," Fi said.

"I just wanted to politely and respectfully suggest that you pull the security footage from tonight and save it somewhere."

"Any particular reason?"

"I don't know what's public knowledge and what's not," Nolan hedged.

"You mean Nash firing Tate for being a bad cop and a shitty human being?" Fi prompted.

"Word travels fast around here. Sometimes it's even the truth," I said.

"Just in case things escalate, it wouldn't hurt to be able to prove a pattern," Nolan said.

"I wouldn't be surprised if he escalated the shit out of things," Fi said on a groan. "He's got a whole lot of artificial self-worth wrapped around that badge. Without it, who knows what he'll do to feel like top dog?"

"Keep an eye out," Nolan advised.

"Will do. Now if you'll excuse me, I'm going to go lie down in the back seat of my minivan for ten minutes. I'll send Max over with a drink for you, Marshal."

We watched her limp away.

"I can't imagine going through something like that every damn month," Nolan said, shaking his head.

"You don't think we're like that with our jobs, do you?" I asked.

"Like what?"

"Like we get our self-worth, our purpose from our careers."

"Oh, you want me to lie to you. Okay. No, we're not at all like that, Solavita."

"Come on."

"Babe, I lost my marriage over this job and I don't even like what I do."

"So why don't you quit?"

"And do what?"

"I don't know. Win back the girl?"

"Right. Because the only thing more attractive than a man married to his job is an unemployed ex-husband begging for a second chance," he said dryly. "Nope. Some of us are just destined to live for the job."

"You don't think there's anything better out there than this?" I asked.

"Of course there's something fucking better out there. Just maybe not for you and me. At least me. If you think for a second I wouldn't quit my job and spend the rest of my life rubbing my ex's feet and packing her lunches if she said she'd take me back, you're dead wrong. But there's only so many times you can shut somebody out before they stop trying to get in."

"But is it worth it? Letting someone in when you know you just made it that much easier for them to rip you apart? I mean, seriously, what could be that good to make that kind of risk worth it?"

"You're asking the wrong guy. I don't know what's on the other side, but I'd sure as hell be willing to risk finding out if I got a second chance."

Nolan's words made me feel just a little bit cowardly. I had no problem confronting a drunken bully, but the idea of opening myself up to someone had my knees knocking together.

"So how did dinner with Sloane go?"

"Good. She's a great girl. Smart. Fucking adorable. A little wild."

"But?" I prompted, reading his face.

"But will I sound like a big girl if I say I might not be over my ex?"

"Yes," I teased. "If it makes you feel better, I

think our little librarian is just looking for a good time. Not wedding bells."

"I don't like to kiss and tell, but after I told her about my ex, she told me she's just in it for after-third-date sex."

I choked on my bourbon. "Well, as long as you're both on the same page."

"Here you go, Marshal. It's a Red Death," Max said, dropping a rocks glass filled with a murky red beverage.

"Actually, can I get a—"

I kicked him under the table and shook my head as Max's eyes narrowed threateningly.

"I beg your pardon?" she said frostily.

"I mean, this looks great. Thank you very much. Here's twenty dollars for your trouble," Nolan said, quickly shoving a bill at her.

Max nodded regally and snatched up the cash. "That's what I thought you meant."

Nolan took a sip and immediately winced. "Jesus, God. It tastes like a hangover."

"How do you feel about trying period cramps on for size?" I asked.

Later that night, I was curled up on the couch with another murdery library book trying not to think about what Nolan had said when I heard a thump against my front door. It was late, after eleven, which was usually when bad things happened.

I slipped off the couch and quietly made my way to the door.

You needed a key to get into the building, but in my line of work, I knew that even a sturdy exterior door and living next to the chief of police wouldn't deter a drunk, determined idiot who'd had his ego dented.

I held my breath and peered through the peephole. There was no one there. Across the hall, Mrs. Tweedy's door was closed. I was debating whether to grab my trusty baseball bat to go investigate when I heard a faint scratching sound coming from the bottom of my door. It was accompanied by a familiar jingle.

Opening the door, I found Piper prancing in place looking anxious. Next to her, slumped against the wall was Nash. He was shirtless, sweating, and shivering.

The guy sure knew how to take a girl on a roller coaster of emotion.

"Hey," he panted, tilting his head to look up at me. "Mind taking . . . Piper . . . for a bit?"

I said nothing as I helped haul him to his feet. There was nothing to say. We'd hurt each other, but he'd come to me when he needed help. And I wasn't quite mean enough to turn him away. Wordlessly, he looped one arm over my shoulders while I slid mine around his waist.

It felt familiar. But I wasn't supposed to have a routine with anyone, let alone *him*.

Tremors racked his body as we shuffled inside with Piper dancing nervously at our feet.

"Bed or couch?" I asked. His skin was hot and sticky against mine.

"Bed."

I guided us into my bedroom and, knowing his preference, pushed him down on the side closest to the door. Piper heroically vaulted onto the mattress and marched back and forth, surveying Nash from head to bare feet.

"I'll get some ice," I said. I didn't have any frozen vegetables in my freezer, and I didn't think cold takeout would do the trick.

Nash's hand clamped over my wrist. "No. Stay." Those blue eyes pulled me in. There were no walls or old wounds in them. There was only an honest plea and I was helpless against it. "Please."

"Fine. But this doesn't mean I'm not still furious with you."

"Same goes."

"Don't be an ass."

I tried to round the foot of the bed, but he stopped me and pulled me back. He jackknifed into a seated position, hooked me under the arms, and pulled me on top of him.

"Nash."

"Just need you close," he whispered.

When he collapsed back against the pillows, he settled me into his side, my thigh draping over his hips, my head resting on his chest just below the scar on his shoulder.

I could hear the thunder of his heartbeat, and I splayed my palm across his chest. He shuddered once and then his muscles seemed to lose some of the tension they held so rigidly.

He let out a tremulous sigh, then wrapped both arms around me, pressed his face to my hair, and held on tight.

Piper claimed her space at Nash's feet, resting her head on his ankle and shooting sorrowful glances up at us.

With nothing left to do, I breathed with him.

Four. Seven. Eight.

Four. Seven. Eight.

Over and over again until the tension left his body. "Better now," Nash whispered into my hair. We lay there, breathing together, being together until sleep drifted over us both.

29

Winning Career Day

Nash

I woke up to the dreary light of dawn and the sound that haunted me, the persistent brittle crunch that drove me to madness in my sleep. This morning, it was accompanied by the soft click of Lina's front door closing.

The sheets next to me were still warm, a ghost of the woman who'd been there all night, curled into my side, anchoring me with the rise and fall of her chest.

She'd been there for me when I needed her most. And then she'd made a point to leave her own damn bed so I'd wake up alone.

I dragged my hands over my face. Something had to give between us and I had the sinking suspicion that "something" was gonna be me.

A weight hit the mattress, and a second later, Piper pounced on my chest. I grunted. Kibble dust stained her white muzzle, which meant Lina had fed her breakfast.

"Mornin', bud," I rasped, wiping the sleep from my eyes.

She nudged at me until I gave her a half-hearted scruffing.

"Don't look at me like that. I'm fine," I said.

Piper didn't look like she believed me.

But it felt true. Sure, I had a lingering headache at the base of my neck and every muscle in my body felt like it had gone a few rounds in the ring. But I'd slept deep and woken with a clear head.

I picked her up and held her aloft over my head. "See? Everything's fine." Her little tail blurred with enthusiasm as she pawed playfully at the air. "All right. Let's start the damn day."

The dog tip-tapped after me into the bathroom where I found a note taped to the mirror.

N,
Fed and walked Piper. Be gone by the time I get back.
L

I remained amused by Lina's terse note until I returned to the bedroom and spotted her suitcase sitting open on the floor. It was empty, thankfully. But I had a feeling the fact that she'd left it out meant she was still considering leaving. If she thought she was going anywhere, Lina Solavita had a rude awakening coming. We had business to settle. Scales to balance. Deals to make.

Any doubt I'd had about my feelings for her had been erased last night. She didn't have to open her door. She didn't have to let me in. And she sure as hell didn't have to fall asleep in my arms. But she did, because despite the fact that I'd pissed her off, she cared about me.

And I was gonna use that to my advantage.

"Come on, Pipes. Let's go home. We've got some thinkin' to do," I said on a yawn.

I was still yawning when we let ourselves out of Lina's place only to find Nolan raising a fist to knock on my door.

"Brought you a coffee," he said, eyeing my appearance. I was wearing nothing but sweatpants and was in desperate need of a shower. "Shoulda got the bucket size," he observed.

I took the coffee and opened my door.

"Long night?" he asked, following me inside as I guzzled caffeine.

I grunted. "Why are you here? Besides to play coffee fairy."

"Ran into your soon-to-be sister-in-law at the café, who did order the bucket size. She said Knox is pullin' out all the stops for Career Day."

"Fuck me. That's today?"

"Today in"—he paused and checked his watch—"two hours and twenty-seven minutes. Figured since I had to tag along anyway, we could strategize. Can't have law enforcement takin' a back seat to some lottery-winning, bar-owning barber. No offense."

"He's my brother," I said dryly. "None taken.

How's he gonna make paperwork interesting?"

"Naomi doesn't realize how deep male competition runs. She told me the whole plan. He's gonna let the kids mix virgin drinks and then shave the vice principal's head."

"Damn. That's good."

"We can be better," Nolan said with confidence.

"Hit the siren, Way," I instructed, gripping the wheel tight.

Waylay grinned wickedly and punched the button. The siren wailed to life.

"Anybody back there get car sick?" I asked the passengers in the back seat.

"No!" came the giddy chorus.

"Then hang on tight."

I turned the wheel hard, sending the back of the cruiser into a gentle slide around the last traffic cone. Then I stomped on the gas.

"Go! Go! Go!" Waylay screeched.

I crossed the makeshift finish line inches ahead of Nolan and his cruiser full of kids.

The back seat erupted in wild cheers.

I brought the car to a stop and that thing hurting my face, stretching muscles that hadn't been used lately was a God's honest grin.

It was safe to say we'd blown Knox's stupid presentation out of the water.

"OMG! That was the best!" Waylay's friend Chloe said as I opened the back door for her. She and two other sixth graders piled out, all talking at once.

"I'd have had you on that last cone if Barfy McGee hadn't asked me to roll down the windows," Nolan said, hooking his thumb in the direction of a freckled redheaded boy as he headed my way.

"Don't be a sore loser and blame Kaden. The kid drives go-karts on the weekends."

"Think we won?" he asked.

We surveyed the elementary school parking lot.

The kids were in an uproar, begging my officers for the next ride. The teachers were grinning ear to ear. And Knox was flipping me the bird.

"Hell yeah, we did. Gotta say, the driving obstacle course was not a terrible idea."

"Your murder mystery game wasn't half bad either," he said.

"I didn't expect Way to be quite so dramatic with her death scene."

"Speaking of the recently deceased," Nolan said, nodding as my niece skipped our way.

She stopped in front of me and looked up. "Uncle Nash?"

"Yeah, Way?"

"Thanks." She didn't say anything else, just hugged me around the waist and then ran off with her giggling friends.

I cleared my throat, surprised by the emotion I felt. A hug from Waylay Witt was like one from Lina. Unexpected, hard won, and damn meaningful.

"You still love what you do," Nolan observed.

"Yeah. I guess I do," I admitted.

"Hang on to that," he advised.

"What? You don't love spending your days babysitting my ass?"

"Not even a little bit."

"Maybe you should do something about it."

"That's what Lina and I were talking about last night."

"You were with Lina last night?" But that was as far as I got with the questioning before we were interrupted by Waylay's teacher.

"Congratulations, gentlemen. I have it on good authority that this was by far our most memorable Career Day, Chief," Mr. Michaels said, handing me Piper's leash.

It turned out that while Piper was shy around adults, she loved kids, the louder and crazier the better. I'd never seen the damn dog so happy before.

"Happy to help out," I said.

"I have a feeling you just inspired the next generation of Knockemout police officers," he said, stretching an arm out to encompass the sixth-grade frenzy.

Mr. Michaels headed off to talk to some of the other Career Day losers and Knox took his place. "Way to show me up in front of my own kid, jackass."

I smirked. "Can't help it if my job is cooler than yours."

"Your job is ninety percent paperwork."

"Look who's talking, Mr. Inventory and Payroll Hell."

My brother snorted and turned to Nolan. "Appreciate the help with Dilton and his crew last night. Maybe you don't totally suck."

"Lina did most of the dirty work. I came along just in time to help with the cleanup."

"What the hell are you two talking about?" I demanded.

Nolan looked at me. "You come walkin' out of her apartment this morning half naked with bedhead and you don't know?"

"Talk. Now," I snapped.

"Did you unfuck things with her?" Knox asked.

"What happened with Dilton?" I repeated, ignoring my brother.

"He and his buddies were gettin' a little rowdy at Honky Tonk. They pissed off Max the server, which given the timing of the month was pretty fucking stupid. Then Lina caught his eye," Nolan explained.

Of course she did. She'd catch any man's eye.

"What happened?" I reached for my phone. I was going to track Dilton down and kick his ass. Then I'd track Lina down and yell at her for an hour or so for not telling me she'd tangled with my problem.

"Slow your roll, Romeo. Fi said Lina eviscerated the moron with words. Now, back to what you were doin' sneakin' out of her place. She didn't say jack about you this morning when she borrowed my truck," Knox said.

"Goddammit. Why did she need your truck?"

"Lina was holdin' her own," Nolan continued. "But another customer—big guy—stepped in when it looked like Dilton might be too drunk to make good choices. Your manager threatened to call the cops just as I walked in. So I got to escort the assface outside."

"What did he say to her?"

"Dunno. She just said he was being a dick," Nolan said. "After my chat with him, I assumed it was drunken misogyny. Hey, do you guys think I should lose the 'stache?"

"Yes," Knox said. "It makes me want to punch you in the face."

"Damn it. It was supposed to be my freedom facial hair. You know, get divorced, grow some hair, magically turn into a new person."

"I've got a barbershop and a straight razor. Just say the word."

I left the two of them to their facial hair and walked away already dialing.

30

Surveillance with a Side of Drama

Lina

T he smell of pizza wafted through the open windows of Knox's truck. I was camped out in a strip mall parking lot in Arlington. Across the street was a block of row homes that had seen better days.

I was waiting for Wendell Baker, a.k.a. Chubby Goatee Guy. He was beefy, white, balding, and an enforcer for the Hugo family who wore too many gold chains and always had a toothpick in his mouth. According to Tina's questionable intel, Baker collected a paycheck from Anthony Hugo but was tight enough with Duncan that his loyalties were divided.

Authorities hadn't been able to tie Baker to the abduction and shootout, which meant he was free to go about his business. And I was free to follow him . . . hopefully to a pristine 1948 Porsche 356 convertible.

So far, however, Baker had gotten out of bed at 11:00 a.m., grabbed a Grande at Burritos to Go, and then paid his brother's girlfriend a visit that involved unzipping his fly on the front porch before she even answered the door.

Classy guy.

My phone rang again.

"Seriously, people? When did I get so popular?"

I'd already had calls from my mom about Dad's birthday gift, Stef wondering if I was planning to sweat with the oldies at the gym this week, and Sloane, who had forced me to volunteer for something called Book or Treat the following night at the library. Not to mention the text from Naomi telling me she'd given my number to Fi and hoped that was okay. That was followed by a group text from Fi, Max, and Silver from Honky Tonk recapping all the best fictional versions of my run-in with Tate Dilton.

Apparently I had broken a bottle over his head, then shoved him backward into a vat of fryer oil. No one was sure where the vat of oil came from but everyone agreed that it was hilarious watching him crawl out of the bar like human escargot.

That was when I saw the caller ID.

I almost let it go to voicemail before deciding that was the coward's way out.

"I assume you found your way out of my apartment," I said by way of a greeting.

"Why the hell am I hearing about you and Dilton from a U.S. marshal and my dumbass brother instead of you?" Nash demanded.

"First of all, I'd like verification that you did leave my place. Second, when exactly did we have time for a conversation last night? Third—and this is the most important one, so pay attention—what business is it of yours?"

"We spent the night together, Angelina." His voice went gravelly on my name and I pointedly ignored the delicious shiver that rolled up my spine. "That's plenty of time for you to say 'Hey, Nash. I was accosted in public by the asshole you suspended.'"

His impression of me was terrible.

"And then what? You'd have said 'Don't you worry, little lady. I'll make sure you're never alone so the big, drunk wolf can't be a dick to you'? Also, I don't remember it fostering a chatty atmosphere when you showed up mid panic attack at my door."

"Dilton is my problem, not yours. If he's trying to make it yours, I need to know."

That at least made sense. "Fine."

My agreement temporarily shut him down. "Well, okay then. Now, I heard that he approached you, then you threw him through a plate glass window," he said, sounding amused.

I snorted at that one. "Really? Because I heard I dunked him in a vat of fryer oil."

"But what I'm most interested in is he approached you and started running his mouth. Why and about what?"

"I made eye contact with him. He was drunk and disorderly and getting rammy so I looked at him until he looked at me back."

"Need I remind you that with great female power comes great female responsibility?"

I rolled my eyes. "I wasn't trying to become a target or start shit, Chief. I was just trying to distract him from riling up the staff. Max definitely would have deep-fried his ass last night."

"Still don't like it, but fair enough."

"How generous of you."

"Tell me what he said to you."

"He asked if I was your bitch and then gave me a message to give to you. Said it was time to take you down a peg or two. I, of course, insulted his intelligence."

"Of course," Nash said dryly.

"Then he tried to pretend he was a cop who could take me downtown until I found my manners. I may have mentioned that I knew he didn't have a badge anymore and wondered how you'd feel about him impersonating a police officer. Then he insulted me and the women of Knockemout, and just when things were getting interesting, as in fried food being thrown, a bystander and Nolan stepped in."

There was a stony silence on Nash's end.

"You still there, hotshot?"

"Yeah," he said finally.

I didn't know it was possible to pack so much anger into one tiny syllable.

I rocked my head back against the seat. "It was fine, Nash. He was never going to get physical. Not in there. Not with me. He was drunk and stupid but not drunk and stupid enough to forget that a physical altercation with a woman in a public place would be the end of him."

There was more silence.

"Nash? Are you stabbing that spot between your eyebrows right now?"

"No," he lied, sounding a little sheepish.

"It's your tell. You should do something about it."

"Angelina?"

"Yeah."

"I meant what I said. Dilton is my problem. If he tries to contact you again, I need to know."

"Got it," I said softly.

"Good."

"How are you feeling? Not that I care," I added quickly.

"Better. Solid. I kicked Knox's ass at Career Day," he said smugly.

"Literally or metaphorically? Because with you two, it could go either way."

"Bit of both. You sleep okay?" Nash asked.

I'd slept like the dead. Just like I did every time I was in bed with Nash.

"Yeah," I said, not willing to give him more.

"What's that psychology minor say about a girl who doesn't like to be touched except by the guy who just keeps pissing her off?"

"That she has serious emotional issues that need to be addressed."

His laugh was soft. "Have lunch with me, Angel."

I sighed. "I can't."

"Can't or won't?"

"Mostly can't. I'm not in town."

"Where are you?"

"Arlington."

"Why?"

I wasn't falling for the "come on, you can tell me anything" tone. But I also had nothing to hide.

"I'm waiting for Wendell Baker." I told him.

"You're doing what?" He was back to using his cop voice again.

"Don't be dramatic. You know what I mean and who he is."

"You're surveilling muscle for an organized crime family?" he demanded.

And there he was, my pissed-off, overprotective-for-no-reason, next-door pain in the ass.

"I'm not asking for permission, Nash."

"Good. Because I sure as hell wouldn't give it," he said.

"You are infuriating, and I want off this merry-go-round."

"Convince me this is a good idea."

"I don't have to. It's my job. My life," I insisted.

"Fine. I'll come down there running lights and sirens."

"Jesus, Nash. I run trainings on surveillance strategies. I'm damn good at it. I don't need to justify my job to you."

"It's dangerous," he countered.

"Need I remind you that *you're* the one who got shot on the job."

There was a noise on his end of the call.

"Did you just *growl* at me?"

"Shit," he muttered. "I don't know. Every day with you is a new fucking surprise."

I took the tiniest bit of pity on him. "Look, with the heat the feds have brought to Anthony Hugo's activities, no one is doing anything. I've been sitting on two of these guys for days. All they do is eat, have sex with women who should know better, and go to the gym. Maybe hit a strip club. I'm not looking to catch them committing a crime. All I need is for one of them to lead me to a stash house. Even if Duncan is long gone, that car might still be here."

"I still can't believe you're doing all this for a damn car."

"It's not just any damn car. It's a 1948 Porsche 356 convertible."

"Fine. All this for a small, old car."

440

"That small, old car is worth over half a million bucks. And just like everything else we insure, its cash value is one thing. The sentimental value is something else entirely. This car is part of a family's story. The past three generations have gotten married and driven off in this car. There's a vial of their grandfather's ashes in the trunk."

"Shit. Fine. Damn it. I want you checking in with me every half hour. If you're even one minute late, I'll show up and blow your cover so fast it'll make your head spin."

"I don't have to agree to any of this," I pointed out. "You keeping acting like we're in some kind of relationship when we're clearly not."

"Baby, you and I both know there's something here even if you're too scared to acknowledge that."

"*Scared?* You think *I'm* scared?"

"I think I have you shaking in those sexy high-heeled boots of yours."

He was not wrong, which pissed me off more.

"Yeah. Shaking with rage. Thanks for making me regret answering the phone."

"Every thirty minutes, I want a text."

"What do I get out of this deal?"

"I'll go through whatever crime scene files I can get from the warehouse. See if there's anything in those files that might lead you to your damn car."

"Really?"

"Yeah, really. I'll give you whatever I find over dinner tonight."

It was like a dance number we were locked in. Two steps forward, two steps back. Get drawn together. Get pissed off. Rinse. Repeat. Sooner or later, one of us had to end the dance.

"I don't like that you don't think I can do my job."

"Angel, I know you're damn good at your job. I know you can handle yourself better than most. But eventually, someone will sneak past those defenses. And in your line of work, the consequences are a hell of a lot more serious."

He was speaking from personal experience.

"I have to go."

"Every thirty minutes. Dinner tonight," he said.

"Fine. But you'd better bring me something useful and the food better be good."

"Don't get involved. Don't do anything to draw attention to yourself," he warned.

"I'm not an amateur, Nash. Now leave me alone."

"Don't do anything to draw attention to yourself," I said, mimicking Nash. I was in the same spot, just one hour more bored and more uncomfortable. I'd texted the man twice with his stupid, required proof of life, selfies with the middle finger. He'd responded with pictures of Piper. Baker had yet to show his face again. And my ass was asleep.

I was starting to wonder if the thrill of the hunt was only exciting because the rest of the job was so damn boring by comparison. Was it really worth it?

I thought about the position opening up in the company's High Net Assets department. Bigger risk, bigger reward, bigger thrill. But did I *really* want to dedicate the rest of my working life to chasing the thrill? On the other hand, the idea of supervisory work gave me the heebie-jeebies. All those people needing to be managed? Ugh.

But what else could I do? What else would I be good at?

Those were questions that had to wait for another day, because a man in leather and denim carrying a bouquet of grocery store flowers strolled up onto the row home stoop like he owned the place.

Apparently he did, because he produced a key and opened the front door.

I sat up straighter and grabbed my binoculars just as Wendell Baker's brother headed inside.

"Oh shit. This isn't good."

The shouting started shortly after that.

Okay. This wasn't great. But as long as they kept it verbal—

The brother exited his house . . . through the front window . . . which was closed.

"Fuck." I groaned and reached for my phone as glass shattered.

Buck-naked Wendell Baker stomped out the front door. A woman in a rock band T-shirt and nothing else appeared behind him and started screaming. The leather and denim-clad brother got to his feet in time to take a right cross to the jaw.

"911. What's your emergency?"

"This is Lina Solavita. I'm an investigator for Pritzger Insurance. There's a naked man assaulting someone on the sidewalk." I gave the dispatcher the address, and as she repeated it back to me, the woman vaulted over the railing onto Baker's back and got an arm around his throat. He bucked forward trying to unseat his attacker, which unfortunately afforded me a front row seat to view both of their butts.

"Now there's a woman assaulting the naked man."

"I have two units in the area responding," the dispatcher said. "Is the woman naked too?"

"She's wearing a Whitesnake T-shirt and nothing else."

"Huh. Good band."

The brother got to his feet again and rammed his shoulder into Baker's gut, driving the man back against the concrete steps. I thought of Nash's bruised jaw and Knox's black eye and wondered if all brothers fought like this.

"Does anyone have any weapons?" the dispatcher asked.

"None that I can see. Naked guy definitely didn't come armed."

The brothers broke apart and Whitesnake lady slithered off Baker's back. The brother reached behind his back and produced a large knife.

"Shit," I muttered. "Now there's a knife in play."

Just then, two kids exited the house next door and stood transfixed by the scene before them.

"And now there are two kids watching."

"Officers are en route. Two minutes out."

Someone could poke a lot of holes in two minutes.

The brother jumped forward and made the wild slashing motion of an amateur.

Nash's words rang in my head again. But it was either do nothing or let two idiots murder each other in front of children.

I tossed my phone on the seat, opened the door, and laid on the horn.

When I had their attention, I stood on the running board and shouted, "Cops are on the way."

Both brothers started toward me.

"Seriously?" I muttered. "Why are criminals so stupid?"

I was laying on the horn again as they crossed the street when I finally heard the sound of distant sirens.

They stopped in the middle of the street,

debating whether they had enough time to get to me.

I heard the squeal of tires behind me. A white panel van rolled up behind Knox's truck and the door slid open.

A man in a ski mask hopped out, grabbed me by the wrist, and dragged me toward the van.

The brothers were running at us now.

"Get in," Ski Mask said, pulling a gun out of the waistband of his pants. But he didn't aim it at me. He aimed it in the direction of the advancing brothers.

"Um. Okay."

31

Would You Like Onion Rings with That?

Lina

"You guys didn't grab me just to murder me, right?" I asked the van's occupants. "Because you probably could have just let those guys back there do your dirty work."

The driver and the passenger who grabbed me exchanged a look through their ski mask eye holes.

"No one's gettin' murdered," the driver assured me. The sirens were getting louder behind us.

"Might want to hang on," the passenger suggested. Just then, the driver took a hard left turn that had me hitting the floor.

"Ow."

"Sorry about that."

For abductors, they were pretty polite.

"Heard you've been trying to get a meet with Grim," the driver said.

"Is that a problem or are you the welcome wagon?" I asked, rolling into a sitting position and wedging myself against the wall.

The van veered hard to the right as the driver

cut across two lanes of traffic to catch an on-ramp.

"We're clear," the passenger reported.

They both pulled off their ski masks.

"Wait. Don't you want to keep those on so I can't identify you? Or were you lying before when you said you weren't going to murder me?"

The driver was a woman with thick, natural hair that waved voluminously around her head. "Relax," she said in the rearview mirror. "Those were for CCTV cameras, not you."

The passenger, a lean, tattooed guy with a shaved head and a blond beard pulled out his phone and dialed. "Yo. Fifteen minutes out."

He hung up, put his feet on the dash, and turned on the radio.

Coldplay boomed through the vehicle.

They didn't take me to a cool, abandoned warehouse or a seedy motorcycle club house. No. My friendly abductors drove me to a Burger King.

The driver pulled into a parking space and they both got out. A second later, the door slid open and the guy gestured for me to get out with a mock bow.

I followed them inside and was struck with an instant craving for onion rings.

We walked past the registers toward the restrooms.

There in the last booth was the one and only Grim. He was tattooed from knuckles to neck.

The gray T-shirt he wore looked like it had been vacuum sealed to his torso. His silver hair was slicked back from his face, and he wore sunglasses despite the fact that it was an overcast day and he was indoors. He was picking at a salad with a plastic fork.

He pointed at the seat opposite him with the fork and I sat. With a jerk of his head, my friendly abductors were dismissed.

"What can I do for you, Investigator Solavita?" His voice was one of those sandpapery baritones.

"First of all, you can tell me how you found me."

His lips curled in amusement. "My guys were just bringing up the tail end of the parade."

"What parade?"

"We were watching you and the feds watching Hugo's man. Gotta stay abreast of what goes down in my territory."

"Where were the feds?"

"Set up in the empty storefront a block down."

"And they were just going to let the Baker boys knife it out on the street?"

He shrugged his massive shoulders. "I don't waste my time trying to understand why the law does what the law does. I'm more interested in *your* interest in the matter."

"I'm looking for something Duncan Hugo stole and probably stashed locally before he skipped town."

"The Porsche. Sweet ride."

"You're well-informed."

"Pays to know what's going on in my backyard."

"I don't suppose you could tell me where to find that car?" I ventured.

Grim speared a tomato with his fork and ate it. "It never made it to his shop before the bust, and it didn't show at the warehouse prior to his little abduction spree either. Don't know where he's got it."

I let out an irritated sigh. "Well, thanks for your time. Just so you know for future purposes, this abduction could have been a text or an email."

He pushed the remains of his salad to the edge of the table. Within seconds, a biker appeared and cleared it. "What's the fun in that?" Grim asked. "Besides, I've got something more important than info on a car."

"What's that?"

"Rumors. Whispers."

"I didn't dip that guy in fryer oil. I don't know what's wrong with that town's gossip phone tree, but things seriously get lost in translation," I insisted.

His lips quirked again. "Not talkin' about that. I'm talkin' about Duncan Hugo still hangin' around, plotting some pretty big moves."

I blinked. "Hugo's still here? But that would be . . ."

"Stupid?" Grim filled in. "Not necessarily. Not if everyone, including his father, thinks he skipped the country. Not if he's so far underground no one's seen him since he hightailed it out of that warehouse."

"But why would he stay? Everyone from his father to the FBI are looking for him."

"If you were him, why would you stick around?"

I chewed on my lip and ran through the scenarios. "Either I'm an idiot and I think this is all going to blow over or . . ."

"Or," Grim repeated.

"Oh shit. Or I see this as my opportunity to take over the family business. If I can get rid of Daddy, I take his place on the throne."

Grim nodded approvingly. "Smart girl. He doesn't even have to go to war for it. He can just sit tight and wait for the feds to make their move. All he has to do is tie up a loose end here and there."

I had a sinking feeling in the pit of my stomach. "What kind of loose ends?"

"Nash Morgan."

Crappity crap. I looked down at my watch, then winced.

"Can I borrow your phone?"

451

32

A Courtesy Warning

Nash

I wanted to punch something. Anything.

I glanced to my right. Knox was still wearing the fading remains of the shiner I'd given him. Lucian was on my left, legs braced, arms crossed. In all our years of friendship, I'd never thrown a punch at him. I'd also never seen him get physical. I knew he was capable of it. I'd seen the aftermath of it. But I'd never witnessed him in action.

These days, he preferred to unleash that pent-up boyhood fury in other ways.

But for me, I knew there was only one way to get this out of my system.

"Here they come," Knox said.

The half circle of grizzled bikers in front of us parted as a bike roared into the lot. I recognized Grim immediately, but it was his passenger that had me curling my hands into fists.

The bike came to a stop directly in front of me. Lina released her arms from the biker's waist and swung one long leg over in a graceful dismount.

She had barely pulled off the helmet before I

was yanking her into my side, then pushing her behind my back.

"Nash—"

"Don't start," I ordered.

Knox, Lucian, and Nolan closed ranks, and together we formed a wall between her and Grim.

The seconds ticked by as I stared him down.

"Give me one reason why I shouldn't arrest you right now," I growled.

"Saved your girl from getting her ass kicked for one," Grim said smugly.

The first check-in she'd missed had Nolan and me heading for my vehicle. We hadn't even made it out of the parking lot before Grave alerted me to the 911 call in Arlington. I was on the road by the time Lina called me . . . from Grim's phone.

Knox and Lucian showed up at the biker's headquarters about five minutes after we did.

"Gentlemen, I hate to break up this thrilling staring contest," Lina said. "But I *really* have to pee and Grim has information he's graciously willing to share."

"Let's do this inside," Grim said. "Except for him." All eyes turned to Nolan. "One cop is bad enough. I don't need two of you stinking up the place."

Nolan didn't look like he liked that idea.

"It's fine," I assured him.

"Don't do anything stupid in there," he muttered. I nodded.

"So, boys and girls, what do we do while we wait? Shoot some hoops? Play some Scrabble?" Nolan asked the remaining bikers as we followed Grim inside.

Knox grabbed my arm. "Try not to be a law-abiding dick in there, okay? You don't want Grim as an enemy."

I jerked free of his grasp. "Try not to be an asshole in there."

"Both of you behave," Lina hissed.

I took her hand and anchored her to me. No one was getting near her.

I had to admit, this wasn't what I'd expected from a motorcycle club headquarters. Instead of smoke-stained drywall and beer-soaked floors, the interior of the one-story block building resembled more of a club and gallery. The floors were stained concrete. The walls alternated between stark white and dark gray with large, chaotic canvases adding brilliant pops of color.

Grim pointed Lina in the direction of the restroom and I stood guard outside while the others entered what appeared to be some sort of conference room.

When the bathroom door opened and Lina stepped out, I straightened away from the wall.

"Are you okay?"

"I'm fine. I swear. Grim and his biker minions are actually pretty nice. And before you even say it, none of this was my fault."

Every time I looked at her, her beauty struck me like a hammer. Every time my eyes found her, something inside me lit up. I wanted to touch her, to back her into the wall, cage her in, and run my hands over every inch of her body. But if I did that, I didn't know if I would have the strength to stop. So I kept my hands at my sides.

"Nash?" she prodded.

"I know," I said.

She went still, then shook her head in disbelief. "You *know?* What do you know?"

I gritted my teeth. "That it wasn't your fault."

"Gonna be honest. I wasn't expecting that."

"Doesn't mean I'm fuckin' happy about you being in that situation in the first place. Even though I get to say I told you so. Because I fucking told you so. And it sure as hell doesn't mean I enjoyed having no fuckin' clue what happened to you after you called 911. And you can bet every expensive pair of shoes you own that I was the opposite of thrilled to find you were pulled out of that situation by men in ski masks."

"Actually, the driver was a woman," she pointed out.

But I wasn't finished. "And I'm *definitely* havin' issues with seeing you ride up to a god-damn motorcycle club on the back of a goddamn known criminal's bike."

"Look at the bright side, hotshot. Remember

how you hated the numbness? Look at the colorful range of emotions you're experiencing right now."

I started to rub my thumb between my eyebrows, then stopped. "Think I wanna go back to numb."

"No, you don't." Her soft smile disappeared and her eyes went serious. "You need to hear Grim out. I called you for a reason."

She'd called me this time. And that counted for something.

"I'll hear him out, but I can't guarantee I won't take a swing at him or slap cuffs on him."

"Pretty sure a motorcycle club president willingly inviting an officer of the law into his lair is a big deal. Maybe leave the cuffs out of it," she suggested.

We found the others in what was indeed a conference room seated at a long wood table with raw edges and black metal legs.

Grim sat at the head with two of his crew at his back, a short, tatted white guy with a barrel chest and a tall, willowy Black woman with bloodred nails.

Lina waved to the woman and she nodded back.

Knox and Lucian were seated across the table on Grim's left. I claimed the seat to his right and pulled out the chair next to me for Lina.

"Let's get this over with. Don't much care for cops in my house," Grim announced.

"It's not exactly a picnic for me either," I said.

Knox rolled his eyes and Lina kicked me under the table.

I gave her thigh a warning squeeze.

"What Nash means to say is he appreciates you sharing this information," Lina said pointedly.

Grim grunted.

"What have you got?" I asked in a marginally more polite tone.

"My club has had an interest in Duncan Hugo's operations since his split from the family business. We keep our ears to the ground and keep our eyes on wild cards like that little prick," Grim began.

"Especially after he decided to set up a chop shop in your territory," Knox pointed out.

Hugo's original shop had been raided. He'd set up another in the warehouse where Naomi and Waylay had been taken and terrorized. Grim had been the one to alert Knox to where they were being held.

That combined with the fact that Lina was unharmed were the only two reasons my fist hadn't met the man's face.

"That was a factor," Grim admitted. "Our interest remained even after he disappeared. And when a certain persistent insurance investigator made it clear she wanted to chat about Hugo, our interest deepened and we started listening to the whispers."

I didn't have the patience for this tap dance. "What whispers?"

Grim put his elbows on the table and steepled his fingers. "The official word on the street is that Duncan Hugo left town immediately after the shit that went down and bought a one-way ticket to Mexico."

"What's the unofficial word?" Lucian spoke for the first time.

"He never left. He went to ground and started thinking."

"That would be a real stupid move on his part," Knox said.

"The feds are still looking for him. I've got a U.S. marshal up my ass, and Hugo decides to stick around?" I prompted. "It doesn't make any sense."

"It does if he's planning to move on the family business," Grim said.

Lucian and Knox exchanged glances.

Lina's hand found mine on her leg and squeezed.

"You're talking about an organized crime war. You can't raise an army without someone running their mouth. No one makes moves that quiet," I said.

"Not necessarily," Lina cut in. All eyes went to her. "All Duncan needs to do is sit tight until the feds move on his father. He doesn't need an army for that. Just a few loyal soldiers to ease the organization through the transition of power."

Fuck.

"Do the feds know about this?" I asked.

"According to my sources, they've been receiving anonymous information that's helping build their case against Anthony Hugo," Lucian said.

I didn't want to think about how Lucian had sources in the FBI.

"That information could be coming directly from Duncan," Lina pointed out.

"Fuck." My brother combed a hand through his beard. "So he feeds the feds info on Daddy's operation, and when they lock him up, Duncan steps into Daddy's shoes?"

"That's what it looks like."

"Why wouldn't the feds just move on both assholes?" Knox asked.

"Anthony Hugo has been running a criminal empire for decades. His son is small change by comparison," Grim pointed out.

"He tried to kill my brother," Knox barked.

"The feds cut deals all the time to get what they want. They've had a hard-on for Hugo Senior for years. They're not gonna waste resources on a small-time car thief, especially not if he's a valuable enough asset to them," Grim said.

"So what the hell am I supposed to do with this information?" I demanded.

"You're supposed to watch your fuckin' back,"

Grim said. "If Duncan Hugo decides he wants to step in as head of the family, all he has to do is clean up a few loose ends."

Lina's leg tensed under my grip.

"And those would be?" I asked, already knowing the answer.

Grim looked at me. "You." Then he shifted his gaze to my brother. "And your girls."

Knox growled.

"Awful hard to build a case if none of the witnesses can talk," Grim said ominously.

33

Book or Treat

Lina

Me: How's my favorite researcher in the world?

Zelda: Leave me alone unless you have anything else on Burner Phone Guy.

Me: I take it you haven't found him yet?

Zelda: Even my superpowers have limits. Without Hugo's burner phone records or a name or at least a description, I've got a whole lot of jack bubkes.

Me: Define jack bubkes.

Zelda: I have a list of 1,217 people (856 of them are men) affiliated with this guy either through family, school, sports, or miscellaneous. That includes neighbors from every address I've found for him, neighborhood liquor store clerks, his father's employees (both incarcerated and not), mail carriers, etc. Unless you have a way of narrowing it down, we're shit out of luck.

Zelda: Any luck on getting your hands on the crime scene report? Maybe there's something in there that'll help.

Me: No. Nash is MIA since yesterday's visit to Biker World. And now I have to go dress up like Nancy Drew.

Zelda: I have so many questions.

The library's annual Book or Treat event turned out to be an excuse for Knockemout to gather for Halloween-themed snacks and drinks without the chaos of trick-or-treating, which would be here soon enough.

Every October, the street in front of the library closed to traffic for one night to make room for a band, dance floor, food trucks, and, of course, a mobile bar. Library patrons bought tickets to the party, business sponsors badgered by Sloane donated the food and drinks, and the library kept the profits.

Unfortunately for me, the scents of freshly popped pumpkin spice popcorn and hard cider weren't helping me forget how annoyed I was. Not only had Nash bailed on dinner the night before, he'd failed to deliver anything from the crime scene report.

He also hadn't called, texted, or even knocked on my door to demand another sleepover. Which I absolutely would have said no to.

According to the Knockemout grapevine, he, Knox, Nolan, and Lucian had holed up in Knox's secret lair office.

This was monumental because, to date, the

only person Knox had ever allowed to enter such hallowed grounds was Naomi.

Of course, the grapevine also had theories about why the four unlikely amigos were on lockdown. These included the secret disposal of a body, a twenty-four-hour high-stakes poker game, or—my personal favorite—Knox had finally pissed Naomi off over floral arrangements and now he was waiting out her wrath.

But I was pretty sure I knew the truth. The menfolk were strategizing, and they'd left me out of it.

Okay, yes. I preferred to do things on my own. And yes, I didn't love being part of a team. But I was already involved. I was the only one running an active investigation. And those four macho shitheads *still* didn't think to include me.

I realized I'd just crumpled the paper in my hand.

"Uh, here's your receipt. Sorry about the mangling. Thanks for your donation," I said, handing over the balled-up paper to Stasia. The stylist at Whiskey Clipper had just donated a jumbo-sized bag of hardbacks to the library's book drive.

"You doing okay, Lina?" she asked, stuffing the receipt in her bag.

Damn. I really needed to work on my poker face.

"I'm fine," I insisted.

463

"If you're worried about Knox and company, don't be," she said. "I heard they're taking secret ballroom dance lessons to surprise Naomi at the wedding."

I grinned. "You know what I heard?" I paused and looked both ways before leaning across the table.

Stasia leaned in too. "What?" she whispered.

"I heard they're choreographing a flash mob dance. Something involving tearaway pants."

"Oh. My. God. I can't *wait* for this wedding!"

A few minutes later, I was spelled from my book donation duties by Doris Bacon of Bacon Stables, who had come dressed as the Horse Whisperer.

My community service had earned me one glass of spiced wine, I decided. And once I enjoyed it, I was going to go to Knox's office and pound on the door until the Four Dumbasses of the Apocalypse let me in.

I had just acquired my wine when a pretty blond who looked vaguely familiar stopped in front of me. "Lina? Lina Solavita? It's Angie from high school."

Angie Levy, the second highest scorer on my soccer team and the reason I'd started going by Lina in high school because having two Angies on the team was confusing. She was a biology whiz who drove her dad's hand-me-down Excursion that held half the team for ice cream runs. She'd lived on Diet Cokes and peanut butter crackers.

She was older now, prettier too. Her once long blond hair was now cropped in a swingy bob. She wore jeans, cashmere, and a chonky diamond on her left hand.

"Angie? What are you doing here?" I asked, dumbfounded.

"My husband and I work in DC. What are you doing here?"

"I'm just . . . passing through," I hedged.

"You look amazing!" she said, opening her arms as if she were about to hug me.

"Thanks," I said, warding off the hug by gesturing with my glass of wine. "So do you."

"No. Really. You look wonderful. Stunning even."

This coming from the girl who'd canceled my standing invitation to sleepovers at her house.

"Thanks," I said again.

She shook her head and grinned, showing that long forgotten dimple. "I'm gushing. I'm sorry. It's just I've thought about you so often over the years."

I couldn't think of a single reason why. She and the rest of the team, the rest of my friends, had essentially abandoned me.

It wasn't like faulty heart valves were contagious, but being linked to me was apparently deadly for teenage reputations.

"Mom!" A boy with fiery red hair and milkshake staining his jacket launched himself into the midst of our conversation. "Mom!"

Angie rolled her eyes but somehow did so with affection. "Hey. Remember that whole manners conversation we had yesterday and the day before that and the day before that?" she asked.

The boy's eye roll was an exact copy of his mother's. He heaved a world-weary sigh before turning to me. "Hi. I'm Austin. I'm sorry to interrupt."

"It's nice to meet you, Austin," I said, not quite able to smother a smile.

"Cool." He turned back to his mother. "*Now* can I ask you my very important, worth-interrupting-you question?"

"Fire away," Angie said.

He took a deep breath. "Okay, so Davy said there was no way I could beat him at the balloon dart game. Which is totally stupid because I'm way better at throwing things than he is. Only I didn't do so good in the first round because he cheated and poked me in my tickle zone. Which is *not* fair. And I need a rematch."

"So you need more than the ten bucks I gave you in the car that came with an explicit warning not to ask for more because you weren't going to get another dollar out of me," Angie summarized, shooting me an amused look.

He nodded enthusiastically. "Yep!"

"Why didn't you ask your father?"

"He's in a grudge match with Brayden at Whack-a-Mole."

Angie closed her eyes and then looked up at the night sky. "Is it too much to have asked for a little estrogen in my house?" she asked the universe.

"Mom," Austin said on a desperate whine.

"Did you take the garbage out last night?"

"Yes."

"Did you do all your homework for Monday?"

"Uh-huh."

"Are you willing to pull the weeds in the front flower bed without complaining or asking for more money?"

His nod was even more vigorous. "I'll even fold my own laundry for the week."

"Five bucks," Angie said, producing her wallet from her purse.

"Yes!" Austin pumped his fist victoriously.

She held out the bill but pulled it back when her son reached for it. "Hold it, buster. When Davy goes to throw his dart, wave and say 'Hi, Erika.' "

Austin frowned. "Why?"

"Because your brother has a crush on her and he'll be distracted." She held out the five-dollar bill again.

He snatched it out of her hand, his freckled face lighting up. "Thanks, Mom! You're the best."

I watched him dash off into the crowd, cash held triumphantly over his head.

"Sorry about that. My entire life for the past

467

decade has been nothing but interruptions," Angie said. "Three boys who go to bed every night and wake up with all manners erased from their brains so you have to start over with feral cave babies every morning. Anyway. What was I saying?"

"I should probably head out," I said, looking for an escape.

"Oh! I know. I was saying I've been thinking about you a lot."

And we were back to awkward. "Ah. Yes. That," I said.

"I always regretted not trying harder to force my way over those walls after . . . you know."

"My cardiac arrest in front of half the town?" I filled in glibly.

The dimple flashed again. "Yeah, that. Anyway, even in the midst of my teenage narcissism, I knew I should have tried harder. I should have made you let me be there for you."

"Made me?" My shoulders tensed. "Look, it was a long time ago, and I'm over it. I'm not going to blame a bunch of teenage girls for not wanting to hang out with the 'dead girl.'"

"Ugh. If I were Wayne Schlocker's mother, that boy would have been grounded until college."

Wayne was an athletic, God's-gift-to-girls-and-football turd. It didn't surprise me that he'd been the one to come up with the nickname.

"You do know that Cindy punched him in the

468

middle of the cafeteria for that, don't you? And then Regina squirted an entire bottle of ketchup on him. The whole team started calling him Wayne Shit Locker after that."

"Seriously?"

"Of course we did. You were our friend and you were in the hospital. What happened was never a joke to us."

I had to ask. I needed the answer to my first unsolved mystery. "Then why did you just disappear?"

Angie cocked her head and gave me a mom look. "We didn't. At least not at first. Don't you remember? We were there every day while you were recovering. In the hospital, then at your house."

I did vaguely recall swarms of teen girls crying, then laughing in my hospital room and then my bedroom. But the swarms had gotten smaller and smaller until there were no visits.

"You know what? It's not important. It happened a long time ago."

"The fault is mine. Teenage me expected teenage you to bounce back. To go back to normal," Angie admitted.

But normal hadn't been in the cards for me. Not for years after.

"I kind of expected that too," I admitted.

"Instead of the 'normal' I expected, you went into a dark place. Which now, after Austin, I understand. I didn't then. Neither did the other girls. And because we didn't understand, we let you push us away."

Another memory surfaced. Angie and our friend Cindy lying on my bed, flipping through magazines, debating how much cleavage was too much for a school dance. Me sitting in the window with bandages on my chest knowing not only wouldn't I be showing cleavage, I wouldn't be going to the dance.

Instead, I'd be traveling to see a specialist.

Worse, no one had asked me to the dance in the first place.

"God, is that all you idiots care about?" I'd snapped at them. *"Dates and boob tape? Do you know how vapid you sound?"*

I winced at the long-buried memory.

I'd felt abandoned, but I hadn't accepted responsibility for the role I'd played. I'd all but evicted my friends from my life.

"What happened with Austin?" I asked.

"Leukemia," she said. "He was four. He's seven now, still in maintenance chemo. But the kid is amazing, minus being an asshole to the twins. I had this aha moment during a playdate we forced Austin into. My husband and I were trying to deliver as much 'normal' as possible."

"My parents went the opposite route," I said wryly.

"I remember it. Your poor mom would stick her

head in your bedroom door every fifteen minutes when we were there. I thought it was over-the-top smothering at the time. But now?" She blew out a breath. "I don't know how she was able to restrain herself. I thought we were going to lose him. And for a few minutes, your mom really did lose you."

"Well, I'm glad your son is doing better," I said, feeling all kinds of awkward.

"With the help of his friends. He and his two best friends were outside throwing rocks into the creek. Something upset him and Austin had a pretty epic fit. Called them names. Told them he didn't want to play with them anymore. And you know what they did?"

"Started throwing rocks at each other?"

Angie grinned and shook her head. Her eyes glistened. "Those little doofuses hugged him." A tear slipped free and slid down her cheek. She wiped it away hastily. "They told him that it was okay that he was feeling bad and that they were going to be his friend no matter how bad he felt."

I felt a stinging in my eyeballs. "Well, crap."

"Ugh. I know, right? You wouldn't think little boys would have more emotional maturity than teen girls, but they did." Angie swiped away another tear. "Anyway, that was a turning point for Austin. He stopped fighting his treatments so hard. His temper tantrums got fewer and farther between. And he started enjoying 'normal' again.

That's when I realized how badly we'd messed up that turning point for you. We didn't dig in. We didn't accept the bad and we weren't patient enough to wait for the good to come back. And for that, I'm so very sorry. What happened to you wasn't fair and neither was how we handled it. But because of you, I was able to be a better mom to my son when he needed me the most."

I couldn't blink, because if I did, the hot tears would escape and wreak havoc on my kick-ass eyeliner.

"Wow," I managed.

Angie dug a wad of tissues out of her mom purse. "Here," she said, offering me half of it.

"Thanks." I took it and dabbed at my eyes.

"Well, I didn't expect to be doing this tonight," she said with a sniffly laugh.

"Me neither." I blew my nose and took a swig of wine.

A handsome ginger guy in a ball cap strode up. "Hey, babe, the boys conned me into—oh shit." He looked at Angie, then to me, then back to Angie. "Is this an I-need-a-hug-and-alcohol-right-now moment or a funnel-cake-will-fix-it moment?"

Angie let out a soggy laugh. "Definitely funnel cake."

"I'm on it," he said, pointing at her with both hands. "I love you. You're beautiful. And me and the boys are so lucky to have you."

"Extra powdered sugar," Angie called after him. She turned back to me. "That was my husband. He's pretty great."

"I guessed."

"Can I give you a hug now? Or I guess, more accurately, can you give me a hug?" she asked.

I hesitated for the briefest of seconds and then decided. "Yeah."

I opened my arms and she walked right into them. It was weird how not weird it felt to be hugging an old friend who I'd thought I'd lost. Dozens of memories of better times surfaced and I realized how deep I must have buried them.

"Hey, Lina! Get your ass over here. We need you in the photo booth," Sloane shouted from the sidewalk. She was dressed as Robin Hood, and the long feather in her green felt cap was already broken.

"Hurry up before my fingers get frostbite," Naomi called, wiggling a boozy milkshake at me. She was dressed as *Pride and Prejudice*'s Elizabeth Bennet in an empire-waist gown with some impressive cleavage.

"Or before we bring all the boys to the yard," Sloane added.

On cue, Harvey the biker raced up to them and started dancing.

I laughed and released Angie. "I'd better go."

"Yeah, me too. Who knows what the twins conned my husband into."

"Twins? You poor thing," I teased.

"The worst. Don't ever do it," she joked. "Anyway, we live forty-five minutes from here. Do you think I could give you my number and we could get together someplace that doesn't allow children?"

"I'd like that."

"It's great to see you. I'm glad you found some real friends," Angie said with that proud mom smile.

We traded numbers and went our separate ways.

I submitted to two rounds of posing in the photo booth and sampled Naomi's milkshake. Sloane handed me a copy of the printout and we laughed at the antics captured.

Real friends. That's what Angie had called them. Naomi and Sloane had accepted all of me, including my less-than-perfect parts.

Was I still holding everyone at arm's length? And was it time to change?

"We should dance," Sloane announced.

"I don't know if I can dance. These gussets make it hard to breathe," Naomi said, fiddling with the ribbing under her boobs.

I felt a tingling sensation between my shoulder blades. There were only two things that created that kind of awareness: trouble and Nash Morgan.

I turned and found Nash flanked by Knox, Nolan, and Lucian, approaching like a team of stoic sentries immune to the merriment around them. The closer they got, the faster my heart beat.

Naomi threw herself into Knox's arms. His eyes closed as he pressed his nose and mouth to her hair and breathed her in. Sloane glared at Lucian like he was the sheriff of Nottingham before smiling and waving at Nolan.

Meanwhile, I pretended not to notice Nash's gaze boring holes in me.

"I missed you," Naomi said as Knox released her. "Is everything okay?"

"Just dealin' with some business. Didn't mean to worry you, Daze," Knox said almost tenderly.

"You weren't really hiding a body, were you?" she teased.

"Angelina," Nash said quietly. His gaze traveled my body. "Who are you supposed to be?"

"I'm Nancy freaking Drew and you're late." I put my hands on my hips and was trying to decide whether I was going to yell at him or ignore him when the universe delivered an answer for me. The band launched into the opening bars of Luke Bryan's "That's My Kind of Night," and suddenly I wanted nothing more than to be far away from this exact spot.

"Let's dance." I grabbed Sloane, who grabbed Naomi, and off we went, leaving the men staring after us.

"I don't know the steps," Naomi said.

"It's easy," I promised, dragging my friends into the center of the crowd of dancers as they lined up. "Besides, with those boobs, no one's going to care if you miss a step. Just follow along."

We slid in between Justice and Tallulah St. John on the left and Fi and her husband on the right. Sandwiching Naomi between us, Sloane and I fell into step with the rest of the dancers.

I'd fallen in love with line dancing in my early twenties thanks to a honky-tonk bar near campus. Country music still reminded me of those early years of freedom when I could just be a girl on the dance floor and not some medical miracle.

We were surrounded by denim, leather, and a parade of Halloween costumes. The sharp clomp of boots echoed off the asphalt. Colors blurred as we whirled around. I forgot about Duncan Hugo. About Nash Morgan. About work and what came next. I focused on Naomi's laughter, the platinum gleam of Sloane's ponytail as we danced.

But I could only block out the real world for so long. Especially with those blue eyes locked on me.

Every time I spun, my gaze was drawn to Nash and company standing on the edge of the crowd, legs braced, arms crossed. Together they formed a wall of unfairly hot masculinity. It should have gone against the laws of nature to allow so many perfect specimens of alpha male to occupy the same territory.

They were all frowning.

"Why are they glaring at us?" I groused between boot stomps.

"Oh, that's Knox's happy face," Naomi insisted, stepping the wrong way before correcting her course.

Sloane clapped in time with the rest of the crowd. "That's Lucian's asshole face."

Dancers whooped as the song came to an end. But just as we all broke ranks, the next song started and Justice claimed me, spinning me out and pulling me back. Laughing, I joined him in a two-step until Tallulah appeared. Justice spun me out again and grabbed his wife. I hooted with laughter as another pair of arms found me. It was Blaze, one half of my favorite lesbian biker couple.

Together we cut an enthusiastic rug, singing along with the rest of the crowd. I barely heard the indignant squeak over the chorus. But there was no missing the shrill "Get your hands off me, asshole." Blaze and I came to a halt on the dance floor, and I spotted Sloane, baring her teeth and struggling against the grip of one of Tate Dilton's friends.

34

Inevitable

Lina

He was a big, sweaty guy who had clearly had more than his fair share of beer. He also didn't look like the type to crack a book, and I was willing to bet he'd crashed this party.

I pushed my way through the crowd.

"I said, back off," Sloane growled as I arrived at her side.

"Now where you runnin' off to, darlin'?" the big man said, flashing a grin with a gold canine tooth. He tried to perform some kind of dance step but only succeeded in twisting Sloane's arm and knocking the glasses off her face.

"That's it. Take a hike, micro penis," I snapped, inserting myself between them and breaking his hold on Sloane's arm.

His attention zeroed in on me. "Why don't you give yourself a feel, sweetheart," he slurred. He grabbed my wrist with a stinging grip and stupidly yanked it toward his crotch.

"I wouldn't do that unless you've got enough sick leave saved up for a testicle retrieval operation," I said, fighting the downward trajectory.

"Woooo wee! I like 'em spirited," Drunky

McBad Choice said, twisting my wrist painfully and leaving himself wide open. "Who are you supposed to be?"

I closed my free hand into a fist. "Get a clue," I said, winding up. But instead of the satisfying connection of knuckle to face I expected, I found myself freed from his grip and airborne thanks to the strong arm that snaked around my waist.

"Hey!" I yelped.

"Hold her," came the terse command as Chief Nash Morgan handed me off to his brother.

"Let me go!" I demanded, fighting against Knox's grip.

In my rage, I noticed that Lucian had Sloane in a similar hold. The man was shooting daggers of the eyeball variety at Biker Big Mistake.

"You got this?" Knox asked Nash as he locked my arms at my sides before I could jump back into the fight. The Morgans were stubborn *and* strong.

"I got this."

The steel in Nash's voice, the arctic chill in his blue eyes had me going still. I'd never seen him so furious.

Hurt? Yep.

Amused? Sure.

Charming? Absolutely.

Stupidly stubborn? A thousand times yes.

But the icy mask of rage he wore now was something new.

There was definitely something wrong with me because that one look at his face made me hot. Like hand-a-girl-a-fresh-pair-of-underwear hot.

I gave one last flail, but Knox's grip was unbreakable.

"*I* wanted to punch him," I whined.

"Get in line, Leens," Knox said.

There was a line, I realized. Nash was at the head, Nolan next with Lucian—still holding Sloane—at his back. Knox and I brought up the rear.

"You're under arrest." Nash's voice rang with authority.

"Arrest? Me punching him would have been a hell of a lot more satisfying," I complained.

"Be patient," Knox said.

Sloane struggled against Lucian's grip. "If you don't get your hands off me, I'll—"

"You'll what?" Lucian interrupted her. "Kick me in the ankle and call me names?"

She growled in response.

"Maybe hand Sloane off to Graham?" Knox suggested belatedly.

"No," Lucian said, his voice colder than an iceberg.

"You can't arrest me! I ain't done nothin'," Booze Breath whined.

Naomi appeared next to us, a bag of popcorn in hand. "I think you can let her go now, Viking," she said.

"Daisy, I know you think that. But this ain't my first rodeo with Bar Fight Lina. I let her go and she's gonna start breakin' faces."

"Oh come on! One time," I spat, renewing my struggles.

"Two times," he argued, locking his arms tighter around me. "You're forgetting that asshole's nose in Pittsburgh."

I got enough room to elbow him in the gut. Unfortunately his rock-hard abs did more damage to my elbow than vice versa. What was it with the men in this town and their muscles? "Ouch! Damn it! You're the one who threw him through a window."

"Calm the fuck down, Lina," he growled.

"Honey, you do know that doesn't work on women, right?" Naomi said, scooping up a handful of popcorn.

"Knox, if you don't let me go, I'm going to start with *your* face," I warned.

"You put your hands on two women who made it clear they didn't want them there," Nash was saying to the unpunched face of the biker. "You're under arrest."

"What seems to be the problem here?"

"Fuck," Knox muttered as Tate Dilton strolled into the situation.

"Yeah, you're gonna want to let me go now," I hissed.

"I got this," Nolan said over his shoulder.

"This has nothing to do with you, Dilton," Nash said, his voice snapping with authority.

Dilton sneered. "Looks to me like you're abusin' your power. Someone's gotta stand up for what's right."

"You sure you know what that looks like?" Nash asked.

"Here we go," Knox muttered. He lifted me off my feet and handed me to Harvey, the gigantic biker with arms the size of my head. "Hold this."

"Sure thing, Knox. How's it going, Lina?" Harvey asked as he wrapped those tattooed pythons around me. I managed to kick Knox in the ass as he left but it was only a glancing blow and did little to soothe my temper.

Lucian deposited Sloane next to Naomi. "Move from this spot and we'll have problems," he warned, looming over her with a finger in her face.

"Bite me, Lucifer."

Knox and Lucian took their stances next to Nash and Nolan.

"Pretty sure you're the only one being investigated for abuse of power, ya jack wagon," someone in the crowd drawled at Dilton.

"You shut your dirty, lyin' mouth or I'll shut it for you," he snarled.

He was drunk, which made him that much more dangerous. I noticed Sergeant Hopper and another officer sidling up behind the first line of defense, ready to step in if necessary. Realizing I wasn't going to get a shot at avenging Sloane or myself, I let myself go limp against Harvey.

He released me, then patted me on the head before stepping up next to Hopper.

Irritated, I joined Naomi and Sloane. Our view was restricted by the ring of Knockemout citizens taking Nash's back.

"Come on," I said, spotting an abandoned picnic table.

"But Lucian told Sloane not to move," Naomi said, lifting the hem of her dress.

"Lucian can kiss my ass," Sloane said and followed me.

The three of us climbed up onto the table.

"Pretty sure he'd like to do more than kiss it," I guessed.

She ignored my comment and squinted at the crowd. "All I can see are pissed-off blobs."

"We'll get your glasses as soon as Nash is done talking these assholes to death," I promised.

Naomi shook her head. "Oh, he's not talking them to death. He's lulling them into a fake sense of complacency. Just watch."

"Tate?" A pretty blond on the edge of the crowd wrung her hands.

"Go back to the car, Melissa," Dilton snapped.

"Mom called. Ricky has a fever—"

"Go back to the fuckin' car!"

The woman scurried away, disappearing into the crowd.

"You're under arrest, Williams," Nash said to the guy who'd grabbed Sloane. "You have the right to an attorney."

But Nash wasn't reaching for cuffs and he also wasn't taking a defensive stance. From my vantage point, I could see Williams getting ready to do something really stupid. He waited until Nash had almost finished reading him his rights before making his move.

I watched in slow motion as the man's fist plowed into Nash's face. A very feminine gasp escaped me as his head snapped back with the force of the blow. But he didn't stagger and he didn't put his hands up to defend himself.

I made a move to jump down from the table, but Naomi stopped me. No one else in the crowd had moved a muscle.

"What the hell is he doing?" I hissed. "Nash just let that guy hit him."

"It's a whole thing," Naomi said. "If he gets hit first, it's self-defense, and according to Lucian, the legal bills are smaller."

"Plus, this counts as resisting arrest," Sloane added.

"Why, I do believe Bronte Williams just assaulted an officer while resisting arrest," Harvey yelled through cupped hands.

"That's what I saw," a woman in flannel agreed. "Same here."

"I feel unsafe with this criminal activity

unfolding in front of me. I might have to defend myself."

A chorus of agreement rang out from the crowd.

"You got your one shot. Now either turn your ass around and put your hands behind your back or try that shit again," Nash said to Williams.

Williams and Dilton exchanged a look and then struck simultaneously. Williams hauled back to hit Nash and found himself taking a face full of pissed-off police chief fist. He went down like an anvil. No swaying. No stumbling. One shot and he keeled over backward, unconscious before he hit the road. It was beautiful.

"Yes!" I said, pumping my arm in victory.

Dilton's swing connected with Nolan's jaw. Nolan spit, then grinned as he raised his own fists.

"What's happening? Did the fat blob just punch Nash? Who are the other two blobs?" Sloane demanded.

Naomi delivered the play-by-play for Sloane as Nolan delivered a one-two combination to Dilton's face that had the man staggering back and tripping over his own damn feet. He landed hard on his ass, which made the crowd laugh.

It was over that quickly.

"Nice shot, Nolan," Sloane yelled.

"Does violence make you want to break your three-date rule?" Naomi teased.

In no time at all, Hopper and the other officer

were loading the two bloodied, handcuffed assholes into the back of a cruiser. Williams was a bit groggy from his recent trip to dreamland, and I felt a sense of vindication when Dilton howled in pain as his ass hit the seat.

I noticed Lucian in the middle of the street pause to pick something up off the ground. He studied it, then tucked it into his pocket. His eyes scanned the crowd, then narrowed when he spotted us on the picnic table.

"Uh-oh," Naomi whispered.

"Uh-oh what?" Sloane demanded. "I can't see shit!"

"Lucian is coming toward us," I said.

"And he looks *mad,*" Naomi added.

Sloane snorted. "Please. He always looks that way. It's a permanent case of PMS."

"Uh, no. I have to agree with Naomi. He looks like he wants to murder someone and that someone might be—"

"I told you to stay put," Lucian snapped at Sloane.

"And I told you to kiss my ass. I guess neither one of us does what we're told," she said, enjoying her vantage point over him.

"Oh boy," Naomi whispered, tilting her bag of popcorn in my direction.

I took a handful.

Lucian reached up, hooked his hands under Sloane's arms, and scooped her off the table. She yelped, then struggled as he held her at eye level for just a beat before lowering her to the ground.

"I love it when a guy can do that," I said.

"Be more careful," Lucian growled. The man was a foot taller than she was and he used that height to loom over her.

Sloane, however, had no intention of being intimidated.

Fire burned bright in her eyes as she went toe-to-toe with him. "Right. Because me dancing is a provocation. I was basically *asking* for some drunk moron to put his hands on me."

Naomi crunched loudly next to me.

"If you don't want me to get involved, stop making it impossible," he snarled.

"Read my lips, Lucian. I don't need you any-where near my life. So you can stop pretending you care. We both know the truth."

"Damn," I whispered, helping myself to more of Naomi's popcorn. "Did his eyes just change color and get more dangerous?"

"Oh, definitely," Naomi agreed.

"He looks like he wants to take a bite out of her," I observed. The fact that neither one of them was writhing on the ground electrocuted by the sparks they fired off at each other was a miracle.

"I know, right? I can't believe they haven't torn each other's clothes off and hate banged yet."

"When they do, I bet it'll shift the earth's axis and send us spinning off into space," I predicted.

Nash stole our attention from the picnic table standoff by clapping his hands in the center of what had been the dance floor. "All right, everybody. It's still a party. What are y'all doing just standing around?"

He gave the band an impatient signal and they immediately launched into Thomas Rhett's "Die a Happy Man."

Knox appeared in front of us. With one tug on Naomi's hand, he had her falling over his shoulder. "Let's go, Daisy." He put a hand on her ass and carried her laughing to the dance floor.

Other couples joined them. I was alone on the picnic table, thinking I could use another drink, when someone snagged my wrist. Nash Morgan looked up at me.

"Get down here," he ordered. His eye was puffy from Williams's fist and there was a drop of dried blood at the corner of his mouth. Two of his knuckles were split and bleeding. He looked so damn heroic I would have swooned . . . if the rest of him wasn't so annoying.

"I'm fine where I—"

He moved fast for a guy still healing from bullet wounds. Before I could fight it, he lifted me off the table and set me on the ground in front of him.

"I'm not dancing with you," I said as his hands settled at my waist.

"Least you can do after that trouble," he said

as he gave another pull that had my hips meeting his. Those blue eyes smoldered and I wondered if my underwear was in danger of catching fire.

"You don't look like you want to dance with me," I said as my arms found their way around his neck.

"What do I look like?"

"Like you want to throttle me."

"Oh no, Angel. I was thinking of something much worse."

For once in my life, I had no intention of poking the bear. I'd seen too much of him, felt too much for him. I was standing on the edge of a precipice that I didn't want to fall from.

We swayed from side to side to the tick-tock beat of the song, never breaking eye contact. He pulled me closer while I used my elbows to push him away, each of us applying more and more force.

"How's your face?" I asked as my arms started to shake.

"Hurts."

"I was handling it, you know. I could have hit him myself," I said as my elbows lost the battle and he pulled me against his chest. Once again, Nash Morgan had gotten closer than I wanted him.

He traced the tip of his nose around the outer shell of my ear. "I know you could, baby. But I was in a better position to do more damage."

"Clearly you've never been punched by me."

We were swaying flush against each other. My elbows were on his shoulders, my hands looped behind his neck.

"Williams has a glass jaw. Everyone knows it. All you need is one shot to the right spot and he goes down like a ton of bricks. Hit him there after he assaults an officer when he's already had two similar charges and the situation cleans itself up real fast."

I pulled back to look up at his face.

"Okay. Maybe I'm a little impressed."

"With what?"

"With you. I was mad. I just wanted to make him bleed. But you were fueled by rage and still had the capacity to run those calculations."

"I had good reason to do it the right way."

"Why's that?"

"He touched you."

He said it so simply, as if he wasn't delivering the truth with the strike of a hammer. As if I didn't feel it inside me like a thousand tiny electric shocks. As if my stupid heart didn't fall right out of my stupid chest and land at his damn feet.

He touched you.

And just like that, I toppled right off that precipice into free fall.

A short, blond Robin Hood popped up next to us. "Hey, Lina? We're running low on raffle tickets and I can't see shit. Do you know where—"

"I'll get them," I volunteered, all but jumping out of Nash's arms . . . out of his gravitational field.

Without waiting for a reply, I hauled ass toward the library. Inside, I slapped a hand to my chest and headed for the stairs. I *liked* my walls. I liked being safe behind them. But Nash was breaking through, and it scared the bejeezus out of me.

I took the stairs at a jog and found the second floor dark, but I didn't want the light. I didn't want to see the truth of what was happening. I couldn't possibly be falling for Nash. I barely knew him. We'd had more fights than civil conversations. Two steps forward. Two steps back.

We hadn't even had *sex*.

I headed for the back office when I heard the footsteps on the stairs behind me and I *knew*.

It was inevitable.

We were inevitable.

But that didn't mean I was ready to face that fact.

As quietly as I could, I raced toward the office. Beyond it was a large supply closet where the raffle tickets were stored. Where I would be cornered.

He was coming fast and I had to decide, but

panic made me foolish. I veered off into the small employee break room.

I didn't make it two steps into the room before Nash caught me. Those big, rough hands settled on my hips as if staking a claim.

My back was flush with his front, every glorious inch of it. And the rightness of it had me wondering why I bothered trying to escape it in the first place.

"I'm gonna turn you around, Angel. And when I do, you're gonna stop running and I'm gonna stop fighting this." His voice was a soul-stirring rasp against my ear. "Do you get me?" he prodded.

A shiver rolled up my spine. I *so* got him. I got him so good.

I nodded and without hesitation, he spun me around so my front met his. My breasts were crushed against his chest. His erection pressed into my belly. His thighs were hard against mine. The only separation was the infinitesimal inch between our mouths.

My world was full of Nash. His clean scent, the heat and hardness of his body. The magnetic field of his attention.

"You're gonna open your mouth for me."

"Excuse me?" I was going for haughty but it came out breathy.

He dipped his head, drawing me even closer. "And I'm gonna kiss you."

"You can't just expect—"

But the man did expect. And damned if I didn't open my mouth the second his lips hit mine. *Inevitable.*

35

Pushed Too Far

Nash

I wasn't cold inside. Not now. Maybe not ever again. I was an inferno of anger, frustration, need.

Everything I wanted, she held the key to, and I'd been waiting my entire life to unlock it.

I crushed my mouth to hers. Hot. Wet. Hard. It wasn't a kiss, it was an act of desperation. Those soft lips that had taunted me for weeks were already parted and I inhaled that sexy little gasp she gave when I backed her against the wall.

I plundered and took. I punished her with my tongue. And when she surrendered to me, I felt power ripple through my veins.

I managed to tear my mouth from hers for a split second. "Am I hurting you?"

"Don't treat me like I'm fragile," she rasped a second before her teeth sank into my lower lip.

My blood simmered. My body roared to life with a need unlike any other. I didn't know if I could survive this and I didn't fucking care.

At least this time survival was a choice.

We devoured each other, breathed each other in, then dove beneath the surface again and again.

My hands cruised her hips, her waist before finding their way to the promised land.

The throbbing in my cock turned painful when I filled my palms with her breasts. Soft, inviting flesh. Her nipples pebbled against my rough hands through her top.

Her moan went thready at the contact. The noise, the shudder that rolled through her, the feel of those peaks straining for more drove me out of my mind. It was *my* hands she wanted on her. No one else's. There was power there. And gratitude.

Lina tugged hard on my belt buckle. The zing of leather against metal made me desperate for more and reminded me what "more" meant.

"Wait." I gripped her fingers at my fly.

"What?" she whispered, her breast heaving against my other hand.

"I need this to be good. Need you to feel good."

"I don't think you have anything to worry about."

I shook my head and tried to get the words out. "I haven't . . . since. I don't know if I can . . . And I *really* need to make this good for you."

That lovely face softened in the shadows. Not in pity but in sweetness. She cupped a hand to my cheek. "Hotshot, trust me. You've already made it good for me."

"Angelina, I'm serious."

"So am I." She looked at me earnestly. Then

winced. "Damn it. You're going to make me say it, aren't you?"

"Say what?" I was having trouble focusing with her fingers an inch from my aching dick.

"Oh my God. You already got me off. Okay?" She squeezed her eyes shut as the words came out in a rush. When I didn't say anything, she opened one of them.

"Baby, I'm pretty sure I'd remember that."

"Not if you were sound asleep. The first time we slept together? When we woke up practically dry humping?"

I held on to her gaze, her words like they were lifelines.

She rolled her eyes. "For Pete's sake. I got off. Okay? Accidentally. My shirt was all bunched up and you were hard and in the right place. All you did was move your hips one time and . . ."

"And what?"

"I–I came apart."

Fuck me.

I didn't need to hear any more. I shoved my hands under her arms and picked her up. She let out a little trill of nervous laughter when I boosted her onto the counter and then wrapped those long, lean legs around my waist, hooking her ankles at my back.

I yanked the buttons of her blouse open as she finally unzipped my fly.

The world stopped when those strong, slim fingers found my shaft.

"God. I've been waiting so long for this," she said on a moan.

So had I. My entire life.

My jaw clenched and my breath caught in my chest. The rise and fall of her high, full breasts was hypnotizing. I wanted to taste, to suck. I wanted to forget everything that I was and take what she was offering.

Her grip on my dick tightened and a haze began to creep into the edges of my vision. Desire. Craving. Need. It pulsed up my shaft under her hand in a frantic beat. Something clawed at my chest, begging to be released, and I realized it was the breath I'd been holding.

She turned me into something primal, primitive, an animal driven by the need to mate. After so much numbness, this tidal wave of emotion scared the hell out of me. At the same time, I wanted nothing more than to dive into it headfirst. But I needed to be careful with her.

She cupped my face with her free hand. "Nash, look at me." Her eyes were glassy with desire. Her lips were swollen and parted as she panted in short, sharp breaths. "I don't want the gentle good guy right now. I want what you have inside you."

God help me. I wanted to give it to her. Wanted to cut myself open and let the pain, the cold bleed out so she could fill me up with fire and put me back together again.

"It's not pretty," I warned, nipping at the base of her throat.

She tightened her thighs around my hips. "I'm not worried about breaking you, hotshot. Do me the same favor."

With that, I dove forward, taking one dusky nipple into my mouth and sliding my hand up her short, plaid skirt.

Jesus. They weren't tights. They were thigh highs. There was nothing between my fingers and her molten core but a pair of silky underwear. I rewarded us both with a long, hard suck, and her nipple swelled in my mouth.

She let out a whimper that had moisture welling up out of my cock, coating her fingers. I was going to lose it. My first time back in the saddle and I was going to come before we'd even gotten started.

I released her breast and pulled back so I could look at her, drink her in.

She was wearing a plain, white thong. The innocence of it drove me wild. I coasted my fingers over the transparent wet spot in fascination.

"Yes," Lina hissed, using her heels to pull me closer until the tip of my cock lined up with the wet spot on her panties.

We both shuddered. One layer of white silk was the only barrier between us. Driven by need,

I tugged the material of her thong up so those soft, wet lips parted on either side. Then I ran my knuckle between them.

Her legs spasmed around me as her head fell back, knocking into the cabinet.

I did it again and then again as I lowered my head to lap at her other pert nipple.

I couldn't get enough of the soft, inviting curve of her breast against my cheek and jaw.

But we were in public.

Anyone could walk in and find us like this.

We had things to settle.

But none of that mattered in this moment. The only thing that did was fucking my way into her until we both lost our damn minds. Somehow I knew once I did, things would make sense.

I dragged the head of my cock between the lips of her sex. Up and down the silk of her thong.

"Oh my God," she chanted. "Oh my God."

My hips gave a short, hard thrust forward and we both stared down, transfixed at the sight of my tip disappearing between her folds. The only thing keeping me from going deeper was that strip of white silk.

"Nash, I need you," Lina whispered before she grabbed me by the shoulders and sank her nails in.

I thrust again and again, nudging the tip of my dick against her clitoris. Her breasts bounced with every short drive of my hips, teasing another shot of precum from me.

"Don't you fucking come until I'm inside you," I ordered.

"Then you better hurry the hell up," she said through clenched teeth.

She didn't have to tell me twice. I was harder than I'd ever been in my life when I yanked the wet silk of her thong to the side. I'd never wanted anything this badly. My hand shook as I guided my aching cock through her silky, soaking folds.

I wanted to go slow, to ease into her, giving us both the chance to get used to the fit. But the second I felt her heat sucking at me, all good intentions burned away.

Holding her by the back of the neck and the hip, I drove home.

Her cry and my shout were triumphant. And loud enough that she slapped a hand over my mouth. Our eyes locked and held. And in hers I saw my future.

Tight. So tight I could barely see, barely breathe. Her inner walls had me in a death grip that felt like agony and ecstasy wrapped around each other. And I never wanted to leave.

"Fuck! Condom," I gritted out against her palm.

I had never once forgotten protection. Liza J's boys were raised right. We might have played fast and loose with the rules, but we were always careful with what mattered most.

Lina's muscles locked down on me as if she

was afraid I was about to pull out even though I couldn't have if my life depended on it.

"You think I'd let you get this far without a condom if I wasn't on birth control?" she panted.

"Are you sure? Are you okay? Am I hurting you?"

The throb in my cock was getting more insistent by the second. If she told me to pull out, I'd come all over those wet panties.

I closed my eyes to ward off that visual. My balls were drawn up so tight they ached. But there was something else here. Something fucking magical.

I was surrounded by heat. Slick, wet fire that had me in its grips. I was finally warm. All the way through. This was what I needed. To be brought back to life, reanimated. She was the lightning strike that cut through the cold and the dark. That cleared out that icy fog that had clung to me.

Lina pulsed around me, an undeniable reminder that I was alive. I was a man.

"Nash, please. Give me more." Her broken whisper from those swollen lips was music to my ears. Every sense I had came online and fired up at once. The shroud of numbness vanished as if it had never been.

It was because of her. Close. I was closer to Lina than I'd ever been to another human being. Not just because I was sheathed in her to the hilt but because she pulled at me, teased me apart, and somehow managed to put all the damaged pieces back together again.

"Hold on to me." It was a command and a plea.

When she tightened her grip, I reveled in it. She was an anchor, keeping me from floating off into the abyss. True north. The way home. And I loved her for it. I didn't have a choice.

Testing us both, I slowly pulled out an inch, then two, only to sink back in.

Heaven and hell intertwined, turning pleasure into an exquisite torture. I wouldn't survive this. But I already knew I couldn't survive without her.

Her brown eyes were glazed with lust, but there was something else in them. Nerves.

"Angel."

She shook her head, reading my mind. "Don't you dare stop."

"Am I hurting you?" I asked again.

"More like scaring the hell out of me," she admitted, her fingers digging into my shoulders. "This doesn't—I've never felt this."

"Baby, if it makes you feel better, I'm scared to death right now that I won't be able to take a breath without you wrapped around me."

I needed someone who didn't need me. Someone who had no intention of sticking. Someone I was guaranteed to lose. And I still couldn't stop myself.

She hitched her knees higher on my hips and I growled.

"Keep scaring me, Nash," she whispered. Her body trembled against mine and then I was moving.

I wanted slow. I wanted control. But neither of those were an option with my cock buried in Lina Solavita for the first time. I imagined it would take fifty or sixty tries before I could manage to take it slow.

Her eyes were locked on mine, those long damn legs wrapped tight. Her fingers dug into my flesh. And I rode. Hard and fast. Out of my mind as I basked in the slick heat she offered me.

It was too much. My muscles screamed as my hips pumped mercilessly. Sweat dotted my skin.

I needed to shift her. I needed to get deeper. So I plucked her off the counter, and still buried inside her, I carried her to the table. I hinged over her, forcing her back just enough to change the angle.

I felt it then. The end of her. Pinning her to the table, I let go and thrusted like a wild animal. The table slammed into the wall.

But her gaze never wavered from mine.

A pleasure so intense I knew I wouldn't survive it swept over me and I didn't fucking care. The only thing that mattered was that Lina had let me in. She'd surrendered to me. Given herself over. She trusted me with her body.

The table banged into the drywall with every hard thrust I delivered.

Her walls quickened around me, those muscles dragging against me each time I pulled out and fighting me on every thrust. I felt *powerful*.

"Angelina." Her name was a snarl that abraded my throat.

"Now, Nash. Now!"

On instinct, I covered her mouth with my hand as I slammed home.

"Fuck. Fuck. Fuck. Angel!"

I couldn't stop. The churning in my balls had won out. Heat streaked down my spine, then up my shaft and erupted.

Just as I ejaculated, she closed around me, vise tight. Our releases—thank fucking God—detonated together.

Her cry was muffled by my hand, but I felt it in the depths of my soul.

Lina didn't come delicately. Her entire body locked down, wrenching more semen from me. Over and over again. She demanded it all, even as her arms and legs went slack.

I kept coming, kept pumping into her as she closed around me, holding me to her, in her. Endless. Warm. Glorious. Fucking beautiful.

I'd never felt this. Never lost myself inside a woman like this.

Angelina was my goddamn miracle. And I would absolutely step across the line of black and white into the gray to protect her.

36

High Fives and Orgasms

Lina

"Mornin'." Nash's voice was a rasp from behind me.

My eyes flew open, and last night, all of it, came flooding back to me in high-definition with surround sound.

Five orgasms.

"You're gonna stop running and I'm gonna stop fighting this."

Nash on his knees between my legs. His tongue working miracles.

"I need you."

Inevitable.

And then circling right back to the five orgasms.

Not just any run-of-the-mill, I-could-have-done-better-with-a-vibrator orgasms. No. Nash Morgan had blown my previous peak sexual experiences out of the water. Hell, out of the stratosphere.

It was like the moment his penis came out, my body was programmed to explode.

Just what the hell was I supposed to do about that?

Oh, and then there was that whole thing about me falling in l—

Yeah, my brain wasn't even willing to think the word. This couldn't be real. This had to be some kind of delusion. Maybe the whole town had a radon problem? Or there was some sort of hallucinogen in the water?

A chuckle rumbled in his chest, which was pressed against my naked back. My stupid body thrilled at the sensation.

"I can feel you freakin' out."

"I'm not freaking out," I lied.

"Angel, your body is so tense I might find a diamond with my dick next time," he said, tracing the edges of my tattoo with a finger.

"There's not going to be a next time," I decided, trying to scooch my way to the edge of his bed.

The sheets were rumpled from our sexathon before we'd passed out from dehydration and orgasm supersaturation.

His arm tightened around my belly and he dragged me back against him in a delicious show of strength. I was plotting defensive maneuvers when he nuzzled his face against my hair and sighed. "I was right."

I paused my plotting. "About what?"

"Best way to wake up in the morning by far."

I went limp.

Great. After a night of Nash the Sex God, now

I had to deal with Nash the Sweetheart. I didn't have the weaponry to defend myself against either, let alone both.

"You can't keep me here," I warned him, stretching my leg straight until my foot found the edge of the mattress. "Eventually someone will come looking for one of us, and I'll be forced to tell them that you held me captive."

A heavy, hairy leg slid over mine. He hooked my ankle with his heel and dragged it backward.

In another second, I was on my back and an amused Nash Morgan was ranging himself over me. His hips pinned mine to the mattress with the aid of what I identified as his usual impressive morning wood. "Angel, any man who walked in and saw you lookin' like you look wouldn't blame me."

My escape plan fell out of my head.

Those blue eyes were sleepy and satisfied. His hair was tousled. The fresh bruises on his face tarnished his all-American good guy handsomeness, giving him an even sexier rakish appeal. There was a self-satisfied smirk playing on the lips that had turned me into a writhing puddle of need.

Without thinking, I traced my fingers over his pecs where a dusting of light hair tickled me. God, I loved chest hair.

Those two garish pink welts stood out against the rest of his smooth skin, reminding me that the man on top of me was nothing short of a hero. He had such a beautiful body.

"What's going on in that head of yours, beautiful?" he asked.

"How's your shoulder?" I asked. "I wasn't careful last night."

"Shoulder's fine," he said. "I wasn't careful with you either."

I grinned against my will. No, he hadn't handled me like I was a delicate flower in danger of being trampled. I hadn't felt like a glass figurine. He had used me. *Hard.* And I'd freaking loved it.

"I guess I didn't mind it."

Nash slid down my body and placed a light kiss to each of the trio of surgical scars surrounding my breast. It was painfully sweet. My toes curled against the hair on his legs.

"Tell me what you need," he said, just before using his mouth to tease my nipple.

"Coffee. A huge breakfast. Some ibuprofen."

His head came up and those blue eyes were serious now. "Tell me what you need to feel safe with this. With us."

If I hadn't already lo—liked him, I would have fallen hard just for that. No one had ever asked me that question before. I wasn't sure I had an answer.

"I . . . don't know."

"I'll tell you what I need," he offered.

"What?"

Nash slid off me onto his side and propped his head in his hand. The fingers of the other trailed over my breasts and stomach. His swollen cock rested against my hip, scrambling my brain.

"I need to know that you're okay with what happened last night and that you want it to happen again."

"Done and done. Wow. That was easy. Now about that coffee . . ."

"I need to know that you're in this with me for however long it lasts," he continued. "That you're willing to admit there's something between us that adds up to a hell of a lot more than just chemistry."

"Pretty sure we experienced a very chemical reaction last night," I reminded him.

He trailed those talented fingers up my neck, through my hair, combing it back from my face. "I need more pieces of you. As many as you're willing to give. And I need you to talk to me, honestly. Even if you think I'm not going to like what you have to say."

I shifted uncomfortably. "Nash, we don't know where this is going or what the future holds."

"Angel, I'm just happy to be back among the living. I'm more concerned with enjoying right now than worrying about tomorrow. But I need us to be on the same page."

It wasn't a big ask.

I brushed my fingertip over the scar on his

shoulder. "This sounds like you're trying to turn this into a relationship."

His smile was like the first peek of the rising sun. "Baby, we're already in one whether you like it or not."

"I've never done the relationship thing. At least, not as an adult."

"And I never had sex in a public library before. First time for everything."

I contemplated my options, and for once, telling the truth seemed like the straightest path to what I wanted.

I needed Nash to understand what he was getting himself into. To recognize the pitfalls that lay ahead.

"I live alone and I like it. I hate sharing the remote. I like not having to consult with someone else before ordering dinner. I don't want to have to move the seat of my car every time I drive. The idea of passing my decisions through an 'us' filter leaves me feeling vaguely nauseated. I love my parents but their constant need to check up on me drives me insane, and that problem could become yours if this goes anywhere. I like to splurge on clothes and bags and shoes, and I'm unwilling to justify that. I get up early and I work a lot. I don't want to have to change that to accommodate someone else."

Nash waited a beat. "Okay then. The only TV I watch is the occasional football game.

The remote can be yours the rest of the time. I don't mind cooking, but if you tell me you want takeout burgers, I'll get you takeout burgers. I promise to always move your seat back to the original position after I drive. I wouldn't mind having some nosy parents worry about me for a change. I like the way you dress just fine so I've got no problems with your shopping habits. Long as you let me spoil you once in a while. As for the schedule thing, I think you're just reachin' because, Angel, I'm a cop. Enough said. And when it comes to making decisions together, I need a say in your personal safety. I expect you to want a say in mine. Any decisions that affect us together, we make together."

He was saying all the right things and it was scaring the shit out of me. "I travel a lot for work," I reminded him.

"And I might spend Christmas morning on the scene of an accident. Baby, give us a chance to deal with it. At least agree to this for the time being. We can revisit it after I've got Hugo in a cage."

He really wanted this. And I was downright shocked to realize I did too. I was definitely getting this town's water tested.

"There's one more thing," I said.

"Name it."

"I need to know what you, Knox, Nolan, and Lucian have been up to since our talk with Grim."

He didn't hesitate. "We've been hashin' out a plan to flush out Hugo."

I sat up. "What kind of plan?"

"The kind of plan that uses me as bait."

"What?"

I was up on my knees, ready to do battle, when Nash struck, tackling me back to the mattress. His hands held my shoulders down. His hips pinned mine to the bed. And his erection notched into the exact right place. Like a key fitting into a lock.

We both went still.

My mind may have been in fight mode, but my body was ready for orgasm number six.

He grinned down at me. "Know this makes me sound like an asshole, but I don't mind you worryin' about me."

I tried to heave him off me, but my flailing only succeeded in inserting the first two teasing inches of his cock inside me. I stopped fighting and tried to focus on the problem at hand and not how much I wanted the rest of his inches.

"Nash! You were worried about me doing surveillance but you expect me to be fine with you acting as bait to a man *who tried to kill you?*"

"I'd be disappointed if you were fine with it. And I'd like to point out, you got yourself abducted while doing surveillance."

I bared my teeth at him. "If you think I won't

fight with you while your dick is in me, you're about to be sorely mistaken."

"Let's try something new," he suggested. "Instead of fightin' and stormin' off and pretendin' we both don't exist, let's hash it out right now."

My thighs were starting to shake from their grip on his hips. At this point, I didn't know if I was trying to keep him from sliding further in or preventing him from pulling out. "Fine. Talk."

"If Hugo is feeding intel to the FBI to help build their case against his father, there's a damn good chance they're gonna feel pretty friendly toward him. Maybe friendly enough to offer up immunity. But I'm a loose end to him no matter what. So are Naomi and Waylay. Right now, he's just waiting for the feds to make their move. But sooner or later, he's gonna have to snip those loose ends."

"And you want him to try sooner?"

"That's right. And I want him focused on me."

"You think if he makes another attempt on you, his deal—if he has one—will fall through."

"That's the idea."

I swear I was listening, but my body was multitasking. I was getting wetter by the second and my inner walls kept rippling around the tip of his penis.

Nash's eyes closed and he groaned low. "Angel, if you wanna keep talking, you're gonna have to stop beggin' for more."

To be petty, I contracted the muscles of my sex as hard as I could. "How are you going to force his hand?"

He gritted his teeth. "Shit, sweetheart. I'd tell you anything just to feel you grip my cock like that."

"Then tell me," I demanded.

"I'm gonna get my memory back."

I went still under him, understanding and appreciation dawning. "You're going to fake it."

"That's the plan," he said, nuzzling my breast. "We done talking?"

I slid my hands down his back and sunk my nails into that perfect ass of his. "Not yet. Spill the details."

His eyes were half-shut, his stubbled jaw clenched. "We're gonna spread the word that my memory is back and that we've got a lead on the suspect's whereabouts."

My pulse quickened. He was bearing down against my thighs. I wasn't going to be able to hold out much longer. Especially since I didn't want to.

"What precautions are you taking?"

"Angelina, I came inside you three times last night. So zero."

I pinched his ass. "I *meant* what are you doing to make sure Duncan Hugo doesn't get a second shot at you?"

He was starting to sweat. And there was a heat blazing in those denim-blue eyes. "Still workin' on that."

"I want in."

"What?" he gritted out.

My thighs quivered and he sank another inch into me.

I was on fire. My vision was starting to blur. I wanted all of him. Needed all of him. But I needed this first. "I want to be in the loop."

"Do you want in the loop because you want to find that damn car or because you're worried about me?"

"Both," I admitted.

"Good enough for me. I'll keep you in the loop. Deal?" he said.

"Deal," I repeated and let my knees fall open to the sides.

He sank the rest of the way into me, filling me with a long, low groan.

I was deliciously sore from last night. But that didn't stop it from feeling so damn good.

"When are you going to let me be on top?" I demanded as he pulled almost all the way out and then surged back in.

"When I know for sure watching your perfect tits bounce in front of my face won't make me go off before I get you off. I'm out of practice."

There was nothing out of practice about the way he drove that cock into me.

"Practice makes perfect," I said, shoving him onto his side.

He rolled, taking me along for the ride until I was straddling him, impaled on him, my knees in the sheets, my hands on his shoulders.

His gaze locked on my breasts. His erection pulsed once inside me and his fingers dug into my hips. "Yeah. Not gonna last like this. Unless you take it real slow."

I leaned down, brushing my nipples against that glorious chest hair. "That's not gonna happen." I nipped at his lower lip and started to ride.

"Jesus. Fuck. Damn it," he cursed, bucking under me.

But even with me on top, he still managed to wrestle back control. His hands gripped my hips as he set a new pace. He pistoned his hips up and yanked me down to meet his thrusts. Hard. Fast. My heart was in my throat, every muscle in my body poised for the orgasm that was building.

I grabbed the headboard and held on for dear life as Nash bucked into me, hitting that secret spot with brutal accuracy over and over again. The flutters started, my inner muscles curling in on themselves, dragging over that thick, hot shaft.

"So fucking tight," he muttered against my breast. "Have to fight my way in every damn time."

"Nash." It was a broken whimper as my walls clamped down on him as he thrust home.

"Give it up, baby. Give it to me." The cords on his neck stood out. His jaw was locked, nostrils flaring as he fought his way through my orgasm.

I couldn't breathe, couldn't see. I couldn't do anything but *feel*.

I needed to win. Needed to take him over the edge. With the echoes of my own release still trembling through my core, I bore down on him.

"Damn it, Angelina," he snarled.

Sweat slicked my skin and his. His eyes were wild as my thighs gripped him harder, his fingers digging into my hips. He knew what I was doing and let me have my way. I rode hard, making my muscles burn. Then suddenly Nash curled into a sit-up, and with a look of agonized ecstasy, he went rigid under me.

I felt him come, felt the first hot spurt of his orgasm deep within me. It was endless. Inevitable. Perfect.

We both collapsed, my head resting on his shoulder, his fingers now gentle as they stroked my hair.

This wasn't what I'd been looking for. This wasn't what I'd thought I'd needed. But the body didn't lie. I wasn't capable of feeling this kind of connection to a man if there wasn't something essential, elemental there to build on.

"Let's have all our fights like this," Nash panted.

"Neither one of us will be able to walk after a week," I predicted.

"Thank you," he said after a long beat of silence.

"For what?" I asked, shifting to look up at him.

"For taking a chance on me. For being with me now. We can worry about after later."

"After?" I repeated, stroking my hand over his chest.

"Do we have a deal?" he prodded.

The man was still inside me.

"Fine. Deal."

"High-five?" he offered, grinning.

37

A Hole in the Wall

Nash

I strolled into the station with a spring in my step and a dozen chocolate éclairs. Piper trotted along next to me, her new favorite toy—one of Lina's socks—clamped in her teeth.

I had my own souvenirs. Shallow scratch marks lined my back like tiger stripes. And there was the tiny, purple love bite that was mostly hidden by the collar of my shirt.

"Mornin' . . . Chief?" Bertle's greeting sounded more like a question.

"Mornin'," I returned. I slid the bakery box onto the counter next to the coffee maker.

Piper started her customary sniffing lap around the bullpen.

"Did you do something with your . . . face?" Tashi asked, looking concerned.

I ran a hand over my now smooth jaw. "I shaved. Why?"

"You look different."

"Different good or different 'dear God, please grow the hair back to cover up the ugly'?"

She looked at me as if I'd rode in on a unicorn

519

preceded by a marching band of leprechauns.

"You're not makin' me feel good about my grooming, Bannerjee."

"Different good," she said quickly.

Grave wasted no time in breaking into the box of éclairs.

"How'd it go with our overnight guests?" I asked him.

"They bitched and moaned until Dilton's wife showed up and posted bail," Grave reported. "You pressin' charges?"

"If Dilton doesn't go quietly, I will."

Grave nodded. "We've got him dead to rights on three cases and we've only gone back eight weeks. Affidavits are on your desk. If he don't go quietly, he's a bigger idiot than we gave him credit for."

I was both glad to have the proof we needed to build our case and pissed off that I'd given him the opportunity to abuse his power. There was no telling what kind of damage he'd already done behind the badge. But it ended here.

Grave gave me a closer look. "Why's your face look like you got laid? Is that a hickey on your neck?"

"Shut up and eat your éclair."

I spent an hour buzzing through paperwork, including the incident report from the night before and the three affidavits from Dilton's victims. His presence on the force was only a formality at this point. He was never going to wear a badge again. I'd see to that.

I topped off my coffee, took a lap around the bullpen, and then scratched out a quick letter to my dad.

When I got back to my office, I found Piper passed out cold in the dog bed under my desk. I reached for my phone and snapped a picture of her, then opened my text messages.

There was nothing from Lina, which I'd expected.

I'd taken advantage of her sated, walls-down state to get what I wanted. A commitment. At least a temporary one. Now that I'd had her, all of her, I wasn't letting go. I just had to hang on tight and wait for her to catch up.

I fired off the picture of Piper and followed it up with a text.

> **Me:** Still freaking out? Or are you still in bed too exhausted from orgasms to move?

I held my breath, then blew it out when those three telltale dots appeared below my message.

> **Lina:** What did you do to me? I tried to go for a run and my legs wouldn't work.

I grinned, my anxious ego immediately soothed.

> **Me:** Hopper just told me my face looks like I got laid.
> **Lina:** Justice said I was glowing and Stef asked me if I got one of those placenta facials.
> **Me:** Hope you weren't planning on keeping this a secret.
> **Lina:** Is that even possible in this town?
> **Me:** Nope. Which is why I'm taking you out to dinner tonight.

If I asked, it would give her too much time to think. The more she felt and the less she thought, the better.

> **Lina:** "Out to dinner" as in no nudity and orgasms?
> **Me:** Yes. Unless you're planning to get us arrested on our first date.
> **Lina:** *sigh* How quickly the thrill fades. What next? Game night?

My exhausted cock flexed behind my zipper. Twelve hours ago, my main concern had been whether I could perform at all. Now I had to worry about overuse.

> **Me:** I can think of a few games I'd like to play with you.

Lina: Since you're taking me to dinner instead of fucking me senseless, I can only assume you mean charades or checkers.

Me: Be ready at 7. Wear something that makes it hard for me to stop thinking about what you've got on underneath.

With that business taken care of, I moved on to the next item on my list.

"I knew it!"

Busted. Sloane stood in the doorway of the library break room, arms crossed and a triumphant grin on her pretty face. She was wearing a different pair of glasses today. These had bright blue tortoise-shell frames.

Piper retreated behind my back, unsure of what to do with the gloating woman blocking the exit.

"Knew what?" I asked, giving the sage-green paint a stir. The dent in the wall was going to need more than a coat of paint, but until I patched the drywall, paint would at least make it less noticeable.

"You, Chief Morgan, scuffed my wall with table sex!"

I shot her an irritated look. "Jesus, Sloane. Keep your voice down. This is a library."

She closed the door and then regained her victorious stance. "I *knew* there was something up with you two last night. My sex radar never fails!"

"Lina didn't . . . mention anything?" I asked casually.

Sloane took pity on me. "Didn't have to. She left here walking funny and looking all dazed and feverish. Even without my glasses, I could tell."

I turned my attention back to the gouge in the wall so she wouldn't see my manly pride on display. "Maybe she had a stomach bug."

"You think I don't know the difference between a woman leveled by an orgasm and one trying to keep her dinner down? I know what I saw. Then you tore out of here not thirty seconds later looking all sweaty and hungry—and not in the food way, mind you. You looked like you were about to devour something . . . or someone."

"Maybe I had the stomach bug too."

"I say this with love. Bullshit."

"I had official police business."

Sloane tapped a finger to her chin. "Hmm. Since when is getting naked considered official police business?"

I jabbed the brush into the paint, then slapped it against the wall. Maybe if I ignored her, she'd go away.

"You rattle her," Sloane said behind me.

I stopped painting and turned to look at her. "What?"

"Lina. You rattle her. It takes a lot to do that."

"Yeah, well, the feeling's mutual."

Her smile was bright and smug. "I can see that."

Hoping the conversation was over, I turned my attention back to the wall.

"It's good to have you back, Nash," Sloane said softly.

On a sigh, I dropped the brush. "Now what's that supposed to mean?"

"You know what it means. I'm glad to see you returning to the land of the living. I was worried. I think we all were."

"Yeah, well, I guess it takes some of us longer to bounce back. So what's with you and Lucian?" I asked, changing the subject and stabbing the brush into the deepest part of the gouge.

"Don't you mean Nolan? Who, by the way, is currently sitting in my office eating all my candy."

"No, I mean Lucian. You and Nolan might be havin' a few laughs, but he's not Lucian."

She was too quiet. I looked up and saw she'd carefully rearranged her face into a mask.

"I don't know what you're talking about," she said.

"You're not supposed to lie to a cop," I reminded her.

"Is this an official interrogation? Should I get a lawyer?"

"You know my secret," I said, nodding toward the wall.

The tension went out of her shoulders and she rolled her eyes. "It happened a long time ago. Water under the bridge," she insisted.

Piper tiptoed around me to sniff tentatively at Sloane's sneakers. The librarian crouched down and offered her hand to the dog.

I went back to the wall. "You know what I remember from back in the day?"

"What?"

"I remember you and Lucy sharing these long, meaningful looks in the hall between classes. I remember him ripping the helmet off Jonah Bluth and putting him on his ass during football practice because Jonah said something about your body that I as an adult man with great respect for women won't repeat."

"It was about my boobs, wasn't it?" Sloane quipped. "The price you pay for developing early."

I gave her a long, steady look until she flinched.

"Did Lucian really do that?" she asked finally.

I nodded once. "He did. I also remember driving home after curfew from some particularly heavy making out with Millie Washington and seeing someone who looked a hell of a lot like Lucian climbing the tree outside your bedroom window."

Sloane had been a sophomore and next-door neighbor Lucian a senior. They'd been as much opposites then as they were now. The broody bad boy and the pretty, peppy nerd. And as far as I knew, neither had ever officially acknowledged the other beyond "hey" in the hallowed halls of Knockemout High School.

But outside those halls was another story. One neither of them had ever shared.

Sloane focused on coaxing Piper closer to her hand. "You never said anything."

"Neither of you seemed to want to talk about it so I left it alone. Figured it was your business," I said pointedly.

She cleared her throat. The noise sent the dog scampering back to the safety of my reach. "Yeah, well, like I said, that was a long time ago," she said, standing back up.

"Doesn't feel good to have people shoving their noses in your business, does it?"

She gave me a chilly librarian glare and crossed her arms. "If I stick *my* nose someplace, it's because *someone* isn't doing what they need to be."

"Yeah? Well, from where I sit, this animosity between you and Luce isn't healthy. So maybe I should start inserting myself into that situation. Help you two come to a resolution."

She blew out a breath through her nostrils like a bull facing off against a red flag. The stud in her nose twinkled. The standoff lasted all of thirty seconds. "Ugh, fine. I'll stay out of your business and you stay out of mine," she said.

"How about this?" I countered. "I respect your privacy and you respect mine."

"Sounds like semantics to me."

"Might sound that way, Sloaney Baloney. But we're friends. Have been for years. Far as I can tell, our lives are gonna stay tangled up. So maybe instead of butting in and being nosy, we focus more on bein' there for each other when needed."

"I don't need anyone to be there," she said stubbornly.

"All right. But I might need a friend if I can't convince Lina to take a chance on what we've got." She opened her mouth, but I held up a hand. "I probably won't want to talk much about it if I lose, but I sure as hell am gonna need a friend to help keep me from disappearing again."

Sloane's face softened. "I'll be there."

"And I'll be there for you if and when you need me."

"Thanks for fixin' my wall, Nash."

"Thanks for bein' you, Sloaney."

I was just closing up the paint can when dispatch called for me over my radio. "You out and about, Chief?"

"I am."

"Bacon Stables has a horse on the loose again. Had a couple of reports of a big, black stallion galloping its ass southbound on Route 317."

"On my way," I said on a sigh.

"I can't believe you won him over with a damn carrot," I said as Tashi Bannerjee handed the reins of the big-ass Heathcliff to Doris Bacon, who was holding an ice pack to her ass.

We were standing in waist-deep weeds in the east pasture of the foreclosed Red Dog Farm, a fifty-acre horse property that had sat empty for going on two years since its owner's multi-level marketing skincare business went belly-up.

Heathcliff the stallion had decided he didn't feel like riding around the ring today and had bucked Doris off on her ass before heading south.

The seventeen-hundred-pound son of a bitch had kicked the passenger door of my SUV and tried to take a bite out of my shoulder before Tashi had distracted him with a carrot and snagged his reins.

"You handle the snakes, Chief, and I'll take the horses."

"I seem to recall you riding one of Heathcliff's relatives through a drive-thru your senior year," I teased.

She grinned. "And look how that paid off."

I kept my distance as Tashi and Doris coaxed the humongous horse up the trailer ramp.

Something tickled between my shoulder blades and I turned around. Two deer jolted, then disappeared into the woods. There was nothing else out there. Just weeds and trees and broken fences, but I still couldn't shake the feeling that something or someone was watching us.

Doris slammed the gate shut on the trailer. The sound of hoof meeting metal rang out. "Quit acting up, you big ninny."

"Maybe it's time to sell Heathcliff to a farm with higher fences," I suggested.

She shook her head as she limped around to the driver's side door. "I'll keep that in mind. Thanks for your help, Chief, Officer Bannerjee."

We waved her off as she maneuvered the truck and trailer onto the property's driveway and headed for the road.

The stallion let out an earsplitting whinny.

"I think he just put a curse on you," Tashi teased as we headed for my dented vehicle.

"Like to see him try."

My phone buzzed in my pocket and I pulled it out.

> **Lina:** You won't believe what the town grapevine is reporting now. According to a not-so-reliable source you spent your afternoon herding a horse around town with your SUV.
>
> **Me:** It wasn't just any horse. It was Heathcliff the Horrible.

I attached a picture of the horse in question and another one of my dented door.

Lina: You better not smell like horse when you pick me up for dinner.

Me: I'll see if I can squeeze in a shower between now and then. Have you picked out what dress you're gonna torture me with?

38

First Date

Nash

"T his is so cliché," Lina said when she opened her door.

"A first date is not a cliché." I was glad I got the words out because the second I clocked what she was wearing, my power of speech vanished.

Her red lips pursed in a flirty pout. "It is when you've already had sex."

I needed a minute to catch the breath she'd knocked out of me.

She was wearing a short black dress. The sleeves were long, but the skirt showed off so much leg I wanted to back her up and bend her over the first flat surface I could find just to see what color underwear she was wearing. Her fuck-me stilettos had a crocodile pattern that proudly said "man-eater." She'd gone heavier on the makeup, adding some kind of smoky bronze to her lids that made her eyes look even bigger and more sinful.

She was beautiful. Confident. And vaguely annoyed that I was taking her to dinner instead of bed.

I was the luckiest son of a bitch in the world.

"You shaved," she said when I remained silent.

I ran my hand over my jaw and grinned. "Thought it would make for a smoother ride."

Her eyes sparkled wickedly and a pink tinge warmed her cheeks. "I don't mind it rough," she reminded me.

"I've got the scratches to prove it, Angel," I teased.

"Why don't we skip this whole date thing and go straight to testing out that baby-smooth face of yours?" she suggested.

My dick reacted like a puppet with its master at the strings.

"Nice try, baby. But you're getting the full first date experience."

"Ugh, fine, but I'd like to point out that society says I'm not supposed to sleep with you on the first date," she reminded me.

"Since when do you follow the rules?" I teased.

"Only when it suits me."

Which was exactly why I couldn't afford to play fair.

I produced the small gift box I'd been hiding behind my back. "Got you something."

She eyed the box like she might a bomb.

"Go on now. Don't be scared."

"Scared?" she scoffed and snatched the box out of my hand.

Her face went soft for a second when she pried open the lid. Then her careful mask slid back into place. She was letting me in, but only in inches, and I wasn't about to lose any ground.

"I'm not supposed to sleep with you on a first date and you're *definitely* not supposed to give me jewelry."

I'd swung by Xandra's again to talk to her about the initiative I was rolling out and to drop off a toy deputy badge for Alex.

I glanced down at the earrings nestled inside the box. Delicate gold chains ended in sharp, sparkly sunbursts. "I saw them, and I thought of you. Made by the woman who saved my life, worn by the woman who reminded me it's worth living."

The mask slipped away again and I saw nothing but pure female enjoyment. "Well, how am I supposed to say no to *that?*"

"They're just earrings, Angel. Not a wedding ring. Besides, a portion of the sales go toward a local autism foundation."

She took a breath and handed the box back to me. "Why do I get the feeling you're playing me?" she asked as she removed the hoop from her right ear, then liberated an earring from the box.

She expertly found the hole and secured the earring in place, then did the same with her left ear.

"How do they look?" she asked, giving her head a shake.

"Fucking beautiful."

• • •

I chose a swanky Italian place in Lawlerville. Not because they had the best homemade bread in the tricounty area or because I was hoping to keep the whole "us" thing secret. I just wanted a quiet dinner without any distractions. If I'd taken Lina out in Knockemout, we'd be dealing with a whole town of gossips, and if I'd cooked for her at my place, we wouldn't have made it past appetizers before I'd gotten her naked.

Unfortunately, this meant I had to bribe Nolan with his own dinner at the bar since the marshal wasn't willing to take the night off.

But at least he was far enough away from our table that I could pretend he wasn't there. We'd been given a circular booth tucked away in a quiet corner of the dining room, which meant instead of sitting across from each other, we were next to each other on the bench. Beneath the pristine tablecloth, my thigh was pressed intimately against hers. Her foot was hooked companionably behind my ankle.

"Are you immune to the fact that every man in this restaurant watched you walk in and sit down?" I asked her as she dragged a piece of bread through the plate of olive oil.

She glanced up, a sparkle in those beautiful eyes. "If you're wondering if I notice attention, I do. If you're asking if I like it, it depends on the situation. Tonight I didn't hate it."

I liked that she didn't pretend. I was starting to understand her brand of honesty. She didn't lie or tell the truth. She either opened herself up to you or closed herself off from you. And I was starting to get the difference.

"You're so goddamn beautiful, sometimes I can't look directly at you," I confessed.

The slice of bread tumbled to her plate and landed olive oil side down. "Damn it, Nash. Stop sneaking up on me."

I smirked and reached for my own slice, surprised when I didn't feel the familiar twinge in my shoulder. I hadn't really noticed it at all the night before either. It looked like Lina's miracles weren't limited to mental health.

"I thought of something else that I need from you," she announced.

"Name it."

"I don't want to sit on the sidelines while you and the boys have all the fun. I want to be on the team. I want to help find Hugo."

"Angel, you'll get your car," I insisted.

Her eyes narrowed as she picked up her glass and sipped. "I *know* I'll get the car. What I want to make sure of is that you get your man. That you don't have to live with the fear that at any point, Duncan Hugo could wake up one morning and decide today's the day he's going to eliminate witnesses."

I said nothing. Mostly because I was afraid to

spook her. Maybe she didn't realize what she was saying. But I did. She wanted me safe. And she wanted it enough to play on a team to make it happen.

Whether she realized it or not, she cared about me and I wasn't above exploiting the hell out of that to get what I wanted.

"I already promised to keep you in the loop," I reminded her.

"And now I want you to promise me more. I've planned over two dozen asset retrieval operations," she continued. "I've been on hand to actually execute half of those operations. I'm a pro at working in tandem with law enforcement agencies. And I never quit."

"You packed a suitcase," I pointed out.

She pinned me with a look.

"What?" I asked.

"I'm debating."

"Debating what?"

"Whether to tell you the truth."

"Don't waste the energy deciding, Angel. Always tell me the truth."

"Fine," she said with a delicate shrug. "I packed a suitcase because it hurt too much to be that close to you when you hated me. I was going to move back to the motel, wait until work could send a replacement, and then I was going to leave town."

It was like a knife to the gut, knowing how

537

close I'd come to losing her for good. If it weren't for Naomi and Sloane stopping her, last night wouldn't have happened. And this conversation wouldn't be possible. I owed them flowers or maybe a spa gift certificate.

"I'm sorry, Angel," I said. "I was falling fast and I grabbed on to any excuse I could to break that fall. I'm sorry for making you feel like you couldn't trust me. I won't make the same mistake twice."

Her fringe of lashes was thick and dark against her skin, and when those heavy lids raised and she looked at me, she stole the breath right out of me.

"When you say falling," she said softly.

"Head over heels, Angel. I'm really regretting taking you out to dinner instead of taking you to bed again."

Her laugh was husky, and when she leaned in, her breast was soft and tempting against my arm. "Mission accomplished. Now tell me you'll use me, Nash."

My fingers tightened on the stem of the wineglass. I knew what she meant, but the double entendre was impossible for my dick to ignore. It was time to take back control.

"First things first. I wanna hear those words coming out of your mouth again once I'm inside you. And I want you to mean them."

Her lips parted as her breath quickened. "Deal."

"Second, if you want in, I need you to take every precaution *I* deem necessary to keep you safe. That's nonnegotiable," I said.

"Deal," she said again.

I gave her a wolfish look. "You know, last time we made a deal, I was inside you."

"And instead of being naked in bed, we're out to dinner on our first date. Guess you'll just have to settle for the high-five," she said smugly.

It was a first date to end all first dates. I knew it in my gut. There was something about Lina Solavita that drew me in, that captivated me. I wanted all her secrets, all her trust. And I wanted her to willingly hand them over to me. Forever.

This wasn't just an attraction. This was something more.

We talked, we laughed, we flirted, we sampled bites of each other's entrees. The longer the meal wore on, the closer we inched.

By the time the waiter was describing the desserts, my right hand was on her thigh just below the short hem of her dress. My fingers drew tiny circles on her warm skin.

Lina looked as if she were riveted by his description of the bourbon bread pudding, but beneath the table, my bad girl opened her knees wider for me.

Inviting me, testing me, *teasing* me.

I wanted to look down. Knew if I did, I'd finally

see the color of her underwear and experience a whole new level of torture. However, it was time I delivered a little torture of my own.

She didn't think I'd do it. But there were a lot of things Angelina Solavita could tempt me into.

As the waiter rhapsodized about the hazelnut cheesecake, I trailed my fingertips all the way to the promised land. Lina jumped and tried to close her knees, but it was too late. I'd found what I was looking for. That damp spot on the silk I'd yet to see. But I could *feel* it.

Her thighs trembled around my hand.

"What sounds good to you, Angel," I asked her.

The look she shot me was a beautiful combination of shock and naked desire. "Wh-what?"

"Dessert," I said, pressing two fingers to that delectable wet spot. "Tell me what you want."

She blinked twice, then shook her head. The smile she shot the waiter was not her usual man-eater. "Uh, I'd like a piece of the hazelnut cheesecake. To go."

"And for you, sir?" he asked me.

I used my index and middle fingers to squeeze the lips of her sex together through her thong.

"Just the check."

With a nod, he disappeared and Lina fisted her hands on the tablecloth.

"Open your legs." My command was a harsh whisper.

She didn't hesitate before spreading her thighs.

"Wider," I commanded. "I want to see."

She obeyed, sliding her ass to the edge of the cushion, giving me the permission and freedom to play. My cock was rock-hard and begging to be let out.

Red. Her thong was bad-girl red. I slid my fingers under the band that covered her sex.

"Nash," she whispered, her voice trembling.

I loved the way she said my name when she needed me.

"Think you can play your bad-girl games in a fancy restaurant and I won't call you out?"

"Well . . . yeah," she admitted on a shaky laugh. Under the table, she bucked her hips forward, begging for more pressure.

I wanted to bend her over this table and shove her dress up to her waist.

I circled her slick little bud with the pads of my fingers. "If I take the edge off for you right here, right now, promise me—"

"Anything," she whimpered, writhing against my hand.

God, I loved the sound of her surrender. It made my dick ache.

I leaned even closer so her breast was plastered against my arm, my lips brushing her ear. "Promise me you'll still take me as deep as I can get when we get home."

"Yes," she hissed instantly. Then she smiled wickedly. "If you can make me come before my dessert gets here, I'll be sure to return the favor."

Challenge accepted.

"Spread as wide as you can, Angel."

She hooked her knee over my thigh to accomplish it, but once she was splayed open, I drove two fingers into her slick, wet channel.

Her low moan made my cock twitch painfully. So I added a third finger.

"Oh Jesus," she groaned.

"Don't ride it," I warned, brushing what looked like an innocent kiss to her shoulder. "Stay still or everyone in this restaurant will know what's happening under this table."

She bit her lip and stopped moving.

"That's my girl," I whispered and then brushed my thumb over her clit.

"Oh God," she whimpered.

The telltale quivers that teased my fingers told me everything I needed to know. "You're ready to come already. Aren't you, Angelina?"

"It's your fault," she hissed. "You in that damn good guy suit. With your damn first date and your damn 'I saw these and thought of you' earrings."

She was rocking subtly against the thrusts of my hand, her thighs straining to stay open. My fingers were coated in her wet. I added just a little more pressure with my thumb and it was like pulling a trigger.

She closed her eyes and I had the privilege of

feeling everything inside her locking down hard before releasing. Lina went off like a firework on my fingers, making me feel like a goddamn hero. I kept pumping into her, kept swiping my thumb over that sensitized bud. Her legs shook and she leaned heavily into me as she came and came and came.

I jammed my other palm against my erection, praying I wasn't as close to blowing as it felt like I was.

"Oh fuck," Lina said, still panting, still gripping my fingers inside her.

"Your cheesecake and your check," the waiter said.

"Am I reading this wrong, or are you pissed off?" Lina asked me as I slid behind the wheel of her car.

I'd had to half drag, half carry her to the parking lot because her legs were still shaking from my finger fucking. Thankfully, Nolan had been in the restroom and missed our escape.

"I'm not mad," I snapped. I still had her wetness on my hand, a fact that wasn't helping my fucking situation.

"I was only teasing you. I didn't mean for it to go so far. But damn, hotshot. You continue to surprise me."

"Baby, the only thing that's mad right now is my dick at how fucking far we are from home."

543

I could feel the pulse of it hammering in my head. How the hell was I supposed to last the thirty-minute drive home?

"Ohhhhhh." She drew out the word as I shifted into gear and stomped on the accelerator. The car fishtailed as I pulled out of the parking lot and hit the road.

"Shouldn't we wait for Nolan?" she asked.

My answer was a growl. If I didn't get some relief soon, I was worried I'd lose my fucking mind. She'd spread so wide for me. Come so hard. In a restaurant full of people. Now I had a zipper tattooed on my shaft.

"I think I can help with that," she said, releasing her seat belt.

"What are you doing?" I demanded harshly. "Put your seat belt back on."

"But if I do that, I can't do *this*."

She reached across the console, and when her fingers closed around my belt, I knew I was in serious trouble.

I sucked in a breath as my cock turned to motherfucking granite.

"Angelina," I warned.

Those nimble fingers had my belt and fly open in seconds. "You're not going to abide *all* the laws tonight, are you?" she teased.

"Take off your bra," I snapped as I eased up on the accelerator.

"I'm not wearing one." She relayed this information just as she wrapped her hand around my throbbing erection.

"Goddammit!"

"Just keep your eyes on the road, hotshot."

That was going to be impossible. Especially after I hooked my right hand in the neckline of her dress and yanked it down so I could see those perfect breasts.

With a wicked smile, she lowered her head into my lap. The second those hot lips spread over my crown, I was a goner. That hot tongue, that slick mouth, the way she gripped me in her tight fist. Angelina Solavita was going to deliver a religious experience.

I groaned, long and ragged as she used her mouth and hand on me. Confined by my pants, the seat belt, the steering wheel, I couldn't do anything but let her work me. The lonely, moonlit highway stretched out before us, but I barely saw it.

My attention was stolen by the hot mouth on my cock.

I shoved a hand under her just to grab a handful of bare breast. Her moan vibrated down my shaft. The back of my head was drilling itself into the seat. My knees pressed outward against the door on one side and the console on the other.

She'd hit the perfect rhythm and I knew I was about to lose my mind and my load. The release was churning dangerously in my balls, causing them to tighten.

"Fuck."

I wanted to thrust. I wanted to move. But I couldn't.

Without warning, Lina's mouth popped off my erection. She peeked up at me with an arched eyebrow and red, wet lips. "Seriously, hotshot? Thirty-five in a fifty-five?"

I grabbed her none too gently by the hair and pushed her back down in my lap. "Shut up and suck, baby."

The second her mouth hit my dick, I jerked the wheel to the right and pulled over onto the shoulder of the road. It took some maneuvering to downshift around her, but I managed to bring us to a complete stop. Dumping the car into neutral, I pulled the parking brake. The dust was still rising around us when I hit the lever on my seat to recline.

Both of my hands came to her head and I set the pace. She scrambled farther over the console, her tits bouncing in the light of the dash, her mouth never leaving my shaft.

It was building.

I wanted to warn her, but I couldn't get the words out. I couldn't even draw in the breath required to form them. In a way, this was how the panic felt. But this was a world away. This was something I'd give up everything for. Lina was someone I'd give up everything for.

On that terrifying thought, I ejaculated *hard*. It

raced up my shaft like fire and burst free into her waiting mouth. I must have shouted. I must have hit the gas pedal because the engine revved into the red line. I was fisting her hair in a too-tight grip, but I couldn't seem to stop. Not as long as I was coming.

It was endless. Her mouth sucked me off, capturing every spurt of my release as if she couldn't live without it.

"Baby," I panted, collapsing back against my seat.

Her mouth stayed fastened to the sensitive tip until I tugged her up. Her hair was a mess. Her eyes were big and glassy. Her full tits swayed hypnotically with each breath she sucked in. Her mouth, that fucking mouth, was swollen and rosy and wet.

I'd never seen anything so beautiful in my entire life.

Hooking her under the arms, I dragged her across the console into my lap and tucked her head into my chest. She curled into me, both of us breathing like we'd just sprinted a mile.

"Jesus, baby. You should have to register that mouth of yours as a weapon," I said.

She let out a low, sultry laugh. "Consider it payback for making me come in the middle of a restaurant."

I stroked a hand over her hair. "Don't know about you, but I'd say this was a pretty successful first date."

"I wouldn't say no to a second one."

I palmed her breast and squeezed. "We'll order in," I decided.

It was right about then that I noticed the flashing lights in the rearview mirror.

"Fuck."

39

The Gang's All Here

Lina

Y ou're a bad influence," Nash complained, fumbling with his keys.

"At least it was only Nolan," I reminded him as I waited for him to unlock his apartment door.

Nash's U.S. marshal babysitter had been none too pleased to return from the restaurant bathroom to find us gone. He'd only found the situation slightly funnier when he walked up to the driver's side window. It hadn't taken a brain surgeon to know what we'd been up to.

Nash opened the door and gestured for me to enter first. Piper met me at the door, proudly carrying a small, stuffed police dog in her mouth.

"That one's new," I noted, leaning down to ruffle her wiry fur.

"Saw it on Amazon," Nash said, shutting the door and hanging his keys on the hook.

"Are you ever not hard?" I asked, noting the obvious situation in his pants.

His grin was downright evil when he reached for me. "You have a choice."

"Explain."

"Either I go down on you here against the door or in the bedroom." His hands were already reaching for the hem of my dress.

"Wait. Wait. Wait."

To his credit, he stopped immediately. "What's wrong?"

"As much as I really, *really* want to take your new, smooth face for a test drive . . ." I shook my head. "I can't believe I'm saying this. But I think we need to talk."

Nash's lips quirked. "Just what the hell did they put in that wine?"

I shoved my hands into my hair. "Obviously, I've been abducted by aliens and replaced with a not-very-convincing clone. But we've been too busy orgasming to talk."

"About what?"

"About the plan to take down Hugo. I was serious when I said I wanted in. And as much as I want in your pants again and again, this is important. Important enough not to let you distract me with your magic penis."

His eyes went from a blazing intensity to amused. "You're one of a kind, Angel."

"Uh-uh, Studly Do-Right. No distracting me with compliments. Rally the troops while I take Piper out."

"Now?"

I grabbed Piper's leash from the hook. "Yes. Now," I said firmly.

I returned from my walk around the block with Piper and a nagging guilty conscience. "Nash? Before everyone gets here, there's something I need to tell you."

Nash was hanging Duncan Hugo's photo on the whiteboard he'd set up next to the table. "What's wrong?"

I was pretty sure I'd done the right thing, but I had a feeling he might not see it that way. "Okay. So in school after the whole heart-stopping thing, I didn't really fit in. And besides work, I never really belonged socially."

He was watching me intently now.

"I guess what I'm trying to say is I'm new at this. I'm new to whatever is going on between us. I'm new to having friends like Naomi and Sloane."

Nash's eyes closed slowly and then reopened. He rubbed the spot between his eyebrows. "What did you do, Angelina?"

"Just hear me out," I began. But I was interrupted by a loud knock. Piper went scrambling for Nash.

"It's nine o'clock on a school night," Knox complained as I let him in.

"I'll take Words by the Domesticated Knox Morgan for two hundred, Alex," I quipped. I was just shutting the door when Lucian appeared in it. "How the hell did you get here so fast?" I asked him.

"I worked remotely from here today."

"You worked remotely in a suit?"

"Nice earrings," he said.

I narrowed my eyes in suspicion. "Why are you being nice to me?"

"Because of that." He nodded over my shoulder at Nash, who was offering his brother a beer and smiling while doing it. "Don't fuck it up."

He crossed to his friends and I closed the door feeling guilty. "So, guys. Before we start, I should probably tell you all—"

I was interrupted by another knock.

Lucian stopped trying to coax Piper out from behind Nash's legs and frowned. "Is that Graham?"

"We know you're in there." Sloane's voice carried from the other side of the door.

Nash headed for me and the door.

"That's what I wanted to tell you," I said, grabbing his arm.

He looked through the peephole and then shot me a "you didn't" look.

"I did," I confessed.

"Did what?" Knox asked, crossing his arms.

"This," Nash said, opening the door to Naomi, Sloane, and Mrs. Tweedy.

"Okay. To clarify, I didn't text Mrs. Tweedy," I said.

Knox looked concerned. Lucian looked ready to commit murder. And Nash, well, Nash looked at me and rolled his eyes.

"Daisy, baby, what the fuck are you doin' here?" Knox demanded, closing the distance between them.

She crossed her arms over her pretty violet sweater. "Lina texted us."

Sloane, dressed in plaid pajama joggers and a matching top, put her hands on her hips. "You penises aren't shutting us out of whatever the hell this is."

"I'm just here 'cause it looked like a party from my peephole. I brought booze," Mrs. Tweedy announced, holding up a bottle of bourbon.

I winced as three grumpy, male gazes landed on me.

"Angelina," Nash began.

I held up my hands. "Hear me out. This involves all of us in one way or another except for Mrs. Tweedy. And Naomi and Sloane deserve to know what's going on. The more heads we can put together on this, the more eyes and ears we have around town, the better prepared we'll be."

The men continued to glare at me.

"No one knows this town and what goes on in it better than Sloane. And Naomi earned her way here by being a target. She shouldn't be kept in the dark. The more she knows, the safer she can be and the better she can protect Waylay," I insisted.

"You're not leaving me out of whatever this is. If it has anything to do with my sister or her shitty ex, I deserve to know what's going on," Naomi insisted to Knox.

"You don't need to worry about this, Daze," he assured her, gripping her gently by the biceps. "I've got this. I've got you and Way. You need to trust me to take care of this."

Naomi's face softened momentarily before going grumpy again. "And *you* need to trust *me*. I'm not a child. I deserve full disclosure and open lines of communication."

Sloane hooked her thumb in Naomi's direction. "Yeah. What she said."

"This has nothing to do with you. When are you going to learn to mind your own business?" Lucian said, addressing Sloane in a tone so icy I almost shivered.

Well, at least the big guy was pissed at someone besides me for once.

Sloane, however, appeared to be immune to the Rollins freeze. "Shut it, Satan. If it involves my town and people I care about, it involves me. I wouldn't expect you to understand that."

The stare off began and I wondered whose neck would get tired first, given their height difference.

Nash strode over and took me by the wrist. "Excuse us for a second," he announced and dragged me into the bedroom. He shut the door, pushed me against it, and then boxed me in with his palms on either side of my head. "Explain."

"You seem mad. Maybe we should talk later?"

"We'll talk now, Angel."

"They had a right to know."

"Explain why you talked to them before you talked to me."

"Honestly?"

"Let's try that for a change," he said dryly.

"I'm not really sure what the hierarchy of loyalty is in this situation. Naomi and Sloane are my first real friends in a long time and I'm out of practice. But I know how much it hurt you when I kept you in the dark. I got a taste of that when you were off plotting without me. And—"

He pinned my hips to the door with his with a thump.

"Are they fucking in there?" I heard Knox ask from the other room.

"And what?" Nash asked me.

"And they should know. And I get that you're mad and I'm sorry for not raising this with you first."

"I appreciate that and you're not wrong," he said, brushing my hair back from my forehead in a gesture so gentle my knees went weak.

"I'm not?"

A smile tugged on the corner of his mouth. "No. But next time, let's have the conversation first."

He was so damn handsome and so damn . . .

good. No wonder I'd fallen in L-word with the man.

I managed a nod. "Yep. Got it."

He cupped my face in his hand. "You and I are in this together. When our decisions affect each other, we *make them together.* Understand?"

I nodded my head vigorously.

"Good," he said, pulling me away from the door. He gave my ass a stinging slap. "Consider that a low five."

"Ouch!"

"She either slapped him or he spanked her," Sloane said in the other room.

"Now, let's get back out there and figure this shit out. *Together,*" Nash said firmly.

"Okay."

He paused. "Is there anything else you need to tell me before we go back out there?"

I opened my mouth just as another knock sounded on the front door. "I swear this one isn't me," I insisted.

He grinned and opened the bedroom door.

Nolan strolled inside and Knox closed the door behind him. The marshal stopped and eyed the gathering, the whiteboard, and Mrs. Tweedy mixing up a pitcher of old-fashioneds. "I'm gonna hate this, aren't I?"

"Not as much as I already do," Knox told him.

"Hi, Nolan," Sloane said with a pretty smile.

"Hey, cupcake."

Lucian remained silent, but the "I'm about to explode" vibes were a tangible presence in the room.

"I'll get more beers," I said, deliberately stepping between Lucian and Nolan, who seemed unaware that his life hung in the balance.

"You know the basics. This is your last chance to bail before shit gets real," Nash said to Nolan as I headed for the kitchen. "In or out."

"In," he said without hesitation.

"Nolan, this could get you in serious trouble," I warned, pulling a six-pack out of the fridge. "Your bosses won't like your involvement in this."

Nolan spread his arms. "I don't know if you've noticed, but my job sucks. It cost me my marriage. It ruined any hope I have for the world in general. And sleeping in one-star roach motels has destroyed my back. I already have my resignation drafted. I'm just waiting to get drunk enough or fed up enough to send it up the chain. Besides, I'm tired of babysitting."

Nash and I exchanged a look and he nodded. I handed Nolan a beer. "Welcome to the team."

"I don't know what the hell you kids are talkin' about, but I'm on the team too," Mrs. Tweedy announced.

I shrugged at Nash and he rolled his eyes. We both knew there was no easy way of giving her the boot.

"Fine," Nash said to her. "But you can't repeat anything you hear tonight. Not to your gym buddies. Not to your poker pals. No one."

"Sheesh. I got it already. Let's talk turkey."

"Let's get this over with," Knox muttered and pulled a chair out for Naomi.

We sat around the table with bourbon and beers and listened as Nash walked us all through the events of the past few days, then laid out the basic plan they'd come up with.

"I hate it," Sloane announced when he was finished.

Naomi was wide-eyed and gripping Knox's hand. "You can't be serious, Nash. You can't just dangle yourself out there as bait. He almost killed you once."

"And this time, I'll be ready for him," Nash said gently.

"We all will," I promised.

Naomi turned beseeching eyes to Knox. "But if Nash is a target, a loose end, so is Way."

"So are you," Lucian said.

Knox dragged her into his side. "Look at me, Daze. No one is getting near either of you. I promise you that. They'd have to get through me first, and no one is fucking getting through me."

"He shot Nash," she said, her eyes welling with tears.

"He's not gettin' a second chance there either,"

Knox promised. His gaze went to his brother and they shared a long look.

Naomi closed her eyes and leaned into Knox's chest. "I can't believe all this is happening because of my sister. I feel like I brought this on all of you."

"You can't take responsibility for another adult's bad decisions," Nash told her. His gaze shifted to me. "All you can do is try to make good ones for yourself."

"I want one thing straight," Knox said. "None of this goes down before the wedding Saturday. Nothing fucks up Daisy's day."

"It's your day too, Knox," Naomi said, leaning into him.

"Damn right it is. And nothing and nobody is going to ruin it. Agreed?" He looked around the table, making sure each of us nodded our agreement.

"We'll put everything in motion Monday," Nash said.

"Okay. Then we should talk about preparation," I suggested.

Nash nodded. "We're all part of the team. We've all got a job to do, otherwise why are we here?"

"Because Lina opened her big mouth and dragged them into it," Knox said.

"Lina saved you a week of sleeping on the couch, which is exactly what you'd deserve if you'd gotten away with keeping me in the dark on this one. So you should be thanking her," Naomi pointed out.

Knox looked at me and used his middle finger to rub at the corner of his eye. "Thanks, Leens," he said.

"You're so welcome," I said sweetly, lifting my glass with middle finger extended.

"Let's get back to assignments," Nolan suggested.

"Go on," Nash prompted me.

I blinked. "I don't really . . . I'm not comfortable . . ."

"But you know what needs to be done," he insisted.

"Right," I said. "Okay then. Nash, you're going to get access to the case file the Lawlerville PD started before the feds muscled their way in. Maybe there's something in there that will tell us where Hugo went."

He nodded his agreement and I blew out a breath. "Keep going," he prompted.

I turned to Nolan. "Nolan, you use your charm and connections to see what information you can get on the case the feds are building against Anthony Hugo. Who's feeding them information, and how are they getting it?"

"On it," he said, stroking his mustache.

"Sloane?"

"Lay it on me," she said, holding a pen poised

over the notebook she'd dug out of her purse.

"We need people in town on the lookout for Duncan Hugo and his henchmen. The earlier the warning we have, the more time we have to prepare. Grim already agreed to continue keeping tabs on the Hugos' men. If any of them head in our direction, we'll know. But we need people here who can keep their eyes and ears open and their mouths shut."

"Oooh! Pick me! Pick me!" Mrs. Tweedy said, coming halfway out of her seat, hand raised like an eager student.

"Okay. Mrs. Tweedy is our first official spy," Sloane agreed.

"That means you can't be blabbing about this to anyone," Knox reminded his elderly tenant.

"I know when to blab and when to keep my trap shut," she shot back.

"Choose people you know you can trust not to run their mouths about this. The last thing we need is a whole town looking for a fight," Nash cautioned Sloane.

"Maybe we can spin a few tall tales to a couple big-mouthed gossips so they can be on the lookout without knowing exactly why," Mrs. Tweedy suggested.

"How would that work?" I asked.

"Take Face Tattoo Guy. I can casually mention to Neecey at Dino's that I heard a guy with face tattoos is looking to buy up acres of farmland to build a bunch of hipster condominiums and vape shops."

"That's not a terrible idea," Lucian and Sloane said at the same time. They shared a long, simmering glare.

"Knox," I continued.

He still had Naomi glued to his side with one tattooed arm around her shoulders. "Let's have it, boss."

"Local security. Beef up the system at your place and here at Nash's. Lucian, can you find a way to track Nash, Naomi, and Waylay in case they get separated from their phones?"

Nash's eyes swung back to me. "Now hold on a minute. I've already got a federal shadow—"

"Don't bother arguing," Naomi said to him. "If it's a precaution Waylay and I have to take, you have to take it too."

"I have access to some interesting technology that might help," Lucian volunteered.

"Great. Knox, work with Lucian on that," I said.

"What do you want me to do?" Naomi asked me. "And don't even think about leaving me out of this."

I looked at Nash for help.

"Self-defense," he said. "You and Waylay are gonna sign up with Fi's jujitsu instructor for private lessons." Knox opened his mouth to argue, but Nash shook his head. "Hugo's not going to get near either of you. But we're taking zero chances."

"I look forward to building on my knee-balls-nose repertoire," Naomi said.

Sloane yawned and looked at her watch. "Okay. We have our assignments. Let's nail this asshole."

There was a murmur of agreement around the table.

Mrs. Tweedy noisily slurped up the remainder of her bourbon.

"Come on, Daze. Let's get you to bed," Knox said.

The way he said it and the way she looked at him made me think sleep was the last thing either of them had in mind.

Sloane stuffed her notebook back into her bag. "I'll start a WhatsApp group so we can keep everyone updated."

"Good thinking," Nash said.

"Graham," Nash said to Nolan, jerking his head toward the kitchen.

"A word," Lucian said, appearing at my elbow.

"What's up?"

"What's my real assignment?"

My smile was slow and smug. "I didn't want to make the ask in front of a U.S. marshal, even if he is batting for our team."

"I gathered as much."

"Can you dedicate your creepy shadow network of intel gathering to finding a man with no name and no picture?" I explained Duncan's faceless, burner phone friend. "He's the only one I couldn't track down, and that makes me think he's the one we need to find."

"Send everything you have over to me, and I'll get my team started immediately."

"Good. Oh, and how do you feel about keeping an eye on Sloane? The rest of us are either trained to deal with this or live with someone who is. Sloane's by herself, and since you stay next door to her when you're in town, you're the most convenient candidate."

Icy fire danced in Lucian's eyes. "No one will get near her," he promised.

"She'll probably give you shit about the attention," I warned.

Something that almost looked like a smile played over his handsome face. But then it was gone. "I won't be run off as easily this time."

Personally, I was dying to know what other time he was thinking about and how a five-foot-two-inch woman had run off Lucian "Lucifer" Rollins. But it didn't seem like the time for questions.

We said goodbye as everyone except for Nolan filed out the door, a buzz of purpose and anticipation between them.

Sloane paused in the open doorway. "Still up for being my date to the wedding Saturday?" she called to Nolan, who was lounging against the kitchen island.

"Wouldn't miss it for the world, cupcake."

"Pick me up at—"

Lucian slammed the door, cutting Sloane off midsentence.

"Those two are going to implode one day. Right, Pipe?" I asked the dog that was tap-dancing playfully at my feet.

"Angel, I need your key," Nash called.

"Door's unlocked," I told him, meeting him and Nolan in the kitchen.

"Good. Go get your stuff and bring back your key," he said.

"My stuff?"

"Graham's taking over your place until this is over. It'll help to have him closer than the motel."

"Not gonna lie. I'm lookin' forward to a real bed and not having to stomp on half a dozen roaches before my shower," Nolan said cheerfully.

"Uh, you get the couch, my friend," I told him.

"No. He gets your place," Nash countered. "You're staying with me."

"You expect me to *move in with you?*" My voice went up an octave. I instantly began to sweat.

"On that note, I'll go get my shit. Be back here in however long it takes to scare the rats out of my suitcase," Nolan announced and ran for the door.

"Fight me on this," Nash dared me.

"I can't just move in with you, Nash. That's insane. We barely made it through the day without fighting, and you want to share a bathroom with me? Do *not* smile at me like *I'm* the crazy one!" I could hear the hysterical tinge to my words but there was no dialing it back.

He was still smiling, but now he was heading toward me.

I held up my hands and began to back away. "It's one thing to accidentally fall asleep after sex, but to bring my clothes here and . . . Do you even have closet space? I can't just leave my things in a suitcase. They need to breathe."

I needed to breathe.

Nash caught me, his hands settling on my hips and tugging me closer. I hated the fact that I instantly felt calmer.

"Take a breath," he insisted.

I sucked in a tiny, useless inhalation.

"You're adorable when you freak out."

"I'm not freaking out. I'm . . . processing your ludicrous suggestion."

"If it makes you feel better, this is just temporary," he said, his voice annoyingly calm.

Temporary. Temporary. Temporary. Just like our relationship. One day at a time until . . . *after.*

Nash brought my hands to the back of his neck and then began to sway.

"Why do you keep slow dancing with me?"

"Because I like being close to you even when we have all our clothes on."

"This can't be the best solution," I insisted. "Why don't we all move in to the motel?"

"He wasn't joking about the rats," Nash pointed out.

"Okay, fine. We'll all move in with Naomi and Knox. They've got room."

"You don't think that'll get the entire town talking? The whole point of this is to make things look as normal as possible from the outside."

"What is *normal* about this?" I demanded. "Besides, won't people start talking about Nolan staying at my place? I mean, they'll think I'm sleeping with you both. Or that we're in some weird throuple."

"Or they'll think my federally issued protection is staying with me to protect me. Or they'll think you and I are serious and Nolan wanted to get out of the roach motel."

Damn it. He'd thought of everything. The sneaky, conniving son of a bitch.

I was impressed.

And terrified.

"I'm not going to become Suzy Homemaker and suddenly learn to cook," I warned.

"Noted."

"And you better not use your bathroom floor for a hamper. I saw Mount St. Dirty Clothes the day we brought Piper home."

"Do I need to get the broccoli out of the freezer?" he asked, rubbing his cheek against the top of my head.

"No. Maybe."

40

Smile Pretty for the Camera

Lina

I can't believe you're making me do this," Nash said as a makeup artist dabbed powder across his brow. Out of patience, he dodged her hand. "Can we be done? Please?"

I was perched on the counter in his office, enjoying the hell out of his discomfort under the heat of the photographer's lights.

For the past few days, I'd been the one suffering discomfort, being forced to move in with him . . . temporarily, I reminded myself. But that meant in the meantime, me, my clothing, my makeup, even my damn houseplant were now living in Nash's apartment.

For the last forty-eight hours, I'd slept in Nash's bed, brushed my teeth at his sink, and gotten dressed in his bathroom. Then I'd sat at his table and eaten the breakfasts and dinners he made me.

I drew the line at pooping while he was home. To be safe, I'd temporarily cut back on fiber.

To be honest, minus my fear of sharing a bathroom, the living situation hadn't been *as* weird as I'd expected. But that was probably because most of our quality time was spent naked and the rest of it was working out details of the Nash's-fake-memory-recovery-to-lure-Duncan-Hugo-out-of-hiding plan.

The makeup artist packed up her gear and hustled out of the room. I slid off the counter and approached Nash. He was in uniform and scowling, a combination I found utterly appealing.

"Need I remind you? This was your idea," I said, running my palms across his broad chest. He'd been putting weight back on, steadily adding muscle to his frame. And I'd noticed him using his bad shoulder with fewer grimaces. My heart had given up on its nervous PVCs for the most part, and I wondered if earth-shattering sex was some kind of miracle cure-all.

"My idea was to spread the word that my memory was back. Not shout it from a national online magazine with a goddamn photo shoot," he complained.

"Poor baby. But we have to make sure the news spreads far and wide in case Duncan is in hiding across the country."

"How did Stef even pull this off?" Nash demanded, tugging irritably on his collar.

"He's got a PR firm on retainer. Naomi called him, he called them, and here we are."

"Remind me to drop a weight plate on his foot at the gym next time I see him."

I grinned.

"What?"

"I kind of like it when you're surly. It's cute," I confessed.

"I'm not surly and it's not fucking cute."

"Okay. You're broody and it's sexy."

His jaw ticked as he pondered that one. "I can live with that."

"Are you worried?" I asked, cuddling up to him.

Nash slid his fingers into the back pockets of my pants. "He's unpredictable. I could be putting myself out there as bait and he could still ignore me and go after someone else."

"Knox isn't going to let Naomi or Waylay out of his sight for the foreseeable future. You're the one who's going to be drawing Duncan's attention. You're the biggest threat. He won't be able to resist trying to finish the job." I shook my head and closed my eyes.

"What?" Nash asked.

"I can't believe I'm comforting my live-in lover with the fact that the man who tried to murder him once will make a second attempt," I said. "Nothing about this situation is normal."

"Live-in lover?" he repeated.

"Boy toy? Man friend? Emotional support fuck?"

"Boyfriend," Nash decided. He grinned when I winced. "For a badass, you sure spook easy."

"I'm not *spooked*," I lied.

"You think I can't tell when my girlfriend is panicking?"

"Now you're just being a Nashhole," I complained, stepping out of his grasp. "Let's table the labeling of whatever this is until after."

He leaned against his desk, still grinning. "I like knowing I can rattle you."

"Yeah? Well, I like it better when you're freaking out over cosmetics and a photo shoot for a national magazine."

He winced. "Now who's being mean, Meana?"

"Here, have a mint," I said, handing him one of the wrapped candies I'd snagged from the restaurant's host stand on our first date.

"I don't want a mint. I want . . ." He trailed off as the wrapper crinkled in his hand. He frowned down at it, lost in thought.

"What?" I asked.

He shook himself. "Nothing. Just felt like I was remembering something."

"About the shooting?" I prodded.

"Maybe. It's gone now."

"If you're a good boy, I'll take you for ice cream," I offered, changing the subject.

His fingers hooked into the waistband of my pants and tugged me closer.

"Your pepper spray is digging into my stomach," I warned him.

"How about instead of a photo shoot and ice

cream, I sit you on my desk and spread those long, sexy legs of yours wide? I'll go down on my knees and kiss my way up your thighs."

A delicious shiver worked its way up my spine as he slid one hand lower to cup my rear end. His hand was warm, the grip possessive.

"You'd be begging me for it until I'd take my tongue and—"

"Okay! Sorry for the delay. I'm locked and loaded." The photographer didn't seem to notice that my knees had quit functioning or that Nash was glaring at him with the heat of a thousand suns.

"Rain check?" I whispered.

"What the hell am I supposed to do with a hard-on?" he growled in my ear.

I glanced down and grinned. "Hide it behind your pepper spray. And your flashlight. And your Taser. But whatever you do, don't think about me screaming your name when you go down on me."

"Fuck."

Nash suffered through twelve whole minutes of photos—most of them with a barely disguised erection—before pulling the plug on the shoot like a grumpy man bear. It was six minutes longer than I thought he'd last.

I shifted Piper in my arms and pulled out my phone.

Me: You owe me $20. Nash just gave the photographer the boot.

Stef: Damn it! I thought he'd make it to fifteen.

Me: Sucker. Venmo me. Also, thank you for arranging this while you're busy doing whatever it is you do in New York. I owe you.

Stef: You can repay your debt by feeding me intel on Jeremiah.

Me: Aren't you in contact with him?

Stef: Of course I am. I just want to know if he's lifting weights like a sad, sexy panda while I'm gone.

"Hey. You wanna get out of here?" Nash said, poking his head in the door of his office. His face was scrubbed clean of the makeup artist's powder. He looked exactly like an all-American hero. Piper thought so too if her tail wagging was any indication.

"Where are we going?" I asked, slipping my phone into my bag and putting the dog on the floor.

"To see a girl about an ass," he said cryptically.

"After you," I said, gesturing for him to walk ahead of me. I admired his posterior in those sexy as hell uniform pants as he led the way into the bullpen.

"Did they take any pictures of your face or was

it all ass?" Nolan asked, shrugging into his jacket and following us out the door.

"Bite me," Nash said.

It was a beautiful fall day for a drive. Nash cued up a country playlist and off the three of us—plus Piper—went in his department-issued SUV. I focused my attention on the updates in the WhatsApp group. Naomi and Sloane were taking their assignments seriously.

Sloane had recruited a tiered network of spies on the lookout for Hugo and his henchmen.

Naomi and Waylay had their first jujitsu lesson scheduled for this evening. Knox and Lucian had ordered seven million pounds of security equipment that they would be installing this week.

"Fun field trip, Chief," Nolan said from the back seat.

I glanced up and saw the women's correctional facility looming in front of us.

"Figured it was about time I had a sit-down with her," Nash said, eyeing the prison through the windshield. "Anything I need to know before we go in?"

"She won't talk if Nolan's in the room, and she has a crush on you."

"Tina? On me?" Nash looked like I'd just whipped out a badminton racket and slapped him in the face with it.

"It's the butt, isn't it?" Nolan asked.

"Mine or hers?"

"Come on, Chief," I teased. "You know that every female in Knockemout loves to watch you leave a room."

Nash's ears were turning an adorable shade of pink.

"Can we please not talk about my ass?"

"We can stop, but I don't think you're gonna shut the whole town up, Studly Do-Right," Nolan warned.

Muttering under his breath, Nash got out of the SUV and tossed his keys to Nolan. "Stay here and keep Piper entertained. We'll be back."

"Try not to get shanked," Nolan called out.

I stiffened when Nash slung his arm around my shoulders as we headed across the lot.

"What's wrong?" he asked.

"We're working," I pointed out.

"And?"

"And it's not professional of us to be hanging on each other, making out."

"I think we're gonna have to revisit your definition of making out."

"You know what I mean," I said, hating how bitchy I sounded.

Nash pulled me to a stop just shy of the entrance. "You've been busting my balls all day, and when you aren't busting my balls, you're turning me on. And when you're not doing either of those things, you're locked away in that head of yours thinkin' deep thoughts. Now, I'm gonna go out on a limb here and guess that you're still in a tailspin over the whole extended sleepover thing."

"I'm *not* in a tailspin."

"Did you know you overemphasize words when you're freaking out?"

"I do *not*." Okay. He had me there. I'd never spent enough time around a man for him to detect my tells before. This was *annoying*.

And now I was doing it my head. *Great.*

"Listen to me, baby. You freak out all you want. I'll still be here when you're done. It's an extended sleepover. That's it. You're not locked in a dungeon. You're not being held against your will. You're just keeping your clothes in a different closet. We'll deal with the real decisions after. Okay?"

I was nodding with overemphasis now. Baby steps. "Okay. Yeah. Okay."

"Good girl. Now help me crack Tina like a walnut."

I shook my head to clear it. "Fine. Let me think. She likes that you were always nice to her. She said you never treated her badly even when you arrested her."

"Then why'd she let her boyfriend put a few rounds in me?"

"She says she didn't know until after the fact. And I'm wondering if Hugo may have decided to start with you because Tina had heart eyes for your ass."

Nash looked over his shoulder. "Is it really that nice?"

"Yes. Yes, it is."

Tina strolled into the room with her usual attitude but came to a halt when she spied Nash next to me. Hastily, she brushed her hair out of her face and then approached the table with shoulders-back-boobs-out posture.

Nash did not glance at the bust line beneath the khaki prison garb, but he did smile. "Hey, Tina."

"Chief." Tina's laceless shoe met the leg of her chair and she stumbled, catching herself against the table.

"You all right?" Nash asked.

"Fine as fuck. I mean, yes. I'm fine." The tough girl trying to be strong enough to resist falling for the cute guy. I didn't care for the obvious parallels.

"Nash has a few questions for you," I said.

Tina's eyes came to me as she sat. She looked startled as if she hadn't realized I was in the room. "Oh, uh, hi, Lona."

"It's Lina," I said, shooting Nash an I-told-you-so look.

He cleared his throat. "Tina—"

"Look, I didn't know nothing about him shooting you," Tina said. "Least, not beforehand.

And I laid into him after. He said he did it to make his dad start takin' him seriously. Why people give a shit about their parents' opinions I'll never know. Waste of time if you ask me."

This coming from a woman with two delightful parents who wanted nothing more than for Tina to find happiness . . . and stop acting like a criminal.

"I appreciate that," Nash said.

She bobbed her head. "Like I said, I had nothin' to do with that."

"Why is that?" I asked.

She shrugged. "Dunno."

Nash leaned in and Tina mirrored him. "Do you have any idea where he would go if he needed to hide out but still wanted to stay close?"

"Told her I never met the guy, but whenever he needed a new place, he always called Burner Phone Guy," Tina said, nodding at me without taking her eyes off Nash. "He'd hook us up with a place to crash or find Dunc a place to stash the cars he was stealing."

"How would he pay Burner Phone Guy?" Nash asked.

"Cash. He'd put it in one of those media mail boxes from the post office and send it."

"You've been real helpful, Tina," Nash said, making a few notes on his pad before putting the pen down.

"If you have any questions about that night

in the warehouse, ask Waylay. Kid's got one of those memories like a trap. Don't ever mention going for ice cream unless you're serious about takin' her 'cause it's all you'll hear for the next two years of your life if you change your mind."

And just like that, I was back to not liking Tina.

Nash and I got to our feet.

"We appreciate your time," Nash said.

Tina looked panicked for a second and then a sly look crossed her face. She slapped Nash's pen off the table like a cat. "Oops. I dropped your pen."

Nash went pale and looked at me for assistance.

"You're closer," I said.

I barely managed to choke back a laugh when he crouched down, keeping his rear end far away from Tina.

"You have yourself a good day," he said, pocketing the pen.

"See you, Tina," I said, then followed Nash as he kept his ass to the wall and skirted toward the door.

We found Nolan and Piper sitting in the sunshine on a strip of grass playing tug-of-war with Piper's stuffed police dog.

"I'll show you mine if you show me yours," Nolan offered.

Nash reached down to ruffle Piper's fur. "Hugo's unidentified henchman might be less of a henchman and more of a property manager or real estate agent. He got paid in dirty cash through the mail."

"Mail fraud. Nice."

"I'll have my researcher narrow down the search of known associates by those with a connection to real estate," I said.

"Your turn," Nash said to Nolan.

"I got hold of an old friend in the Bureau. And no, I'm not sharing his name. But he had some insider knowledge he was willing to share. Says the anonymous intel is coming in through the mail, addressed to Special Agent Idler. It's handwritten notes on Anthony Hugo's operations. Nothing huge yet, but so far it's all checked out. The not-so-anonymous sender has hinted that he's got more where that came from in exchange for an immunity deal."

"That lines up with Grim's intel. Sounds like Duncan Hugo wants to work with the feds if it means getting his father out of the way and taking over the family business," Nash said.

"Should I be worried about our national security if there are this many leaks at the FBI?" I wondered.

"Nah. It's probably fine," Nolan said with a wink.

I opened the WhatsApp chat to fill everyone in on our progress.

"Oh good. Knox and Lucian installed more

cameras on the building exterior and added some to the interior. They'll be adding window and door sensors tomorrow and Lucian left a tracker that looks like a condom for you at the station," I read.

"I don't know about you guys, but all this forward momentum is makin' me hungry," Nash announced.

"I wouldn't say no to an open-faced hot turkey sandwich," Nolan said.

"Hey, Nolan. Tina dropped a pen just to watch Nash pick it up," I tattled as we got in the car.

41

Words of Wisdom

Lina

Ninety-six hours. Nash and I had officially survived four whole days of living together *and* the intense local scrutiny of our budding relationship. I hadn't even choked on my latte yesterday morning when Justice asked me how my "boyfriend" was doing.

The wedding was four days away—my bridesmaid dress was pretty damn stunning—and Nash's article was slated to be published the following Monday.

If all went to plan, news of Nash's recovered memory would draw Duncan Hugo out of hiding, he'd fall into the trap, and then it would all be over.

I just wasn't sure how much of the "all" I wanted to be over.

The ambiguous "after" was suddenly looming large, which meant decisions would have to be made. If we found the car when we found Duncan, the job would be done and I'd be heading back to Atlanta to wait for my next assignment.

Or . . .

I slowed my legs to a jog before coming to a stop in Honky Tonk's parking lot.

Bending at the waist, I tried to catch my breath in the early morning chill. Steam rose from my sweaty face.

Everything was moving so fast. There was a momentum, a sense of urgency we all felt as the days ticked down. It made me feel nervous and just the slightest bit out of control.

"Never understood why people run for fun," a voice said behind me.

I straightened and found Knox with a gym bag slung over his shoulder.

"What are you doing up so early?" I asked, my breath still coming in pants.

"Dropped Way off at school. Grabbed last night's deposit and figured I'd hit the gym after the bank."

"Couldn't sleep?" I guessed.

"Not a fucking wink."

"Wedding or Hugo?" I asked, stripping off my headband and using the hem of my shirt to mop my face.

"Fuck Hugo. That asshole's gonna end up behind bars or in the ground."

"So wedding then."

He swiped a hand through his hair. "She's gonna be mine. Officially. I keep waitin' for her to come to her senses."

"You're scared," I said, surprised.

"Fuck yeah, I'm scared. I'm shaking in my goddamn boots. I need to lock her down now before she realizes she could do better."

"She couldn't," I said. "No one in this world could ever love her more than you do. And I'm not saying she's not lovable. I'm saying you love her that much."

"I do," he said hoarsely.

"And she loves you that much."

His lips quirked. "She does, doesn't she?"

I nodded.

He tossed his gym bag into the back of his truck and I leaned against the fender.

"Tell me it's worth it," I blurted out.

"What's worth it?"

"Letting someone in. Letting them get close enough that they could destroy you if they wanted to."

"I might sound like a goddamn greeting card, but it's worth everything," he rasped.

Goose bumps rose on my rapidly cooling skin.

"I'm not kidding. What I had before compared to what I have now?" He shook his head. "It doesn't even compare."

"How?"

"Don't know how to explain it. I just know there's nothing ballsy or brave about living your whole life behind walls. The real good shit doesn't start until those bricks come down and you invite someone in. If you're not scared shitless, you're doin' it wrong."

"But what if I like walls?" I asked, kicking at a rock with the toe of my sneaker.

"You don't."

"Pretty sure I do."

He shook his head. "If you liked your walls so much, you wouldn't be scared shitless right now."

I rolled my eyes. "So how does this work? I'm just supposed to dump my deepest, darkest secrets, the ugliest parts of me, on everyone and then hope it doesn't all go to hell?"

He gave me that bad-boy smirk. "Don't be a dumbass. You don't let everyone in. Only the ones who matter. The ones you want to trust. The ones you want to let *you* in. That vulnerability shit is just like respect. It's earned."

I wondered if maybe that was why I'd failed as a team member before. I didn't trust anyone to have my back and I'd given them no reason to trust me with theirs.

"I think being with Naomi has quadrupled your daily word count," I teased.

"Being with Naomi made me realize how miserable I was before. Everything I thought I wanted was just me trying to protect myself from really living. Like pushing people away," he said pointedly.

I looked down at my toes and let his words

rattle around in my brain. Did I want to keep living the way I always had? Or was I ready for more? Was I ready to stop pushing?

I blew out a breath. "I'm really proud of you, Knox."

"Yeah, yeah," he grumbled. "Now stop fucking asking me about relationship shit."

I bumped his shoulder with mine. "You're gonna be a great husband and dad. A grumpy one with a foul vocabulary, but a great one."

He grunted and I started for the door to the stairs.

"Lina?"

I turned back. "Yeah?"

"Never seen him like this with any other woman. He's in deep and he's hopin' you are too."

I wanted to smile and throw up at the same time. To be on the safe side, I bent at the waist again.

Knox smirked. "See? Scared shitless. Least you know you're doin' it right."

I gave him a friendly middle finger.

I had the whole day to roll things around in my head. By midafternoon, I was so sick of my own thoughts I headed to the grocery store and bought fixings for turkey clubs.

Sandwiches didn't count as cooking, I assured myself.

Back at Nash's, I watered my plant, checked in with work, and—after a brief internet search—managed to cook the bacon in the oven without turning it into charcoal.

I assembled two sandwiches like they were works of art and then sat there staring at the clock. Nash wasn't due home for almost another hour. I'd seriously mistimed my food prep.

On a whim, I pulled out my phone and called my mom.

"Well, this is a nice surprise," Mom said when she came on-screen. The pure joy on her face over me reaching out to her spontaneously felt like a billion tiny guilt darts embedding themselves in my skin.

I leaned my phone against the jar of dog treats Nash kept on the counter. "Hey, Mom."

"What's wrong? You look . . . Wait. You look happy."

"I do?"

"You have a glow. Or is that a filter?"

"No filter. I'm actually . . . I'm seeing someone," I said.

My mother didn't move a muscle on the screen.

"Mom? Did I lose you? I think you're frozen."

She leaned closer. "I'm not frozen. I'm just trying not to startle you with any sudden moves."

"So there's this guy," I said, deciding to get it all out. "He's . . ."

How was I supposed to explain Nash Morgan?

"Special. I think. I mean, he really is and I like him. Like a lot. A whole lot. But we *just* met and I have a life in Atlanta and a job that requires a lot of travel and am I completely losing my mind for thinking that maybe he might be worth changing all that for?"

I waited a beat and then another. My mother's mouth was hanging open on the screen.

"Mom?" I prompted.

She started blinking rapidly. "I'm sorry, sweetie. I'm just processing the fact that you willingly called me to talk about your love life."

"I didn't say love. You said love," I said, feeling the panic crawl up my throat.

"Sorry. Your like life," my mother amended.

"I *really* like him, Mom. He's just so . . . good. And real. And he knows me even though I tried to keep him from getting to know me. But even with everything he knows about me, he *still* likes me."

"This sounds serious."

"It could be. But I don't know if I can do serious. What if he gets to know all of me and then he decides I'm too much or not enough? What if I don't trust him enough and he gets tired of that? What would I do for a living if I quit my job and moved here for him? He doesn't have nearly enough closet space."

"Take the risk."

"What?" I blinked, certain I'd misheard my mother.

"Lina, the only way you're going to know if he's the one is if you treat him like he's the one. He can either earn the title or lose it. That's up to him, but you're the one who has to give him the chance to earn *you*."

"I'm confused. You've always seemed so . . . risk averse."

"Honey, I was a hot mess for years over what happened to you."

"Uh, no shit, Mom."

"I blamed myself. I blamed your father. The pediatrician. Soccer. The stress of high school. So I dedicated myself to trying to protect you from everything. And I think putting you in that bubble did worse long-term damage than your heart condition."

"You didn't damage me." I hadn't grown up a risk-averse little chicken. My job involved actual danger.

"You've viewed every relationship since as a potential prison."

Okay, that rang a little true.

"If you really like this guy, then you need to give him a real chance. And if that means moving to Knockemunder—"

"Knockemout," I corrected.

"What's going on? Are we pausing this game or what?" My dad bellowed in the background.

"Lina has a boyfriend, Hector."

"Oh great. Let's tell everyone," I said dryly.

My father squished into the frame. "Hi, kiddo. What's this about a boyfriend?"

"Hey, Dad," I said lamely.

"Where are you? That's not your kitchen," Dad said, leaning in to look at the screen, essentially blocking everyone else from the camera.

"Oh, I'm . . . uh . . ."

I heard the key in the lock.

"You know what, I should go," I said quickly.

But it was too late. The front door swung open behind me and Nash, looking all kinds of fine in his uniform, and Piper in a new orange sweater walked in.

I spun around to look at him.

"Hey, Angel," he said warmly. "Holy shit. Did you cook?"

"Uh." I spun back around and stared at the two slack-jawed adults on my screen. "Oh boy."

"I think that went well," Nash said through a mouthful of turkey club.

I put my head down on the counter and groaned. "Did you have to be so charming?"

"Angel, it's in my DNA. It's like asking Oprah to stop loving books."

"Did you have to give them your phone number? They call me every day!"

"I couldn't come up with a polite way around that one," Nash confessed. "What harm could it do?"

I sat up and covered my face with my hands. "You don't understand. They're going to get on a plane and show up here."

"I'm lookin' forward to meeting them."

"You don't know what you're saying. You're delusional. I obviously undercooked the bacon and pork amoebas are eating your brain as we speak."

"If they're important to you, they're important to me. They show up and we'll deal with it together. You, me, and the amoebas."

"You have no idea what you're signing up for," I warned him.

"Why don't we worry about this after?" he offered, his blue eyes sparkling with annoying amusement.

"Because we have to worry about it *now*."

"There you go emphasizing again."

My eyes narrowed. "Don't make me slap you across the face with undercooked bacon."

Nash had finished his sandwich and picked up half of mine. "You know, something struck me as you were telling your folks that you were just visiting me at my place."

"Cramps from pork amoebas?"

"Funny. No. I was thinkin' about honesty."

"Fine. I've been meaning to tell you I've been using your toothbrush to brush Piper's teeth," I joked.

"Explains the dog hair in the toothpaste. Now

592

it's my turn. You gotta stop lyin' to your folks."

I stiffened on the stool. "That's easier said than done. And I don't have the energy to explain to you why."

"Nope. That's not happening, baby. I'm not letting you push back on this. Hear my words. You have got to trust your parents enough to be honest with them."

I rolled my eyes. "Oh, sure. It'll go something like this. 'Hi, Mom. I've been lying to you for years. Yeah, I'm actually kind of a bounty hunter, which involves some dangerous investigations while staying in seedy roach motels with flimsy doors. I'm really good at it and the rush makes me feel alive after so many years of feeling smothered. Also, I didn't give up eating red meat like I told you. What's that? Oh, you're so devastated you just had a heart attack? Now Dad's ulcer is acting up again and he's bleeding internally? Cool.'"

He grinned at me. "Angel."

I gave the sandwich thief a shove. "Go away. I'm mad at you."

"This is you pushing me away and this is me stickin'," he pointed out.

"I changed my mind," I decided. "I like keeping everyone at arm's length."

"No, you haven't. No, you don't. And I get that what I'm suggesting is probably downright scary. But, Angel, you have got to trust your folks

593

to handle their shit, which includes but is not limited to their reactions to you and your shit."

"There's too much shit in that metaphor. It stinks."

"Ha. Look, I'm not sayin' it's gonna be easy. And I'm not sayin' that they're gonna have the exact right reaction. But you have to do the best you can do and trust them to do the same."

"You want me to confess to every single thing that I've lied to them about?"

"Hell, no. No parent needs to hear about sneakin' out at night and stealin' booze. Start with now. Tell them about work. Tell them about us."

"I *did* tell them about us. That's *why* I called them."

He stayed where he was, sandwich halfway to his mouth, eyes boring into me with the kind of heat that made my stomach feel like it was attached to a pair of flip-flops.

"What?" I dared him.

"You told your mom about me."

"So?"

He dropped the sandwich and pounced on me.

I squealed and Piper barked playfully.

"So that deserves a reward," he said, picking me up.

42

Chocolate Chocolate Chonk

Lina

W hen you said ice cream, I thought you meant a date," I teased Nash as he lowered the tailgate of his truck in the parking lot of Knockemout Cold, the town's premier ice cream establishment.

I'd spent the day poring over the crime scene reports from both Nash's shooting and the warehouse. I also answered a few follow-up questions from the Arlington police detective who was wrapping up his report on the Baker brothers' naked knife fight. To top it off, I'd watched the dashcam footage of Nash's shooting, looking for clues.

I was a wreck on the first watch, and by the third, I was so sick to my stomach I tackle hugged him as soon as he walked in the door.

"Look who's learning to like dates," he said smugly before setting the sweater-wearing Piper in the bed of the truck with her vanilla puppy cuppy. "Think of this as a double date plus one."

I handed his cone back to him. "It's hard to get to third base when we have an audience." I made sure he was looking in my direction before I took a leisurely lick of my salted caramel ice cream.

"Shouldn't have gotten you a cone," he groused.

I sent a smug smile in his direction and perched on the tailgate. He stepped between my legs and planted a chilly, chocolate-flavored kiss right on my mouth.

"Gross. You guys are as bad as Knox and Aunt Naomi," Waylay complained. She was flanked by Nolan and Sloane—on their second date—and carrying a towering ice cream cone.

"How many scoops is that, Way?" Nash asked.

"Three," she said.

"Naomi is going to murder us," I whispered.

"You're in trouble," Sloane sang as she and Nolan wandered over to his SUV.

Waylay shimmied her way onto the tailgate next to me. "Okay. You guys busted me out of soccer practice and gave me ice cream before dinner. I'm not stupid. What do you want? Did your laptop get a virus? 'Cause my rates have gone up," the girl said before taking an enthusiastic slurp of her chocolate chocolate chonk.

"We want to talk to you about the night your mom and Duncan Hugo took you," Nash said.

"Is this because he's still out there and you guys want to catch him?" she asked.

"Pretty much, yeah," he said.

I liked that he wasn't sugarcoating it. That he

trusted Waylay to handle the truth even if it was ugly and scary. My parents had tried to hide so many things from me because they were afraid I wasn't strong enough to handle the bad. But every time the real truth had been revealed, it felt like another tiny betrayal.

I'd hated it . . . and holy shit, I was doing the same damn thing to them now. I didn't trust them to be able to deal with truth so I lied to protect them.

Which meant Nash was right. Again.

"Damn it," I muttered.

Nash and Waylay both looked at me with concern over their cones.

"Don't mind me. Brain freeze," I said.

Brain freeze, life-altering epiphany—same difference, right?

"We talked to your aunt and Knox and they said it was okay if we asked you some questions about that night," Nash continued. "Are you all right with that?"

Waylay shrugged carelessly and chased a drip with her tongue. "Sure. Why not?"

"What do you remember?" I asked.

She shot me a duh look. "Uh, everything? You don't get abducted by your mom and her crazy boyfriend every day. It's kinda burned into my brain."

"Let's focus on when you were in the warehouse alone with Duncan," Nash suggested.

"What did he say or do before your mom came back with your aunt?"

"Well, he fed me some *disgusting* pizza. It was, like, burnt and cold at the same time. Then when I tried to climb out a window with Waylon, he tied us both up."

Ever the hero, Nash's shoulders tensed almost imperceptibly. I reached behind Waylay and rubbed his back with my non-ice cream holding hand.

"What did he do while you were tied up?" I asked.

"Mostly played video games. He ate a lot. Mostly shitty—I mean crappy pizza and some candy. I think he's a nervous eater. Aunt Naomi would *freak* if she saw his diet."

"Did he talk on the phone at all while you were there?" Nash asked.

Waylay wrinkled her nose. "I don't think so. He mostly just yelled while he played *Dragon Dungeon Quest.*" She looked back and forth between us, then added, "That's a video game where you shoot people with arrows and blow sh—stuff up."

"Did anyone else come into the room while you were there?"

"I guess a couple of . . . what do you call the bad guys who work for the bad guy in charge?"

"Henchmen?" I supplied.

"Yeah. A couple of henchmen came in. Every

time Duncan had to take his headset off, he got mad and yelled at them for interrupting him."

Waylay walked us through everything she remembered that night, including Naomi diving through the air to save her and Knox squashing them "like pancakes" until Uncle Nash saved the day.

"My mom has the worst taste in guys." Waylay finished her recap with a sardonic shake of her head. "Not like you and Aunt Naomi," she added, looking at me.

"Oh, uh, we're just . . ." I looked to Nash. "Help?"

"Yeah, me and Knox are pretty great. Well, mostly me. Knox is okay. If you're into growly grumps who pout all the time," Nash said, nudging Waylay with his elbow.

It was sweet to watch him with the guarded girl. He was good with kids. And why in the hell was I thinking about that? "Good with kids" had never once been a criterion for me.

"Thanks again for Career Day. Don't tell Knox, 'cause he really will pout, but you and the 'stache definitely won."

"Yes! I knew it!" Nolan, who was clearly eavesdropping, straightened away from the front bumper of his SUV and celebrated his official victory with an arm pump.

"You have ice cream in your mustache," I called.

Sloane: Question. Does following Nash and Lina on their ice cream interrogation of Waylay count as a second date for me and Nolan? Asking for a friend who only puts out after the third date.

Naomi: It most definitely counts. You are one date away from Sexville!

Me: When are you seeing him again?

Sloane: Not before I get a wax, apply a thick coat of sunless tanner, heal from said wax, change my sheets, and buy some underwear.

Naomi: What do you mean buy some underwear? Don't you mean buy some sexy underwear?

Me: My God. Is our quirky librarian a commando??

Sloane: I have revealed too much.

When we got back to Nash's place, I freshened up Piper's water dish and gave her her prebedtime gourmet treat. Then I went into the bedroom and changed into a sexy little silk number that showed more than it hid.

I found Nash standing in the dining room holding up a photo of the interior of the warehouse.

"Whatcha got there?" I asked, sidling up next to him.

"Something Waylay said got me thinkin'—Holy shit," he said, noticing my outfit.

"Thinking about what?"

"Your boobs." He shook his head. "No. That's not what I was thinking about. I mean, I'm kind of always thinking about them. But not in a pervy way. More like a worshipful way."

I took the photo from his dangling hand and glanced at it. "It's a gaming console."

Nash said nothing, and I realized he was still staring at my chest. I held the picture over my breasts. "Focus, hotshot. Talk to me."

"Hugo's gaming console," Nash said, slowly coming out of his boob fugue.

"Looks like it was shot to hell. Do you think anyone could get anything useful off it?"

"We might not need them to."

I met his gaze and it hit me. "Because he wasn't yelling at the TV. He was yelling at other players."

"Because he was playing online," Nash said with a slow grin.

"Now who's Nancy Drew?" I teased. "This is good. Really good. We could trace his location, couldn't we?"

Nash pulled out his phone and dialed. "Hey. I need a favor."

He listened briefly and rolled his eyes.

"Shouldn't you be saving that for the wedding night?"

There was another brief pause and Nash winked at me.

"Then put your pants back on and go ask Way what Hugo's username was on *Dragon Dungeon Quest*." Nash waited a beat. "Yeah, the three scoops of ice cream were my fault."

Nash reached for me and pulled me up against him. But instead of grabbing a handful of boob as I expected, he held my hand and kissed each one of my fingers while he waited for his grumpy brother.

"Yeah, I'm here," Nash said into the phone. "She remember?"

His gaze held mine. I wondered if I'd ever seen eyes that blue before.

"Yeah. Got it. Thanks . . . No. You can take your pants off again. I'm about to."

"She remembered it, didn't she?" I asked when he hung up.

"Sure did. KingSchlong85."

"Gross."

Nash opened up his text messages. "If he's using the same user name, Lucian's creepy stealth team should be able to track down an IP address."

"God, you're hot when you're all sleuthy."

"And you're sexy as hell when you're investigating in lingerie."

He tossed his phone on the counter and took a step toward me, a dangerous, determined gleam in his eyes.

I held up my hands and started to back away.

"Hang on. We just had a break. Shouldn't we wait to see what Lucian says?"

"No one says we have to wait with our clothes on," he said as he kept coming.

I pulled out a dining chair and put it between us.

"But there's work to do," I reminded him.

"And there will still be work to do once I get you out of that outfit," he said devilishly.

With a squeal, I turned to run, but he was faster than me. And I didn't mind it one bit when he tossed me over his shoulder and marched us into the bedroom.

The pounding woke us both out of a dead sleep. Sometime after falling into a post-sex coma, I'd actually crawled on top of Nash, which was embarrassing to say the least. But there wasn't any time to wallow in it with an extremely insistent middle of the night knocker.

Nash reacted more quickly than I did. He dragged on a pair of sweats and hauled ass to the door while I was still rubbing the sleep out of my eyes and hoping I hadn't drooled on his chest.

I managed to stumble after him, barely avoiding stepping on the anxious Piper, who was growling and trembling at the same time.

"It's three in the fucking morning. Someone better be bleeding," Nash said, swinging the door open.

Nolan prowled inside in pajama pants, running shoes, and, well, that was it.

"I think this was meant for you," Nolan said, handing me a freezer bag with a large rock and a piece of paper inside.

"Me?"

Nash snatched the bag out of his hand but not before I read the note.

Back off, Bitch.

"Where the hell did you find this?" Nash demanded.

"Mixed in with a nice shard of glass salad on her dining room floor," Nolan reported.

"What?" I squinted at him, processing.

He looked to the heavens when I didn't pick up what he was putting down fast enough. "They threw it through the damn window about two minutes ago."

Nash sprang into action and bolted barefoot through the door.

"Damn it," I muttered.

"Nice nightie," Nolan said, throwing me a smirk and a salute before jogging after him. "There's no one out there. They peeled out about five seconds after they broke the window," he called after Nash.

I ran back to the bedroom, pulled on my shoes, a sports bra, and Nash's sweatshirt over the nightgown, then sprinted after them.

The night air was damp and cold. The streetlights bathed the eerily silent street in golden yellow light that pooled in the thickening fog. I spotted tire marks in front of the building.

"Get back inside," Nash growled at me when I caught up to them in the middle of the street.

"It was meant for me—"

"Which makes you the goddamn target. So get your ass off the street, *now,*" he barked.

"Now who's the one overemphasizing words?" I muttered under my breath as I marched back inside.

Annoyed, I waited shivering in the vestibule as Nash and Nolan canvassed both sides of the street.

"Well?" I demanded when they finally returned.

"They were long gone," Nash said, his voice tight as he brushed past me and headed up the stairs.

"Chief doesn't seem to like having his girlfriend threatened," Nolan said to me as we trudged up behind him.

"I'm not his girlfriend. I'm . . . We're . . . whatever."

"You're living together and wearing shit like that to bed. Pretty sure in some parts of the country, you'd be considered married."

We'd made it to the top of the stairs when Mrs. Tweedy's door burst open.

"It's like a circus full of elephants escaped out here. What's with all the thundering feet? You're interrupting my beauty sleep," Mrs. Tweedy said. She was wearing a housecoat and holding what looked like a martini.

"You sleep with a martini?" Nolan asked.

"This is my middle-of-the-night nightcap."

43

Bad Day, Bad Advice

Nash

A fter the rock through Lina's window and Grave's arrival to take our statements, I'd lain awake staring at the ceiling for an hour, listening to the steady rhythm of Lina's breath next to me. But instead of the comfort I usually found from her proximity, I was left with a gnawing anxiety.

Someone had threatened her.

If something happened to her . . . If I couldn't protect her . . .

I'd finally managed to drift off only to dream of dark pavement, the menacing crunch, and the echo of gunshots.

When I jolted awake with a racing heartbeat and thundering headache, I'd given up on the idea of chasing more sleep and slipped out of bed.

It was a dreary gray morning with a slow, icy rain that somehow settled into your bones.

I took my first cup of coffee standing in front of the case board in the dining room and pushed aside the anxiety that threatened to choke me.

Either Tate Dilton had decided not to go so quietly or somehow this Duncan Hugo mess had

607

spilled over onto Lina. Either way, I wasn't going to wait and see what happened next.

I pulled out my phone and opened my messages.

> **Me:** Meet me at the station. ASAP.
> **Knox:** Jesus don't you ever sleep? Lucian needs at least an hour to put on his fancy ass suit and commandeer a helicopter to get up here.
> **Lucian:** I'm already dressed and I've conducted two teleconferences from the back room of Café Rev so far this morning.
> **Knox:** Kiss ass.
> **Lucian:** Sweatpant-wearing whiner.

I beat them both to the station and nodded a curt greeting to the night shift.

I'd left my place without a goodbye just to prove to myself I didn't *need* to start my day with her.

My head felt fuzzy and my gut burned from coffee and nerves. Uneasiness crawled through my veins like a thousand spiders.

To distract myself while I waited for Knox and Lucian, I opened the mail sitting on my desk. I didn't realize until I'd already opened it and unfolded it that one of the envelopes contained a letter from my father.

Just seeing his signature at the bottom ratcheted up my anxiety.

How many times had I wanted something from him, needed something from him? How many times had he let me down because his addiction was greater than his love for me? Duke Morgan needed pills just to get through the day. To survive. To numb himself before the world and its realities could put him in the ground.

Despite the morning chill, I broke out into a light sweat.

Was that what I was doing?

I swiped a hand over my mouth and stared unseeing at my father's handwriting.

Even after all this time, it was as recognizable to me as my own. We made our *e*'s with the same slashing angle. We had the same eyes, the same *e*'s. What else was the same?

My heart pounded louder in my head. But now it wasn't fear that threatened to choke me. It was anger.

Anger at myself for following in his footsteps.

I knew better. I knew that leaning on a crutch just to get through the day was the beginning of the end.

And wasn't that exactly what I was doing with Lina? Using her? Turning to her to help push the pain and fear aside? It didn't have to be drugs or alcohol or whatever else people used to numb the pain of existence. It could be anything, anyone you needed just to survive, to wake up and start the whole horrible cycle all over again.

"Everything all right?" Lucian strolled inside and I stuffed my father's letter, unread, into the top desk drawer.

"No, it's not. But I'd rather wait for Knox to get here before I get into it."

"He's fuckin' here," Knox said on a snarly yawn.

"Someone threw this through Lina's window last night." I tossed the bagged rock and note on to my desk.

"Well, fuck," my brother said.

"Guess those exterior cams are now a priority," Knox said to Lucian after I finished filling them in.

"I'm assuming Lina should be outfitted with her own tracker," our friend suggested.

Knox smirked. "She'll love that."

"Good. Then you can deliver it to her," I said.

"Why can't you fucking do it? You're the one sleeping with her. Or, according to Way, 'making heart eyes' at her."

"I'm busy today. Just drop one off for her and yell at her until she agrees to carry it," I said.

Knox's eyes narrowed. "Somebody pissed in your wheat bran this morning, sunshine?"

"I don't have time for this. Just get it done."

Knox thankfully wasn't as combative early in the morning, so he left my office swearing under his breath.

Lucian, however, remained seated.

"Aren't you breaking out in hives by now?" I asked him. He wasn't a fan of cops or police stations and for good reason.

"You're exceptionally pissy this morning. What's wrong?"

"Besides a 3:00 a.m. warning rock through the window?"

Lucian sat and stared blandly at me. I decided to wait him out and turned my attention to my emails. Our standoff lasted three and a half messages.

"Do you think we're all doomed to repeat the sins of our fathers?" I asked finally.

"Yes."

I blinked. "You don't wanna think about that for a minute?"

He crossed his arms irritably. "I've thought of little else for the past few decades. It's impossible to outrun your genes. We were made by flawed men. Those flaws don't just dissolve out of the bloodline."

Rain pelted the windows, ensuring I couldn't forget the misery outside.

"Then what the fuck is the point of anything?" I asked.

"How the hell should I know?" He absent-mindedly patted the jacket pocket where he stowed his single daily cigarette. "My only hope is if I keep getting out of bed every morning, someday it will all make sense."

"You know, I was already feeling pretty shitty before you brought your cloud of doom in here," I told him.

Lucian grimaced. "Sorry. I didn't get much sleep last night."

"You don't have to move your entire life up here for this, you know." His parents' house held ghosts for him.

"I'll stay where I want to stay and work where I want to work."

"Someone must have been pissing in wheat bran all over town," I quipped.

It was right about then that my office door flew open.

"Why the hell am I finding you here instead of at your damn door? I swear to God, Morgan. You're worse to babysit than that little old church lady in Ala-fucking-bama," a disheveled Nolan announced, storming into the room and kicking my trash can for emphasis. "It's two steps forward, thirty-seven thousand backward with you, and they don't pay me enough to put up with this shit."

"Why don't you quit then?" I snapped, feeling too sorry for myself to spread it around to anyone else.

"I quit and you end up full of holes. Then I'm supposed to live with the guilt of it? Great fucking plan."

"I might have a position for you," Lucian

announced. He had that crafty bastard look about him that should make anyone on the receiving end very, very nervous.

"Oh, really?" Nolan said, still pissed off.

"Really."

"What's the catch?"

"Catch is such an ugly word. Let's call it an addendum."

Nolan didn't look impressed.

"Stop seeing Sloane and the job is yours."

"You've gotta be fuckin' kidding me," Nolan said.

"Okay, seriously? You hate her guts but you don't want her dating anyone else? Even you have to realize how unhealthy that is," I said.

"I never claimed to be healthy," Lucian said in his scary voice.

"Then why the hell am I taking advice from you?" I demanded.

"How the hell should I know?"

"Bunch of feral assholes," Nolan muttered, storming out of my office.

Lina: Hey. Everything OK? I woke up and you were gone. Not that you need to clear all your movements with me. Or whatever.

The rain made for slick roads, and slick roads made for accidents. The first call wasn't bad. A fender bender with an anxious new mom and her infant on the way to the pediatrician.

Bannerjee calmed both mom and baby while the tow truck was called. Meanwhile I dealt with the traffic and cleanup, forcing myself not to think about the woman I'd left warm in my bed.

We hadn't even dried off from the first call when we got the second.

There's a mode of operation first responders learn to shift into so the trauma they witness doesn't haunt them. It works. For the most part.

But given the mood I couldn't shake, the circumstances, the cruel coincidence . . . I knew I was already spiraling before things got worse.

It was dark and I was thoroughly frozen by the time I trudged up the stairs to my apartment. My shoulder and head were battling it out for which could ache more.

I just wanted a hot shower so I could stand under the water until my soul thawed. And then I wanted to go to bed and sink into the blackness until I could forget about the pain that I hadn't been able to save anyone from.

There was a husband and two little boys holding vigil in the ICU waiting room hoping their wife and mom would wake up.

I'd arrived after the fact. Generally how things worked. Something bad happened and then the cops came. I'd helped the fire crew and paramedics pull her from the mangled prison of twisted metal, held a poncho over her motionless body while they belted her onto the gurney, and felt fucking helpless.

I was supposed to save people, but I hadn't even been able to save myself. It was dumb luck that I was still here. A lucky coincidence that Xandra had been there at the exact right time.

I unlocked my door with frozen fingers, anxious for the dark, the quiet.

Instead, I was met with light and warmth and the smell of something cooking on the stove.

There was music, an upbeat country classic playing loud. Memories of her pulling me or Knox or my dad into a dance in the kitchen assailed me, making my chest ache.

Jayla Morgan was the light and laughter of our little family.

When she didn't come home that day, part of me died. Part of all of us died. We were never the same.

Piper trotted up to me growling playfully through a stuffed snake.

"Hey!" Lina called cheerily from the kitchen. "Before you panic, I didn't actually cook. Mrs. Tweedy made a triple batch of chili and I found a box mix for cornbread in your pantry that I managed not to burn. I figured it was the perfect, miserable day for it."

She was in leggings and a long-sleeve white top that was cropped at the waist and open with crisscrossed straps at the back. Her skin was dewy and her short, dark hair tousled. The earrings I got her dangled from her ears.

In that moment, I knew a longing so intense I felt my knees buckle.

In that moment, I understood my father.

In that moment, I realized I was my father.

"Do you like Piper's new toy? The mayor dropped it off. Said you'd get the joke," she continued.

I wanted to take off my shoes, peel the wet clothes from my body, and stand under the showerhead until I felt human again. But I was frozen to the spot. Because I didn't deserve to feel warm. Not until I'd let her go.

"Nash? Are you okay?" her voice sounded like it was far away. Like it was floating to me over country music and the smell of fresh cornbread.

Something rose up in me. Something dark and determined. I couldn't do this.

If I stayed, if I kept her, kept leaning on her, I'd be no better than my father.

And if I loved her too much, I would lose her.

"I think you should go." My voice sounded thin and shaky, like my father's when he needed a fix.

The ladle fell from her hand and landed on the floor.

"You think I should do what?" she demanded, meeting my icy numbness with her fire.

Was this why we fought? So I could provoke

her and steal her heat? Would it all just be finding new ways to use her?

"This isn't working," I insisted. "I think you should go."

Those whiskey-colored eyes scanned me from head to toe as if looking for injury. But she'd never see it. It was too far beneath the surface. The wound that never healed.

She threw the ladle in the sink and crossed her arms. "What's wrong?" she asked again.

I shook my head. "Nothing. Just . . . I need you to go."

"Did you have another panic attack?" She was coming toward me, and I knew if she touched me, it would be game over. I'd cave. I'd burrow into her body and take what I needed from her.

"I didn't have a fucking panic attack. Okay?" I exploded.

She flinched but kept coming at me. "What happened? Are you all right?"

"I just don't want you here anymore. I can't make it any more clear than that. I'm over it. You were right. This was a really fucking stupid idea. We barely know each other."

She stopped in her tracks and the look in her eyes nearly leveled me. The shock. The hurt. I'd put them there. But it was better this way. Better than dragging her down with me. Better than her leaving me.

"You're serious, aren't you?" she whispered.

Piper whimpered, dropping the stuffed snake at my feet. I kicked it away. "Not now, Pipe," I said quietly. "You were always going to leave. Might as well be now," I said.

She lifted her chin and took a shaky inhale. "Okay."

"Just okay?"

Why couldn't I leave it alone? I was getting what I wanted. Lina would go. She'd be safe from the things I couldn't protect her from. And I could go back to whatever the hell I had before her. Yet I was baiting her, trying to make her share in the responsibility for this spectacular flameout.

She didn't say a word to me, didn't rise to the bait. She just walked away.

I followed her into the bedroom and watched as she pulled her suitcase out of my closet.

"I'm sorry this is how it worked out. You're probably relieved."

Her jaw was tight, making the hollows under her cheekbones even more pronounced. Still she said nothing as she efficiently unzipped the bag and laid it open on the bed.

Piper hopped onto the bench, then onto the mattress, where she sniffed at Lina's suitcase.

"You should take her too. I can't deal with her right now," I said, gesturing at the dog.

Both sets of female eyes hit me and made me feel like King Asshole of the Planet Asshole.

Lina put her hands on her hips. "Okay. You almost had me. I was buying it until that."

"Until what?"

She pointed at Piper. "You love her, you idiot."

"I do not."

Lina opened the nightstand drawer and withdrew a short stack of papers. "You bought her a bench to help her get on the bed. You have a basket full of toys to entertain her. You dress her in sweaters to keep her warm outside. You love her."

"That's not love. That's taking care and I'm tapped out. I don't have the capacity to take care of anyone or anything else." *Myself included,* I added silently.

"Bullshit."

"Don't you get it?" My voice snapped like the crack of a whip. "I can't take care of her. I can't protect you. Hell, I couldn't even protect myself."

She tossed the papers down on the bed and took a challenging step toward me. "For the record, this is you pushing me away and this is me sticking."

"I don't want you to stick." The words burned like acid in my mouth.

"Who didn't you protect, Nash?" she said quietly.

Piper curled up in a tight ball in the suitcase and wrapped her tail over her nose.

"Are you forgetting the rock someone threw through your window last night?"

"No one got hurt."

"Can't say the same for the woman on a fucking ventilator in the ICU. She's got a husband and two boys wondering what they're gonna do if she doesn't wake up."

Lina took another step forward. She was too close. I had to fist my hands at my sides to keep myself from grabbing her and holding her to me.

"Does that remind you of your mom?" she asked quietly.

"How the fuck could it not? It happened on the same stretch of road less than two hundred yards away."

"Baby," she whispered, inching closer like I was some kind of skittish fucking horse.

"Don't," I hissed.

"You can't get there in time to save everyone," she said.

"I can't save anyone. I really need you to go, Lina. Please."

Her eyes looked glassy, and when she nodded, her earrings shimmered, the golden sunbursts catching the light.

"Okay. You're exhausted. You've had a god-awful day. I'm going to give you some space. I'll stay next door with Nolan tonight. We'll talk tomorrow after you've had some sleep."

"Fine," I rasped. I'd promise her anything

just to make her leave before I broke down and touched her.

I stayed where I was, rooted to the spot as she packed a few things into her bag and then wheeled it out around me. I heard her go into the kitchen and turn off the burner. And then I listened for the front door to open and close softly.

She was gone.

And I was alone.

But instead of relief, a wave of panic crashed over me, shoving me under, forcing me down deep.

She was gone.

I'd made the woman I needed, the woman I loved, leave.

I left the bedroom, the sight of the bed we'd shared making me sick. I *loved* her. I'd known it for a while. Maybe since the moment I found her on my stairs. I'd wanted her. Needed her. And now I'd thrown her away.

But it was the right thing, wasn't it? She deserved more than to be someone's crutch, someone's emotional support fuck. She deserved something real and good. And I couldn't offer that. Not like this.

Piper sat next to the front door and whimpered pathetically.

I put my hands on my head and headed for the bedroom as the band around my chest tightened to the point of pain. I spotted the papers Lina had left and picked them up. They were from the dog rescue. It was an adoption application. The sticky note on top said in Lina's bold scrawl, "She's yours. Make it official."

It felt like a punch to the gut. I dropped the papers and walked back to the living room. The plant in the window drew my attention. Lina's plant. It had been nothing but a pot of glossy leaves when she'd moved in, but now it was covered with delicate white bell-shaped blooms.

Lily of the valley, I realized.

My mother's favorite.

"Fuck."

44

Eye Water

Lina

I pushed through the exterior door and stepped out into the rainy night Main Street had to offer. Raindrops pelted my head, soaking my shirt. But I didn't care. I was angry and hurt and sad and confused. Also hungry. Was this why women in movies always ate ice cream out of the carton after getting their hearts broken?

Feeling the cold stab of each drop was better than feeling the pieces of my stupid heart splinter apart.

This. *This* was what I got for being vulnerable. I put myself out there. I opened up. And I got punched in the goddamn heart. Which was *exactly* what I'd predicted. I blamed Naomi. Smug soon-to-be-married women were not to be trusted. Neither were sexy, broody next-door neighbors with great asses and heroic scars.

I knew this. Yet here I was, taking a stroll in the icy rain after *making fucking cornbread.*

Nash was hurting, and that devastated me in a way I was unprepared to handle. But I couldn't fix him. I couldn't open up those wounds of his and force them to heal.

I could only go for a stupid walk in the stupid rain so my stupid eye water could mix with the stupid sky water.

A shuddering sob ripped its way out of my throat.

If he didn't change his mind, if he couldn't venture out of his black-and-white thinking and meet me in the gray, I would lose him forever. The thought of that reality was terrifying. And stupid. We barely knew each other, and I was crying in the damn rain over a man who had kicked me out of his apartment.

Or did we know each other better than anyone? a nagging inner voice interjected.

"I *hate* having feelings," I muttered to the empty, soggy street.

Everyone else was at home or inside, staying warm, being happy, eating hot food. And once again, I was left on the outside.

I started to walk, crossing my arms over my chest and hunching my shoulders against the cold. I'd barely made it past the warm glow of Whiskey Clipper's storefront when I heard the door to the apartments burst open.

"Angelina."

Oh no. No thank you. Nope. I was not letting the man who brought me to literal tears see me in those tears. I was too vulnerable right now. I wouldn't survive.

Swiping at my wet face with my sleeves, I broke into a run.

He wouldn't follow me. The man had just tried to dump me. It wasn't like he was going to chase—

Fast footsteps sounded behind me.

I poured on the speed, my feet slapping at the water on the sidewalk, and thanked my lucky stars that it was a dark, miserable night, which meant there was no one else to witness my tearful humiliation.

He was tired and cold and spiraling. Any second now, he'd decide I wasn't worth chasing after.

My heart pounded in my chest as my arms pumped harder. I was faster than he was. I could outlast him, outdistance him. If I could just make it to the corner, I wouldn't have to witness him giving up on me. On us.

A hand closed in the material of my shirt, jerking me backward. Then strong arms wrapped around me hard, banding me to him.

"Stop," Nash panted in my ear as he pulled me against him. He burrowed his face in the back of my neck. "Just stop."

A new panic set in. "Let go of me!"

"I tried. I can't."

I went still in his arms even as more tears coursed down my cheeks. "I'm . . . confused."

"I'm an idiot. An asshole. An idiot asshole who doesn't deserve you, Angel."

I tried to pry his hands loose, but the man wasn't

giving an inch. He was squeezing the breath out of me. "If you're looking for an argument here, you're gonna be disappointed."

"All day, all I could think about was what if something happened to you."

"Nothing happened to me. Nothing is going to happen to me," I whispered, my breath hitching. How many conversations had I had with my parents that started the same way and ended with me making promises we all knew I couldn't keep?

"Lucian said we're doomed to repeat the mistakes our fathers made."

I fought against his grip and he finally allowed me to turn in his arms. When I looked up into his face, I wished I hadn't. So much pain. So much sadness. I ached for him.

"You went to Lucian for advice? That guy is one typewriter away from *The Shining*. I mean, it's great that he owns his fucked-upness, but he's the guy you go to for stock tips or to make someone disappear. He's not the guy you go to for advice on women."

Nash's lips quirked as the rain pattered down on our heads. "I repeat. Idiot asshole. I think I was looking for someone to confirm my darkest fears."

"Well, you went to the right place."

"My mom asked me to go with her to the store that day. I didn't feel like it. I was too busy doing whatever kid shit kids do. I could have been there. But I wasn't. So she died alone in that car. I could have helped her if I'd been there. Maybe I could have even prevented it. But I wasn't there."

My heart ached for him when his voice broke.

"After, I made sure I was there every fucking day and I still couldn't save my dad."

Tears burned paths down my cheeks. Seeing them, Nash hooked a hand at the back of my neck and pressed my face to his chest. I wrapped my arms around him and held on tight.

"We lost him too," he continued. "No matter how good my grades were, how hard I worked on the football field, nothing was enough to make him choose us. He wanted something more than he wanted us."

I let out a shuddering sob, my heart shattering for the boy who wanted to save everyone.

His arms tightened around me until I could barely breathe.

"I wasn't there when Lucian was arrested. We found out after the fact. He didn't deserve to be punished for defending himself against his own fucking father. I thought becoming a cop would mean I could finally fix it all. I could protect the ones who needed protecting."

"That's what you're doing. Every damn day, Nash," I murmured against his damp uniform shirt. His badge was icy against my cheek.

He gave a bitter laugh. "Who am I protecting? I couldn't even save myself. If not for dumb fucking luck, I wouldn't even be here."

I wrestled my arms free so I could cup his face. "On your darkest days, you drag yourself out of bed and you choose to go protect your town, your people. That's what a hero does, you idiot. What you do is nothing short of heroic."

Eyes closed, he bowed his head to mine.

Tears continued to spill free onto my cheeks, scalding hot against the icy raindrops. "I'm so proud of you, Nash. You face down your own demons every damn day so you can show up and be there for everyone else. You single-handedly made your entire town safer. Hell, even Tina respects you."

"My family doesn't."

My heart ached for him. "Baby. Your brother and grandmother are two of the worst communicators in the world. Maybe Knox doesn't understand why you do what you do, but he is so fucking proud of you for doing it. Just like you're proud of him for using his money to help support the same people you protect. Not that you'd ever tell him that. But you're the one who stands between your people and danger. You're the one who's there immediately after to restore order. You're the one who does whatever he can to make sure it doesn't happen again."

He crushed me to him again as the rain pelted

us. "I miss her," he whispered. "I–I think maybe she would have been proud."

I held on to him like he was dangling off a cliff. "She *is* proud of you."

He took a shaky breath, his chest rising against mine. "They used to dance in the kitchen. My parents. They used to be happy. He loved her so much. And when she was gone, he didn't love us enough. He chose booze and pills over and over again. He *needed* them."

"And that sucks, but it was never because of you. It was never because of anything you did or didn't do."

"I *want* you like that. I *need* you like that."

"You are *not* your father, hotshot. And I am not some unhealthy habit that needs to be kicked. We are all very different people from the ones who made us. You didn't turn to me to numb yourself to the pain. You turned to me to remember what felt good. To give yourself a reason to fight through the pain."

"Jesus. Why in the fuck did I talk to Lucian and not you?"

My laugh was half hiccup. "I think it has something to do with the idiot asshole thing."

He started to sway with me, side to side in the rain as the reflection of streetlights danced over rivulets of water trickling into the gutters.

"You know this is crazy, right? *That's* what we should be freaking out about instead of all our stupid baggage. I've known you only a few weeks," I reminded him.

Nash rested his chin on the top of my head. "Doesn't mean this isn't real. My parents met, fell in love, and got engaged in three months."

"They were happy? Before?" I asked.

His hands shifted on my back, pressing me closer. "Yeah. We all were. Before they got married, Dad got 0522 tattooed on his arm. May twenty-second. Their wedding date. He said he knew even before it happened it would be the happiest day of his life."

"Wow."

"When we were kids—before—we all celebrated that day like it was a national holiday. Hell, their wedding date is my PIN number. I never changed it. It felt like the only way I could hang on to those good times."

"Maybe . . ." I began, but emotion made the words stick. I cleared my throat and tried again. "Maybe your good times are yet to come."

"If I haven't fucked up my chances already."

"Nash—"

"No. Listen to me, Angel. I'm so fucking sorry. I let you walk out that door, but that's as far as I'm willing to let you go. Please don't take another step away from me. Please be patient with me."

"Nash, I wasn't trying to leave you. I was trying to give us both some space."

"You ran," he pointed out.

"I was trying to give us both a lot of space very quickly," I amended.

"You're cold," he said, noticing my shivers. "Come home with me."

I could feel the shift in gears from wounded soul to take-charge hero.

"Okay."

"Thank God," he murmured. "I was afraid I'd have to pull a Knox and carry you back."

He led me straight to the shower. After carefully undressing me and then himself, Nash guided me under the hot water. He followed me in and we stood there, my back to his front, letting the hot water take the chill out of our bones.

His hands were gentle as they combed through my wet hair and slid down my body. Soothing. Reassuring.

I felt raw, vulnerable. And when I felt the brush of his erection against me, I felt a new kind of warmth spiraling through my body. I wanted to reach out and touch him, to make him feel as good as he made me feel. But I understood that he needed to give. So I surrendered to his touch.

He stroked and kissed his way up, then down my body. And when he turned me to face him, I found him on his knees in front of me.

Those callused hands pressed me against the tile wall.

He watched me with solemn eyes as he slid one hand from my ankle up to my thigh. Our gazes held in a way that was so intimate it made me tremble. Hooking me behind the knee, he draped my leg over his shoulder, baring me to him.

My head thumped against the wall, breaking our eye contact.

Steam rose around us, but I barely noticed, because Nash used two fingers to part the lips of my sex.

"Such a pretty pussy, Angel," he said, his voice barely audible over the water.

Gah. Who knew the law-abiding man with the shiny badge would be such a dirty talker?

It was the last coherent thought I had before his tongue traced everything his fingers had just bared. My knee went week and nearly buckled at the first swipe of his tongue. Every muscle in my body seemed to contract at the same time as all my consciousness coalesced to the nerves at the apex of my thighs.

He licked his way up and back, driving me wild with his mouth, tender and loving, yet determined to conquer. When my supporting leg shook again, he merely wedged his shoulder behind my knee so I sat astride him, my back to the tile.

I let out a long, low moan as he devoured me.

My thighs trembled as his tongue alternated between thrusting into my opening and laving my clit with a fervent kind of worship. He was magic. *We* were magic. And I knew, deep down, something that felt this good couldn't be wrong.

"Nash," I whispered brokenly as things inside me began to give way.

He groaned against my sex as if hearing his name from my mouth was too much to bear. Mindless now, I bucked against him, then gasped when he thrust his fingers inside me again. His tongue concentrated on the desperate need that kept building and building.

Without warning, I came. My inner walls clamped down on his fingers as he licked and sucked my swollen bud through the orgasm.

I rode his face shamelessly, relishing the way his tongue forced the pleasure to spiral on and on. I was still feeling the echoes of it when he withdrew from me and spun me around to face the wall.

He caged me in with his arms, his palms flat against the tile. His erection was hot and hard against my back.

Nash's need made me feel both powerless and powerful.

His head dipped and I felt his lips trail over my tattoo.

"Need you," he murmured before using his teeth against my skin.

I needed this too. "Hurry," I whispered. "Please."

He didn't make me wait. Those big, rough hands of his slid down my hips, canting them at just the right angle. He guided the blunt crown of his penis down the cleft of my cheeks. I went still and tensed when he eased the head over my anus, reminding me just how intimately vulnerable this position was. He let out a guttural groan and then he was dragging the tip lower still, between my spread thighs, sliding through the lips of my sex.

I could feel the pulse of him against me, and a fresh wave of longing crashed over me.

"I lose my mind when I have you like this," he murmured, sliding one hand up my stomach to cup a breast.

I dropped my head against his shoulder. He wasn't the only one losing their mind here.

My thighs trembled. My palms flattened against the tile. My hips had a mind of their own, pressing against him, begging for more as if I hadn't just come mere moments ago.

His hand kneaded my breast, squeezing and plumping. "I can't let you go, Angel."

"Why would you have to let me go?" My knees were knocking now. From excitement. From need. From the weight of his body pressing me down, down.

"Just lettin' you know it's not an option now. You'll move here or I'll move with you. Maybe we'll find someplace to start over. But I can't. Let. You. Go."

"Nash," I whispered as a hot tear slid down the side of my nose.

"You breathed life back into me. You brought me back to the light. Let me have you. Let me take you. Say you're mine," he demanded.

He thrust his erection through my slick folds.

"Y-yes," I managed. I'd worry about the consequences of what I'd promised him after. I needed this, *him* now.

"Thank God," he said, dropping an openmouthed kiss to my shoulder. The shift of his weight had me angling my hips for more.

"Nash!" I gasped.

His grip tightened at the back of my neck as he dragged his erection back and then surged forward again, the crown of his cock nudging against my clitoris.

He needed this. And I needed to give it to him.

"I can never decide which way to take you," he rasped, continuing those short, measured thrusts. "I fucking love watching you come. Watching your tits bounce while I move in you. But I love you like this too. When you give it all up and just surrender."

I love you like this.

I can't let you go.

His words echoed in my head like a mantra. A mantra that I had no right repeating. He didn't mean it like that, I told myself. And then I stopped telling myself anything because Nash lined up the head of his cock with my eager opening and surged inside me.

Our shouts echoed off the tile.

Full. So full. He snaked one arm across my abdomen. His other hand closed in my hair, holding me to him. And then he began to thrust.

Hot water pelted me from above. But it was Nash's heat that warmed me from the inside out. He powered into me, bringing me up on my toes with every drive of his hips until we both came, shaking and panting as each wave sent us tumbling. Each warm wash of his release branding me, soothing me from the inside.

45

A Perfectly Good Parachute

Nash

I woke to warm, female flesh pressing against me.

"Wake up, hotshot. It's time for some fun," Lina murmured in my ear.

Me and my cock both gave her our full attention.

She kissed me hard, nipping my bottom lip with her teeth. "Sorry, handsome. We don't have time for that kind of fun this morning. Time to get up."

I guided her hand under the covers to my erection. "I am up."

Her husky laugh was warm against my throat. "After," she promised. "Come on. Get that cute ass out of bed."

She slid off me before I could capture her and convince her to stay. My hard-on pitched a worthy tent under the sheet.

"No amount of fun is going to be better than staying in bed with me," I warned, rubbing the sleep out of my eyes.

A pair of athletic pants hit me in the face.

"We'll see about that," she said smugly. "Get dressed. We've got an appointment."

"No fucking way, Lina."

She grinned from behind the wheel and said nothing as she turned the Charger onto the lane after the sign that said Just Jump Aviation and Skydiving.

The paved lane ran parallel with a small airstrip tucked between acres of cornfields just south of the Virginia-Maryland border. Unlike the misery of yesterday, the morning sun burned bright in the cloudless sky over the oranges and golds of autumn leaves.

Lina whipped the car into a parking spot against the cavernous red hangar with a white-and-blue logo painted on it.

Still grinning, she lowered her sunglasses to look at me. With those red lips, she looked like a temptress, a siren trying to lure me to my death.

"Planes are meant to land," I insisted.

"It *will* land. We just won't be on it when it does," she said, shutting off the engine and unbuckling her seat belt.

I refused to move. Nothing was going to get me out of this car and anywhere near a goddamn parachute. "It's irresponsible to jump out of a moving vehicle. Especially one that's several thousand feet above the fucking earth."

Lina reached between her legs and slid her seat back.

Before I realized her intention, she managed to climb over the console into my lap. "I'm not going to make you do anything you don't want to do, Nash."

"Great. Let's go get some breakfast and then we can go buy caulk to fix the loose tile in the shower."

She shook her head, still smiling that siren's smile. "I'm going up. And I would love for you to go with me."

Fuck.

"You're not throwing yourself out of a goddamn plane." A cold sweat erupted in my armpits.

She slid my sunglasses on top of my head and cupped my face in her hands. "Nash, I've done this more than a handful of times. This is one of my favorite things to do, and I want to share it with you."

Double fuck.

How in the hell was I supposed to say no to that?

"Come on, hotshot. Have some fun with me," she coaxed.

I'd put her through hell yesterday and this was my punishment. Death by gravity.

Less than a minute later, I was—reluctantly—following her toward the huge open garage door on the side of the building. Her hand gripped mine in a way that suggested she wasn't going to take no for an answer.

"Doesn't this require a license or some kind of complicated paperwork that takes weeks to get approved?" I asked desperately.

She looked over her shoulder at me, smirking. "Not for a tandem jump."

"What the hell is a tandem jump?" My back was turning into a Slip 'N Slide with sweat.

"Newbies jump attached to pros," Lina said, pointing to a giant poster just inside the hangar's open door. In the photo, a guy too stupid to be scared was grinning like a lunatic. He appeared to be harnessed to another man from behind.

"There's no way I'm dying with another man strapped to my back."

"Of course not. You're jumping with me."

I stopped in my tracks and dug my heels in, putting an abrupt end to Lina's forward momentum. She rebounded into my chest.

"I'm certified," she said.

Of course she was.

"Nash." There was laughter in her tone.

"Angel."

"Tell me what you're feeling right now," she insisted.

Abject panic. A little delirious.

"Just sit through the training video and then decide. Okay?"

A training video. If it was long enough, I could

pray for a thunderstorm to roll in. Or a cloud of locusts. Or some kind of mechanical failure that would be discovered while we were still safely on the ground. *Oh, two flat tires and a hole in the propeller? Too bad. Let's go get some breakfast.*

"Please?"

Fuck. Me.

I had two options. I could put my foot down and wuss out, in which case I'd have to sit here alone on the ground and panic until Lina floated back to earth. Or I could sign my own death warrant, defy gravity in a tiny tin can, and then hurl myself out of it with her. *For* her.

I was vaguely nauseous and extremely sweaty. But those brown eyes locked on my face. Her cool hands pressed against my chest.

She wanted this from me. And I had the power to give it to her.

"Fine. But if we plummet to the earth and create a tandem crater in a cornfield, I will never forgive you."

She let out a little squeal and launched herself into my arms. She may have knocked me back a step, but I still managed to catch her, holding her so her feet dangled off the ground.

Her mouth crashed into the side of my face and she gave me a loud kiss.

"You're not going to regret this. I promise."

I was busy regretting every single thing about the day, starting with the decision to get out of bed, when a guy in cargo shorts casually rolled up the flimsy door in the plane's fuselage.

"It's time," Lina said in my ear. We were straddling a bench that was bolted to the floor. I was hog-tied to her with a series of nylon straps that didn't look like they would hold Piper, let alone a full-grown man.

Every cell in my body screamed for me to cling to the bench. Instead, I stupidly forced myself to crab walk toward the gaping hole in the side of the plane. This was by far the dumbest thing I'd ever done for a woman.

"Are you sure about this?" I yelled to her over the rush of air.

"I'm positive, hotshot." I could hear the smile in Lina's husky voice.

We balanced in the opening, each gripping a handle on the inside of the door, and I made the mistake of looking out and down.

My knuckles went white on the handle.

"You can let go. Trust me, Nash," she said.

So I did. One finger at a time. I hoped Knox wouldn't put something stupid on my headstone.

And then Lina was tilting us to the right and we were falling into nothing.

I squeezed my eyes shut and waited for the panic, but it was too late for regrets. The wind buffeting my face, the drop in my stomach like an endless downhill of a roller coaster, told me that.

"Open your eyes, hotshot."

I didn't know how she knew I had them closed. Just another bit of her magic.

"I don't want to see myself die," I yelled back.

I felt her laugh against me, and her amusement had me prying one eye open and then the other.

My heart did a slow roll in my chest.

We were suspended above the earth. Autumn rolled out in a carpet of reds, oranges, and golds that went on forever beneath us. Ribbons of river, grids of roads, the smooth rise and fall of mountains all formed a patchwork quilt of nature and civilization thousands of feet below.

It didn't feel like we were careening to our deaths. It felt like we were suspended in time. Like gods surveying the world they'd created. Above it. Apart from it.

A bird's-eye view. The big picture. There was nothing between me and the entire world, and it was fucking breathtaking.

The world wasn't dark and terrifying. It was beauty unfolding all around us.

"Well?" Lina demanded in my ear, her hands squeezing my arms.

I gave the only answer I could.

"Holy shit." My roar of laughter was instantly swallowed up by the wind.

"I *knew* you'd love it!"

I wrapped my hands around hers on the straps and squeezed. "This is fucking amazing. *You're* fucking amazing!"

Lina whooped triumphantly into the wind.

I followed suit, reveling when the sound was snatched from my throat.

"Ready for the best part?" she asked.

"What's the best part?" I yelled back.

I'd barely gotten the words out when the free fall stopped abruptly and we were jerked up and back. One second, we were flying, belly down, and the next, we were suspended like marionettes as a bright red parachute billowed into being above us.

The rush of the wind in my ears stopped instantly, leaving nothing but an unearthly silence.

We were so far from everything that seemed so important on earth. Up here, we were removed from the minutiae of daily life. Here was only silence, peace, and beauty.

Emotions that I'd thought long dead welled up inside me, clogging my throat, making my eyes sting behind their goggles.

"I wanted you to see this. To feel it," Lina said.

I could have missed this. I could have died that night. I could have chosen to give up on her, on us. I could have said no on the ground. But instead, everything had led me to this moment. To Lina Solavita.

I was awestruck.

"This is . . . I can't believe I'm saying this, but I'm glad you didn't have sex with me this morning."

Her laugh was music in the silence.

"Wanna know a secret?" she asked.

"You have more?" I quipped.

"I don't jump for the rush. I jump for this. Everything makes sense up here. Everything is always beautiful and quiet. And I remember that, even after my feet touch the ground."

I got it then. Really got it.

I loved her. I wasn't using her as some crutch to avoid the world. She was reintroducing it to me one experience at a time.

My heart belonged to this woman and I was going to go buy her the biggest fucking ring I could find.

46

Blame the Candy Penises

Lina

"Y ou didn't kick him in the balls for that?" Sloane demanded. She was sitting cross-legged on Naomi's living room floor, stuffing pouches of flower seeds into mini burlap bags.

In an attempt to be a better, more vulnerable friend, I was recapping my relationship drama for Naomi, Sloane, Liza J, and Amanda during what appeared to be the lamest bachelorette party in history.

The rehearsal and ensuing dinner were over. In less than twenty-four hours, Naomi would be Mrs. Knox Morgan, and Nash and I would hopefully be having tipsy sex in a closet during the reception.

But for now, we were putting the finishing touches on the guest favors and watching the bride panic about last minute RSVPs in her living room. Piper and the rest of the dogs were outside running off the evening crazy with Waylay.

"I couldn't," I confessed. "He was already hurting and that made me hurt. It was basically horrible. Why people do relationships is beyond me. No offense," I said to Naomi.

She grinned. "None taken. That's how it was with Knox. I knew he was struggling with something I couldn't fix. Not even with a kick to the testicles."

"What did you do?" I asked, closing one of the burlap bags with a rust-colored ribbon. I'd arrived in town post-breakup, mid-fallout, and didn't know the details.

"He ended things so abruptly, my head spun. I already knew I loved him, but he had things to work through on his own. I couldn't force that. And I also couldn't wait around for him to come to his senses." She glanced down at her engagement ring and smiled softly. "Thankfully, he came around before it was too late."

Sloane blew out a breath that fogged up her glasses. "I don't think I have that gene in me."

"What gene?" I asked.

She shrugged. "I don't know. The ability to take a punch to the gut without swinging back. I can't just forgive someone for the baggage they're lugging around. Especially not after they bash me over the head with it."

"Someday, with the right person, you'll get there," Amanda assured Sloane.

"Yeah. Hard pass on that," Sloane said.

"My boys are stubborn as the day is long," Liza J said. "Knox always tried to distance himself from every single problem while Nash got in there and tried to fix everything. He always wanted to make things right, even when there wasn't a damn thing he could do about them."

She looked at me and then Naomi.

"You two have been good for my grandsons. Maybe even better than they deserve. And I'm speakin' as a woman who loves the crap out of those boys."

"I'm thinking about quitting my job," I blurted out.

All eyes came to me.

"Really?" Naomi asked hopefully.

Sloane frowned. "Don't you make a butt ton of money?"

"Yes. I do make a butt ton of money. But . . ." I trailed off. Nash had used a moment of preorgasm weakness to get me to admit that I wanted more with him. But was I really considering leaving my job and my choose-your-own-adventure lifestyle to settle down?

I thought about Nash standing in the rain, holding on tight.

The free fall before the chute opened.

The tip-tap of Piper's little nails on the floor as she pranced around with some new toy.

The bluest eyes.

The biggest heart.

I blew out a breath. Yep. I really was considering it.

"Would that mean you officially moving here?" Naomi prodded.

I was saved from answering when Waylay tromped into the room wearing waterproof boots and holding a shivering Piper. "The dogs got in the creek and Piper tried to follow," she announced. "She didn't seem to mind it too much until the current got her."

"Brave girl," I crooned, taking the dog from her. Despite her soggy shivers, Piper's little tail wagged heartily. "Thanks for pulling her out."

Waylay shrugged. "No problem. What are you guys doing?"

"We're finalizing the seating chart, finishing the favors, and choosing between these three Knox-approved tablescapes," Naomi said, pointing at the pictures she'd taped to the wall next to her sticky-note seating map. "What do you think about the denim and daisies one?"

"This is what bachelorette parties are?" Waylay asked disdainfully. "I knew Jenny Cavalleri was lying when she said her aunt got arrested in Nashville during her bachelorette party!"

"Actually that was true," Sloane said. "She had a little too much to drink, flashed an entire bar from the back of a mechanical bull, and then got caught peeing in the gutter."

"I think you guys are doing this bachelorette thing wrong," Waylay observed.

"This isn't really a bachelorette party," Naomi explained. "Knox and I didn't want bachelor and bachelorette parties."

"But the guys went out," Waylay said.

"They're just having a few drinks and some baskets of fried food," I told her.

"The kid's right," Liza J announced, slapping a hand to her thigh. "This sucks."

Naomi pouted prettily. "But what about the seating chart?"

Amanda snatched the remaining sticky notes off the coffee table and slapped them onto the wall in all the empty seats. "Voilà! Everyone has a seat."

Naomi chewed on her lower lip. "But you didn't even read the names. What if someone needs to sit closer to the restroom, or what if they don't get along with their table mates? We can't just make big decisions like this on a whim."

I reached out and squeezed her hand. "Actually, you can."

"What about the tablescapes?" she asked.

"Naomi, it's always been the daisies," I told her.

She bit her lip and stared at the photo for a long moment and then her eyes started to sparkle. "It has, hasn't it?"

I nodded. "Sometimes you don't have to weigh every single pro and con. Sometimes the answer is the one that just feels right."

I wasn't sure if I was telling her that or myself.

She pursed her lips, then grinned. "We're going with the daisies."

Naomi's mother clapped her hands. "Okay, people. We need wine, snacks, face masks, and one to two romantic comedies."

"On snack and wine duty," I volunteered.

"If you're getting snacks, I'm coming with you," Waylay insisted.

"If you're getting wine, I'm coming," Liza J announced.

"Team Shopping reporting for duty," I said.

"Perfect," Naomi's mom said. "Sloane, you can help me turn the living room into sleepover central. We need all the pillows and blankets that don't belong to dogs."

"What should I do?" Naomi asked.

"You should drink a large glass of wine and review your packing list for the honeymoon." I nudged the pink notebook titled Honeymoon on the coffee table in her direction.

"I don't think Grover's sells candy penises, Liza J," I said, grabbing a shopping cart as we entered the freshly painted grocery store. It was late, minutes from closing, and the parking lot was almost empty.

"Ew! I thought we were coming here for snacks," Waylay complained.

"Gummy penises *are* snacks," Nash's grandmother said.

"Hey, at least I didn't say broccoli florets," I told the girl.

"Aunt Naomi made me eat beets last night at dinner," Waylay said with a shudder. "Beets!"

"Well, there won't be any beets tonight," I promised, heading for the candy aisle. "Have at it."

Waylay's face lit up and she started tossing bags of candy into the cart. "We'll get snack cakes for Grandma, and Sloane likes Sour Patch Kids."

"I'll go ask where they keep the penises," Liza J said and ambled off.

"Oooh! These are good. You ever have them?" She handed me a bag of individually wrapped brightly colored discs.

"Sunkist Fruit Gems," I read out loud. I'd never had them, but they looked vaguely familiar.

"Yeah. Gettin' kidnapped wasn't all bad. These are the candy things that Hugo guy was obsessed with. He musta ate half a bag before my mom came back with Aunt Naomi. There were wrappers everywhere. He let me have some. The yellow are my favorite."

It all coalesced in my head in an instant. I knew where I'd seen this candy before and I knew who bought it.

I patted my pockets and dug out my phone.

"What's wrong? You look all hyper. You're not gonna call Aunt Naomi and ask her how many bags we can buy, are you?"

I shook my head and dialed Nash. "Nope. I'm

calling your uncle to tell him you just identified our henchman."

"I did?"

Nash's phone was ringing. "Come on. Come on. Shit," I muttered when it went to voicemail. "Nash. It's me. Burner Phone Guy is Cereal Aisle Guy. Mrs. Tweedy was with me when we met him in the grocery store. He was buying the same kind of candy that Waylay said is Duncan Hugo's favorite. There were candy wrappers all over the warehouse floor in the crime scene pictures. I saw him again at Honky Tonk the night Tate Dilton caused a scene. I know it's not much to go on, but I feel it in my gut. Call me back!"

"Whoa," Waylay said when I hung up. "That was a *lot* of words real fast. You sound like my friend Chloe."

I clapped my hands on her shoulders. "Kid, I'm buying you a cartload of candy."

"Cool. So who's Cereal Aisle Guy?"

"I hope you're not talking about me." The deep rumble of a male voice behind me had dread sinking to the pit of my stomach.

I squeezed the girl's shoulders. "Waylay, go find Liza J and go outside," I said as quietly as I could.

"But—"

"Go. Now," I said, and then I turned around and pasted a flirtatious smile on my face.

Cereal Aisle Guy was dressed in track pants

and a long-sleeve T-shirt. His cart was once again full of healthy produce and lean proteins. The only thing missing was the candy.

"So we meet again," I said coyly. "I was just telling my short friend how I met a cute guy in the cereal aisle."

"Were you? Because it sounded to me like you figured out something you shouldn't have."

Well, shit. So it was going to go down this way? Okay.

"I don't know what you're talking about. Now if you'll excuse me, I have to go disappoint a twelve-year-old's dentist," I said.

A large, meaty hand closed around my bicep. "The dentist will have to wait, Lina Solavita."

My heart wasn't just cartwheeling, it was trying to climb out of my throat.

"I'm not a fan of nonconsensual touching," I warned.

"And my friend isn't a fan of you following his boys around and getting one of them arrested."

"Hey, *I* wasn't the one who decided it was a good idea to bang my brother's wife. Maybe you should be having this conversation with him."

"I would, but he's in jail because *you* called the cops on him."

"In my defense, the whole naked thing really threw me."

"Let's go," he growled.

His grip was cutting off my circulation.

654

"I'm going to give you one chance to take your bear paws off me and leave. One chance for a head start before I kick your ass and then my boyfriend, the chief of police, shows up to finish the job. You're legit. At least partially. If you drag me out of this store, there goes that life. You'll be a full-time criminal."

"Only if I get caught. You caused too many problems and now it's time to face the consequences. Nothin' personal. It's just business."

"Leave her alone, you gigantic shithead!" Waylay appeared at the mouth of the aisle and savagely hurled a can of kidney beans at my captor.

It caught him in the forehead with a satisfying *thunk*. I used the surprise canned good beaning to my advantage and kneed him in the groin. He released my arm to grasp his balls with one hand and his forehead with the other.

"Fuck!" he wheezed.

"Run, Way!" I didn't watch to make sure she listened. Instead, I landed a jab to the man's jaw. My knuckles screamed in agony. "Damn it! Is your face made out of concrete?"

"You're gonna pay for that one, sweetheart."

He was still off-balance, so I planted both hands on his chest and shoved as hard as I could. He stumbled backward into the endcap display of Diet Coke, sending cans of soda everywhere. A shopper holding a box of cereal in each hand screamed, threw both boxes in her cart, and then ran away.

Liza J appeared out of nowhere on one of the store scooters. She rammed him from behind at full speed. It knocked him close enough to me that I could make my next move. I brought my heel down on his thigh with an axe kick, making sure to lead with the stiletto.

He howled in pain.

"Take that, you son of a bitch!" Liza J crowed.

The store manager, Big Nicky, himself appeared, holding a mop like it was a jousting lance. "Leave the lady alone, sir."

"For fuck's sake," the bad guy muttered. He reached into the waistband of his track pants and produced a gun.

I put my hands up. "Easy there, big guy. Let's talk this out."

Apparently, he was done talking. Because he aimed at the ceiling and fired two shots.

The store went dead silent for a second and then the screaming started. It was followed by the sound of stampeding feet and the incessant beep of the automatic door opening.

"Let's go," Cereal Aisle Guy said stonily. He picked up the bag of Fruit Gems and grabbed me by the arm.

"Umm." The manager was still standing there wielding his mop, though he looked significantly less confident now that firearms were involved.

"It's okay. I'll be all right. Go make sure everyone else got out," I assured him.

Cereal Aisle Guy dragged me toward the front entrance, both of us limping, him from the injury I'd inflicted with my boot and me because his hard-ass thigh broke the heel right off.

I took a mental inventory of the situation. Getting taken to a second location was almost always a very bad thing. But in this case, I was finally going to see Duncan Hugo's hideout. I had my phone in my jeans and Lucian's ridiculous condom tracker in my jacket pocket. I'd left a voicemail for Nash, and I'd missed a call from my mother during the rehearsal dinner.

Help would be on the way soon.

We stepped outside into the dark parking lot, and he held the gun to my neck. "That's a really small gun," I noted.

"Too hard to carry concealed. The bigger barrels stick halfway down my ass crack. It's uncomfortable."

"Bad guy problems, am I right?" I quipped.

47

Pantsless and Ass Up

Nash

Dear Nash,

This feels awkward. Writing you a letter. But I guess most things have been awkward between us for a good portion. Why stop now?

Things here are pretty good. Three squares a day, which means I'm putting on weight. I have my own room for the first time in two decades.

The group therapist looks like he's twelve years old, but he's assured us he graduated from medical school.

Anyway, he was the one who suggested we write letters to our families or the people we've let down the most. Looks like you and your brother are both. Lucky you. This is an exercise in apologizing and taking responsibility. You know, getting the words out and putting them down on paper. We don't have to send it. I probably won't send it.

And since I'm not gonna send it, I might as well be fucking honest for once.

I don't know if I can kick this habit or addiction or disease. I don't know if I can survive in the world without something to numb the pain of existence. Even after all these years, I still don't know how to "be" in this world without your mom.

But I am still here. And so are you. And I think I owe it to the both of us to give it a real shot. Maybe there's something else on the other side of all that pain. Maybe I can find it. Whether I do or don't, I want you to know my brokenness was never yours to fix. Just like it wasn't your mom's job to hold me together while she was here.

We're each responsible for our own damn mess. And we're each responsible for doing what it takes to be better. I'm starting to understand that maybe life isn't something to get through with the least amount of discomfort possible. Maybe it's about experiencing it all. The good, the bad, and everything in between.

Hope you're well. Not that it should mean anything to you, not that it's my place to say it. I'm damn proud of the man you've become. I've worried over the years that you and your brother would follow the piss-poor example I set. Hiding from the light. But that's not who you are. You stand up for what's right every damn day and people respect you for it. I respect you for it.

Keep being braver than me.

Yeah. I'm definitely not sending this. I sound like that Dr. Phil guy your mom used to love watching.

Love,
Dad

"This blows," Stef announced from his bar stool.

"I'd rather be home with Daze and Way," my brother grumbled.

"You're not getting married without a bachelor party," Lucian said. "Even if you wouldn't let me hire any strippers or flash mobs."

"Or flash mobs of strippers," Nolan added.

We were bellied up to the bar at Honky Tonk, drinking beer and bourbon in what really was the lamest bachelor party in Knockemout history. I'd once had to arrest half of the Presbyterian congregation when Henry Veedle's bachelor party fight club got too rowdy and spilled out onto the streets.

Lou, Knox's soon-to-be father-in-law, harrumphed. "In my day, we didn't need bachelor parties or ice sculptures or engagement brunches. We showed up at the church on a Saturday, said 'I do,' someone fed us some ham salad sandwiches, and then we went the hell home. What the hell ever happened to that?"

"Women," Lucian said dryly.

We raised our glasses in a silent toast.

I'd had a long day, and going the hell home to Lina sounded a hell of a lot better than anything else. That morning, I'd formally fired Dilton after making sure every *t* was crossed and every *i* dotted. It had been ugly, as predicted, but there hadn't been time to celebrate the win thanks to a tractor trailer losing its load of Alfredo sauce on Route 317.

I'd spent the afternoon helping with the cleanup and had just enough time to squeeze in a shower before showing up at the rehearsal only a few minutes late. There had barely been time to drag Lina into my brother's dining room and kiss the hell out of her before it was time to head out for drinks.

I wanted time with her. I wanted normal with her. I wanted to make up for the near disaster I'd caused. But the wedding was tomorrow. I still didn't know who'd thrown that rock through Lina's window. And the clock was ticking down with the "hometown hero" article set to run on Monday.

"After" was nearly here. The only thing standing between us and "after" was Duncan fucking Hugo. I'd end this. I'd put him behind bars. And I would do whatever it took to convince Lina that I deserved a place in her future.

I thought about my father's letter that I'd read after Dilton's official firing.

"Did Dad send you a letter?" I asked Knox.

"Yeah. You?"

"Yeah."

"This open family communication is so touching," Stef quipped, pretending to wipe away fake tears.

"He might come tomorrow," Knox said.

I blinked. "Really?"

"Yep."

"And you're okay with that?" We'd both had our own version of a strained relationship with our father over the years. Knox cut his hair every few months and gave him cash. I checked in on him and supplied him with essentials he couldn't trade for oxy.

He shrugged. "It's not like he's ever showed up for anything before."

Silver appeared with another round of drinks. She frowned and wrinkled her nose. "Does anyone else smell garlic and cheese?"

"That's probably me," I said.

Everyone leaned in closer to sniff me.

"I'm suddenly craving Italian," Lucian mused.

"It's Alfredo sauce. A rig full of it tipped on the highway."

"Sorry I'm late." Jeremiah strolled up, shoving

a hand through his dark, curling hair. "Why are we smelling Nash?"

"He smells like Alfredo sauce," Stef supplied.

Jeremiah dropped a kiss on Stef's cheek and they both smiled shyly.

"Whoa. When did that happen?" Knox demanded, pointing back and forth between the two of them.

"Why? Are you gonna give them shit too?" I asked my brother.

Knox shrugged. "Maybe."

"Why don't you want anyone to be happy?" Stef teased.

"I don't give a shit if you're happy. I just don't want to deal with you if you're fucking miserable," Knox clarified. "Take this dumbass. He looks at Lina with wedding rings in his eyeballs, and she's gonna rip his heart out and accidentally stomp on it with those stilettos when she walks out the door."

"I might walk out the door with her. As long as she doesn't hold my dumbassery against me."

The silence was deafening as seven pairs of eyes landed on me. "What?" Jeremiah asked, recovering first.

I picked up my beer. "I fucked up after a shit day."

"How did you fuck up?" Knox demanded.

"I tried to break things off," I admitted.

"You're an idiot," Nolan said helpfully.

"No. He's a fucking idiot," Knox said.

Lucian merely closed his eyes and shook his head.

"That's an interesting approach," Jeremiah volunteered.

"I thought *he* was the dumbass in the family," Silver said, dropping a drink in front of Jeremiah and nodding her head at Knox.

"Need I remind you who signs your pay-checks?"

"Apparently dumbass number one of two," she quipped.

"But you had your tongue down Lina's throat after the rehearsal dinner," Stef pointed out.

"She didn't let me push her away. She stuck. And then she made me jump out of a plane."

"Jesus. Why in the hell would you jump out of a perfectly good plane?" Knox asked, looking bewildered.

"Because when the woman you're going to marry asks you to do something, you fucking do it."

Lucian was rubbing his temples now. "You barely know her."

"*I* know her. She's too good for you," Nolan said.

"I agree with porn 'stache," my brother said.

"Lina's a peach. You planning on having more shit days?" Lou demanded.

"No, sir," I assured him.

He nodded. "Good. Back in my day, shit days happened and we didn't try to give our ladies the boot. We just drank too much, passed out on the couch watching *Jeopardy!*, and woke up the next day trying to suck less."

"God bless America," Stef said into his drink.

"She's the one," I said to no one in particular.

"You can't possibly know that," Lucian argued. "I'll admit, she's a pretty package. But better men than us are fooled by pretty packages every day."

"Don't talk about my girl unless you're prepared to face the consequences, Rollins," I warned. "Besides, Knox is the one getting married. Why aren't you heaping shit on him?"

My brother frowned. "Hang on. Why aren't you?"

"Besides the fact that Naomi is perfect in every way and you're the luckiest man on earth to have found her," Stef prompted.

"Hear, hear," Lou agreed.

Lucian rolled his eyes. "It's not Lina. It's you."

"What the fuck is wrong with him?" Knox demanded with an irate kind of brotherly loyalty.

"He's in a dark place. When a man is in the dark like that, he can't trust himself, let alone someone he barely knows. You put your trust in the wrong place, and those betrayals are nearly impossible to come back from."

"No offense, Lucy, but this sounds kind of like you're applying your shitty past to your friend's happy present," Jeremiah said.

"Listen to the hot barber. He's practically a psychologist," Stef said.

"You know nothing about my past," Lucian said darkly.

"Maybe we should change topics before this turns into Henry Veedle's bachelor party," I suggested.

"She really stuck?" Knox asked me.

I nodded. "Yeah. And as soon as I can get her warmed up to the idea of forever, I'll need that jeweler's phone number."

"Christ," Lucian muttered under his breath, signaling for another bourbon.

"What's standing in the way of warming her up?" Jeremiah asked.

"Besides barely knowing each other and coming from an emotionally damaged place?" Lucian said to his fresh bourbon.

"I fucked up less than forty-eight hours ago. I need to figure out some kind of grand gesture to make her believe in me. In us."

She's yours. Make it official. Lina's words echoed in my head.

"Are you serious enough?" Stef prompted.

"Serious enough to make Bannerjee show me how to use Pinterest so I could save a few dozen ring designs."

Lucian dragged his hands over his face in horror but said nothing.

"Sounds serious to me," Lou decided.

"So what qualifies as a grand gesture?" Jeremiah asked.

"Flowers?" Knox guessed.

Stef snorted. "That's the opposite of grand. That's a petite gesture. You busting in to Duncan Hugo's warehouse to save the damsels in distress was a grand gesture."

My brother nodded smugly. "That was pretty epic."

"Me surprising Mandy with a three-week cruise was a grand gesture," Lou said.

"That's a good one. Take her on vacation," Nolan suggested. "My wife loved it when we got away just the two of us."

"Didn't your wife divorce you?" Lucian pointed out.

"A, fuck you. And B, maybe she wouldn't have if I'd taken her on more vacations instead of working all the fucking time."

"That's good, but I need something I can do now. Even before we settle this thing with Hugo."

"Get the oil changed in her car?" Jeremiah suggested.

"Too small," I said.

"Fly her family in to surprise her?"

"Overstepping."

"Buy her one of those purses that cost a fucking fortune," Knox suggested.

"Not everyone has lottery winnings to throw around."

"You would have if you kept what I gave you instead of putting my fucking name on a goddamn police station, dumbass."

"Point taken."

"Why not just get a tattoo of her name on your ass?" Lucian said dryly.

Knox and I shared a look.

"Well, it is a family tradition," my brother mused.

And that was how I ended up pantsless and ass up in the chair at Spark Plug Tattoo. Knox was in the chair next to me shirtless, getting his wedding date tattooed over his heart.

"You do realize I was being sarcastic," Lucian muttered from the corner where he lurked like a pissed-off vampire.

"That was not lost on me. But it was still a damn good idea."

"You're going to feel like a fool when she leaves and you've got a permanent reminder on your ass."

But even Lucian's pessimism couldn't dampen my spirits.

Nolan was paging through a design album with Lou at the counter while Stef and Jeremiah cracked open another round of beers for everyone.

"I've been waiting years to get my hands on this ass," the tattoo artist said gleefully. Her name was Sally. She was inked from neck to knees and had been a nationally ranked equestrian champion in her early twenties.

"Oh, honey, you and every other woman in this town," Stef said.

"Be gentle with me. It's my first time," I said.

She had just started when I heard the click of a camera shutter and turned to glare at Nolan. "What? I'm just documenting the evening."

"Maybe you should trade the trash 'stache for a tat," Knox suggested.

"You think?" Nolan asked. I could practically hear him stroking his mustache like it was a pet cat.

"I think you could pull off something cool. Like maybe a wolf. Or what about a hatchet?" Lou suggested.

"Give y'all a group rate if you do decide you want one," Sally said over the buzz and stabbing needle of the tattoo gun.

I was listening to the hum of dueling tattoo guns when Stef let out a yelp.

"Shit. Oh shit," he said.

"What?" I demanded.

"Stop clenching," Sally instructed.

I did my best to relax my ass cheeks.

"You know that article that wasn't supposed to

go out until Monday?" Stef said, still peering at his phone.

"What article?" Jeremiah and Lou asked in unison.

Dread creeped into my gut. "What about it?"

Stef turned his phone so I could see the screen. There I stood next to the American flag in my office, looking pissed off as hell under the headline *Small Town Hero's Comeback.*

"It went live early," he said. "Apparently they lost the feature that was supposed to run today and posted this in its place two hours ago."

"Gimme my phone. Now," I snapped. "Sal, we're gonna have to finish this later."

"Roger that, Chief. I won't complain about getting to see this masterpiece again."

I waited impatiently while she slapped a piece of gauze over the work in progress.

"Holy shit. It already has fifty thousand likes," Stef commented. He looked at me. "You're America's goddamn sweetheart."

My phone was already ringing by the time Lucian dug it out of my pants pocket.

It was Special Agent Idler.

"This is not what I meant by lying low," she snapped when I answered.

"I don't know what you're talkin' about, Special Agent," I said pointedly as I vaulted out of the chair and grabbed my pants.

Nolan made the universal "I'm not here" slashing motion over his throat.

"Police chief recovers from gunshot wounds and memory loss to rid his force of a dirty cop," she read out loud. "I distinctly remember telling you I wanted to know if and when you regained your memory. And where in the hell is your protection detail?"

I shoved my leg into my jeans. "You know what I don't recall? I don't recall you telling me you were gonna cut a deal with the criminal who tried to put me, my niece, and my sister-in-law in the ground."

"Who said anything about a deal?" she hedged.

"The FBI has more leaks than the goddamn *Titanic*. You're willing to look the other way on attempted murder and kidnapping charges to land the bigger fish. Well, news flash, Special Agent. I'm not putting my family in danger because you can't build a case the old-fashioned way."

"Now you listen here, Morgan. You do anything to jeopardize this case and I'll make sure you end up behind bars."

I zipped my fly. "Good luck with that. I'm America's goddamn sweetheart right now." I disconnected before she could say another word and dialed Lina. It went to voicemail.

Knox was on his phone, presumably dialing Naomi. "She's not answering," he said, his voice tight.

"I'll call Mandy," Lou volunteered.

Lucian was looking at his phone. "According to the trackers, Naomi is at home. Waylay and Lina are in the grocery store parking lot."

I had a missed call from Lina and a new voicemail.

I stabbed the Play button and headed for the door, the rest of the wedding party behind me.

Lina's voice came out of the speaker. "Nash. It's me. Burner Phone Guy is Cereal Aisle Guy. Mrs. Tweedy was with me when we met him in the grocery store. He was buying the same kind of candy that Waylay said is Duncan Hugo's favorite. There were candy wrappers all over the warehouse floor in the crime scene pictures. I saw him again at Honky Tonk the night Tate Dilton caused a scene. I know it's not much to go on, but I feel it in my gut. Call me back!"

Candy wrappers.

And just like someone had snapped their fingers, I was transported back to the side of the road on that hot August night.

Bang.

Bang.

Two gunshots echoed in my ears as a strange stinging sensation started in my shoulder and torso. I was going down . . . or the ground was rushing up.

I was sprawled out on asphalt as the driver's

door swung open. Something thin and transparent floated to the ground, glinting in the headlights of my cruiser. And then it was gone. The crinkle of plastic wrapper rang in my head as a black boot crushed it under foot.

"Been waitin' for this a long time," said the man in the hoodie. He sneered, his mustache twitching.

A fucking candy wrapper. That was what had been haunting my dreams for weeks. Not Duncan Hugo. A candy wrapper and Tate Dilton's finger on the trigger.

"Call her the fuck back," Knox snarled, snapping me out of my head.

"What in the hell do you think I'm doing?" I dialed again.

"I need a status update, now," Lucian barked into his phone.

"Someone wanna tell me what the hell is going on?" Lou said.

Lina's phone was ringing.

"Come on. Pick up, Angel," I murmured. Something was very wrong and I needed to hear her voice.

The ringing stopped, but instead of her outgoing message, someone answered.

"Nash?"

But it wasn't Lina. It was Liza J.

"He got her, Nash. He took her."

48

They Kidnapped the Wrong Girl

Lina

My job had put me into some pretty interesting situations, but this was a first. Not only had he zip-tied my hands behind my back, Cereal Aisle Guy also tossed my phone, watch, and coat—with Lucian's tracking device —in the grocery store parking lot.

Then he'd shoved me into the trunk of a late-model sedan.

So much for Lucian's team of creepers being able to follow my signal. I closed my eyes tight and thought of Nash. He would move heaven and earth to find me. So would Knox and Nolan. Even Lucian would lend a hand. And if they couldn't do it, my mother would hunt me down.

I just needed to keep my wits about me and find a way to escape. This asshole had kidnapped the wrong woman.

Pep talk complete, I spent the first few minutes of trunk captivity trying to find the emergency trunk release only to discover that it had been disabled.

"Damn it," I muttered. The car took a hard right

turn. I banged my head and rolled awkwardly on my back, cringing at the binding at my wrists. "Ouch! Learn to drive, jackass!" I gave the trunk lid a half-hearted kick.

Over the noise of the road, I could hear him talking to someone but couldn't make out what he was saying.

"Plan B," I decided.

I could kick out a taillight and signal to other motorists that the asshole driving the vehicle had a hostage in the trunk.

The road changed. Instead of the smooth glide of asphalt, I could hear the crunch of gravel under the tires as we bumped along. This wasn't good. Either Duncan Hugo was closer than we'd thought or Cereal Aisle Guy was taking me out into the woods to give me a tour of the inside of a freshly dug shallow grave.

I was trying to feel my way to the edge of the carpeting without pulling a neck muscle when the car came to an abrupt stop.

I flopped back onto my belly. This was definitely not good.

The trunk lid opened, and before I could roll into a striking position, I was hauled out unceremoniously.

"Jesus. Where'd you learn to drive? The bumper cars?" I complained, shrugging him off.

"Quit whining and start moving," he said, giving me a shove forward.

We were on what had once been a gravel drive but was now overtaken by nature. In front of us was a huge barn-like building ringed with tall weeds. Beyond it, I could just make out the outline of a split rail fence.

"Are we still in Knockemout?" I asked, fighting off a shiver. No coat plus a healthy dose of fear made the night air feel even colder.

The henchman didn't bother answering me. Instead he shoved me forward again.

"If you let me go now, you probably won't have to do any prison time," I said as I limped along in the shadow of the barn.

"I'm committed now, sweetheart. There were witnesses. There's no going back for me."

In the shadowy night, my abductor no longer looked like a handsome gym-going accountant. He looked like a man who enjoyed making babies cry.

"You sound like you blame me for this."

He shook his head. "I warned you at the bar. I said, 'Don't make yourself a target.'"

"I do recall something like that," I said as he unlocked the heavy exterior door of the barn. It was the only opening I had, so I took it.

I spun around and took off into the dark, but my broken heel and the uneven gravel made running impossible. I felt like I was in the middle of one of those nightmares where you're trying to run but you've forgotten how.

A big, meaty hand closed around my shoulder and I was yanked backward.

"You're a real pain in my ass, you know that?" he told me as threw me over his shoulder.

"I get that a lot. So you're in real estate, aren't you?"

"Shut up."

He carried me back to the door, then dumped me on the floor inside.

It was pitch-black and I froze, trying to get my bearings. "You know real estate doesn't land people in prison often. Not like abducting women from grocery stores," I said as I got to my feet.

"Bigger the risk, the bigger the reward," he said in the dark.

That was Pritzger Insurance's unofficial motto.

I heard a *snick* and then an overhead light fixture illuminated the space. It was a fancy foyer for a barn. The floor was stamped concrete and the wood-clad walls were nicer than my place in Atlanta. Electricity. That was good. Maybe it meant there would also be a phone somewhere inside.

On the wall directly across from me was a large metal sign that said Red Dog Farm.

Realization dawned. This was the foreclosed property where Nash had found the runaway horse. Had Hugo been this close all that time?

I was only a few miles outside town. I could run that easily under normal circumstances, but

I'd need different footwear and I'd have to stay off the road.

Not ideal, but definitely a possibility. I calculated my other options.

There were three doors that led in different directions and a utilitarian staircase that went up to what looked like a dark loft area. Definitely not a viable escape option, I decided.

The henchman clamped a hand on my shoulder and marched me over to one of the heavy wooden doors. "Let's go," he said, opening it.

It was a wooden staircase that led down a level.

"Really? A basement lair? How cliché." It was actually kind of genius. Finding an abandoned property far enough outside town that no one would notice any activity? Maybe my captor wasn't a complete idiot after all.

"Move," he told me.

I took my time, hobbling down all fifteen stairs.

I had to keep my wits about me. I had to stall. The longer I kept them distracted, the more time it would give Nash to find me.

Cereal Aisle Guy guided me to the left at the foot of the stairs and through an open doorway.

There, seated with his muddy boots propped carelessly on top of a beautiful oak desk, was Tate fucking Dilton.

Shit.

"Well, well, well. Look who we have here. If it isn't the leggy bitch from the bar."

I'd been prepared to face down a junior organized crime lord, not a dirty, disgraced cop.

Dilton tossed his phone down on the desk and chewed his gum smugly.

"What's the matter, sweetheart? Not who you were expecting?"

"Wait. Let me get this straight. *You're* the mastermind here?" I said to Dilton, wondering how hard it would be to separate him from his phone.

"Damn straight I am."

My kidnapper cleared his throat pointedly behind me.

Dilton's gaze moved to him. "You got somethin' to say, Nikos?"

Nikos the grocery store kidnapper.

"Where is he?" Nikos replied.

"That's need to know, and you don't need to know, son," Dilton said.

Okay. The bad guys were in-fighting. This could either go really well for me or really, really *not* well. Either way, I needed a plan.

There was an ancient-looking monitor on the counter behind the desk. Unfortunately, there was no phone or laptop or conveniently placed flare gun.

On the opposite wall was a huge flat-screen TV with a couch in front of it.

"Don't you know you seem more threatening when you pretend like you're so in synch you can read each other's minds? Haven't you ever seen a James Bond movie before?"

"Go get him," Nikos said, ignoring me.

"Fuck you," Dilton shot back. "I'm in charge here. You go get him."

"You can't keep me here," I said, drawing their attention back to me.

Dilton gleefully chomped on his gum. "Looks like I can do anything I want with you and your bitch mouth."

"Charming. Why am I here? Is this what you do to every woman who tells you to grow up and be a man? I mean, it would explain why you need such a large facility."

"You're here because you and your fucking friends are done pissing me off."

Judging from Nikos's eye roll, that was not exactly why I was here.

"Hold on. You had *me* kidnapped because *you* got fired for being a racist misogynist? Are you one of those perpetual victims who blames everyone else for what a shitty human being you turned out to be?"

"Told you a rock through her window wasn't gonna cut it," Nikos muttered.

"You're fuckin' here because you ran your bitch mouth in the wrong place at the wrong time," Dilton snarled. "Plan was to take the other two bitches first. Tina's kid and her tight-assed twin. But you just had to go and make yourself a shinier target, shopping by yourself and figuring things out."

I glanced at Nikos. He'd seen Waylay with me. He could have easily taken us both. Well, not easily. I still had another stiletto and he still had another leg. But he'd decided against kidnapping a child. Maybe he wasn't the worst bad guy in the room.

Nikos avoided my gaze and I decided it was probably best for both of us if I didn't mention it.

"So we'll start with you and then take care of the other three problems," Dilton continued. He pointed at me like his finger was a gun and mimed pulling the trigger.

"We don't need to discuss the plan with her."

Dilton scoffed. "Why not? Not like she's gettin' out of here alive." He looked at me with a sick kind of excitement in his eyes.

"Hey, asshole, how are you gonna motivate her to lure her cop boyfriend here since you just told her you were gonna kill her no matter what?" Nikos demanded. "Jesus, do you even know how motivation works?"

"You actually work for him?" I asked Nikos, jerking my head toward Dilton. "I would have stuck with real estate."

"I don't work for him," Nikos snapped.

Dilton sneered. "We'll see about that." He turned his attention back to me. "As for you, I'm not a man to be truffled with. Your boyfriend should have known that."

"Trifled," Nikos corrected. "Truffle is a goddamn mushroom, you fucking idiot."

"Fuck you, dick."

Dilton took his boots off the desk and made a show of wandering around to the front. He leaned casually against it, his legs stretching out toward me.

"So what now? What are you going to do with me?"

He leaned forward menacingly until I could smell the stale beer on his breath. A fat finger hooked in the neckline of my shirt and tugged. "Anything I fuckin' want."

Rage licked its way up my spine, making me shake.

Headbutt, knee to the balls, break the zip tie, run.

"Well, well, well . . ."

We all turned as a freshly showered Duncan Hugo entered the room. He was wearing a black T-shirt and jeans with a handgun tucked into the waistband. His hair, originally a fiery red, was now dyed a dark brown. But the freckles, the tattoos, everything else I'd memorized from photos was exactly the same.

"Your boy here already used that bad guy line," I informed him.

I didn't miss the way Hugo's eyes narrowed at

the dirty cop's ass planted on the desk, the dried mud sprinkled across the surface. He prowled into the room and caught the bag of candy Nikos tossed at him.

"Ass off the desk, Dilton."

Dilton took his sweet time complying.

"You've caused me a few headaches recently," Hugo said to me as he took a seat behind the desk.

"Me?" I asked innocently. My wrists were starting to ache from being restrained behind my back. I needed to get loose, but there was no way I'd make it to the door with three of them in the room.

"Not only did you follow my men, you got one of them arrested. We don't need that kind of attention right now. Yet you failed to heed the warning."

"Like I told your pal in the candy aisle, that arrest wasn't my fault. Your guy was the one who tried to murder his own brother in broad daylight. Naked."

"Good help is hard to find," Hugo said with a careless shrug.

"Yeah, not sure what you're paying this one over here, but you should demand a refund," I said, nodding in Dilton's direction.

I saw the backhand coming and braced. Dilton's knuckles connected with my cheekbone, snapping my head back. My face felt like it was on fire, but I refused to make a sound.

I focused instead on adding concealer to my mental shopping list and imagining what Nash was going to do to Dilton's face soon.

"Time you learned some manners," he snarled in my face, his eyes wild and his lip curled under the mustache. An unpredictable madman with something to prove was worse than a calculating bad guy any day.

"Does that make you feel like a big man?" I hissed through clenched teeth.

"Enough," Hugo snapped. He peeled open a piece of candy and popped it into his mouth. "We have work to do. Nikos, make sure we're ready for our friend Chief Morgan's arrival."

With an ominous nod, Nikos left the room.

I was down to two bad guys, but I still didn't like those odds.

"You're on cleanup," Hugo said to Dilton.

"I fuckin' know."

"Get your shit together. Once you're in position, call me, then wait for my signal. You don't get to fuck this one up."

"Least I had the balls to pull the trigger," Dilton spat.

"You fucked up is what you did. You're lucky you're getting another chance."

"You might have to pull your own trigger someday," Dilton warned him.

"And when I do, I'll make sure I finish the fucking job," Hugo said ominously.

They glared at each other for a long beat before Dilton backed down. He flashed me one last lecherous look before storming out of the room.

"Fruit Gem?" Hugo offered, tilting the open bag my way.

"It was Dilton, wasn't it?" I said quietly.

"What was?"

"You hired Dilton to shoot Nash." The dashcam footage was grainy and the shooter was wearing a hoodie and gloves. But Tate Dilton and Duncan Hugo had similar builds, came in at similar heights.

Hugo shrugged. "Leaders delegate. And that's what I plan on being."

"Good help is hard to find," I said, repeating his words.

"I stole the car, gave him the gun, and told him when and where to do it. He was supposed to lure your cop boyfriend farther out of town, do the deed somewhere quiet."

"Instead he shot him in cold blood on the highway," I filled in.

"Can't be helped now. He's got one shot at redemption, and if he doesn't get this right, he'll be done," Hugo said, unwrapping another candy.

Nervous eater.

"You're planning to use me to lure Nash here. And then what?"

685

He looked at me and said nothing. He didn't have to.

I shook my head as a tidal wave of nausea hit me. "Naomi is getting married tomorrow and Waylay is a *child*. You don't have to do this."

He shrugged. "Look, it's nothing personal. Well, Dilton's hard-on for your boyfriend is very personal. Apparently he didn't like your boy's brand of law and order. I think he would have shot him for free. But everything else? That's not personal. You're all just collateral."

Naomi, Waylay, Liza J, Amanda . . . Even if Hugo managed to lure Nash here, everyone else would be at that house. In the line of fire.

Panic was rising in my throat. "All this so you can what? Push your father out of the way and take over the family business? Why not start your own? Build something yourself?"

His fist slammed into the desk. "Because I'm going to take everything my father owes me and watch him rot behind bars while I enjoy it all. I want him to know that the 'sensitive pussy son,' the 'waste of DNA,' was the one who manned up and stole everything from him."

My brain was scrambling for ways out of this. "You can't trust Dilton. He's hotheaded and thinks he's the one who should be calling the shots. He tried to start shit with an entire bar full of women and Nikos had to stop him. You need to call him off."

Hugo got up from behind the desk. "What I *need* is for you to sit down and shut up until it's time to be useful."

I was going to be sick. And then I was going to be dead.

"Why Nash? Why was his name on that list? He didn't have anything to do with your father's business."

Hugo shrugged. "Maybe he pissed off the wrong person."

"Meaning your father or the person who made the list?"

"Guess you'll never know for sure." He crossed to the worn couch in front of the TV and looped a gaming headset around his neck. "Might as well make yourself comfortable."

The TV screen bathed the room in a nuclear green.

I leaned against the desk, my knees quaking, stomach churning.

It had to be now. I had to find a way to warn Nash before Dilton left. Before he got anywhere near Naomi and Waylay.

"Happy fuckin' Friday. Let's shoot the shit out of some cowboys," Hugo said.

I blinked and stared hard at the screen. He was playing *online* . . . which meant he was talking to other players.

My heart was slamming against the walls of my chest. He was wearing the headset, but I still needed to be quiet. I had one shot to get this exactly right.

I blew out a breath slowly and watched the screen for my opening.

"On your left. No! Your *left,* dumbass. Didn't you learn that in kindergarten?" Hugo said, dodging and weaving on the cushion with the controller.

The characters on screen were battling a snot-shooting ogre and a fire-breathing dragon. This was as good an opportunity as I was going to get. I couldn't screw it up.

I raised my hands away from my back as high as they could go and hinged forward.

Adrenaline spiked and I brought my wrists down as hard and fast as I could. The plastic tie snapped, freeing my hands.

"Quit fucking around, Brecklin, and stab him in the fucking foot," Hugo said as I charged him from behind.

49

A Score to Settle

Nash

Twenty-seven minutes.

That was how long it had been since a man had shoved Lina into the trunk of his car and driven off.

Grave was running the partial plate number Waylay had memorized.

Knox drove Waylay and Liza J home to Naomi.

And I was flying down Tate Dilton's street as a light, misty rain began to fall. I swung the wheel and came to a screeching halt at the base of his concrete driveway. There was a shiny red bass boat parked on a brand-new trailer in front of the garage.

I didn't bother closing my door, just barreled up to the front door of the white Cape Cod bathed in blue and red from my lights.

The door swung open before I made it past the hay bales and pumpkins on the front porch. Behind me, tires squealed on the street as another vehicle came to an abrupt stop.

Melissa Dilton, Tate's pretty blond wife, stood in the doorway, one hand clutching the neck of her blue bathrobe.

She had tear-stained cheeks and a fat lip.

Fuck.

"Where is he, Missy?"

She shook her head, eyes welling with tears. "I don't know, but I swear I'd tell you if I did."

I wanted to push my way inside, to search the house from top to bottom, but I knew she wasn't lying.

Nolan and Lucian climbed the porch steps looking grim.

"How long's he been gone?" I asked her, ignoring them.

"A couple of hours. He packed a bag like he might be gone for a while. I–I saw him take a stack of cash out of the crawlspace access in Sophia's bedroom."

"What are you doing, Morgan?" Nolan asked quietly.

"Where was he the night I was shot?"

Melissa swallowed hard as twin tears slid down her cheeks. "H-he said he was working."

"He wasn't. He called in sick that day." I'd checked on the way here.

"He said he was working. He didn't come home until late and I . . . I could tell he'd been drinking. I asked him about you. I heard about the shooting from my parents. I asked him if you were gonna be okay and he . . ." She looked down at her bare feet in shame. "He hit me," she whispered.

I heard Lucian swear darkly behind me.

"It's okay, Melissa. You're not in trouble here. But I need to find Tate."

She looked at me with tears swimming in her eyes. "I don't know where he is. I'm sorry, Nash."

"Not your fault," I told her. "None of this is your fault. But I need you to get the kids and go to your parents' house tonight. I need you to stay there until I say it's safe to come home. Understand?"

She hesitated, then nodded.

"Go wake up the kids. Tell them they're having a sleepover with Grandma and Grandpa. Lucian will drive you. I'll have officers watch your parents' house."

"It's all over, isn't it?" she whispered.

"It will be tonight," I vowed.

She squared her shoulders and nodded. And for the first time, I saw a spark of determination in her pretty green eyes. "Good luck, Nash."

I turned and hooked a thumb over my shoulder. Lucian nodded and followed Melissa inside.

"Wanna tell me what the fuck is going on?" Nolan demanded as he followed me off the porch.

"Hugo didn't pull the trigger. Dilton did," I said, sliding behind the wheel of my SUV. "Ouch! Damn it." I'd forgotten about my new ass art until now.

Swearing, Nolan jogged around the hood and

got in on the passenger side. "What does that mean?"

"It means either Dilton did this on his own or he's mixed up with Hugo. Either way, he's going down."

I threw the vehicle into drive and made a U-turn, the headlights cutting through the misty layer of fog.

"Where to next?" Nolan asked.

"The station."

"We're coordinating with the state police and setting up traffic stops here, here, and here," Officer Bannerjee said, pointing at the map as we walked into the station. It looked like every first responder in Knockemout was already here. "All units have been advised to be on the lookout for Lina Solavita, the unsub, and a tan 2020 Ford Fusion."

Lina was out there somewhere, in the dark, in the cold. And I wasn't going to fucking rest until I found her.

I opened the folder on Grave's desk and snatched the first piece of paper out of it, then headed up to the board. Tashi stepped aside as I stuck Tate Dilton's photo next to Lina's.

A round of whispers rolled through the crowd.

"All officers will be on the lookout for Tate Dilton, former police officer. He's wanted for attempted murder of a law enforcement officer, domestic violence, and assault. Anyone with information on Dilton's whereabouts needs to talk to me."

I didn't wait for questions. I headed straight for the armory. Nolan was still on my heels.

"What's the plan?" he asked me when I handed him a shotgun.

"We knock on the doors of every one of Dilton's fucking friends until we find someone who knows where the hell he is. We find him, we'll find Lina."

"What about Hugo?"

I shook my head and threw two magazines and a couple boxes of bullets into a duffel bag. "Don't know if he's part of this or if it was all Dilton from the start. But my gut says they're in this shit together."

Nolan calmly loaded the shotgun and threw another box of bullets into a bag. "Think she's made them regret it yet?" he asked.

My lips quirked as I tossed two more boxes of ammo inside. "I guaran-damn-tee it."

"Ball retrieval surgeries are gonna be at an all-time high in this state after tonight," he predicted.

I zipped the bag shut and looked at him. "You don't have to come," I told him.

"Fuck off."

"I'm not doing this by the book. I'm not going to follow fucking protocol. I'll do whatever it takes to get her back."

"Then lead the way."

We cut through the bullpen and almost made it to the door when it opened. Wylie Ogden entered wearing one of the department's old rain slickers.

"Nash. I mean, Chief," he said. He looked older than I'd ever seen him. His face was drawn and pale. "I just talked to Melissa and she told me what's goin' on." He shook his head. "I didn't know. Had no idea. We were friends, but . . . I guess you never really know anyone. It ain't right. What he did to you, to his wife."

"No, it's not," I said stonily.

"I'm here to lend a hand wherever I can," he said. "Make things right."

"See Bannerjee for an assignment," I said, then stepped around him and headed for the parking lot.

I opened the hatch of the SUV, and while Nolan tossed the bags inside, I loaded a second shotgun, then strapped two full clips to my belt.

My phone rang.

Lucian.

"Any problems getting Melissa and the kids to her parents?" I asked.

"No. They're safe and there's a patrol car already in the driveway. But I thought you should know KingSchlong85 just logged in to *Dragon Dungeon Quest*," Lucian said. "My team is running a trace on the IP address. They've narrowed it down to within five miles of here."

Fuck. If Duncan Hugo was close, that couldn't be a coincidence.

I chambered a round in my Glock and holstered it. "Let me know when you find him."

"If we find him this way, it won't hold up in court," Lucian warned.

"I don't care. I'm not building a case. I'm settling a fucking score. Find him," I ordered.

50

Brecklin Is the Worst

Lina

My first attempt at choking someone out hadn't gone well. But I had managed to steal the headset, inflict some windpipe damage, and get out of the room before he could pull a gun on me, so it wasn't a total fail.

I heard him yelling when I hit the stairs to the second floor and hoped that he was calling Nikos and Dilton. If the three of them were busy looking for me, they couldn't go on a murder spree.

I burst into the foyer where Nikos and I had entered and looked around. I could make a run for it outside, but more than an escape route, I needed a phone or someway to contact Nash. I propped open the exterior door to make them think I'd made a break for it, then chose a door at random. It led to a long, dark hallway.

I was using my hands to guide me down the hall as quickly as possible when I heard something.

A faraway voice coming from . . . my hand.

Holy.

Shit.

Duncan's gamer headset was still connected to the Wi-Fi signal.

I slipped it over my head, wrenched open the door closest to the office downstairs. If I could stay hidden and connected to Wi-Fi, I could call for help.

"Hello? Can you hear me?" I whispered into the microphone.

"What's with the heavy breathing? Did someone let a creeper perv into the quest?" An unfamiliar, childlike voice said in my ear.

I heard the door I'd entered through bang open.

"Shit," I muttered.

My hands found another wooden door just as the lights in the hallway blazed on.

I caught a glimpse of a furious Hugo running toward me before I shouldered my way through the door.

The door—thank you, lucky stars—had a dead bolt on the inside. It wouldn't hold him long, but it would at least slow him down. I slid it in place just as the door handle jiggled.

"The longer you make me chase you, the more I'll let Dilton hurt you," he snarled from the other side of the wood.

I hurried away from the door, holding the microphone close to my mouth. "Hello? Is anyone there?" I said as loud as I dared.

The flooring was different in here. It felt like brick and there were windows high up on both walls. It was a dark, cavernous space with what I realized were a dozen horse stalls divided down the middle by a wide brick aisle.

"Are you gonna stop screwing around, King-Schlong, and help us kill these ogres, or am I gonna need to use my stunner spell on you again?"

It was a child's voice. From the sound of it, an annoying child.

"My name is Lina Solavita and I'm being held at gunpoint by Tate Dilton and Duncan Hugo at Red Dog Farm in Knockemout, Virginia," I whispered into the mic as I hustled down the aisle between the stalls.

The doorknob jiggled behind me and then there was a loud thud.

I sprinted to the end of the dark room and ran into a chest-high wooden wall, knocking the wind out of myself.

"Ow. Fuck," I wheezed.

"Is this real?" a snotty prepubescent voice demanded.

"It's probably just KingSchlong messing with us, Brecklin," another kid said.

"Listen, *Brecklin,* do your parents know you're playing online video games with a criminal?" I hissed as I got back to my feet.

Another loud thud came from the far end of the room, accompanied by the splintering of wood. It sounded an awful lot like a body trying to break down a door.

He was coming and I didn't have time to find a way out. My only option was to hide as long as I could before making my stand here.

"Narc," a kid muttered in my ear.

"Oh my God. I swear to you on Justin Bieber or Billie Eilish or whoever you're into, I'm telling the truth. I need one of you to call 911 *now*."

There was another loud thump and more wood gave way.

A loud bing-bong noise in the headset startled me.

"Jesus. What the hell was that?" I whispered.

"Chill out, lady. WittyInPink just joined our quest," Brecklin said.

"I'll chill out *after you call 911!*"

"Lina?"

The familiar voice almost brought tears to my eyes. "Waylay?"

"Where are you?"

"I'm close. Are you safe? Is Naomi safe? What the hell are you doing on here?"

"After Uncle Nash called and asked me what Duncan Hugo's username was, I figured I might be able to help find him through the game."

"Waylay, you beautiful little genius! I'm very, very proud of you and also you're probably in huge amounts of trouble."

"Yeah. I figured," she said, sounding bored by the concept.

"Listen to me, you need to call your uncle Nash

and tell him that Duncan Hugo is sending Tate Dilton to your house to . . ."

How was I supposed to tell a twelve-year-old someone wanted to murder her?

"To take out me and Aunt Naomi?" she guessed.

"Whoa," one of the other kids gasped.

This time when Hugo hit the door, broken pieces of wood fell to the floor.

"Shit, yeah. Listen, I'm trying to distract them, but Nash can't come here, because they're setting a trap for him. He needs to go to your house and make sure you're safe."

"Where are you?" Waylay demanded.

"It doesn't matter. Just tell him that I love him."

"She's at Red Dog Farm," Brecklin's snotty little voice announced.

"Shut up, Brecklin!" I hissed.

Two shots rang out.

"Ready or not, here I come," Hugo sang as the door smashed open.

I chose a stall at random and yanked the bottom half of the door closed behind me as quietly as possible.

"Listen, I gotta go. Duncan is coming. Tate Dilton is with him," I whispered, easing deeper into the stall to duck behind a stack of plastic tubs. "Tell Nash I love him."

"Wha—"

"Break—up . . ."

Crap. The Wi-Fi signal was weakening. I

crawled forward on my hands and knees toward the stall door.

"You're supposed to say AFK," Brecklin's snooty voice crackled in my ear. "It means away from keyboard."

"I don't have a goddamn keyboard, *Brecklin!*" I hissed.

But there was only silence in my ear as the signal dropped again.

Great. I wasted my last words yelling at a child. Oh well. She'd deserved it.

"You can't hide in here forever." Hugo's voice echoed eerily through the space.

I flattened myself against the wall and realized it was cool and smooth. Like tile.

Memories of my short-lived experience at summer horse camp surfaced. I was in the wash stall, essentially a shower for horses.

As the soles of Hugo's shoes scuffed against the brick, my fingers found what they were looking for. Horses were bathed with a hose and nozzle, but some stables had pressure washer wands installed for cleaning the stall itself.

A loud crash scared the bejeezus out of me. It was the sound of wood and metal crashing into stone. I fumbled the hose and smacked my elbow off the faucet. Pain radiated up my arm.

A flashlight beam cut through the dark. "Not in this one," Hugo sang to himself.

There was another crash, this one a little closer.

He was yanking open stall doors one by one until he found what he was looking for.

My heart was doing its best to explode out of my chest.

I crouched down, trying to calm my breath. I needed to stay alive, stay hidden. In that order.

Silently, I whipped off the headset and tossed it toward the front of the stall, hoping it would reconnect to the Wi-Fi signal. I really didn't want to traumatize a bunch of kids with making them listen to my death. Except Brecklin. She seemed terrible. But hopefully one of them was smart enough to record the audio so Duncan wouldn't get away with this.

I closed my hand over the faucet handle and held my breath. The door to the stall next to me smashed into the exterior wall, and I used the noise as cover to give it a good twist.

Please let there be water. Please let there be water.

He was close enough that I could hear his heavy breathing.

Now or never. I had to time it perfectly or I'd never have the chance to tell Nash to his stupidly handsome face that I loved him.

The door to my hideaway yanked open and splintered against the exterior wall. I didn't hesitate. As the flashlight beam swept over me, I gripped the wand and squeezed the trigger.

A gunshot rang out.

51

When Did You Stab Him with a Pitchfork?

Nash

A familiar pickup truck squealed into the station's parking lot, sending water everywhere as its headlights slashed across us. Knox got out and slammed the door. He strode up to me, his jaw tight.

"What are you doing here? You need to stay with Naomi and Way," I said.

He shook his head. "I'm with you."

"I appreciate that, but you need to keep them safe. Hugo could decide to move on them tonight."

Knox crossed his arms. "Lou's got two shotguns. Liza J dusted off Pop's rifle. Stef is mixing drinks and handing out pepper spray. Jeremiah and Waylay are marching around with our old Little League bats."

"You're getting married tomorrow."

"Not without you and not without Lina. Call Naomi if you don't believe me. This wedding only happens with us all."

"Chief?" Grave appeared in the door. "Ford Fusion belongs to Mark Nikos. Guy leases commercial properties between here and DC. He's got a local address. Had it since this summer. Got two patrol cars swinging by his place now."

I nodded. "Thanks, Grave."

He wouldn't be there and neither would Lina, so I wasn't wasting my time dotting those i's.

I turned back to my brother. "This is your shot at something good. You're not fucking it up to play big brother. Not tonight."

He gripped my good shoulder. "You had my back last time. You're not going out there without me."

"Looks like the three of us are goin' to jail together," Nolan said.

"For fuck's sake," I muttered. I pulled out my phone and dialed.

"What?" Lucian demanded.

"I need you to go to Knox's and keep everyone there alive."

"I have a security team en route."

"Great. And now I need you to be there since my idiot brother is standing here in the parking lot with me."

Lucian swore colorfully and I heard the telltale snick of his lighter. "I'll be there in five minutes."

I heard a beep and looked at my screen. *Naomi.*

"I gotta go. I have another call," I told Lucian and disconnected. "Naomi, I don't have any updates but we're doing everything—"

"Uncle Nash? I know where Lina is."

"I see a redneck pickup with smokestacks and a gold Ford Fusion parked next to the barn," Nolan reported. He was on his belly at the edge of the tree line, peering through binoculars.

Thanks to Waylay's heads-up, we'd accessed the property through the woods, coming up behind the house and barn. The rain had brought with it a thick fog that lay like a blanket, making the property look ghostly.

"Dilton and the car that took Lina," I said, trying to put a lid on the emotions that were boiling up inside me.

Knox and I exchanged a look. For better or worse, the men we were looking for were here. And none of them were getting another chance to hurt someone we loved.

"I got movement," Nolan said quietly.

We stilled and peered through the rain and gloom.

"Big guy. Just burst out of the open side door. Gun drawn. He's looking around."

"For us?" Knox asked.

We were two hundred yards away, but my ears still picked up a faint sound. It sounded like someone shouting. We watched as the man ran back inside.

"Lina," I said.

Nolan grinned. Even Knox's mouth managed to curve. "Bet she's givin' them hell," he predicted.

"Tell Lucian Dilton's still here," I told my brother. "I'll call for backup."

I was just dialing Grave when the gunshot rang out.

My heart stopped. My brain emptied. The only thing left was instinct. I was on the move, racing through waist high overgrowth.

I heard Knox and Nolan behind me, but I wasn't going to wait. Not with Lina inside.

I covered the distance to the barn easily, vaulted over the fence, and remembered to lead with my good shoulder when I smashed through the door.

It gave way easily and I paused long enough to clear the foyer before moving on. Two doors were open. One led downstairs, the other to a long hallway.

Lina wouldn't let herself be trapped in a basement with no easy escape, so I took the hallway at a dead run. Something tickled at my gut. I ducked just as a door on my right opened and a huge fist swung at me.

I rammed Mark Nikos, the man who'd dragged my woman out of a grocery store and thrown her in the trunk of a car, with my not-so-good shoulder, catching him in the ribs and knocking him back into the doorframe.

"Got him. Go," my brother said behind me. I didn't even bother looking back. If Knox said he had him, he did.

I continued down the hall until I reached an

open doorway. The door itself was cracked and dented, its hardware useless on the floor.

I felt for light switches and found a row of them. I flipped them all and raced into the illuminated stable. The gates to each stall on the left-hand side were open on their hinges.

I did a fast sweep of each stall, hurrying down the line. She was here. She was close. She had to be. I could feel it.

"What's that?" Nolan demanded, catching up to me. We both looked down at the liquid pooling on the brick outside the next to last stall. In the middle of it was a single shell casing.

For a split second, my heart stopped. Then I heard a faint hiss and spotted the wand and hose, still spraying a fine mist of water.

"Water," I rasped.

"Two sets of footprints," Nolan observed.

We followed them to where they seemed to jumble and combine against the stone wall. Discarded in the middle of the wet prints was a pitchfork. The tines were stained red. There were rusty, red droplets dotting the floor.

"Bet you a hundred bucks Lina stabbed him with the pitchfork," Nolan predicted.

"I'm not takin' that bet." Something like pride pushed at the bubble of fear in my chest. Lina could and would handle her own until I found her.

We followed the trail of blood and water to the

end of the room. A tall wooden fence with a gate opened into another darkened space.

Light from the stables spilled into the pitch-black, and I could see the floor was covered in a thick layer of sawdust.

"I think it's an indoor riding ring," Nolan said. "There's gotta be a switch around here some—"

There was a noise in the dark. A strangled kind of yelp, followed by a thump and a grunt. I didn't care that I couldn't see. I knew she was in there and I would find her.

"You fucking stabbed me with a pitchfork!" howled a disembodied man's voice.

"You were asking for it, you stupid fucking moron," Lina shot back scathingly.

She was okay. At least okay enough to talk shit.

"Angelina!" My voice cut through the blackness like a dart.

"Nash! Get out of here! Ouch! You son of a bitch—"

I was getting closer. I could tell by the sounds of the scuffle growing louder. I dodged my way around a large, shadowy object. A vehicle or farm implement under a tarp, I realized. There were more of them lined up between me and her, creating an obstacle course.

I was almost on them. I could feel her near me. And my stomach churned at the sound of a fist hitting flesh. But the ensuing howl wasn't hers.

The lights came on, illuminating the ring. I was

six feet from her. Hugo was on his knees in front of her, blood pouring from his leg, more from his nose.

"You fucking bitch," he screeched and raised the hand that held the gun.

I didn't think. Didn't plan. Didn't calculate. I acted.

"Nash!" Lina's scream echoed in my head as I went airborne.

Hugo's head turned toward me in slow motion, followed by his arm. But it was too late for him. I hit him with the force of a freight train, leading with the shotgun I carried. His handgun went off and we rolled into the sawdust. I rolled him, pinned him, and smashed my fist into his face. Once. Twice. Three times.

"Okay, hotshot." Lina's voice was soft and calm at my side. "I think you got him."

But it wasn't enough. Nothing short of ending him would be. I pulled my arm back again to let my fist fly, but her hands were on me.

"Morgan!" Nolan's warning shout had both of us looking up in time to see Tate Dilton leveling his gun at us from ten yards away.

Dilton turned toward the running Nolan, and both men fired almost simultaneously.

I was aware of Nolan dropping to his knees, of Lina's horrified scream as I grabbed her under the arms and dragged her behind a big blue tractor.

I pushed her down behind the tire and fired

two shots over it to draw Dilton's attention. Lina clawed at me and dragged me back down. Her touch brought me back into my body.

My breath was coming in vicious pants. Sweat was running down my back. My fist throbbed. My heart thundered in my chest.

"Nash," she said, pressing herself against me. "Can you see Nolan?"

I scanned the arena and shook my head. "He must have found cover." I glanced down, checking her for injuries. "You're bleeding, baby."

She held up her left arm where a piece of her sleeve was missing. The surrounding material was soaked with red. "I hit Hugo with the pressure washer in the face and pulled a Nash Morgan when he fired."

I tore the sleeve off my shirt and tied it over her bicep. "What's a Nash Morgan?"

She grinned at me and I'd never loved anyone more than I did in that moment. "I did just what you did when you walked up to that car. Saw the gun and turned sideways. The bullet barely grazed me. I don't think it even qualifies as a flesh wound, but it stings like hell."

"Jesus, Angel."

"It's a scratch," she assured me.

"When did you stab him with a pitchfork?"

"After he shot at me."

"He didn't shoot *at* you. He shot you." My

vision was going red. "I think I need to shoot him," I decided.

"If you shoot Hugo, I get to shoot Dilton. He's the one who shot you," she said.

"I know." I chanced a peek around the tractor's wheel and saw Dilton disappearing behind a mountain of plastic totes. Nolan was nowhere to be seen.

"You know?" she hissed.

"Memory came back when I got your voice-mail."

"Wait a minute. Why are you here? You're supposed to be protecting Naomi and Waylay."

"Lucian and a private security team are guarding them."

"You two gonna talk all day or come out so I can shoot you in the head?" Dilton shouted.

A bullet zinged off the metal body of the tractor.

I pushed Lina lower and pointed at the tarped vehicle next to the tractor. It was shorter and lower. "Go," I ordered.

She shook her head vigorously. "No."

"Get your ass out of here, Angel."

"I'm not leaving you," she hissed, knocking me off balance.

I winced when my ass hit knobby tread of the tire.

"What's wrong?" she hissed. "Are you hit? If that guy shot you in your perfect ass, I'm going to kill him."

"I'm not shot. I'll explain later."

A bullet whizzed over our heads, ruffling the edge of the tarp.

I caught a glint of blue as I fired back blindly.

"I'm not leaving you," she said again.

"Angel."

"What?"

I gripped her chin and turned her head. "Found your Porsche."

Her mouth fell open and a high-pitched squeak came out.

"You get the car out of here. I'll take care of unfinished business."

She looked to the car, then back at me. "Damn it. I can't do it. I'm not leaving you here."

"You love me."

Lina blinked. "Excuse me?"

"You fucking love me," I told her.

"Oh? And I suppose you *don't* love me?"

"I fucking love you back. So much that we're not waitin' until after."

"What?"

"We're getting married."

"People are shooting at us and you want to *propose?*"

Another shot rang out. I rolled low and fired one back in Dilton's direction.

"You got a problem with that?" I asked, pulling out a fresh magazine and slamming it into my gun.

"This is so typical of you. You wait until we're in the middle of a heated situation to coerce me into doing what you want. There are about a thousand decisions we have to talk through. Where would we live? Whose job is more important? Who takes out the garbage?"

"And they all start with the first. Are you gonna marry me, Angel?"

"Ugh, fine. Yes. But when the adrenaline crash happens and you realize that you just stuck yourself with me from here until the end, that's on you. I don't wanna hear any whining."

My heart leapt and I grinned at my beautiful girl. "I'm gonna kiss you real hard after."

"You're damn right you are," she said.

I heard a whiff and a clunk. I pushed Lina flat to the ground as Duncan Hugo landed face-first in the sawdust at our feet. Knox appeared from the front of the tractor, shovel in hand. He had a cut on his forehead and bloody knuckles.

"Now we're even," he said.

"Dunc! You out there?" Dilton called.

Knox knelt next to Lina. "Nolan's bleeding bad. Got him stashed under some hay wagon, but we need to get him out fast."

I looked between my brother and my girl. "Get him out of here. I'll take care of Dilton," I said grimly.

"Nash, no." Lina gripped my arm.

713

"Baby, I'll be right behind you," I promised her. "I've got a lot to live for."

"And a ring to shop for," she pointed out.

"Did you seriously propose on my fucking wedding day?" Knox demanded.

Lina slapped a hand to Knox's chest and he winced. "Ow!"

"Jesus, what's with you two?" she demanded.

My brother smirked. "You didn't tell her?"

"I've been a little busy," I said dryly. "Take her and Nolan and get them out. I need to end this."

Knox nodded and picked up the unconscious Hugo's gun. "See you outside."

"Dammit, Nash. I can't leave you here," Lina said, her voice breaking.

"Angel, this is my fight. I'm the one who has to end it and I'm counting on you to get my brother and my friend out of here in one piece. Trust me to do my job like I'm trusting you to do yours."

She scrubbed her hands over her face and swore quietly. "Fine. But don't you dare get shot," Lina said finally.

"I won't," I promised.

Knox took her by the arm and started to pull her away.

Her brown eyes locked on mine and held. "I love you."

"I love you too. Now get the hell out of here so I can go be a hero."

"I'm moving here," Lina told Knox as they ducked down.

"Great. What happened to your arm?" Knox asked.

"The guy you hit in the face with the shovel shot me."

"You fuckin' kidding me?" I heard my brother snarl.

I waited until Lina had uncovered the Porsche and Knox loaded a white-faced Nolan into the passenger seat.

My brother threw me a salute then turned and ran low toward the barn door at the end of the arena.

Nolan flashed me a weak middle finger as Lina slid behind the wheel of the Porsche. I returned it grimly. "See you after," she mouthed.

I blew her a kiss then took aim as the Porsche's engine roared to life.

Dilton popped up from behind his cover aiming in Lina's direction. I fired a split second before he pulled the trigger. He disappeared back behind the totes, clutching his arm.

He was a decent shot. But I was better and I knew his weakness.

"Nikos? Where the fuck are you?" Dilton bellowed as Lina hit the accelerator and the Porsche leapt forward. My girl's triumphant "woohoo" carried to me on a cloud of dust left in the car's wake. I grinned and used it as cover.

Staying low, I left the safety of the tractor and moved toward Dilton's location. I needed to get eyes on him.

I ducked behind a smaller tractor with a post hole digger and peered under its belly.

Dilton was sweating and chewing his gum like his jaw was a piston. He was on his knees bellied up against a short stack of hay bales. His arms—one bleeding—were stretched out on top of the hay. In his hands, he clutched his prized Smith & Wesson six-shooter.

I fucking had him.

I took aim and fired, sending up a puff of rotting hay inches from him.

He fired an answering shot in the direction of the tractor.

"Dilton."

He scrambled around on his knees in the sawdust as I stood up.

I stared into the eyes of the man who'd tried once to take my life, and looking into them, I knew he wouldn't get a second chance.

"You know I gotta kill you now," he said, gnawing nervously on his gum.

"I know you tried once."

"Guess you really did get your memory back, didn't you?" he said, gaining his feet.

"What I don't get is why."

"Why?" he scoffed. "You stole that job from a real man and pussified the entire fuckin' department. I shoulda been chief. I did more for this goddamn town than you ever did."

"Then why wait all these years before taking your shot?" I took another step closer.

He was sweating like my great-aunt Marleen at a Fourth of July cookout.

"I don't fuckin' know. Stay the hell where you are," he said, holding his gun with both hands. The long, shiny barrel revealed the tremor in his grip.

"Maybe you didn't think about doing anything until Duncan Hugo came along and put a bug in your ear."

"What makes you think I didn't put the bug in his ear?"

"Because you've never had an original thought in that pea-sized brain of yours. I know none of this originated with you."

Dilton's lip curled, lifting his mustache. "You really have no fucking clue."

"Why don't you enlighten me?"

He was aiming low, the weight of the gun pulling the barrel down. "Shit. You expect me to confess to everything right before I put you in the ground."

"Why not? Tell me how smart you are before you pull that trigger again."

"I'll tell you as you're bleedin' out since I can stick around this time."

I was ready for it. I read the twitch and watched his finger pull the trigger in slow motion. There was a click and the stupid stunned look as Dilton realized he'd already fired his last bullet.

The son of a bitch never could keep track of his rounds.

A split second later, three patches of red bloomed on Dilton's torso. The echo of the three rapid gunshots rang out in the cavernous room and inside my head.

Dilton's sweaty face went slack as he looked at me, then down at the holes in his chest. His lips moved but no sound came out. The red was still spreading when he dropped to his knees and then fell forward on his face.

Behind him stood an ashen-faced Wylie Ogden. His hands shook as he kept the gun trained on him.

"H-he was gonna kill you," Wylie said in little more than a whisper.

"He was out of bullets," I said. I don't know if he heard me, because he was staring down at Dilton like he was afraid the man was going to get back up.

I remembered then, in Wylie's two-decade career, the man had never had to discharge his weapon in the line of duty.

"Put the gun down, Wylie. We're all friends here," I said, moving toward him slowly.

"He was gonna do it," he said again.

I heard the sirens then, the long, urgent whine drawing closer and closer.

"It's over now," I told him.

"It's over," he whispered. He let me take the gun out of his hands and then sank to his knees in the blood-soaked dust next to Tate Dilton's body.

Dawn was just beginning to break over the trees by the time I stepped out of the barn. The long, dark night was over. A new day had begun.

The entire property was crawling with cops, feds, and other first responders.

I was surprised to see my brother push away from the side of the barn and head my way. He had a bandage over the cut on his forehead and more on his knuckles.

We stood shoulder to shoulder in the open door, taking it all in.

"You did good in there," he said finally.

"What?"

"You heard me. You seem pretty okay at your job. When you don't have the rule book shoved up your ass."

It was the nicest compliment my brother had paid me since he came to my senior homecoming football game and told me I hadn't "sucked too bad" on the field.

"Thanks," I said. "And thanks for having my back."

He flashed me a Knox Morgan smirk. "When are these assholes gonna learn, you don't mess with the Morgan brothers?"

"Hey, happy wedding day."

"Gonna be the best day of my life."

As if on cue, the reason for that appeared.

"Knox!" Naomi and Waylay broke through a ring of state cops and started running.

"Don't be fuckin' late," Knox said to me with a parting thump on the back. And then he was loping across the gravel to them. I watched my brother sweep the two most important women in his life into his arms and swing them around.

"Apparently you don't know the meaning of the phrase 'lie low,'" Special Agent Idler said dryly as she approached. Frosted leaves crunched under her feet as she left Nolan behind.

He was strapped to a gurney, a red-soaked bandage taped to his chest, his phone glued to his ear. He caught me staring and pointed to the phone.

"Wife," he mouthed, looking delusionally happy.

My lips quirked and I tossed him a salute. He grinned and held up a friendly middle finger.

"He gonna be all right?" I asked.

"He'll be fine. Missed all the vitals. But you know what that son of a bitch just did? He quit."

"You don't say?"

"Don't know why he's telling me since I'm not his boss. But seems he got poached by the private sector," she said, shooting a pointed look to where Lucian was standing, arms crossed, in a huddle with a handful of agents.

"You don't seem too broken up about having to fire my ass," I observed.

"Maybe it's because sometimes the greater good comes at too high a price tag," she said, watching my brother kiss his bride-to-be as she clung to him. "Of course, maybe it's also because Duncan Hugo knew less about his father's operations than a midlevel employee," she continued. "Or maybe it's because your friend Lucian agreed to put his extensive resources at our disposal to help us take down Anthony Hugo once and for all. So you can see how I might be a little too busy to worry about whether some small-town chief of police keeps his job."

"Back away from my chief, Special Agent," Mayor Swanson said. It would have been more threatening had she not been wearing jack-o'-lantern pajama pants and clutching a Snoopy tumbler of hot coffee.

"We're just having a conversation, Mayor," Idler said.

"You make sure you keep it friendly. I'd hate for the seventy-two thousand people who liked this article about our hometown hero to find out the FBI hung him out to dry." She held up a stack of printouts and waved them around.

I snatched them out of her hand, then regretted it immediately when I saw the first few comments.

He can protect and serve my ass any day.

721

Thinking about committing a misdemeanor in northern Virginia. BRB.

"Christ," I muttered.

"If you think the FBI has the time and money to handle the PR fallout, by all means, go for it. But I'll make it my personal mission to go on every morning show between DC and New York—"

"Mayor Swanson, Chief Morgan's job isn't in any danger. At least, not from my end."

Nolan's ambulance pulled away and I was rewarded with the kind of sight a man wouldn't soon forget.

Angelina Solavita.

She was leaning against the side of that goddamn navy-blue Porsche, her long legs stretched out in front of her, hands shoved in her pockets. Her face was bruised, her clothing was muddy, and she was standing there in borrowed firefighter turnout boots.

She looked like a beautiful badass. My beautiful badass.

She spotted me and those full lips curved knowingly.

I stepped between Mayor Swanson and Special Agent Idler without seeing them.

"About time he got his head out of his ass," I heard the mayor say as I walked away from them.

Lina pushed away from the car and launched herself at me.

I caught her and boosted her up. She wrapped her legs around my waist.

"Hey there, hotsh—"

I didn't let her finish. I dragged her mouth down to mine and kissed her like it was the first time. Like it was the last time. Like it was the only time.

She went soft in my arms and I went hard. The taste of her, the feel of her, the reality of her was too much. I was never going to get enough.

I pulled back from the kiss. "It's after."

"Yeah, and you're still buying me a ring."

"You didn't change your mind?"

"I told you. You're stuck with me. I drafted my letter of resignation on my phone while I was waiting for you to kick Dilton's ass."

"How's your arm?" I asked her.

She rolled her eyes. "It's fine. I don't even need stitches."

"I said you could probably use a few stitches," one of the paramedics yelled from the open window of their vehicle.

Lina shrugged and grinned at me. "Eh. Same thing."

"I fucking love you, Angel."

Her face softened. "I love you too, hotshot."

"You gonna marry me?"

There was so much love in her eyes that I felt like I almost couldn't breathe. "Yeah," she whispered.

"Good girl."

I pulled her mouth down for another kiss, then winced when she dug her heel into my ass cheek.

"Are you sure you didn't get shot in that perfect ass?"

"Shot? No."

"What happened?"

"I'll show you later. First, why don't you give me a ride home?"

She let out a little squeal and unwound her legs from my waist. "I thought you'd never ask."

My phone vibrated in my pocket and I tugged it free.

I grinned and turned the screen toward Lina.

"Why is my mom calling you?"

"I'm guessing you missed a few calls."

"I figured we could tell them about our night together," she said, looking guilty.

"You big, beautiful chicken," I teased.

I snatched the keys out of her hand and tossed her my phone.

"I'll drive. You talk."

"Fine, but as my fiancé, I hope you're mentally prepared for parents with no sense of personal boundaries or privacy descending on Knockemout to meet you."

"I can't wait, Angel."

Epilogue

Nash

It was a damn miracle that we were still standing . . . let alone standing *here*. Tate Dilton was dead. Duncan Hugo was in custody. I hadn't lost my job. And everyone I loved was safe and here. Some of us were a little banged up. But we were here and that was what counted.

My brother's backyard was decked out for the occasion with a little help from Mother Nature. The sun was shining. The sky was blue. Fall leaves showered the guests in showy colors as the creek burbled over rocks and around bends, adding a familiar music to the lively guitar.

The rows of rustic benches full of excited guests faced the wooden arbor Knox and Lou had made together.

My brother was facing down the pumpkin-lined aisle, looking like he was about to puke all over his suit and tie. He had a cut on his forehead, a bruise under one eye, and several knuckles bandaged. I myself was rocking a few new bruises and a sore-as-hell shoulder.

Under the arbor ready to officiate was Justice St. John, who cleaned up nicely for the occasion, trading in his usual coveralls for a charcoal-gray suit.

Lucian, with a smirk, and Jeremiah took their places next to me. Together, we had my brother's back.

Naomi's mom, pretty in gold, flashed me an enthusiastic thumbs-up from the front row. Across from her, Liza J pulled a flask out of her shit-brown cardigan and took a nip. Beside her, I was surprised to see our dad. He looked . . . good. Healthy. Present. He was decked out in a suit and tie that he kept fiddling with. Next to him was a man I didn't recognize.

I didn't have time to draw any conclusions because the music changed and there she was.

Lina appeared at the end of the aisle in scarlet that draped over her like paint from the brush of an enchanted artist. She had a black eye not quite hidden by makeup, ruby-red lips, a bandage on her arm, and a halo of flowers in her hair.

I'd never seen anything more beautiful in my entire life.

My throat closed up on me as she sauntered my way. And I knew for certain I couldn't wait for her to be walking down a different aisle to me. Our aisle.

I wanted to go to her. To touch her. To drag her up to Justice and make it official. But there'd be time for that. *After.* We had all the time in the world now.

Her eyes were on me, and that sly, knowing smile of hers warmed every corner of my soul.

Mine.

She tore her gaze away from me and stopped in front of Knox. "Congratulations, Knox," she whispered. He reached out and pulled her in for a hard hug, his throat working hard to swallow.

The crowd "awwed" as my brother managed to whisper a broken, "Thanks, Leens."

She pulled back. "They're both so beautiful," she added. And then she was standing in front of me.

"Looking good, hotshot," she said. It was lily of the valley in her hair. For the first time in a long time, I felt the presence of both my parents.

I shocked the hell out of her and everyone else by hooking her around the back of her neck and pulling her in for a fast, hard kiss. The crowd twittered with sighs and laughter.

"Right back at you, Angel," I said after breaking the kiss.

She grinned up at me with a thousand promises in her eyes before she moved on to high-five Lucian and Jeremiah. Lucian made room for her between the two of us and I felt her hand stroke my back.

Fi strutted down the aisle next in a fitted gold dress like it was a runway. She wore her thick, dark hair down in wild curls tamed by a headband of flowers. She blew Knox a kiss before peeling off toward the opposite side of the arbor. Stef and

Sloane were next in the processional. Stef, in a suit, tossed Jeremiah a flirty wink before pointing two fingers at his own eyes before pointing them at Knox.

Sloane, in a rust-colored gown with a full skirt, floated toward us looking like a forest fairy. Her blond hair was swept up and back. A headband of white blossoms perched on her head. She kept her eyes straight ahead until she got to us.

Then she gave Knox a watery smile filled with so much love and hope. I heard Lucian's sharp intake of breath behind me and wondered if seeing that smile had pierced through his armor somehow.

And then there was Waylay. That brave, beautiful girl was happier than I'd ever seen her as she all but skipped down the aisle in yellow tulle. Her hair was curled into princess ringlets with daisies woven throughout.

In front of me, Knox's shoulders shuddered once as he fought back a wave of emotions. He held out as long as he could, breaking rank when his daughter reached the front row. Knox picked her up in a crushing bear hug. Waylay's arms came around his neck and held tight. Two tears slipped down her cheeks before she buried her face in Knox's shoulder.

After everything the kid had been through, it was the first time I'd ever seen her cry.

Amanda let out a hiccupping sob and started handing out tissues like they were candy.

"Love you, kid," Knox murmured, his voice cracking.

He set her back on her feet and she swiped the tears away. "Yeah. I guess I kinda love you too and stuff."

Fi blew her nose noisily while Sloane stared up at the trees and tried not to blink.

"You and your aunt are the two best things that ever happened to me," Knox said, tipping her chin to look up at him.

For a second, I thought she was going to burst into tears, but Waylay mustered an inner stubborn strength and smothered the emotion. She was going to make a fine Morgan. "Don't get all mushy. If you get all mushy, this is gonna take forever, and I want cake," she instructed.

"Got it," Knox croaked.

She started to move away from him and then gave in to some impulse and wrapped her arms around his waist.

I wasn't sure if I heard her correctly, but it sounded like she said, "Thank you for loving me."

Lucian, Jeremiah, and I took turns clearing our throats in a manly attempt to suffocate any feelings.

"Shit." Lina sniffled behind me. I pulled a wad of tissues out of my jacket pocket and handed them to her. Her eyes were glassy with unshed tears. "Thank you," she mouthed.

My girl cried at weddings.

Lina Solavita was full of surprises.

When Waylay finally let go of Knox and took her place, my brother looked up at the sky, trying to get control of himself. Dad tentatively rose from his seat. He hesitated—twice—then made the short journey to the arbor and pressed something into Knox's hand before returning to his seat.

It was a handkerchief. For once in his life, Duke Morgan had shown up when he was needed.

Knox looked down at it, then nodded his thanks.

Comedic relief came next in the form of Waylon in a doggie tux galloping down the aisle as the official ring bearer.

Once the dog plopped his ass down at my feet, courtesy of the fancy dog treat I bribed him with, the music changed again. As the guitarist strummed the first chords of Tom Petty's "Free Fallin'," the crowd got to its feet.

I heard the sigh run through the guests as Naomi, a vision in white lace, appeared on Lou's arm.

Knox took one look at her and dropped to a crouch, his hands shaking as they clutched the handkerchief to his face.

From then on, there wasn't a dry fucking eye in the yard.

Even Liza J had to wipe her nose on her sleeve between nips from her flask. When Knox all but wrestled Naomi out of her father's grip, when he held her to him like she was the most precious thing in the world, I had to turn around to thumb away a stray tear.

Lina was waving her hands in front of her eyes as if the breeze would help her tears dry.

Lucian stood with red-rimmed eyes, looking like his heart had been shattered into pieces. But he wasn't looking at the bride and groom. He was looking past them at Sloane, who was openly crying.

"Don't you dare fuckin' cry, Daisy," Knox ordered his bride.

Naomi grinned through her tears of joy. "Too late, Viking. I love you so damn much."

The muscles in Knox's jaw and throat worked. "You're everything I always wanted and never thought I deserved."

Naomi's broken sob was echoed by Lina and Sloane. I couldn't take it anymore. I shifted and put my arm around Lina, pulling her into my side. The delicate blooms in her hair tickled my face like a caress.

Naomi looked up at Justice, who was brushing away a tear or two of his own, and grinned. "I always knew I'd get you to marry me somehow, Justice."

With the I dos said, the tears dried, and the drinks served, there was nothing left to do but enjoy the day.

Waylay held court next to the creek with a huge slab of cake, her friends from the soccer team, and the dogs.

Lina was in the photo booth again with Sloane and Fi. The photographer was still frantically looking for Naomi and Knox, who had been suspiciously absent for the last twenty minutes or so. No one had the heart to tell her the bride and groom were probably getting it on somewhere in the house.

"Wanna push an old lady around the dance floor?" Liza J asked, appearing at my elbow when the band shifted into George Strait's "All My Ex's Live in Texas." It was one of Mom's favorites, which made it one of mine.

"I'd be honored," I said, offering her my arm.

We found a spot on the dance floor surrounded by friends and family. I knew every single face here and recognized what a miracle that was. What a privilege it was not just to be part of this town but to serve it.

"So I'm just gonna get this out," my grandmother announced. "I was thinkin' during the ceremony when everyone else was bawling like a bunch of babies. If things had worked out differently, there wouldn't have been a wedding today without you. If that Dilton asshole had better aim, we wouldn't be standing here watching your brother marry a woman who's so far out of his league he'd better never quit trying to earn her. You taught Knox how to be brave. To do the work. And I'm real damn proud of both of you."

I was so taken aback I actually missed a step. Morgans didn't talk about feelings, especially not to other Morgans. "Well, shit, Liza J."

"Shut up. Not done yet. Your mom wasn't yours to save, Nash. It was her time. Nothing you or anybody else could have done to stop it. She lived as big and loud and colorful as she could in the short time we had her. We were damn lucky to get those years with her. And I'm damn lucky to have the grandsons she made. I don't know if you know this, but when she was little, your mama wanted to be a cop. Eventually, real life got in the way. But I know for sure Jayla's up there tickled pink watching you serve and protect down here."

For the second time that day, my eyes went cloudy.

"Mind if I cut in?" Wraith in his formal motorcycle leathers offered his hand to Liza J.

"Yeah, we're definitely done here," my grandmother announced. She danced away with the burly biker before I had the chance to say another word.

"You look like you could use a drink." Lina came into my line of sight.

"How about a dance instead?" I reached out and pulled her into my arms. "You look happy,"

I observed, moving us to a quiet corner of the dance floor.

"I mean, you'd kind of have to be a heartless monster not to be happy today," she said, swaying with me to the beat of the music. "I just got off the phone with Nolan's ex-wife."

"Oh, really?" I spun her out, then pulled her back to me.

She laughed. "She's at the hospital with him. He's gonna be fine. And I think there's a possibility that they're gonna be fine. Especially since he told her he's moving to the private sector."

"Lucian offered him a job. I still don't know if he did it just to keep Nolan from dating Sloane."

Lina took a fortifying breath before confessing, "He offered me one too."

"Did he now?"

"It's with his research team. It would mean a bigger paycheck. No time in the field. The only travel would be between where I live and DC once or twice a week."

"Sounds like quite an opportunity," I said.

Her eyes sparkled. "Naomi and Sloane also asked if I'd be interested in helping with their new venture."

"Really? What are you gonna do?" I asked.

"I think I might take some time off first. I have a boyfriend I'd like to get to know better before I commit to another job."

"A fiancé," I corrected.

"No second thoughts yet?"

I shook my head. "If you're planning on sticking around, I guess we'd better start looking for a house," I drawled.

Lina blanched and stepped on my foot. I grinned down at her and hoped I never lost the power to rattle her.

"You want to buy a house together?" she squeaked.

"There's no way your entire wardrobe is gonna fit in my closet. Might as well find a place that'll hold all those nice bags and shoes."

Her eyes narrowed as she rose to the challenge. "You know, if we're buying a house together I guess a wedding might be kind of fun," she mused.

"I think so," I agreed amicably.

"And after seeing Knox and Waylay . . . maybe one kid wouldn't be the worst thing in the world."

"One kid definitely wouldn't be the worst."

She rolled her eyes heavenward. "How can you be so blasé about all this? This is your entire future we're talking about. Real estate and marriage and *babies*."

"Angel, as long as you're by my side, none of that scares me."

She shook her head and looked up at the canopy of trees and sky above us. "Well, I'm pretty damn terrified. What if you change your mind?"

I dropped her into a dramatic dip and reveled in the way her arms tightened around me. "Too late for that."

"No, it's not. In fact, now's the ideal time for you to change your mind before we do anything permanent."

I righted us both and cupped her face in my hands. "Let me show you exactly how permanent this is right now."

"Lead the way," she said.

I was towing her away from the party when someone called my name.

"Dammit," I muttered.

I turned and found my father standing there. The man who'd sat next to him during the ceremony was behind him.

"I just wanted to say goodbye," Dad said, shifting his weight from foot to foot. He had his jacket slung over his arm and his shirtsleeves rolled up to his elbows. The 0522 was still visible, though faded to a grayish blue on his skin.

"This is Clark, by the way. He's my sponsor," Dad said, making the introductions.

Surprised, I offered my hand. "Good to meet you, Bill."

"You too. Your dad's been making some positive headway," he said.

"Glad to hear it."

Dad looked past me and offered Lina a small smile.

"Dad, this is Lina. My fiancée." I couldn't wait to change that word to wife. *My wife.*

"I figured that one out during the ceremony," Dad teased. "Congratulations to you both."

"It's nice to meet you, Mr. Morgan. Your sons turned out pretty great," Lina said, shaking his hand. She looked down at his arm at the number inked into his skin, then looked at me, her gaze going soft.

"Call me Duke. And I can't take credit for my sons. All the good in them came from Jayla."

I hadn't heard my dad use Mom's name in years. Maybe there really was hope.

"Not *all* the good," Lina countered.

He gave her a small, grateful smile. "Well, figured it was time to hit the road. Don't think I'm quite ready to face an open bar," he said.

"It was good to see you, Dad."

"Good to see you too, Nash. Nice meeting you, Lina." He started to leave, then paused. "I'm real proud of you, Son. Real proud. I know that probably doesn't mean much. But I also know your mom would be over the moon."

I couldn't find the words so I settled for a nod.

We watched them go.

"You okay?" Lina asked, scratching her nails against my back.

"Yeah. I am. Come on." I led her into the house and up the stairs. There was a cheer that went up in the backyard, and I guessed that Knox and Naomi had just made their post-wedding-sex entrance.

"Where are we going?" Lina asked.

"Gotta show you something," I said, opening a door and pushing her inside.

"Oh my God. Is this your room?" she asked, taking in the small bed under the checkered comforter, the shelves of trophies, and other boyhood knickknacks.

"It was. I told Naomi she could redecorate, but I guess she hasn't gotten around to it."

I closed the door and locked it.

"Sex at your brother's wedding?" she said coyly. "My, my, hotshot. I'm impressed."

I unbuckled my belt and she wet her lips. That peek of pink tongue and wet lips was all it took for me to go hard.

"Been thinking a lot lately."

"When have you had time to think? We spent most of the last twenty-four hours dodging bullets," she teased.

"Every waking moment since I found you in my stairwell." I nudged her until she sat down on my old bed.

"That's a lot of thinking."

"You're a complicated woman. It takes a lot of thought and planning when it comes to figuring out how to convince you to make a life with me." I slid my pants down my thighs.

Her eyes were on my groin and I felt the pulse and throb her attention ignited in my dick.

I hooked my thumbs in the band of my boxer briefs.

"If you think your cock—magnificent as it is—is going to count as some kind of grand gesture that proves you're in this for the long haul, you'd better go back to the drawing board."

She was already parting her knees on the edge of the mattress. I longed to push all that silk up around her waist and take her. To show her how much I needed her. To remind her how much she wanted me.

But first I had something else to do.

I turned around.

"I might be willing to accept your ass as a grand—"

Her words cut off as I shoved my underwear down.

"Nash!" she gasped.

I tried to peer over my shoulder at her to get a sense of what she was feeling. "Damn it, this was stupid. I should have gotten it someplace else. Somewhere I could see you."

What had I been thinking? A woman like Lina deserved a midnight proposal on safari with fireworks and fucking lions. Not—

"Angel wings," she whispered, stroking her fingers over the fresh ink.

I winced.

"Poor baby," she teased. And then I felt her lips brush my ass cheek.

My cock responded accordingly.

"I can't believe you got a tattoo for me. On your ass. You realize this makes it official. Your ass is mine. Every woman in town is going to be devastated. Because I'm absolutely telling them about it. In fact, I need my phone. I want a picture of this."

"Angel," I said.

"What?"

"It's not done yet."

"I can see that."

"Someone had to get herself kidnapped in the middle of the inking. But that's not what I meant."

"What's missing?" she asked.

"Our date. The happiest day of my life."

She was silent so long, I turned to face her with my pants still around my thighs. "Knox got today's date done over his heart. Family tradition," I said.

Those beautiful brown eyes were glassy with tears. Her full, red lips trembled.

"Make a life with me, Angelina. You can be as scared about it as you want because I'm not. I'll be strong enough for the both of us."

She nodded and a single tear spilled over. I crouched down in front of her and thumbed it away, then moved in to kiss her.

740

But she stopped me. "I still get a ring though, right?" There was joy and mischief sparkling in her eyes, mixing with the tears.

I grinned. "Already have an appointment with the jeweler scheduled for tomorrow."

She leaned in closer until our mouths were just a breath apart. "Then I guess I'd better schedule *my* appointment."

"Your appointment for what?"

"My Nash tattoo. I was thinking maybe your badge might be appropriate."

I surged up, pinning her to the mattress.

"I fucking love you, Angel."

"I love you, Studly Do-Right," she whispered, stroking a hand over my face.

A loud knock rattled the door, and for a second, I flashed back to my teenage years.

"Knock! Lina? Are you in there?" a voice called.

Lina jackknifed into a seated position. "Is that my *mother?*" she hissed.

"Shit." I stood, frantically trying to pull my pants up.

"Lina? You in there? That Knock guy said you were probably up here."

"Dad?" she squeaked, looking shell-shocked.

"Maybe they're having sex," her mother suggested from the hallway.

"Why do you have to say shit like that, Bonnie?" her dad said.

"Why are my parents here?" Lina demanded as she frantically straightened her dress.

"I forgot to tell you. I maybe kind of invited them . . . after I asked them for their permission to marry you . . . after I already proposed."

She put her hands on my chest and looked into my eyes.

"Prepare to be smothered for the rest of your life."

I was looking forward to it.

Bonus Epilogue

A Few Years Later

Lina

Peel!" Stef announced gleefully.

"Fuck you," Knox snarled as he reached for another tile on our game table in the game room.

Yes, I, Lina Solavita Morgan, had a game room. I also had an entire section of the closet dedicated to expensive lingerie.

My handsome husband shot me a knowing grin as if he could read my mind and flicked a tile toward himself. Piper was sitting in his lap, enjoying the action around the table.

"How are you so good at this?" Lucian demanded. This was the man's first foray into Bananagrams, and he was taking it more seriously than Sloane, who had given up. She had her feet in his lap while she skimmed an article about her program's latest success story on her iPad.

The light from the tablet played over the slim, silvery scar on her jawline. A mark of valor. A mark that reminded us all of how brave our little librarian was.

Lucian, I noted, was playing one-handed so he could rub his wife's feet under the table.

"He cheats," Jeremiah said, winking at Stef.

"You're just jealous, Mr. Three-Letter Words."

"Anyone want a drink?" I asked as I began collecting the empties.

"Sit down, Angel," Nash ordered. His hand snaked out and brought my wrist to his lips. "I'll clean up."

"I feel better when I'm moving," I told him, then leaned down despite the zing of pain in my lower back so I could brush my lips over his.

"You okay?" he asked softly. His hand coasted down my back and over my butt. Unerringly, he found my tattoo and gave it an affectionate squeeze.

I was huge and uncomfortable. My back hurt. My feet were swollen. For the past several hours, I'd been experiencing the occasional sharp cramp that reminded me of what was to come.

"I'm good," I promised.

"Peel, fuckers!" Knox barked triumphantly. The table groaned.

"Game night," I muttered, flashing Nash a wink before I carted the empty beer bottles into the kitchen. Waylon the basset hound lifted his head, ascertained that I wasn't holding any treats, and immediately went back to sleep on the tile.

Somehow, this was my life.

Of course, my life had also included building

this beautiful house on Liza J's land just across the creek from my brother- and sister-in-law. I had an exciting job, a quirky dog, a man I loved more and more every damn day. My parents and I were in a good place. They still called. A *lot*. But I no longer lied to them about my life and they had learned to deal with me spreading my wings. I suspected it was mostly due to the fact that they'd passed the worry torch on to Nash and now relied on him to keep me safe. But I still considered it a win.

To top it all off, our biggest adventure was about to begin.

I dumped the empty bottles in the recycling bin. Naomi came up behind me and slid an arm around my expanded waist. "The dishwasher is running and the leftovers are put away."

"Thank you. I promise when I'm not eight hundred pounds and shaped like a beach ball, I'll return the favor."

"Are you feeling okay?"

I nodded, then grimaced. The weight of my pregnant belly seemed to be riding lower than usual. My back protested everything whether I sat, stood, or lay down. For the first time since my teenage years, I was uncomfortable in my own body.

But I didn't want to complain to my friend. Not when she and Knox had been trying for babies of their own.

"I'm fine," I assured her.

Naomi shot me a knowing look. "Liar," she said affectionately.

"Really. I'm fine." As I said it, another one of those sharp pains sliced through me.

Nash's eyes came to me as if he felt it too. The man had watched me like a hawk since that damn pink line showed up all those months ago. I gave him a weak smile.

"Walk or sit?" Naomi asked.

Both sounded awful right now. "Walk," I decided and started my laps around the kitchen island, my hands at my lower back.

Naomi picked up a dish towel and started wringing it, something like a smile playing on her lips.

"What?" I asked.

"I just need you to know that I'm going to love these babies so much. I'm so happy for you and Nash that sometimes it takes my breath away," she said, her voice quivering. "I don't want you to ever think that just because I'm sad for me and Knox that I'm not happy for you and Nash."

I stopped walking and faced her. "Of course I know that. And I need you to know that I wish these were your babies or that you were an eight-hundred-pound beach ball with me."

She gave a tearful little laugh. "I do too. It makes me feel a little selfish."

"There's nothing wrong with wanting to bring more love into your home. That's not selfish." I released her as another painful pang hit me.

I blew out a slow breath.

"Knox and I have been talking," Naomi said, sliding onto one of the barstools I'd agonized over choosing. Because apparently I wasn't just a diva for fashion and makeup but also home furnishings. "And we made a decision."

"What did you decide?" I asked, trying to keep my words from sounding like I was being strangled as the cramp refused to abate.

"We're not going to do any more fertility treatments."

"Oh, Naomi," I said.

She shook her head, and beyond the tears in her eyes, I saw something beautiful. Something happy and hopeful. "We're going to adopt."

I reached for her. Pregnancy had made me freer with physical contact. It probably had to do with me physically sharing my body with not one but *two* other humans.

"It's a long road ahead, but it just feels right. Like a puzzle piece just snapped into place," she said. "I'm so happy."

I hugged her as tight as my belly allowed. "That's beautiful, Witty. I'm so happy for you. You and Knox and Way are going to find the rest of your family," I promised her.

"I feel it in my heart. Just like I know you're

not the sister I was born with, but you're the sister I choose, Lina," she whispered.

Hot tears blurred my eyes and I hugged her harder. "Crap. Way to make a pregnant lady cry."

Naomi gave a tearful laugh against my shoulder.

"I'm honored to have you as a sister," I whispered.

"Was that a kick?" Naomi asked, bringing her hand to my belly.

"Yeah, one of them wants to follow Waylay's footsteps onto the soccer field."

The next cramp caught me off guard, and I released Naomi to bend forward. "Gah," I gasped.

"Nash!" Naomi called, her voice sharp.

There was a crash in the great room and my husband was at my side in a second.

"Okay, Angel?" he asked, running his hands down my arms.

"Fine," I rasped as the rest of our friends and family tried to enter the kitchen at the same time and got stuck in the doorway.

"I think she's in labor," Naomi announced.

"She's early," Jeremiah noted.

"Twins usually are," Sloane said, arriving at my side, her hand cool on my shoulder. Lucian followed her. Even after all this time, even while my insides were threatening to exit my body, I still found the way he always put himself in her orbit breathtaking.

Painfully adorable.

"What do we do? Do you need some towels and shit?" Knox said, looking panicked.

"Stef, go get the bag sitting on the floor in our bedroom," Nash said. "Naomi, call the parents. Jeremiah, take my keys off the hook and go start the Tahoe."

I shook my head. "No Tahoe."

"What?" Nash leaned in closer.

"My car. One last ride just the two of us," I said through gritted teeth.

He leaned down and looked me in the eye. "Fuck, I love you, Angel. Even though you're a stubborn pain in my ass."

"I love you too. Now please get me out of here before I embarrass myself and start crying and screaming."

"I'm not ready. I can't do this. *Two? Two babies?* What were we thinking?" I said, gripping Nash's arm with both hands.

The hospital bed and gown were enough to freak me out. Add the fact that two human beings were about to explode out of my vagina, and this was a whole other level of freak-out.

"I'm so sorry, baby. I'll never do this to you again," my husband promised fervently. "Get her another epidural or some pain meds or some goddamn horse tranquilizers now! Whatever it takes to fix this," he barked.

I dropped my head back against the inclined mattress and squeezed my eyes shut. Nash's cool hand came to my forehead. I felt his lips against my ear.

"I'm right here, Angel. I'm with you. You can absolutely do this. You have to do the heavy lifting, and I'm real fucking sorry about that. I'd do anything to take this pain from you. Anything. But I swear to you, you'll never have to do anything alone after this. Okay?"

I nodded and opened my eyes. "Okay."

"Get ready. We need a big push, Lina," the nurse said.

"You can do this, baby. You brought me back to life. You can bring another two lives into being. Because you're fucking magic."

I gripped his hand in mine and held tight. His blue eyes burned bright.

"I need you, Nash."

"It's about damn time."

I shook my head. "I've always needed you."

"I'm right here. Let's get this adventure started."

"I can't wait till after," I said through gritted teeth.

The little scrunched face under the blue beanie didn't look like me or Nash as far as I could tell. He looked like a grumpy old man with teeny tiny fingers. I moved my head against Nash's shoulder. He'd climbed in bed with me and we sat holding our son and daughter, enjoying the first few minutes of being a family of four.

Nash was looking down at our baby girl with a look of pure awe on his face. I felt my heart open down the middle to accommodate this new quantity of love.

My heroic husband held it together for the both of us. He'd kept it together until the twins were bundled up, pronounced healthy, and I was safe. Then with a look of love just for me on his handsome face, Nash Morgan had passed out cold.

"It happens all the time," the nurse had said when she went for the smelling salts and butterfly bandages.

I managed to take a shaky selfie with Nash prone on the floor next to my bed. Most of our best moments as a family involved blood and bruises.

"There are about twenty people in the waiting room with more balloons than a carnival," the nurse announced.

"I guess we should let them in before they get kicked out," I said. I felt like my body had been cut in half and stitched back together, and I'd give my left arm for some concealer and mascara. But there was a kind of special joy that I'd found within sharing imperfect moments. An awe-inspiring strength I felt when I let the ones I loved most see me at my rawest.

We were blessed with this beautiful life.

These tiny, perfect babies would be loved and cared for by our whole extended family, even when their human imperfections started to show.

Nash shook his head. "I want a few more minutes just us," he said.

"Okay," I said, knowing he was saying it for my benefit. Always the protector.

I reached over and ran a finger down our daughter's pink cheek.

"I was thinking maybe we could call her Jayla after your mom," I said.

Nash looked up at me with tears in those beautiful blue eyes. He nodded silently for a while as his throat worked. "I think I'd really like that," he rasped finally.

"Yeah?"

"Yeah." He looked down at our son and then back up at me. "What about Memphis?"

"Memphis Morgan," I said softly. Our son squirmed in my arms and I grinned. "I think he likes it."

"You're beautiful, you know?"

I glanced up and found Nash staring at me with a fierce look of love. I was a hot mess and my husband was a dirty liar.

"Please," I scoffed.

"I'm glad you stuck around for the after," he said.

"Even after *this?*" I asked, gesturing with

my chin at the two newborns we were now responsible for.

"There is no one else in this world that I'd do this with," he said, his voice thick with emotion.

I sighed and leaned into his shoulder. "Me neither."

We took our time, our moment together.

My mom was the first to poke her head through the door. I wondered how many people she'd had to trample for that honor. I watched as she embraced Nash in a long, hard hug, rocking him side to side.

"I'm so proud of you," she said, releasing him from the hug only to cup his face in her hands.

Nash beamed at her and pulled her in for another hug.

It turned out that all that love my parents had focused on me wasn't quite as smothering when it was divided up between the two of us. Now the four of us.

My dad stood in the doorway, shyly clutching a bouquet of wildflowers. Even from across the room, I could spot the lily of the valley. Jayla's favorite. We'd planted a whole bed of it alongside the house, and every time it bloomed, I whispered a "thank you" to the woman who'd brought love into my life.

"He looks just like you," Mom breathed, her

eyes filling with tears as I handed over her grandson.

"Look at this little angel," Dad said, trading Nash the flowers and a cigar for his grand-daughter.

There was a knock at the door, and everyone else began to file inside. Knox and Waylay entered with the teary-eyed Naomi between them. "Oh my goodness! They're so perfect," Naomi crooned, waving her hands in front of her eyes. "You have four casseroles in your freezer, the nursery is vacuumed and dusted, and Piper is hanging out with Duke who is watching all of the dogs until we get back and then he'll be in to visit. Now give me one of those babies, please."

Lucian had a protective arm around Sloane and carried a Prada gift bag in his free hand. "Diaper bag," Sloane mouthed at me.

Stef and Jeremiah brought up the rear with the biggest teddy bear I'd ever seen and Liza J.

"You did good, kid," Nash's grandmother said as she eyed her great-granddaughter.

"Her name's Jayla," Nash said.

Liza J nodded, then kept right on nodding. "It's a good name," she said finally, then blew her nose noisily into a bandana.

My husband found his way back and climbed into bed next to me. I tucked my head under his chin and sighed happily while he toyed with the rings on my finger. My engagement ring was a spectacular, fiery diamond, and the band belonged to his mother.

"I don't know how I got to be so damn lucky," he murmured against the top of my head.

I tilted my face up to look at him. "Maybe because you've got an angel or two looking out for you."

His face went soft, his blue eyes tender. "I think you might be right."

He kissed me sweetly on the lips and then the forehead.

"You know," I mused, "it's a good thing you have such a nice, round ass. I think you're gonna need to add another date."

Dear Reader,

The more romance novels I write, the more convinced I am that loving someone is the bravest thing we can do in this world.

It's not just falling for the broody police chief next-door. It's the friends who show up with wine on your best and worst days. The nephew who can't talk yet but melts your heart with a toothy smile. The sibling that always manages to make you laugh. The neighbor surprising you with fresh vegetables from their garden. The happy sigh of a good dog. The knowing looks that have become their own language between long-time lovers.

And sometimes it really is the small-town hero who makes you want to take a chance on getting your heart crushed.

The most important lesson Lina and Nash taught me is that the best kind of love is the one you are brave enough to give freely. Even knowing they could hurt you or disappoint you or break your heart, loving someone exactly as they are is the greatest gift you can ever give.

Now if you'll excuse me, I have to go hug Mr. Lucy and ask him to take me for emotional support tacos.

Xoxo, Lucy

P.S. Lucian's book? *wipes sweat from forehead* *shoves computer into freezer to keep it from overheating*

Acknowledgments

Kristy Rempalski for her generosity in supporting Lift 4 Autism and for her sparkling creativity in helping develop the character Xandra.

Carol and Cora for girl-tripping all the way from Connecticut to see me in Enola, Pennsylvania.

Kari March Designs for once again designing a cover that brings the feels.

Korrie's Korner for your amazing feedback and your diversity editing services.

Kennedy Ryan for always being a beacon of talent and for letting me know if I was getting it right.

All the readers on my Facebook author page who suggested I name the dog Piper.

My amazing partner in crime, Tim, who celebrated his fiftieth birthday this year. Just like a good scotch, you keep getting better, babe!

Joyce and Tammy for championing Nash even when it took me forever to write him.

Team Lucy for keeping the ship afloat while I disappeared into Knockemout yet again.

The teams at Bloom Books and Hodder for bringing this series to a wider audience.

Flavia at Bookcase Literary Agency for walking me through the Year of Chaos.

Every reader who takes a chance on one of my books and doesn't hate it.

Finally, for my author friends who sprinted with me, told me to quit whining, and cheered me on. You guys make a solitary job into a quirky, beautiful community that I'm proud to belong to!

About the Author

Lucy Score is a *New York Times*, *USA Today*, *Wall Street Journal*, and #1 Amazon bestselling author. She grew up in a literary family who insisted that the dinner table was for reading and earned a degree in journalism. She writes full-time from the Pennsylvania home she and Mr. Lucy share with their obnoxious cat, Cleo. When not spending hours crafting heartbreaker heroes and kick-ass heroines, Lucy can be found on the couch, in the kitchen, or at the gym. She hopes to someday write from a sailboat, oceanfront condo, or tropical island with reliable Wi-Fi.

Sign up for her newsletter by scanning the QR code below and stay up on all the latest Lucy book news. You can also follow her here:

Website: lucyscore.net
Facebook: lucyscorewrites
Instagram: scorelucy
TikTok: @lucyferscore
Binge Books: bingebooks.com/author /lucy-score
Readers Group: facebook.com/groups /BingeReadersAnonymous

Center Point Large Print
600 Brooks Road / PO Box 1
Thorndike, ME 04986-0001 USA

(207) 568-3717

US & Canada:
1 800 929-9108
www.centerpointlargeprint.com